Trio:
A Corpus Christi Trilogy

Eve La Salle Caram

Plain View Press
P.O. 42255
Austin, TX 78704

plainviewpress.net
sb@plainviewpress.net
512-441-2452

ISBN: 978-1-935514-20-6
Library of Congress Number: 2010925167

Cover design by Susan Bright

Cover art: *Salt and Fresh*, Thaw Malin III; you can see more of his work at: http://www.thawmalinart.com.

Other books by Eve La Salle Caram:

The Blue Geography
Rena: A Late Journey
Palm Readings: Stories From Southern California (Editor)
Wintershine
Dear Corpus Christi

For Bethel and Neil

Of the two novels and one short novel here, the first, *Dear Corpus Christi*, was published in 1991 (reprinted in 2001), the second, *Rena, A Late Journey*, in 2000 and the third, *Looking For Johnny*, here in *Trio*, 2010, for the first time. The first is Elizabeth McElroy's story, the second the story of her Aunt Rena, and the third, the story of Elizabeth's search for Rena's long lost brother, Johnny. The first two novels are set in Corpus Christi, the third in the Texas Hill Country, Houston, and East Texas, with only a short flashback to Corpus. I, nevertheless, think of all three as my "Corpus Christi" novels because both the joy and the trouble in them begin there and take the characters forward. All three of these books and three others not in this volume (one of them a book of stories I edited) have been published by Plain View Press, which from the fortunate time in the late 1980s when it was recommended to me by the editor of a small Houston magazine which had published an essay I wrote on the work of William Goyen, has not only supported my work, but kept all of it in print, a claim very few people writing currently can make for their presses. Initially I was told that Plain View was the only feminist press in the Southwest and that it was making a name for itself. Although I didn't think of my novel as a "feminist novel" —I have never written to a polemic, but only told stories that came out of character, place and time —I knew that my heroine, Elizabeth McElroy, was a strong woman from a family of strong women, including her warmhearted, life loving Aunt Rena. And so I sent *Dear Corpus Christi*, a novel written in the form of letters Elizabeth is writing to her home town (which represents her youth and a time in which she imagines things were better) to Susan Bright who after some consideration, wanted to publish it. In the spring of 1991 I met Susan in Austin to talk about the book. I signed the contract for it on the Thursday before Easter of that year, the first edition came out in December, and our association which now covers the better part of twenty years was officially begun.

I wrote the first draft of the first chapter of *Dear Corpus Christi*, my first published novel as a journal entry at Yaddo, the writing colony that has provided residencies and inspiration to so many American writers, one morning when I felt discouraged about my work. That was in 1982 in March — supposedly it was spring. The snow was up to the window sills of the house where I was staying and I didn't want to get out of bed and get dressed and trudge through the slush to the house where breakfast was being served. When I looked across my room I saw a world globe with a light in it and that light seemed to come from South Texas where I had gone to high school and when I picked up a pen by the side of my bed what I wrote was, "Is it still spring in March there?" which remains the book's first line.

But later when I began to work with what I wrote in my journal as fiction, altering the characters and their circumstances (in some cases drastically) from those I had actually known when I was a teenager, I had no idea that what I was putting down on paper would become a novel and certainly not that it would be followed by two books with the same characters. I would have laughed at that notion —and it also would have terrified me! I hadn't gone far with my material, however, when I saw the potential for a long narrative, Elizabeth's story set off against her Uncle Bo's parallel story, both of them mavericks, both in the repressive 1950s Texas culture —with opportunities for finding fulfillment in love —shut down.

The first difficulty I had was with the character of Elizabeth. I was stopped from going ahead until I found the ways in which she differed, and was going to differ, from myself. When I realized she would be forever single (and also childless) and would have a vagabond existence as a writer of radio drama, I saw that she was not me, but only the aspect of myself that prizes liberty and truly a character in her own right. (Ever since I discovered this I have told my creative writing students that if they begin a fiction with a character who comes out of themselves they need to look for ways in which the character differs from who they are and, conversely, if the character seems very different from themselves they need to find a connection.) Early in my writing about Elizabeth I took her physical appearance from that of a high school friend who was spunkier than I was and whose independent spirit I admired, a girl whose 15-year-old dark hair was, like Elizabeth's, shot through with gray. This alone helped me see my first person narrator as a character with her own life. Then when Elizabeth became fully herself, the characters around her also took on their own unique identities and I was, as a novelist, set free.

The publication of *Dear Corpus Christi* brought me invitations to speak at book clubs and writers' groups —one of which in an article in the *L. A. Times* mentioned their list as including me along with (to my astonishment) Toni Morrison and Edith Wharton —as well as interest in teaching it from colleagues in Southern California universities and colleges, and also from university teachers in Texas I had never met. And even fan mail! None of which I expected a small press publication could bring. It also literally took me back to Corpus Christi, where I had not been in over thirty years, to give a reading, a trip which shocked me because of the changes I encountered there and which generated the second book in this collection, *Rena, A Late Journey*, a novel set in a contemporary world of drugs and violence, and which of my novels has been taught more than any other.

It was in Corpus Christi in December of 1992 that for the first time I realized that the problems with drugs and gangs were not just the problems of those of us who live in cities on the West and East coasts. A trip back to the neighborhood I had lived in as a teenager let me know that destructive forces were also at work in the place my mother had called "the sweetest town I ever saw, sitting so quietly there on its bay." Not only the street but the very house I had lived in as a teenager was unrecognizable to me —bars were now on its windows, beer cans and trash littering the yard that had once boasted flower beds, chinaberry, willow and pecan trees. Several townspeople told me before I revisited about drug traffic initiated there to and from Mexico. Because I knew deep down that my Elizabeth was not likely to return to this place, her reaction to it was one I didn't even consider when I sat down in a chair near the pool of my waterfront motel and looked over at the Kress's sign still visible on Chaparral Street (this even though the store so many I knew had visited was closed down.) What I wondered was what Elizabeth's Aunt Rena would think of it, and not long after, she began to tell me. And as time passed I almost felt I was taking dictation. (Lest this sound easy, let me say that as she rattled on I had a heavy editing job!)

Teaching and writing have always gone together for me, just as reading and writing have. From the beginning my books were taught. *Rena* lends itself to teaching both in writing and contemporary literature classes because, although it is essentially the story of an old woman who has suffered many losses and is trying to put the pieces of her life together, it also deals with problems urban students can easily relate to: the struggle the poor have in making a living —when I wrote the book I knew about this from my own struggle —that of young people in cities (even smaller ones like Corpus Christi) to steer clear of gangs and to deal with violence and the struggle of families to support one another and stay intact; of people of different ages, ethnicity and gender to respect and make an effort to understand —and even sometimes love — one another. Many of my students at Los Angeles City College, the majority of whom study English as a second or even third or fourth language, connected to *Rena* and asked so many questions about what finally happens to Rena's younger brother, Johnny, who leaves his poverty stricken family early in an effort to find work that will help support all of them, but who never comes back and who Rena can never find, that I was all but summoned to write *Looking For Johnny*, a book that became about a larger question: looking for the lost pieces and a sense of completion of several lives, and which brings my trio of Corpus Christi books to a close.

Because my first two novels are in first person voices —first Elizabeth's and then, Rena's —my early drafts of Johnny began with Elizabeth's much older, wiser and more distanced first person voice, but after I had with great difficulty set down a few pages, that voice didn't resonate, didn't seem to want to tell the story, seemed to want a voice that knew more to tell it. And so I switched into third person, only at first in Elizabeth's consciousness until I felt Rena's nephew, Searcy's, claim on her and on me —his thoughts and feelings welling up in a way that made me realize that part of the story belonged to him, too.

As is apparent from this account of my creative process, one book grew out of another in conjunction with my own responses to them, as well as to responses and questions from readers. Although all my writing has always been intensely personal, sometimes I do feel I am in a conversation with my audience, just as Rena, who speaks to those who hear her is; and in the dialogue between us, the arc of the narrative, and hopefully the understanding of all involved in it, widens.

Working on these stories, and on others, has, with teaching, set me out on a great, perilous, but wonder filled and transformational journey, an adventure of the spirit that has propelled me forward and given me, and I hope my readers, a sense of continuing life.

E. L. C.

Contents

Dear Corpus Christi

All flesh is grass,
And all its beauty is like the flower of the field.

Isaiah 40: 6

*With grateful acknowledgement to
The Ragdale Foundation and to
The Corporation of Yaddo.*

Acknowledgements

Thanks to my mother, Lois, for her aspirations and to all of my family, friends, and teachers who have inspired and encouraged my work. A special thanks to my daughter, Bethel Eve, for her loving support while I was working on this book and for her blithe spirit. Thanks to Robert Love Taylor for his help with the manuscript at the Ragdale Foundation and after; and among those close to me, particular thanks to: Marnell Jameson for her editorial expertise and for giving so generously of her time and talent. Thanks also to Frances Grimes, Lola Hover, Lori Mass Hultman, Roberta Kanesfsky, Mary McFadden and Kate Crane McCarthy. Thanks, too, to Florence Janovich of Sensible Solutions for believing in this book and for her guidance and advice. And thanks to Jacqueline Piatigorsky, an early reader, for enthusiasm which spurred me on. Deep gratitude to Carolyn Waller for her lifelong friendship and to all in her big Texas family. Thanks to Susan Bright, a nurturing editor and publisher, and to Plain View Press. I also salute my mentor-guides, Cecil Dawkins and the late William Goyen. Dear Corpus Christi is dedicated to all of you.

"' Pale horse, Pale rider,'" said Miranda, "(We really need a good banjo) 'done taken my lover away.'" Her voice cleared and she said, "But we ought to get on with it. What's the next line?"

"There's a lot more to it than that," said Adam, "about forty verses, the rider done taken away mammy, pappy, brother, sister, the whole family besides the lover."

"But not the singer, not yet," said Miranda. "Death always leave one singer to mourn. 'Death,' she sang, 'oh leave one singer to mourn.'"

Katherine Ann Porter
Pale Horse, Pale Rider

Upstate New York

*I*s it still Spring in March there? Oh very near the beginning with little green leaves popping out on the pin oaks? And in the fields outside of town, the wildflowers, those pale pink ones and butter cups and, up the country, bluebonnets, and then those deep blues, bluets, Aunty used to call them (that's so Texan). Aunty was from Shreveport, but during thirty years with Uncle Leeland, contracting job to contracting job, she picked up a lot of Texas talk.

Where I am now and in late March, too, it's still snowing; I have a bad cold and hurt all over, hurt in my bones. My grandfather used to say, as he lay on his sickbed on the sunporch (he had cancer, his face eaten up with it, I cotton swabbed it every day with the stuff the doctor left). "The future's right here, darlin', a lot of the country's done for and I don't know why you want to go away." Well, of course, I was young and I had to and it was exciting and is, still, but I think it may now be, as the poet said, that the center's shaky or maybe even shifted. Is that my blue-funk-middle-life-late-winter sickness? I think of myself as a hardy type, think other people get sick, have accidents or operations or even serious malaise. Corpus, I'd like to see you. You know that. But now it's not just miles between us.

Or miles between Joe and me. What lies between Joe and me now is all pure spirit—oceans and stratospheres of it, an everlasting country, though hard for the living to reach.

Joe, Corpus, is an old friend whose life—when he was well into and nearly through it—with mine finally magically linked.

Of all the little frame basementless houses in a "just folks," on the fringe of a "poor folks," neighborhood, ours was always the nicest. That was mostly because of Uncle Bo's love of gardening and his flare for decoration. And because my grandmother and my mother, too, were experts with a needle and a bolt of cloth, although my mother, a musician, hated sewing and complained.

Palm was the name of our street, although most of its trees were pin oaks; some houses did have fat stubby palms in their front yards. In ours only slender trunked pecans shot up through the carpet grass and in back the willow Granddaddy planted the year we came surprised us, it grew so tall, and a big chinaberry hung over the porch we used to eat on and over the lattice work fence with gates that Uncle Bo had painted a bright rose shade he called Watermelon. Uncle Bo liked to make up the names of colors and had a predilection for loud ones he thought the neighbors had never seen. "I like to surprise people," he often said, though shock would come closer to what he did.

From month to month we never knew exactly what was going to spring up out of the flower beds. When I was in my middle teens, he planted the one out back with banana trees and black roses, and the roses were nearly black, too. My grandmother, who didn't know what to think, all of us confused her—the world was becoming a puzzle— took pictures of me standing in the middle of them wearing the dress she'd worked on all summer. I went out on my first date after; I was late to have one and maybe she took the picture because she thought it was the only one I was ever going to have.

I can still hear her saying to my mother, "All summer long we had nothing but bananas and black roses, the roses not even looking like real flowers, but like some cheap cloth kind you could buy at Kress's and the bananas too green and hard to eat."

"Well, he doesn't like to be common, Mama."

"But it scares me, sends my head reeling. I don't know why, but I wonder what uncommon thing he'll think of next."

What he thought of, and I'll tell you about in my very next letter, was to try to bring a girl and then a man, both of whom I think he may have loved, into that house. That was real odd to most people who lived in what you were then, Corpus, and he finally couldn't, couldn't bring himself to marry the girl either. And his nerves broke over it. Over it and Grandma's death.

The vine that wound through the lattice work on the front porch was common enough, the bougainvillea. For the longest time I thought Uncle Bo had its name; he had been christened Evansten Fletcher, and since nobody was gong to say any of that, we just called him Bo, though nobody, not Grandma or Aunty or anybody else, knew where Bo came from. You'd have thought Grandma would.

On the New Year's Eve that I turned fifteen, the one before the autumn when Grandma took the picture, I walked around the porch and out into the front and then into the backyard and right into that bed, though no roses were blooming in it. I was wearing the black evening dress Uncle Bo had bought me. I wasn't going anywhere, the dress was another of Bo's extravagances, but I felt as if I was and to a whole lot of places, too! "God," my best friend from high school, who still writes from where she is now, just told me, "when the rest of us were in our Lichenstein's Budget-Floor $29.95

specials, you waltzed around in designer dresses and tried to enter rooms like a model, though you wobbled more than we did in high heels."

From as early as I can remember, Uncle Bo liked to dress me as if it was my destiny to go everywhere, to places far from Nueces County, out of Texas, even; he'd been to California when he was in the navy (was stationed there) though he never got overseas. He'd often tell me, "I'm getting you ready, Baby, for the world."

I can't remember why I was alone in the house that evening, New Year's Eve and the day before my birthday; we had celebrated that noon with a big dinner. We always celebrated my birthday on December 31st, although I was born at 12:01, January 1. My grandmother wasn't yet sick; maybe Uncle Bo had taken her for a ride down on the waterfront around the yacht basin. My grandfather had died just the previous summer. My mother was with my stepfather and away. When I was small Bud had been a safety engineer with a nearby refinery, but then he'd gone off in the army to Alaska, had been in battle in Attu and when he came back, limping, for he'd been shot in the leg, the refinery was shut down. So he became a land salesman for Tennessee Gas which was covering the country with pipeline; that is, he traveled across the country and tried to talk farmers into selling their land. Because of school I couldn't travel with him and my mother, so I stayed in Corpus with my grandmother and Uncle Bo.

The war was five years over when I was fifteen, my family reunited for the first time since I was small, Aunty with us as often as not; after Uncle Leeland died she married again, but it didn't take, Granddaddy's things still in the house and the ghost of him everywhere. Although my mother and Bud traveled, they came back summers and for a few weeks at Christmas and lived in the garage apartment in back of the house. Bo never would rent it. Bo went into insurance and what we thought of as a "good" job, which meant that it was secure and paid enough money and had nothing to do with whether or not he liked it; he didn't like it at all.

Bo hadn't minded his work before he went off in the navy; he refused to go into Uncle Leeland and Granddaddy's contracting business, too much he said in the way of mathematics and camping out in winter, though in the middle thirties he and my mother had come to South Texas with them; my mother became the music teacher for refinery children while he ran, more or less happily, though he grumbled, the refinery town's general store. And although the depression gripped the country, Grandaddy and Uncle Leeland did all right putting up buildings and bridges after they found their way from hard-hit Arkansas to the Texas coast.

No, I don't know where everyone was that late December twilight or what happened later. Earlier Aunty had certainly been around; at four o'clock in the afternoon we'd sat down with soup bowls full of ice cream and cake. Once the house was empty, I suppose I slipped on the evening gown. I don't know; I only remember lifting the big taffeta balloon of a skirt up by a row of beading and waltzing around the yard. I was barefoot, mind you, and carried the shiny spike-heeled sandals that Uncle Bo had also bought me, in my hand, speaking aloud in the stillness to the rose bed, bereft of flowers and to my life which seemed all ahead. "Hello, hello," I called. "Hello college, Europe, New York."

I wasn't the only girl in town who spoke to a future; a lot of the ones I knew whispered hellos to the boys they were with on the bluff that jutted out over the shrimp boats over on Ocean Drive. Years, half a lifetime, lay ahead before I found Joe's love, but I imagined, and even then, envied those sweet whispers and embraces (cheeks against cheeks, hands that traveled across skin and into hair), but my hello, I thought then, was bigger and reached farther. I figured Dallas, about 500 miles to the northwest of us, was about as far as most of the daydreams of the girls I knew ever got. Uncle Bo had outfitted me and I would go farther, though I didn't yet know where.

The very next summer a Tennessee Gas airplane took me across the continent to visit my mother and Bud in New York. I didn't, however, go out in Corpus Christi, at least not with a boy, (which was, then, the only kind of "going out" that mattered) until very nearly a year later. His name was Ben and he was new in town, half Jew somebody told me and not even a Texan. He'd come to Corpus Christi all the way from Kansas; tall and good looking, wavy, dark hair with olive skin and green eyes with thick, almost girlish lashes. As far as I knew, he was the only boy in our high school who'd read both Tolstoy and the Brontes; he represented what for a long time, until I was well into adulthood, I believed lay north of Dallas, a glittering, but mostly peace-loving and literate world.

A word-loving world. In the beginning was "The Word." You taught me that. Remember?

Hey down there, do you still have Buckaneer Days in April? Could I walk the seawall? Take the steps all the way down to watch the pirate ships come in? How I'd like to hang around one of those booths the high school kids used to run, as we waited for Jean LaFitte, selling kites and homemade candy, a lot of divinity as I remember and sour limeades. I made that by the gallon without a drop of syrup. "Keeps the blood down, you know," I'd tell people who came to visit from other towns: Port Lavaca or Palacios. "Here in Corpus helps keep us cool."

"How're you, Travis and John, hey, want to spend some of that pocket money?"

"Well, maybe, what you selling? Kisses?"

Oh, could I come? Wear a strapless dress in the noon sunshine, feel my shoulders burn? April this year brings nasal voices and snow like in Switzerland, a big wind blowing it up outside the windows where I write, like smoke. Oh, to be in the Texas sunshine, down there near the Bluff, selling coke, lime or lemonade! Just like I used to with my good friend, C.C. (yes, her initials were the same as those in Corpus Christi.)

C.C. and I spent all our free time together, met between periods at school and, afterwards, we'd walk over to get the bus for Chaparral Street, listen to the honky tonk music blasting across the fair grounds, talk our worries out with one another while drinking cokes. On the evenings when we went out, we'd often double date. C.C. went for a long time with a boy named Travis who turned out to be a looker, though he certainly wasn't then and I kept on seeing Ben.

As likely as not we'd been to a Bette Davis picture. One time Ben said, "I hope you won't take this as a compliment, but when you turn your head to the side like that in this neon light, you look a little like Bette Davis; something about you is like her." (He thought complimenting girls, like our Texas boys did, was dumb.) And I said, "I certainly don't take that as a compliment, for while I admired Bette Davis as an actress, I think she is ugly as sin." And he would say, "Oh, I didn't mean it that way, exactly."

And after an awkward silence, C.C. and her date, Travis (more likely than not) would ask if we wanted to go to one of the water front drive-ins. I forget what they were called, but they were all lined up on that street just off the drive by the Seawall where our booths were on festive Springtime days and had names like Ship Ahoy or Treasure Island or The Bucket. Once we got there, we'd look around first thing and call to people we knew; sometimes we even got out of the car and ran around. But, most likely, just the boys would get out, in our case, just Travis; the rest of us would just sit there and smile and call and wave.

Next day the reports would fly around school. "Last night at The Bucket, Nancy was with Erwin, Patsy with Jimmy, C.C. with Travis (again), Elizabeth with Ben." Once the preliminaries were over and the report for the next day had registered, C.C. and Travis ordered hamburgers. Travis, who was then a pale, pimply-faced tow head, always blushed as he said, "Without the onion," and then turned even redder as he asked, "How about you, C.C.? " And she'd say, "I don't believe I'll have any either." And Ben and I sat very still through all of this—we didn't talk or even smile at each other; each of us sat poker straight and looked right ahead.

Because he'd bought it with what he referred to as his "Tombstone money," Travis called his souped up car The Stone. His father owned a monument business, on the wrong side of town we all thought, though half of us lived there. As we sat in The Stone, pulling on our sour limeades in the September heat and later chewing on the straws, Ben would tell me about Kansas. I didn't want to say anything to him about where I'd lived before we came to Corpus Christi, for I was ashamed of the little refinery town. I thought of it as real low down, probably the ugliest and smelliest hole in the United States. I can still hear my mother saying, "If the world was flat instead of round, it would stop right here."

Except for Bud, nobody in my family actually worked for the refinery and I was glad of that, though it was most certainly refinery money that paid them, Leeland and Grandaddy, the builders, and my mother, the music teacher. I thought of Bo as "the supplier." They all did OK until the war came and shut the refinery down and took the men away, but I never wanted to go back, not even for a day.

I did make conversation out of it, though, sometimes, used it to fend off certain boys.

High school dates always ended up in one place: on the bluff that overlooked the shrimp boats just off Ocean Drive. While C.C. and Travis made out, and for a long time they were crazy about one another, I'd spend my time, as often as not, talking a blue streak. "How do you remember all that?" whoever he was would ask me as I went on pulling myself out of the clinches, as gently as possible so as not to hurt his feelings or make him mad. "You sure are a talker." I'd be telling all about Uncle Leeland, he was the pride of the family, and because he drank so much, also its earliest disgrace and Aunty, who always had such a good time, and finally about my Uncle Bo, who never married, most people who lived in you then thought he was the odd one, who brought some fine things and a little beauty to the refinery town. In addition to lumber and hardware, he started to carry Haviland China and several good lines of furniture, including Duncan Fyfe. "How do you tell all that?" whoever he was would ask me, and I'd answer, "I don't know, in our family we just tell stories, just talk." I started to say, "You can remember a lot if you don't want whoever you're with to paw you."

Ben was different; when he kissed me I liked it a lot and just wanted him to go right on. And I kissed him back. Word got out about that, but we never had more than ten or fifteen minutes. If C.C., whose family was strict Methodist, was home one minute after midnight on Saturdays, her dad, a white collar worker at the Post Office with an unused history degree from Rice University and not some red-necked vigilante, would be on the porch with a gun.

Do sixteen-year-olds go to that bluff anymore? Do shrimpboats still dock there and do they bring in a good catch? We surely had all the shrimp we ever wanted. Bowls just loaded with them at Christmas, the big jumbos stuck through with colored tooth picks for me to push into grapefruit or arrange on plates. As often as not, we'd have a crate of grapefruit somebody had brought up and left with us from the Valley, the Ruby Reds, they called them; they were almost red inside and they were sweet too.

At Christmas we ate ourselves sick on boiled shrimp, and on oysters, fried and on the half-shell and every other way. We always knew somebody with a boat who kept it in the basin and found some excuse to board, and before you knew it, we'd made a party; we'd dance on the decks and play cards in the cabins and there were always cokes or maybe a little bourbon, bourbon sours in December, or boiled shrimp and beer. During the holidays, if there wasn't a yacht basin party, there'd be a Mexican supper somewhere with freshly made tamales. One way or another, you'd get that good food.

At any time of year you could go to North Beach and I liked to, though some of my friends thought it was tacky (all the sailors from the naval base hung out there) where you could buy corn on the cob and ride the Ferris wheel and swing out over the bay. When I was on it, tipping back and forth near the top and could see the town lights for miles in all directions, some of them coming, I realized, from that smelly little town which formed me, I thought about going North and East, to Europe maybe, and most certainly, to New York.

And now, here I am with Joe away from me, having accomplished very little of what I intended, and in one of the places I reached for, and a damn cold part.

Do you remember how I used to throw messages—scrawled on Dixie cups that I unfolded and labeled page one and page two—over the side of the Ferris wheel, how on sticky summer nights, the air almost too heavy to breathe, I'd just let them float? "Hey, there it goes!" I'd yell. "Hell, I want to get out of Texas."

Travis would call up from the bottom, "What's the matter, isn't it hot enough for you?"

"Yeah, yeah, it's hot. I want to get out of Hell."

"My name is Elizabeth," my message would say, "and I go to high school here in C.C. I like to go to shows and read long novels and walk the beach and seawall, for miles sometimes, and eat and drink and dance at boating parties. And I like to swim too. Write to me and tell me about where you are and how you like it and what you do."

I'd squeeze all that on a Dixie cup and toss it.

Now I'm trying something much harder, to send messages the other way.

I see my grandfather on the sun porch; his cancer took two years. I painted his face every day. Every day he'd say, "Honey, why do you want to go running? The future's here. If you stay right here, the world will come to you someday."

God, I'd give anything for a fat grapefruit with some boiled shrimp stuck on it or a half gallon of sour limeade, I'd drink it in the snow. Or ten minutes of Ben's kisses, or just one or two. Or to hear Travis saying, "I don't believe I'll have any onions, how about you, C.C.?" That or anything. He's gone now, the first among us. I don't remember which war took him. He was a handsome senior, after his skin cleared up and tanned and his shoulders filled out and his hair grew. He left us, though. "This is a backwater." That's the last thing I remember him saying. "I'm going to come back and get my girl and get out of it." The girl, by that time, wasn't C.C.; she tried to hide the hurt before she and I went off to college and I'll tell you how, soon.

Have you ever read a more disgustingly homesick letter? Oh, but, I'd give anything for the taste and sound and feel of you, your voices, your kisses, for a North Beach Ferris wheel ride that would go on for a long time, or maybe, never stop, turn me again and again toward those little refinery lights and the Gulf of Mexico where I once wrote messages and dropped them over your sometimes smelly, sometimes sweet and sultry bay.

Hollywood, CA

*W*ell, it's taken me some time to get back to you and I've crossed a lot of miles and many thousand, over decades and decades, in memory.

First of all, in catching up from last time, never mind that neither of them had mothers. The thing was, Travis saw more clearly than she did the difference between a Downtown Methodist and an Assembly of God member—his tiny church was on a gravel road just off the highway to Alice and on the far inland fringe of town—or between the offspring of a man with a degree from Rice University and a tombstone cutter's child.

"It won't work ever," he said to her the day she talked about going to The University of Texas. "I'm never going to go there or to any place like it." C.C. was going to major in art so that she could teach it, nothing she liked better to do than draw.

"You could come to see me," she told him. "And at night you could go to college here in Corpus. It would be OK to go to—" And she named it, the junior college none of us wanted. To stay in you, go to school in you, Corpus, was to go to sleep, like a little death, like being left behind. "You think The Stone would make it?"

That just came out; his getting mad was the last thing in the world she wanted.

C.C., I believe now, was really in love with Travis. Love, I've found out, has no regard for ages, but I couldn't have thought that then. Couldn't admit her ready. Or that Christmas she mounted our loud pink steps, "¡Caramba!" or "Hot Damn," Bo called the color, she had come to say goodbye.

I was packing my bags for college. In just a few months, I would be back I told her. We would write all the time and be close; never mind that the college was in New York.

But she had moved away from me even then, had been funny all summer, buying slinky dresses instead of shirtwaists and bangle bracelets which she had never before worn, and peroxiding streaks in her hair.

Began going out with boys who were older, out of high school, grown men some of them, even with an officer or two from the naval air station. I never could find out exactly where she met them, though she threw out an allusion or two. The son of someone T.J. had known at Rice; (T.J. was her father). Now a handsome twenty-four-year-old naval lieutenant and a visitor in the real estate office where she'd taken a summer job.

Two years later, on that same porch when we were both home for Christmas and strange to each other, she showed her tiny diamond to my mother. She hardly looked at me. It was a year after Travis had taken another girl and gone away. "Why, C.C.," my mother asked, "you getting married?"

"Yes ma'am."

"Why, have you thought about it?"

"Yes ma'am."

Corpus, if I came back to you now, would I know you? Or in unfamiliar buildings and on superhighways, just be lost in tangle? As you can see from the letterhead, I left that cold place I was in and, as they used to say in the movies, came on out to "the coast."

Los Angeles is still pretty—if you don't think about what it is, even the brown haze that hangs on the horizon during certain sunset hours—a city of flowers and balding mountain tops and Spanish voices and many flat, dark faces (I imagine a gentle acceptance in some of them), large sections that are, at least in the daytime, like sleepy little towns. When I ride a Sunset Blvd. bus past pink and blue buildings, one of them devoted entirely to some latter day religion, I think: Why I've come full circle, this is Corpus Christi, but my, how it's grown, even the palms are taller, and how much more it has now, though it all looks worn and more than a little shabby, but so much time has passed, I guess we all do.

I know, of course, that only something about it is like, something sent from here, maybe, that got stuck in the culture.

Your palms were thick, Corpus, and except for that bluff half a mile or so back from your seawall, you had no hills of any kind. Yet, ever since I arrived here, stepping first off a Greyhound bus and then onto a city bus, I've been overwhelmed by the familiar. Again and again I've said to myself, I've always known this and yet I never even saw it in the movies. Paris, Rome and I grew up on shots of New York. But Hollywood Blvd? Never. Since I was always geared to radio, did I miss those pictures? Why does it seem I might have been young here?

We had no mountains in South Texas and only a little of the same vegetation, oleanders, with their milky poison and the bitter leaf castorbean, yes.

Corpus, you were certainly duller, flatter, bleaker. Yet, here, too, I find scary, barren places. On one side an inhospitable desert, on the other a cold and treacherous sea.

I never thought of the Gulf as treacherous. As often as not, it seemed sluggish, though, of course, on stifling late summer and early fall days hurricanes grew out of it.

The Driscol Hotel, where the seniors had their dances and I hear that's gone now, sat up on a bluff, wind whipping around it, blowing hard enough to tear hair out of the head. I always tied mine up in a scarf. Tyrone Power, who was a big movie star, stayed there; he was in the marines and several of us from the refinery town rode the bus over and went to the movies, then hung around in the Driscol corridors just hoping to get a glimpse and when we never did, grew bold enough to write love notes and stick them under the door.

My note, though, only started as a love note. I managed always to put love off.

Dear Mr. Power,

I think you're wonderful and a good actor. I'd like to meet you someday. Or talk to you on the phone. And might if I came to Hollywood.

Do you know of any jobs there for a young person with an interest in radio drama? Working in pictures would be all right, too, though I'm mostly interested in sound.

Four or five miles south of the Driscol, the Church of the Good Shepherd, Episcopal, though the Spanish architecture made it look Catholic, or "The Shepherd of the Roses," as my friend, Bartola, a wild Mexican boy I'll tell you about later, called it, sat on a shelf of its own. The young blond minister's name was Reverend Rose (no one said "Father," which possibly gave Bartola his title) a man with pink cheeks and straw colored hair. I only remember Reverend Rose in white, though, surely, in the course of our liturgical year, he must have worn other colors.

I went every Sunday to the Young People's Fellowship and to Evensong, the service I loved best and after spending twenty-five years as an atheist-agnostic, still do, though today I don't know where I'd find one or who I'd take along. Back then, C.C. as often as not, went with me though her membership was with the Methodists downtown. We played board games and down in the rec room, danced to songs like "Harbor Lights" or "Twilight Time," tunes that seemed to go on in you, Corpus, after the rest of the country forgot about them.

But we came for the simple service, too, which without a choir, we sang, kneeling on the crimson velveteen cushions and looking out at the tall, clear windows at the palm branches swaying in a dark wind. The prayers were to God and all bright angels to help us get through the evening in a world shutting down. What I liked, the idea I liked, though I never spoke of it, was that the few of us there, young and ignorant as I knew even then we were, could help God and the angels with that.

> *Keep watch . . . with those who work, or watch or weep this night, and give thine angels charge . . . bless the dying, sooth the suffering, pity the afflicted, shield the joyous; and all for thy love's sake.*

I can't remember now what the old prayer was but it had this same idea. Shield the joyous.

We prayed for ourselves to be shielded then.

Couldn't help what we felt and people can't, can't help their feelings, the life rising in us.

Caused me to sing every morning on my way to the bus stop and after school to run as fast as my strong legs would carry me, sometimes still singing, between the rows of pin oaks to our house.

Bud always said my voice should be trained.

In the house my grandmother lay on her bed doubled up with pain in her stomach no doctor could abolish, no amount of morphine deadened. Weak as she was, she managed to get by us when we weren't looking, pull the step ladder out of the closet in the kitchen, climb up it and reach for the top of the cabinet where Bo thought he had the "medicine" out of reach. In the late afternoons he would stand over her bed asking if she'd like this or that for supper, for a while everything we ate, from macaroni and cheese to oyster stew, was made with milk, and he and Aunt Rena would fix it, Aunty laughing. She was always full of laughter no matter what was going on. "I never saw any proof that life is serious," she'd tell me.

Were she and I, then, among those to be shielded? I asked that question back then.

Today if I went to an Evensong I wouldn't have to ask. But where could I find one? And who could I take along?

I long ago lost track of Bartola Perra and wonder if he's still living. Somehow I never thought of him living long. I don't know why. He wasn't frail looking, only thin with pockmarks. He wasn't accident prone.

Not long ago I heard a terror story about him, heard that last year on the corner of Hollywood and Highland, with a throng in front of Mann's Chinese Theatre watching, watching TV stars arrive for a premier, (not watching Bartola), he was shot through the heart.

Probably just a story although they say he handled cocaine.

"Spic-Wop boy," people said back in you, Corpus Christi, meaning Mexican-Italian (or "Eye-talian") and he was mostly Mexican I think. He wore shirts in bright colors, silky looking synthetics, tied up high like I used to tie mine, all of his mid-section and some of his stomach showing.

"He wants to do you-know-what with his own sex," my friend, Lana, had told me, but in those days I didn't, had only the sketchiest idea of what "you-know-what" was. I knew the sailors who went to North Beach on their Liberties were from lots of places, California as well as New Orleans or Pensacola and that Bartola struck up friendships with some of them, "went off," as he put it, with this one and that, and that sometimes they bought him things.

"I know this town," he'd tell me, "and I show it to them, Baby." Then he would wink and tell me how he showed them the bluffs on the far side of the seawall, his favorite, a deep cavern directly beneath the church, "The Shepherd of the Roses," as he continued to call it, that he was sure no one knew but him.

I wondered if he had an eye for our young minister. And sometimes when we sang or prayed or chanted "Shield the joyous," I wondered if Bartola sat down under the bluff and if he heard and who it was we protected, Reverend Rose or him.

"The person who bought this for me," he'd tell me as he ran his fingers over a silky lapel, "the person has good taste."

Some days he put on lipstick and rouge and a big gold earring, not a fad then, like a movie-star pirate or a movie-star gypsy or a boy-girl. A joy-boy. Into joy, yes, wanting to find it and at the same time, scared he might, scared he couldn't stand it or, worse, that he'd have to steal it and then not be able to stand it and then get caught.

Scared and hiding away a lot of the time, but also receptive. And we were all a little like that; I was like that, but most of the kids I knew wouldn't admit it, so that those who sat around Bartola in speech class got up fast when the bell rang, got out of the room in a hurry.

"He's a disgrace," my friend, Lana, whispered one day just before she disappeared. Lana lived in the house just behind us. Remembering my family chronicle, which I'd learned mostly through my mother and from Aunty, I didn't worry about disgrace; I figured I'd been born in it.

"Elizabeth," Bartola said as I dropped my books slowly into my book bag, we had speech together for two semesters, "Elizabeth, I need to talk to you." We had both had to give speeches in which we used our hands and both gave one on trimming hats. I put flowers on a big white leghorn, he outlandish satin bows on a purple velveteen beret. "I don't care that they all go; you're the only one I care about. They are all so, so—"

"Dull," I said. "And they're afraid of their shadows." Then I grinned at him for he looked surprised.

"You think that, too?" He lifted one of his eyebrows, so black I thought he might have dyed it, and I nodded. "Did you know I went to North Beach last night? Want to know what I did there?"

Here the kids who stand, hands on hips, on Santa Monica Blvd., are often shirtless and seem to like it that way, smiling much of the time, looking happy as if nothing pleased them better than to hustle. Calling out to everybody. Old, young, male, female.

"Hey, lady, I like your body!"

The other day I asked C.C. when I wrote my yearly letter on funny paper I bought as a joke, Sodom and Gomorrah written across the top like a letterhead, if she remembered Bartola and if back in those church days, she thought he'd heard our chanting. She'll probably think I'm nuts.

Asked her, too, if she thought we helped shut those days down.

Now, as then, the world closes.

Here in this improbable place, limos, coliseums, baths, I think of Rome—a poor small town by comparison—of apocalypse. In the summer, fire falls from the air and in the spring whole streets have purple trees. The church I sometimes visit has no children and only a few young people. Cecil B. DeMille, once a member, gave it the Ten Commandments he used in the movie and they're still in the narthex though somebody ripped off the plaque that went alongside.

"I hope they sold it for food instead of coke," the Korean Father says. His church feeds the hungry, opens its doors to the displaced, the jobless and homeless, the addicted.

When I lived in you, Corpus, my church going ran alongside my Grandmother's dying. She was a lifelong Methodist, the other people in the family not members of any church though all believed in what they called a Higher Power and most, like Bo and my mother, in taking communion once in awhile, "joining with The Body," as Uncle Leeland said, though most of the time, whiskey was all he took into his. When I was a child he would leave me at the Episcopal church for Sunday School two doors from the place where he drank, could bring his own bottle, and sometimes where he met women, and all this time, you understand, he was married to Aunt Rena and loved her. He was like all of us, split up that way sometimes, or at least, and how I hated it, like everyone I knew.

I promised I would tell you, but still haven't, have I, about Uncle Bo?

Later

*F*or you to know anything about Uncle Bo, you also have to know about his attachment to my grandmother and how he cared for her through her terrible sickness which began shortly after the start of still another war. The Korean, this time.

I was a senior in high school; during the summer I had, for the first time, flown across the country, to join Mother and Bud, and got my first look at New York. In October, the same month that Grandma began to complain of pains in her stomach, I began regular attendance at The Good Shepherd and Marion Van De Meyer, my Communications teacher, gave me nearly full responsibility for running the radio station at school.

That time preceded so many changes: graduation, our move from Palm Drive and good-byes to many. Some of my friends moved away for jobs or to get an early start on college and half of the boys I knew enlisted in the army or navy.

At the end of my senior year we moved into a new house in a better neighborhood, although we didn't own the house, merely rented, closer to The Good Shepherd which had been a bus trip across town. The church building itself, an unadorned white stucco, gave me a sense of protection, of peaceful harbor.

Bo put our old house on the market because he said he couldn't stand to hear Grandma still in it; he claimed to hear her for months after she died, and in July he sold it, so that two years later, when C.C. came back to show her ring off on our newly colored steps, (¡Caramba!), it was a different house, all the old ghosts gone, she came back to.

"I had to get us out," Bo told me, "your grandmother gone and not gone, clinging on to all of us, trying to take me with her." I, too, thought I'd heard noises, felt threatened. And I blamed her, blamed her for not dying the way I thought she ought to. She went one sticky June afternoon, screaming and clawing the air, saying she wasn't going to do it. Threw up and then choked on part of her insides.

The diagnosis for what she'd called "nervous stomach" came in December; she'd had some stomach trouble for as long as any of us could remember, always eating Tums or asking for soda or Pepto Bismal, but it had grown much worse that fall. She suffered all through those last months in a blue speckled house dress she'd sewn up herself and in an amber one just like it except for the color. "I can just 'wrench' these out myself," she said.

She "wrenched" them both out every weekend and lived her death days in them, alternating the colors all winter when the sun was, as she so often said, pale in the "windas," stopped in June just after my graduation from Corpus Christi High School to which I wore a yellow sashed white eyelet dress, the sun so bright then, all of us, except her, consumed by heat.

My mother always says it's our destiny, and she means by this our family's destiny, to die in summer and that it's fitting then, graduation time.

But I've always thought my death will come, that I will fall into it, a few weeks or months after my New Year's birthday, just before the green budding of trees and before the delicate colors of wildflowers that just crop up in the grass, pale pinks and deep blues and buttercups, that my body and brain will know better somehow than to try to make it through another year and with both earthly and celestial help I can quit before even the earliest breaking of the Texas spring.

Maybe that's because I read somewhere that people who die of natural causes do go a few weeks or months past their birthdays. My old friend, Joe Copeland, did it that way, died a little past his New Year's birthday; in his last years we had celebrated together; Joe had just raised a window on a whole lot of brightness and something, a question, a wonder, had sprung up between us, suddenly as wildflowers and as fragile, gone as quickly, surprising him and me.

That winter my grandmother asked me to paint her face every morning. "Paint my face!" she'd cry and I'd think: Oh, you are so vain and difficult.

"Paint my face!" When she'd yell that my mind would drift to thoughts of Ben, to being held by him or to dancing down in the Shepherd's rec room, to the way the music made me feel there, like I could fly.

Paint my face. My grandfather had asked for the same thing, but he'd meant medicine and she meant make-up, a special cream I filled wrinkles in with, then make-up base, plum colored lipstick, powder, plum colored rouge. "Come here," she called, "Come here and help me."

I translated that to mean: Pay for the room I give you. My mother sends a check every month, I wanted to call back, my mother pays you.

My grandmother came from people for whom life had been hard and who were stingy with one another, not with food or money so much, though they were careful with those, as with affectionate words for one another and with touch.

Only now I remember that frail saving sweetness I sensed rising in her — I try now to focus on what was saving in us — that I saw play around her lips, when she sewed.

My grandmother cared for me through work, the only way she knew how, sewing for long hours, making when I was small, among other things, beautiful organdy dresses. I remember a peach one for Easter, knotted with purply ribbons and garlands of flowers. Though dressmaking was her gift, she cooked for long times, too, making angel food cakes for all our birthdays and homemade ice cream, stirring the custard for that on the wood stove we had when I was little, collapsing in a chair when she was done, calling out to Grandaddy and Leeland to pour it in the freezer and crank it, otherwise uncommunicative, looking martyred, the way she thought she was supposed to be.

One Sunday afternoon when I refused to go on a drive with her, she said I wasn't grateful. The drive was as much a ritual as church and she put on the same hat and gloves for it. And each week Bo, in jacket and tie, got out the DeSoto and drove her down by the waterfront, then up the bluff past all the expensive houses on Ocean Drive.

Aunt Rena, seldom around much on weekends, was off gadding somewhere. She never met a stranger, struck up friendships on city buses and in public parks and movie matinees and during the course of a week, visited more people than the rest of us did in a year. Black hair slicked back and gold-looped earrings stuck through her ears.

On Sundays when she was gone, Bo and Grandma both took pleasure in talking about her and I can tell you, in sometimes calling her some awful names. It was in Grandma's side of the family to do that, the English-German side, not the Black Scot.

I wrote or did homework on Sundays and on that particular one was well into what I thought might be a hot radio drama, a ghost story — always did turn out a lot of them — copied from the format of "Inner Sanctum," a show that always began with the sound of a squeaking door.

"If it weren't for me and for your Uncle Bo, do you have any idea where you would be?" My grandmother asked the question in a level voice and pointed toward the street with the cane she had carried since the summer she broke her hip, before I had even begun grade school.

I threw everything on my desk at her: pens, books and even my ink bottle, all but the typewriter, God knows I didn't want to damage that, and all missed, but the ink and glass made a mess on Bo's newly polished floor.

During the following week I was down on my knees with a steel wool pad, feeling wretched, doing penance. I had just made my first earned radio money from a Saturday broadcast and in addition to trying to get the stain out of the floor, I spent almost all of it on an Elizabeth Arden cream and worked half of Monday afternoon smoothing out the wrinkles in Grandma's face.

"Where's your Uncle Bo?" she asked and I just told her he would be late by a little.

He had called home to say he and Robin Lee were down on the waterfront eating shrimp in a basket. "You tell Rena to go on with whatever she can find for super; there are pork chops in the refrigerator and you can help her peel and mash some potatoes, Mother can eat mashed potatoes, and open some canned green beans."

"I suppose you would rather be off somewhere with that girl friend of yours," Grandma said. "She's boy-crazy."

"She's not boy-crazy, Grandma." No, just Travis-crazy, I thought.

I remembered a time when she and I had hung around the lot with the tombstones in it for half a Sunday morning waiting for Travis to finish helping his father carve birth and death dates into several newly commissioned stones.

Travis's father, a big, silent and I thought probably sullen man, finally pulled five one-dollar bills out of his apron pocket and handed them to Travis who grinned at us and within minutes we were in The Stone on our way to North Beach, Travis's arm around C.C., her head on his shoulder, both of them in my idea of Heaven.

"Well," Grandma said, "God knows where you go or what you do." She picked up the jar of cream I had bought and put it on the night stand and I took it from her — for a moment I thought she might throw it at me— and opened it, dipped my middle finger in and carefully patted her face. "I suppose your Uncle Bo is running around with that boy from the navy."

"No, Grandma, he said he had to work. I guess he's still at the office." I lied because I know she'd be furious if she thought he was with Robin Lee. She tolerated Jay.

Just about that time the nurse we hired to be with Grandma — I must have known her name but I forget it — poked her head in and said she wanted to talk to me. Did I realize Grandma had insisted she change all her bedding and spoon feed the vegetable soup Rena made for lunch? "I'm a practical nurse, not a maid or a keeper," she told me, and then said I could do the chores she had mentioned or Aunt Rena could. "I realize she's in terrible pain, but I sometimes wish you people would find someone else to help her bear it. The old lady sure knows how to dish out abuse."

I said that if she talked to Bo, he might be willing to pay her a little more, but was immediately sorry I had said it. I knew Bo had just enough for our bills.

"Maybe he'll have to," she told me. "Your grandmother expects too much."

Grandaddy hadn't seemed to have expected anything. "Ellen," he asked, the only time I remember his asking for anything except his medicine, "could you please make a dish sometime without noodles and tomatoes in it? Do you always have to stretch everything?"

She stretched food so she'd have money to buy expensive fabric and patterns, though she often sewed from her own.

Now I remember all the dresses she made and sold, some of them for good prices, and how she smiled when she sewed. I saw that same shy delighted smile the day she discovered that I was on the radio, heard my voice coming out of it and onto the sunporch, with my Saturday broadcast for teens.

"Why, how is it?" she asked, tickled, "that I can hear you on the radio when you are also right here with me in this room?"

"It's a recording, Grandma."

I don't know that she ever understood that.

I considered her a domestic, narrow minded and of little curiosity, bigoted, judgmental and opposed somehow to loving, all I swore I would not be. I only half thought of her sickness as serious and only toward the end as "dying," annoyed as I was when I couldn't play my records or type scripts for my broadcasts and worried that I wouldn't be able to give a successful senior party. Successful ones were loud.

And almost every senior gave one, a brunch after which people stayed to play "Oklahoma" or "South Pacific" on the hi-fi and to air frustrations and dreams, or a coke party, which then meant Coca-Cola, or even a formal tea.

The coke parties, held usually on Saturday mornings, were the easiest and the cheapest and allowed for the most people and I was going to have mine with C.C. We planned to have more than one hundred seniors and to use my house since it had the bigger yard. My grandmother's room, however, was practically in it, so I didn't see how we could have any fun.

"You'll just have to ask for quiet," Bo said, "and tell those who know her to drop in and pay their respects."

I don't know why that came so hard. For reasons that aren't clear to me even now I was ashamed, ashamed almost to have a grandmother, ashamed to be living with her and ashamed most all of her terrible sickness. It ran in families we all knew.

The sickness and our knowledge of it was so awful that I sometimes think we held back or misplaced our true feelings and did cruel, and in the manner in which Bo had formed us, even shocking things.

Did we think of her dying as too common, maybe? He doesn't want us to be common, Mama. And had we all in such close quarters been too much for each other, my mother and Bud back by spring? Bo said so.

Coronado, CA

*G*randma died three days after my senior party.

Yes, C.C. and I pulled that off.

Draped all the porches, front and side and even the back patio, with purple and gold crepe paper, Buckaneer colors, our cheerleaders wore purple bell-sleeved blouses, gold satin boleros and sashes. "Colors for thieves," I said to C.C. I always did feel I was one and grew up in the right place, snatching my fun. To guide the guests around the side of the house so they wouldn't ring the doorbell or walk straight through, we made a walkway out of sticks wrapped in crepe paper.

Grandma seemed almost well that day—sat up in bed in a peach colored bed jacket Bo had brought home for her the afternoon he came in late after supper with Robin Lee—smiled, spoke nicely to all who came in to see her and told several she hoped they would stay.

"Elizabeth is a smart girl," she told C.C., "but not always company. Just types."

Here I am still typing and looking out on another bay, shut away from its beauty, although through the window I see the gold glittering on the water, holed up to meet a deadline, forever cranking out radio dramas, this one about adolescence, though it seems more urgent to write to you about my own.

At our party C.C. and one or two others, Lana and Gerry I remember, stayed all day and then that night stayed over. C.C. had several calls from Travis and at midnight, he came to the house and I heard them on the front porch. This was because Gerry had told C.C. that if she wanted to talk to Travis, she'd have to ask him over because she had her own plans for the phone.

We all peeked and saw them nuzzling one another and we heard them, too. Travis, I believe, spoke as little as his father, but his soft voice was very much more appealing and the few words he did use and his very presence, a shy one, said a lot.

"I don't know what to do about you," we heard him whisper that night. Then "I'm in misery." And, of the two of them, I think he may have been the one most in it. And the one who stayed. Both of them somehow were, in spite of their kissing and clinging, a sad sight, not one to watch for long, so after the briefest glimpse, I turned away.

Turned toward the hall telephone and my two other friends, Lana and Gerry—Lana, a strawberry blonde with freckles—she wore a Veronica Lake peek-a-book hairstyle hoping it would hide some of them — and Gerry, a dark, maverick of a girl like me.

Gerry liked to call teachers, always had crushes on the male ones and calling them and pretending to be a poll taker, asked their views on local issues while making thumping noises with the hand she held against the small breast closest to her heart.

That night she also called our famous Baptist preacher, well known on radio all the way to Del Rio, "Brother Blow off," we said, and asked his opinion on certain picture shows—we knew his daughter had to come home from scout camp because she'd seen one—then asked if he thought the Dragon Grill, the newest restaurant in town, ought to be issued a liquor license so it could serve mixed drinks.

Bo, who seemed to feel as festive as we did, stayed in the kitchen mixing his own, even serving us one now and then, a good thing C.C.'s dad never knew it. C.C.'s mother, before she left, drank a lot of Jax beer so drinking, in general, upset him. "I'll never be a drunk like my brother," Uncle Bo said, downing his daiquiri, getting ready to cook short orders.

"Why don't you call up Bartola?" Gerry asked, giggling. "Ask him if he's going to the prom. Ask what he'll be wearing." She saw him, she said, in a sequined dress.

"That's mean, Gerry," I said. "You know I won't do that." I told Uncle Bo I thought we'd all like some scrambled eggs. Scrambled eggs, Bo said, were common. So he baked eggs for us, with hot peppers and cheese on top.

We stayed up all night, of course. Bo, too. Toward morning Grandma started screaming and from then until the end, the agony we were witness to was, for all of us, nearly impossible to bear. The woman we hired to nurse her wouldn't, walked out right after she walked in, early in that day. Later Bo argued with the doctor about giving Grandma heroin.

"Who in the hell cares if it makes her an addict?" Bo asked.

Weeks after she died Bo said he could still hear her screaming; in his sleep he said, that's when he heard her. And when he didn't sleep he heard worse. Heard her dragging what surely sounded like her dead body through one-hundred-degree heat in the Palm Drive house.

I don't know if I heard her or only imagined that I did worn out as I was from my first job which seemed to have nothing to do with anything

I cared about, in the fur department of Lichenstein's, typing numbers day after day.

I had hoped to work for KRIS but Dan Rodriguez who had been my assistant at the high school station took its only summer spot.

The man Bo brought to the house didn't look much older than Dan, light skinned, light eyed, a year or two past twenty. The first time I saw him standing in the screen door that separated the side porch from the breakfast room, he was eating a big chunk of angel food cake, Aunty made that after Grandma died, and he looked like an angel, or the way I had always imagined one, sunlight striking him through the branches and lacy leaves of the Chinaberry tree.

A mistake, I thought at first, for him to have left California where he might have gotten into pictures. I probably got my ideas of what angels should look like from the movies. But he suffered when he first spoke and held his mouth in a pursing way that changed my mind. "We w-w-w-were b-b-b-oth sa-sa-sa-sailors i-n-n-n San Diego." He got the name of the city out whole. He told me how he met Bo who had run the general store at the naval base and was never sent overseas. Another man, someone else he met in San Diego, brought him to Corpus and to work in Las Hadas, Bartola said that meant "The Good Fairy"—my friends giggled about that—where we had eaten once a month since I was small. Just an accident he said that both his navy friends came from the same place.

I could tell Jay's presence made Bo happy. I had never seen Bo look at anyone like that except sometimes at Grandma and now and then at me. I don't know that it was sexual, in the way people usually think about that, although, I guess, in the truest sense it was, only that there was all this feeling in it.

Bo's love for his family we all knew and he knew, too, was excessive, was more akin to passion, because, or so Rena said, he was the baby and pampered, or because family was something he felt he could never get out of, that it was sinful to even want to.

Now some of this same love spilled over to the boy who looked so much like Bo that he might have been his brother.

Bo never looked at Robin Lee that way, or I never saw him do it; most of the time he looked past her, looked away, as if he was afraid. Yet there was no question in my mind that he considered making her his wife.

He would have married her, he said, as soon as he got out of the service, but since he looked after Grandma and Grandaddy, being the only one of their children able to do it, Leeland and Lloyd both dead and my mother as the only girl considered financially incapable, he didn't know how he could also take on Robin Lee.

Aunty said he could have found a way if he had really wanted to, but I could see his side. Robin Lee didn't make much at Bo's insurance office where she worked as a sometimes typist and filing clerk. She would have been an extra burden and was frail besides, susceptible to colds, a touch of T.B. once someone said, and suffered from continual bronchial trouble. Yet, one humid afternoon, I heard him asking her to consider life with him and with us all.

"Mother would like to have you and I would, too," he told her. Then he said that, of course, her mother would also be welcome. "If you were both just here it would help us all so much." A false smile, the one he wore when, inside at least, he trembled, played around his lips.

They were still sitting at the breakfast room table where they had eaten lunch. I was just outside on the porch, (almost all our rooms had porches), but they didn't know.

When Robin Lee asked where she would stay, he said she could have the little extra room just off the hall near Grandma, between Grandma's room and the place on the porch where Bo slept. Or, if she liked, he said she could stay out with her mother in the garage apartment, Leona and Bud would be gone all fall, though I could tell both by what he said and the halting way in which he spoke that he wanted her in the house.

The bed in the garage apartment, he said, was a narrow double and only really any good for man and wife. Then he said he thought he could get her and her mother a tenant for their house for the time it was vacant, maybe an officer from the naval air station so that when the new year came they would be a few dollars ahead.

Robin Lee's mother had spoken of wanting a change, was known by all of us to like excitement; this might be just as good as a trip. As he spoke he looked out the window, his trembling voice almost a whisper and then stopped with, "Oh, please, Robin Lee."

"I don't see how I could," she told him. Her voice also trembled and her freckled hands, both clutching the china cup into which he poured the coffee. He still hovered over her and I now remember where Aunt Rena thought he got his name. From the "Bo" in "bow and arrow."

Grandaddy or somebody had said he was as bent as a bow, that the taller he grew the more he bent over, and thin as a bow string. Now I watched the string that was him quiver as if arrows would soon be shot off.

My mother, who gave him piano lessons at night and behind drawn curtains so that the neighbors wouldn't know a boy of our family was studying music, said that music and not arrows would come from him.

"If you could it would," he said, then stopped so that I, still eavesdropping on the breakfast room porch, wanted to finish for him. Wanted him to say, "It would make me happy."

"It would," he said, "help Mother. Be a help to Mother and to me."

She dropped the cup then and it made a big noise as it hit the glass table top, but didn't break, though the coffee spilled over the glass and on to the floor. He brushed her shoulder with one of his large knotted hands, and she shook like a little yard rabbit shakes and she was shy and plain as one, a funny girl for Bo who, when he was away from the office, and toward the end, in it, wore so many red shirts and red caps and liked so many things bold. "I'll clean it up," he said.

For a second I thought she might dart out of the room and pass me on the porch, but she stayed put, shaking, the coffee a pool on the speckled linoleum floor. I opened the door then, thinking maybe they needed me to help clear away the tension and as I came in I thought I heard her say, "We'll see."

Finally it wasn't Robin Lee but her mother who refused us. Her mother, or so I heard Aunt Rena say, didn't like the proposed location of Robin Lee's room.

By the time the refusal came, half of you, Corpus, seemed to know that Bo Bell had tried to bring a girl he worked with into his house to live with him there and had even had the audacity to also ask her mother.

When many months later Bo invited Jay to live with us, he pointed to the ribbons of light in the bedroom, Grandma's room that he offered. With Grandma's dresser gone— he had given the dresser to me—he said there would be plenty of room for an easel. Drawing was what Jay most liked to do.

I knew the neighbors would talk about Jay living with us even more than they would talk about Robin Lee. Ever since he first came to our house, Lana's mother asked me lots of questions about him; Lana lived right behind us with her mother and brother, her father, a railroad engineer, dead for years, killed in an accident on the SP. And once I heard Brad, Lana's overgrown and I thought overbearing brother, call Jay a queer. Where had Jay come from, Lana's mother wanted to know and where had Bo met him? Who were Jay's people and why on earth was he living in Las Hadas? Even

Lana's mother, who as far as I knew never ate Mexican food, but only collard and mustard greens and the plainest of meat and potatoes, and who had given her children movie magazine names, even Lana's mother had heard about Las Hadas and "that."

Although you weren't a little town, Corpus, not in numbers, not even in those days, you behaved like one.

Bo said it was natural for Jay to live in Las Hadas since he worked there.

"Yes," Aunt Rena said, "but in what capacity?"

She didn't care, was laughing when she asked this.

Still I felt Jay, Uncle Bo, myself, all threatened.

'Oh," I said, "he works as a waiter, handyman, painter." I was quick to give the list.

Still at Coronado

*I*n Las Hadas where we had come for our monthly dinner, we sat at a lacquered table shaped like a tropical flower. Jay had not only done the art work in it and on the red, green and blue chairs we sat in, but he had also painted the mural before us which featured a hillside dotted with pink and blue houses, banana leaves in the foreground, an ocean in the background and a little strip of blue sky. And over it all, a small woman who held a large stick. I had looked at it through several evenings and over a good many enchiladas before I realized the stick was a wand and the woman a fairy godmother. A little magic, a fantasy, Jay said.

I liked the mural and told him so, the way he had done her with just a few curved strokes.

Drawing, not painting, he said to us, stumbling hardly at all over the words, was what interested him most, that and wearing apparel, odd, I thought. Designing clothes was what he really wanted to do; he said he had, in fact, already designed some, had a portfolio he might sometime take to New York.

"I'm going to sell them," he told me, each word as clear as crystal. And I thought maybe he looked into one and saw his future there.

I had never before met anyone with so focused an artistic ambition. In high school I had come in second in the "Most Likely to Succeed" contest. Dan came in first, which was strange to me since he was my assistant at the station, but I suspected he won votes for his position in the Student Council which only made officers of boys, and even more for the wheeling and dealing the kids knew he could do with cars; he even finagled a few spots on our station for them. From my second semester at CCHS I collected all the material and did all the scheduling for CCHS Broadcasting and was sure that radio, either in writing or production, would somehow be my life. My wanting to work at something particular and not just earn a check, was odd to most people and sometimes even to me. I couldn't have explained it and still can't, but ever since I was little and heard voices coming out of our old floor model radio, my grandfather and uncles huddled around it, and only the men listened with consistency, I had wanted to.

When the war was on and the men gone and even Uncle Bo off in the Navy, I listened alone. "Portia Faces Life" to "Lux Radio Theater," "Gang Busters", "The Green Hornet" to "Quiz Kids" to "The Life of Riley" and "Fibber McGee and Molly" to President Roosevelt.

Worked to death, my mother spent her days and half her evenings, too, teaching music in the piano rooms provided for her in the public school.

On Texas stations I heard Joe Copeland's show; he had wonderful dramas, even then got his actors from the Alley Theatre in Houston. From earliest childhood, I had been an admirer of Joe's productions. Some of them were musical, his wife, Kate, was a singer, and some were concerned with the news and local issues, but more were dramatic. Except for the news shows, I listened to them all.

Then I met him. The year I won the teen's contest for radio drama and rode the bus to Dallas with my fans and a few winners in other divisions to get my prize.

"Leona Bell's daughter? Why, Elizabeth, all this is just in your blood." And he opened his arms wide as if to embrace me and my mother at that station. Joe was always one for the expansive gesture. "I still remember your mother opening KTHS."

KTHS stood for Come Home to Hot Springs. And no, I don't know why the initial for "Come" was a "K" instead of a "C." My mother's piano music followed by Governor Terrell's voice from the Arlington Hotel ballroom were the first sounds heard over the Arkansas airways at a time when there weren't more than fifty stations in the United States.

"You heard my mother?" I asked him.

"Everybody did. Queen of the Ivories, that's what they called her up there and even in some Texas counties. She played so many places, I heard her years later on an Okie station, WKY, I think it was and that was an oldie."

"Well," I told him, "I know she did once play in Oklahoma. I know she was with KCRC in Enid in 1926."

"Oh, those were exciting times, Elizabeth," Joe said, "an opening up for sound through the west." He laughed that wonderful deep laugh of his that seemed to come from somewhere near the very bottom of him. "She played in those stations outfitted with only a piano and a Victrola in somebody's parlor. Just a tangle of wires and homemade parts, your mother was a part of all that."

I told Joe I had heard that technicians in those early days found it hard to deal with a piano, that receiving sets wouldn't pick up the high notes, that violins were a better instrument for them to work with. "Your mother knew how to handle a piano for radio," Joe said. "Even with that primitive equipment she got almost all the music across."

It thrilled me that Joe Copeland knew my mother. No one in Corpus Christi knew her; once when I was a child, she had played for KOMA in Oklahoma City and KSD in Dallas, but she had never performed on radio in Corpus, or anywhere else in years.

When I came back from Dallas that spring the school almost elected me "Most Likely to Succeed" and the next fall Miss Van DeMeyer, whom we simply called "Miss V," put me in charge of our school station. Miss Van DeMeyer had been a Wave in the war and her name shortened, the "V" standing less for Van DeMeyer than for "Victory."

I didn't know if Jay's classmates had almost elected him "Most Likely To" anything, but I thought he and I had a lot in common, that, like me, he had probably come in second quite a lot. From the outset it seemed to me that the big difference between us was that he had a chance to realize his dreams, whereas, mine, so often and especially after graduation from high school, seemed thwarted.

I was right about that because an oil man who came to Las Hadas admired Jay's mural—Jay was reworking part of it, this rich man watching—and wanted to know what else he had done. "Do you have any pictures?" he asked. Jay was too practical, and he had been too poor, to have spent time painting pictures not knowing if anybody except his friends would ever see or buy them.

He and I are alike that way. Why I have never written anything but scripts.

"No, I don't paint," Jay told the oil man. Never mind that he stood there with a paintbrush and a tin of blue paint in his hands. "I'm interested mostly in drawing and in wearing apparel."

When the man came back a few days later to see Jay's portfolio, he put money on it and said he would arrange for a Dallas show.

Jay beamed as he appeared in front of us holding pottery plates steaming with rice, beans, enchiladas, the tacos and guacamole already on the table. And he didn't stutter once. "Next month," he told us, "I'm taking my line to Dallas."

Bo looked just miserable about that. But congratulated Jay and ordered Carta Blancas for himself and Aunt Rena and a coke for me.

"Bo Bell," Jay said, "I wish you could come with me."

"Well, I can't." Bo could seldom get away from his company.

"Well, then, hang on; when I get back I'll rent that r-r-room y-y-you sh-sh-owed me."

But he didn't as things turned out.

Bo lost his nerve about that. Later in the summer, after some talk started in you, Corpus, he retracted his offer, and right after, bee-lined it to Robin Lee's. And after talking to her, put the Palm Drive house on the market.

I don't know if he did that because he was too often reminded of Grandma's suffering in it or was just too afraid of Jay's moving in. Or was desperate for money to pay off bills.

Or some combination of all three.

I'm going to save the story about it for a little while. And I'm also going to put off the story of his engagement to Robin Lee.

Coronado,
Flecks of gold
still glittering in
the water and the sand

*M*y memory moves back and forth among these seasons, but what I have to tell you now is that very late in that summer after we moved into the big house that we rented in those hot, final weeks before I went to college, Bo seemed really dispirited, somehow brokenhearted, always walking around with a drink. I longed then to take off for the East, but postponed making a decision about going since I didn't think Bo should spend the money for my tuition and since I knew I could if I chose, even at the last minute, go to UT.

One unbearably hot hundred degree sticky afternoon, Bo studied the sketches Jay left and drank vodka, new for him; he had always talked against vodka, but on this day seemed to like it well enough mixed with grapefruit juice, freshly squeezed and poured over ice. A day came, of course, when he liked it any way, and as often as not, just turned up the bottle.

After he finished the drink and put Jay's sketches in a drawer, he went shopping. For years he had, at the beginning of every season, brought home a bunch of boxes for Grandma and for me, and some of the things for me were always for school and some were for dances and parties.

"But what if I'm not invited to any?" I would ask, pulling on the ashy black hair I hated, cowlicked in all the wrong places, even at seventeen I had grey patches, and he would say, "You're going to be ready to go."

Bo, like my grandmother and like Jay, loved dresses and he brought home several beauties, among them a long-sleeved, calf-length black cocktail dress, a cowl-necked crepe, the kind I dreamed about wearing in some cool foreign fall thousands of miles away from you, C.C. He also brought an expensive grey tweed suit and a number of cashmere sweaters that in my mind epitomized what successful young women wore on the job in New York. Then at the bottom of the box I found a pale grey-blue sleeveless swirly skirted chiffon that seemed more like Texas and home.

I had all month pored over the fashion magazines which in August, as we sweltered, were always filled with pictures of furs and heavy woolens, the kind of clothes people in South Texas sometimes bought for a season that never came. How well I remember every fall on the first sixty-degree morning putting on a corduroy skirt and bolero, or a jumper, over dark cotton, knowing it would be eighty by afternoon. Playing at autumn, feeling disappointed and guilty that it was not as advertised and as if that were somehow my fault.

I hoped when I left Texas I would be less defective, one of the reasons I wanted to go.

Being what the press said I should be was, of course, easier than trying to discover anything about myself or my region on my own. Cost me a lot of time and as I grabbed onto other people's lives and loves, or wanted to, made me even more thieving than I already was, while deepening shame.

"You can have any or all of them," Bo said about the dresses, "but you have to do something about your hair."

I thought maybe I would have my hair dyed cold black. Once and for all, get the ash out of it. Afterwards I would put it all up on rollers and then, to get the cowlicks out, brush like hell.

I told Uncle Bo I wanted only the cocktail dress, the crepe. But when I held the slate blue chiffon next to me, and I wanted to feel contempt for it, I thought for a moment I might go to college in both Texas and New York.

Was New York the center of the world? I didn't know, only knew that it, the center, was cold.

"Well," Bo said, "you might as well know it. They're all yours. I just put them on my charge."

During those August days he not only drank all the time, he spent money all the time, money he didn't have, granted that most of it was on other people, and a lot on me.

"Decide," he said, "which one you want to wear this evening. I'm taking you and Robin Lee, and" (he sighed) "her mother to the Dragon Grill for dinner."

This time I am now telling you about was late August or early September. Mother and Bud left right after we sold the house in mid-July. Jay was in Dallas and, from what we heard, thriving. He sent us copies of his press releases and a few pictures of his show, but he didn't write. I knew he had been rebuffed, and more, deeply hurt and disappointed when Bo turned him away. He had no idea that we were going to move or where, though of course Bo did finally tell him and sent the address.

But he certainly didn't know on that day when we set out for The Dragon. Or on the sweltering afternoon, some weeks before, when Bo had agreed to marry Robin Lee.

Just as, before that, Bo had no idea she was going to propose.

When we were all seated silently around a long table at The Dragon — we were, supposedly, in the dragon's mouth, sitting right at the tip of its tongue — I was nervous and kept fingering the grey-blue lace of my dress and the matching seashell earrings that at the last minute Bo pulled out of his hip pocket. Here we are, I thought, in the dragon's mouth, right on the tip of the dragon's tongue. And yet where are our own?

Then Bo and I began talking. I told him for the first time and to the silence of the others, that in a few weeks I thought if everything was OK I would go on up to Austin and UT. Robin Lee's mother then interjected (Robin Lee had not said a word since we left the house) "Bo, I want to ask you something. I know you and Robin have set a date for next summer, but I want to know why you have put it off 'till then?"

Bo who had just taken an oyster with a lot of hot sauce on it into his mouth went into a coughing fit and when he came out of it, said he had to wait because he had just put his mother in the ground and was not yet in condition to give himself to a marriage partner, nor was his house ready. He said he always had to keep rooms for my mother and for me and that he hadn't had time to get the rest of the house set up for a bride or to assess anything.

He was, I thought, amazingly articulate for one caught off guard and just before Robin Lee's mother ordered the Cornish Hen she murmured, "Oh well, I see."

Robin Lee went on calmly spooning her lemon soup in the lamp light, her freckled hand shining; she probably thought she was through with the subject for good.

To break the silence I said I thought the lemon soup exotic (before I came into The Dragon I never heard of lemon soup), that I thought it must be what citrus growers intended beautiful people to eat in Borneo and Madagascar and the South Seas. Why I said things like that I still don't know.

No one responded. Not even Bo. Silence claimed us through the Cornish Game Hen and that great fifties desert, Baked Alaska.

"Well, did you hear them?" Bo asked when we got home. "These brazen women. My God."

Essie Burnhardt's mother was also brazen, and Bo's most regular caller, that is before Robin Lee proposed and he accepted.

The spring before and, in fact, all the time I was in high school, several of the women in Bo's office, of whom Essie was one, called almost every day. Bo grumbled a lot, but liked the attention. Essie, a tall, long-necked, long-torsoed, long-legged woman was rumored, maybe because of all that length, to be very fast on her feet.

Bo took Essie out a lot during that last Palm Drive spring; she had fiery green eyes and, yes, cold black hair, not ashy like mine, not a touch of grey in it, and one weekend took her as far as Monterrey, Mexico. As I remember, they left on a Thursday and when they came back on Tuesday Bo was sulky and Essie looked like she had been through a bad sickness or a war.

Nevertheless, she insisted on showing us pictures of the trip including several shots of her and Bo on burros. A Mexican boy in one of the pictures seemed to be holding Essie onto the animal's back and I knew immediately she had too much tequila in her, I had seen Essie drink tequila. Had probably been drinking it straight. According to Bo, who decided finally to comment, they had ridden the burros to a spectacular waterfall high in the mountains; Essie didn't seem to remember much about the expedition or, if she did, she didn't say.

That afternoon Bo didn't get out the cocktail shaker which was certainly unlike him, and he seemed considerably relieved when Essie decided to go home.

I knew if Bo had cared deeply for Essie he wouldn't have gone away with her so easily. He would be able to do it now if he was young and living his life all over. But not, not the way he was raised, back then.

Well, anyway, on that afternoon back in the spring Essie hadn't been gone for more than ten minutes when he called Robin Lee. I can still hear them laughing in the backyard.

After planting a whole bed of zinnias, each of them working different rows, they sat down at the table Grandaddy built under the willow to stake tomato plants and consumed with great pleasure Rena's perfectly plain—Rena hadn't ever put sugar in it—pitcher of iced tea.

Still typing,
this time in Ensenada, Mexico

In spring Robin Lee liked working in the yard as much as Bo did, but she had an interest in planting and tending vegetables, even carpet grass, while he only cared for his tropical flowers. Hibiscus. Gardenias.

But, clearly, they had a good time together, were even foolish together and about each other in it, giggling over silly jokes and sayings and, sometimes, playing games like peek-a-boo and hide-and-seek, unbelievable even to me as I watched over my scripts from the sunporch, and at their most sophisticated, guessing games about what sort of animals or birds the people at their insurance office would be if they were animals or birds.

Before I became so busy at the radio station Bo played like this with me.

Essie would be a giraffe, Bo said, except that as far as he knew, giraffes didn't drink booze. Sometimes they sang songs in bad Spanish. Bo often talked to an imaginary character he called "Old Spanish."

His conversations with "Old Spanish" are among my earliest memories. Being here on the Baja brings them all back.

"Well, how are you today, Old Spanish. . . Loco?. . . Loco in the cabeza?. . . Oh, you don't say?"

I thought that someday I would put Old Spanish, or maybe Old Spanish and Bo, on a radio show.

"La cucaracha," Robin Lee sang softly into the flower bed. Although she was a shy girl, she was also fey, possessed I was sure by a fairy spirit which was not delicate but strong.

But during the last months of Grandma's sickness Robin Lee stayed away.

Not that she wanted to. She loved what Bo loved and truly. Too much wild creature in her to "love" out of duty. But her mother had never liked Grandma and liked Grandma even less after Grandma got cancer and it took a good hold. Still Robin Lee phoned the house often enough in the evenings.

"I'm going to my room now," I told Bo after I heard them starting. "I'll leave you and your callers alone."

"What do you do in your room all the time?" he asked me.

"Write love letters," I wanted to tell him. And sometimes I did write them, letters to the soul mate I had not yet met who understood me completely and who I believed was surely somewhere waiting. And one or two to Ben.

Uncle Bo, I write love letters, I wanted to tell him. And I touch myself.

In bed before napping I did touch myself, too. Touched that private part of my body I had not read about in any book and which I had not been told about, what it was for and why touching it was so exciting, and for which I had no name. I wondered if I would get a sickness from it and if the sickness would be as bad as Grandma's.

"Well, answer me," Bo said. "What do you do?"

"Work on radio dramas," I told him.

"More spooky stories?"

"Not anymore. Now I'm writing about you." And I had, in fact, started something on him.

"Oh, Elizabeth, be serious."

"Aunty says life isn't."

"Is that supposed to mean something?" Bo stared at me, incredulous. "Life is real, Baby, life is earnest."

I knew if he didn't most of the time think so he wouldn't stick so close to all of us, wouldn't still be selling insurance, making up all those policies and plans.

Later

from a beach house near Ensenada.
I move up and down this coast.

*D*uring that final high school spring the telephone was once in awhile for me. I still went out with Ben sometimes, but I hesitated to say yes now when he asked me, knew I would be in for some trouble. It was getting harder and harder to pull away from his kisses. Also my hours at the radio station were getting worse. I couldn't go anywhere or see anyone, hardly ever got to see C.C., it was so late when the place shut down. Most nights I stayed there with Dan Rodriguez; Dan and I had started together in Miss V's radio workshop when we were in tenth grade.

Everybody pointed to Dan as Corpus Christi High School's outstanding Latin American student which was possibly because Dan aspired to be all things Anglo. His father, the town's leading used car dealer, had just bought a colonial house near Ocean Drive. Every week or so Dan drove a different car to school, often a year-old Buick or Caddy. When we finished at the station he'd take me home but sometimes before he did, we'd go down to the waterfront for a coke. One Friday when I was griping about the grind at the station, I suggested we close down early and take a waterfront spin in whatever Dan happened to be driving, an Olds as things turned out.

As we were turning into the drive-in which I now think of as The Bucket, whether or not that was its name, the editor of the school paper nearly ran head-on into Dan's Olds and Dan said a few words that surprised me. Two days later we were an item in *The Pirate*, the school paper.

Both our names appeared in the column called "Stolen Treasures." Worse, because this column had won a prize in a statewide high school journalism competition, the entry was reprinted by *The Corpus Christi Caller Times*.

> *Guess what we ran into? Old Dan Rod in his latest, The King of Rods in a new one. Was it a Mercury? And with a late lady? Was she a McElroy? Was it necessary to sit so close, Dan?*

When Ben read that in the *Caller Times* — he never read the school paper—he called up and said he had to have an answer as to whether or not I would go steady.

"It wasn't a Mercury, Ben," I told him. "It was an Olds."

"Never mind any of that," he told me. Then he said if I couldn't go steady, he didn't want to go out at all.

I said I liked seeing him, but I couldn't go steady because of the demands of the radio station and because of my family. "You know," I told him, "I'm at the station four nights a week and, anyway, my family says I can't go steady."

I lied about that.

"Ever?" he asked, sarcastically. "Not when you're twenty-eight? Thirty-two?"

"Not," I stammered, "until I'm nineteen. Or on my own." Whichever comes first.

"By that time you'll be out of high school."

"Well," I said, "I certainly do hope so."

I was wretched, panicked. Although I guess I secretly thought Bo would be jealous, as far as I knew, my family didn't care.

And no one, with the possible exception of Miss V, gave a damn whether I put in time at the station or not.

"I love being with Ben," I told my mother when she was home Christmas. I watched her green eyes, my tiny reflection in them, watched her brushing her wild, wavy dark hair. "I don't know why," I went on, "why I can't say 'yes' when he talks about going steady."

She couldn't answer.

My mother and I were close sometimes. When she was home we would talk for hours, sitting on the patio or in the garage apartment lying side-by-side across the double bed.

Still, I could never go into detail about the strong feelings I had for Ben. Could only repeat, "I don't understand why I can't go steady."

After which, she was mute.

She just looked at me out of her heart-shaped freckled face with those uncommon green eyes. I thought they were beautiful, that she was beautiful with her green eyes and dark auburn hair.

An old friend just wrote me that he remembered my mother as tall, dark-haired and very pretty, "a dynamic woman of the coastal bend."

"Oh, I just don't know," I murmured.

"Well, you have got years for all that."

All she ever said.

C.C. wanted nothing so much as to go steady with Travis. But he didn't ask her. Then she said she knew it was because they lived on different sides of town. "Still," she told me, "I don't understand. I could understand if I lived on Ocean Drive like Dan does."

C.C. and her father lived on Texas Street in a new neighborhood which was undistinguished and treeless; C.C.'s father bought the house with an FHA loan just as dozens of his neighbors had, on the "right" side of you, Corpus, the "right" side of the way in which you were growing.

"I like it out where Travis lives better," C.C. always said.

"But it's what your neighborhood represents," I told her, "white collar jobs, aspiration, respect for education."

"Oh," she moaned, "the status quo."

The space between them was a gulf as wide as the one between us and Florida. I saw the expanse of it, but C.C. didn't, only thought she had to be with him.

She got literally sick to her stomach, nearly threw up in his yard, when she found Travis with another girl who was, like him, a tow-head and who lived on his own gravel road, just the other side of the frame church they all went to, who came by some evenings to put on a pot of pinto beans, which all day had been soaking, for his and his dad's supper and who sometimes boiled some greens and made a skillet of cornbread for them, too.

Travis's mother had been dead for years, died during an epidemic of typhoid fever, and C.C.'s mother was long gone, remarried several times over with a bunch of children C.C. had never seen, but who were, nevertheless, her half-sisters and-brothers.

The girl's dad drove a truck for a nearby lumber yard and her mother did ironing for people, that and mending and little sewing jobs, running up rick-rack over a dress's worn places, taking up or letting down hems. She couldn't make a whole dress, couldn't sew from a pattern.

Considering the way C.C. had been brought up, it was bad enough that she found Travis with a girl at all, much less like she did with this particular one, him on top of her, her blouse up around her neck, his hands on her tiny breasts.

"I only went in the bedroom," C.C. told me, "because I heard those noises. Didn't know what they were. I thought he was sick in it."

She had driven out to Travis's house on the spur of the moment in T.J.'s old car, of course got T.J.'s permission to do it. She never did things like that, hadn't even had her driver's license long, always held out for Travis's invitations, waited for him to call.

That evening, she said, a spell must have been cast on her because after she parked and went up to the door, she just went on in the house. No one had answered her knock and the door was open.

She had just received some pamphlets through the mail from the junior college and she wanted to show him. The courses in draftmanship she was sure he would want to take. Someone told me that after Travis went into the service he became a draftsman.

I had no drama like that, wouldn't let myself. And what I wrote was always for other people to play.

I wanted, I told myself, to preserve something.

But not to bury it. Not to keep it in the ground forever. I wanted blooms.

But did nothing to nurture them.

I went, hell-bent, on my precious business.

Grandma's work ethic had rubbed off, maybe, or worse: I had inherited some of her witholding qualities.

Still in Mexico
near Ensenada

𝐵o and I held ourselves back and although she had been through two marriages, so did my mother.

Did Bo drink, I wondered, so that he might let go?

Back in April, before he began to get into drinking so heavily, Bo told me he had an unhappy dream. Robin Lee, he said, had been in it, all done up in white like some bride. What was weird about it he said was that Robin Lee in her fine white dress swung back and forth, like Nyoka, the Saturday serials queen, in an old jungle movie, from the bottom branch of the willow tree. "Only we all know," he said, "that she's no Nyoka. The poor little brown mouse of a thing."

Then he turned away from me to address Old Spanish. "Don't you think so, too, Old Spanish?" When I was a child I half-believed in Old Spanish—in fact, sometimes, still do—kept looking for him, and I told myself I would know him when I saw him, still do, kept looking for him around corners or through windows to the far side of the yard.

No matter that he complained, no matter what his consolation, both the dream and the telling of it pleased Bo, made him feel more a part of you, Corpus.

Bo knew some of what people said. Once he overheard Lana's mother say to C.C., "Find out all you can about Bo Bell while you're visiting. Any man who would paint his house Spic Pink is peculiar."

As he pulled weeds from the flower beds—he was down on his hands and knees—Bo heard. He worked for hours, for whole days sometimes, back there; fastidious as he was, he loved to dig in dirt, do any kind of yard work, but especially work in flower beds and scratch around the zinnias and black roses with his hands.

Later that same week, as he came in the dining room at the Nixon cafe for the Rotary Club's monthly luncheon, and I guess, staggering a little—his company required his attendance, but he hated the gatherings and finally had to get drunk to go—he heard the blue-suited men near the head of the big table whispering about him.

Heard ugly things said, he told me. Though he never made clear just what.

Told me all this as he poured rum in the limeade he had stirred up for the afternoon's guests. All spring he kept asking his lady friends, with their mothers, to the house for Sunday suppers. But I had noticed that for sometime he focused more on fooling with rum and limes than he did with the food.

"They say I'm odd," he told me. "Well, maybe, I am. If that means I'm not like them, the old bastards, I do hope so."

Then in summer, just after they had met at Las Hadas, after Grandma had died, but before Bo decided to sell the house, he related the dream he had about Jay. In the dream he and Jay were both dead and had gone to Heaven. Only Heaven was really California, a beach near San Diego where they sat naked, staring at each other and making pictures, each of the other, in the sand.

"I looked at Jay and Jay looked at me," he told me, "and when we did, it was as if we saw ourselves through a mirror, we weren't in the glass, you understand, but through it, on the other side. "Do you think that's a strange dream?" he asked. "They say I'm strange, you know."

I told him I thought dreams were strange, and yes, this one. And I did think so.

But even at sixteen I saw how innocently he told it.

In the summer Bo invited Jay over some evenings for ice cream. They sat side by side out on the enclosed sunporch which on the walls that weren't screened had floor to ceiling bookshelves filled with books on gardening and decorating, the relief of those subjects broken with fiction, a few best sellers from The Book of The Month Club.

Bo sat in a hard ladder-back chair, he would never sit in a soft chair, Jay in Grandaddy's old oak rocker, a good looking pair, Jay just a little taller than Bo, but both so long and thin, dark-skinned and light-headed, Jay's hair as blonde as sunlight, Bo's nearly as white as Grandaddy's; it had, a long time ago, as everyone said, turned "prematurely."

After they finished the bowls of vanilla ice cream covered with caramel syrup and with pecans picked from our own tree, they took long walks through the neighborhood streets, since there was nowhere else to go.

From the vacant lot on the corner we could all see, when we walked there, Sinton refinery and oil rigging lights. The putrid smell of gas often in the air.

On his radio show Joe Copeland used to talk about viewing lights like that from a distance, from the window of a house, or, more commonly, from the highway in a car, about the mystery connected to them and the ghostly yearnings they conjured up.

And once Joe said to me, once after he had spent a long time in Europe, right after he had come back and come to pick me up in Dallas where I was working and then drove me out into the country, into the fields, "There. There they are," he said. "I love those little lights."

Even then, Joe, I wondered why. And I thought that only a person who was going to leave this country forever could love them.

Oh, but, Corpus, do I mix you and Joe up sometimes? I was, wasn't I, talking only to you?

Well, we could reach them by car, not that any of us wanted to. From where we were the smell of gas was bad enough.

When Bo and Jay came back into the house from their walks, swinging along side-by-side like two school kids, Bo would get out the cocktail shaker. As far as I knew we were the only family on our side of town who had one.

What was it for? A release from timidity? To help us see a little shine on the land? A promise, like the one the preachers gave, that not too many believed anymore, of the end of travail, an entrance into Glory?

"For awhile," Bo said to me years later, after he was finally off the bottle, "the world seemed very flat and dull." He had put the cocktail shaker away. The poison he had poured into it had eventually sapped his energy and sense. Poison it was, but we had all told the stories of our lives over it.

Later

 nd I can see it so plainly.

The cocktail shaker.

A glass one with one red stripe down the middle and a screw-on top of sterling silver. The focal point of these evenings.

Bo bought it at cost from his own gift shop, the one he had put in the refinery town's general store. During those years, war years most of them, we used it only at Christmas. No one we knew drank anything but beer, though some of the men also took now and then to hard liquor, bourbon usually, which more often than not, they just drank straight.

We came up in the world when we moved to you, Corpus Christi. Though in you, potent drinks of some sort were the highlight of our weekend evenings, just as they had been in the smelly little town.

Around Jay, Bo would refer to our refinery days sometimes. And then, remembering, would tell him stories of the weekends when he and my mother and their friends got together and went honky-tonking in the little clapboard cafes along the side of the highway, those with maybe one neon light and inside a lighted juke box which for a quarter would play five popular country songs.

Oh, Bo wanted to tell Jay all about this. Jay stirred everything up in him, even then I could see that, stirred his memory, excited his imagination. He wanted to tell him things.

Just as in the beginning I wanted to tell Joe.

And now, must tell you.

"The water was new to us," my mother said when she was remembering. "All of us just down from Arkansas and the East Texas woods. When we first came we would swim every night, would pile in the car every evening and take off for Rockport, after Leeland and your Grandaddy were through with jobs and I had taught my last lesson and Bo shut up the store." All of them put in ten hour days. "Finally Leeland even bought a boat and we used to take it out to fish."

Some Saturday nights Bo and my mother and Bo's truck drivers and painters, and maybe one or two others, would go to Ransom Island to dance and drink beer. They would also take me more often than not since they had no one to leave me with and in looking back, I'm glad to have been included, to have been let in on their vices.

The time came, my mother said, when Ransom Island was the only place they would honky-tonk. "The shed out there that sold beer was nice," she said, "quiet, peaceful even, right on the water. You could always hear the water lapping. And there were never really loud people or fist fights like in Sinton or Gregory or other places back in those little towns. We would have to take the ferry north of Aransas Pass and the trip across water helped keep us calm as we were going and certainly sobered us all up as we were coming home."

On Ransom Island they sometimes talked and drank beer and danced to the juke box until nearly morning. Some of the men who worked with Leeland and Grandaddy, when Leeland and Grandaddy were with us, brought their wives and girlfriends and Bo almost always brought workers and their families from his store. One of Bo's truck drivers, a man we called Shorty who delivered lumber and his wife, Gert, and their little boy, Elbert, often came. Elbert and I would sing to the records and dance a little, he leading with big, predictable steps across the splintered floor—all this in an open shed on stilts which raised it high over the water—pumping my hand up and down, copying his father's style and we liked to play like we were his mother and father.

Later on in the lumber sheds he taught me to play like we could do what they did in bed, what it looked like to him; he told me he saw it every night after supper and I thought that was so strange and that what he described was strange, his father lying on top of his mother, but I loved the way what he did to me in the lumber stacks felt, mostly he just rubbed his little body against mine, sometimes after pulling my dress up, or, depending on the season, my shorts and his pants down, one of his legs always moving against me and I suppose, accidentally against that place where I finally touched myself. Got so every day I would say, "Oh, let's go out and play in the lumber like we did yesterday!" And sometimes he would say OK and sometimes he would call for his mother and say, "Mama, Elizabeth is a bad girl and wants to do bad things in the lumber stacks today." And I would say, "Well, you taught me about it, Elbert." And he'd say, "Ummm, she's tellin' a story."

And sometimes he would then turn to me and say, "Elizabeth, you tell stories and one night when you are sleeping, The Devil is going to come to your bed and put you in a sack and take you away."

A Sunday school teacher, I found out later, had told Elbert about The Devil and Elbert had only been to Sunday school once, but that one time carried and lasted as both of us waited for The Devil night after night.

What a patchwork time makes of memory! At Ransom Island we never thought of any of this, but only liked to sing.

"You are my sunshine/my only sunshine/you make me hap-pee/when skies are grey."

That was the song we played and sang the most, and sometimes, even when our dancing was through, Elbert would sing it and pretend he was strumming it out on his toy guitar. Back in Ingleside, and that was the name of our town, we would sing it on street corners, Elbert holding the guitar and me holding a paper cup for donations from the IGA store.

Sometimes Elbert's father and my mother and Uncle Bo would go with us down the steps of the dancing shed and out onto a little strip of sand and then knee high, no farther, into the water. After a dance or two Elbert and I would usually beg to go in and then I, never Elbert, would cry, "Oh, please, Mama, please Shorty, let us take our clothes off and go swimmin'," but they would always say no.

"You young'uns just wade a little, " Shorty would say. "You can't trust the water here. All at once it's over your head."

Then my mother would tell the story, for the umpteenth time, of how Leeland once took them all out in the boat they bought for fishing, took them out from Ransom Island where he kept it, and of how they hadn't gone far when the motor died and a wind came up and it took them all night to paddle back to the shed in the storm and how they then had to take the ferry; there was always that ferry that got us across the water and back to shore.

I would become afraid of the water then and of the dark and didn't see what the grown-ups saw in just sitting there for hours playing the juke box and drinking beer and sometimes I would start to cry.

"Why, are you the same young'un who just a minute ago was beggin' to strip down and go in the water?" Shorty would ask me.

"Here, here," my mother would say, for I embarrassed her as I wailed, "Now you straighten up."

And Elbert would say, "Yeah, Lizabeth, nobody likes a cry baby." And Shorty would pick me up and swing me over his head and cry, "Look up at all them stars, girl, ever see stars like that?" and whirl me around in the air. "Hear all that music?" He would go on, swinging me down toward the steps of the shed. "Let's get to it." Then he'd all but fly up the steps with me and when we were on the splintered dance floor whirl me around some more, his wife, Gert, laughing, then pass me to Uncle Bo who would whirl me and throw me up in the air — once Bo caught me so hard when I was coming down that he sprained my arm — by which time I could see my mother and Elbert coming up the steps. All of this excited and confused me and shut me up and scared me some, too; in the middle of it one of them would yell, "Oh, aren't you having fun?" to make me think I was. By the time Bo put me down, my mother had usually had time to take Fritos and deviled ham sandwiches out of the basket they had brought and set on the table. She might also take out some celery and sweet pickles all neatly wrapped in wax paper. "You children are hungry," she would say, putting the food she had wrapped so lovingly before us, her green eyes gleaming in that face that more and more, because of the way she brushed her hair back, looked like a heart.

If Aunt Rena was along, and once or twice I remember her and Uncle Leeland coming with us, she would bring out a deck of cards. "Want to play Fish?" she would ask us. "I'll play Fish with you." But my mother, who hated cards, never thought to bring any.

Well, anyway, we munched on Fritos as the grown-ups went on dancing, talking and laughing. And louder and louder with all of it as they drank more beer. And, finally, Elbert and I would just give up, would stretch out on the benches built into the walls of the shed and fall asleep while looking at the sky and counting and sometimes giving names to the stars.

Usually, nights were on the hot side, but if a wind came up, my mother or Gert would wrap us in old quilts they had brought along, covers that Rena had long ago pieced together back in Arkansas or East Texas. Then sometimes in sleep the water as I heard it lapping scared me; I'd dream then that we were all lost, drifting in Leeland's boat and I'd pull the quilt close around me.

Rena's mother had done most of the oldest quilt like a star, Rena helping just a little when she was a girl back in Louisiana, before Uncle Leeland met her. Even as a girl she had been married once and before she was seventeen had a child who lived a year, then had to go, died in sleep. This same child had on the day she was born, ripped the womb out of Rena, seeing to it that Rena could never have another.

Some years after her baby died and the baby's father had run away, Uncle Leeland spied Aunt Rena picking berries in a blackberry thicket, or so the story goes, where he and his crew were building a bridge across the Texas-Louisiana border. Leeland dropped everything the minute he saw Aunt Rena, married her a week later and according to my mother, who believes Leeland's spirit lives with us still, has kept her, and her black-Creole spirit, with us ever since.

"So sad," my mother always said, "that they couldn't have children." Sometimes, though, I thought it was because they couldn't that Rena and Leeland were so close to one another. Rena did have two nephews in Louisiana, her dead sister's children, but they were grown men when I was just a child and I thought it was funny that she called them "my little boys." I was also jealous of them, or at least a little.

I always hid when I saw their car coming up our hill as it did only once a year, usually in mid-summer. Aunt Rena would usually find me under the feather bed, that is if I wasn't curled up in one of her wedding ring quilts. "Now come on out here and speak to my little boys, Johnny and his brother." Johnny as the oldest was called by his name. "You all are going to have a lot of fun." I can't remember what they looked like, much less any fun; the whole time they visited I stayed close by the radio and Uncle Leeland, who I sometimes thought liked to listen almost as much as I did. But years later Aunt Rena told me that one of the nephews, the one whose name I never knew or anyway can't remember, carried me on his back to the creek and sometimes even farther, all the way to the spring.

Toward the end of these nights on Ransom Island Bo would talk about Leeland, that is, if Leeland wasn't along, railing against him and all that Leeland had, Bo believed, forced on him in the way of work and ambition. Usually I would fall asleep somewhere near the middle of this; I knew it wore Bo out to go over it again and again and that it was in part because he was tired from the story telling that he had to sleep for half the next day. Mornings after Ransom Island my mother and Bo would let me skip Sunday school and they would stay in bed all morning, wouldn't even get up to go to the door.

With Jay, when he once again told about Ransom Island, Bo would also go over his quarrel with Leeland.

"My big brother would give me these long math problems to work out," he told Jay. "Even calculus sometimes. Can you believe that? Calculus. For me? I would have to struggle with these problems for half a day. And after I finished, Leeland made me camp out. I always hated that, sleeping on the wet ground. 'Come on,' Leeland would always say, 'be a man.' From the time I was little I heard that from him, and yes, from my other brother, Lloyd, and from my father, too. Made me hate them, all of them sometimes, and just want to stay in the house with my mother."

"Why," my mother told me on Sunday evenings when Uncle Bo was getting his stock straight so as to begin another work week in his store, (my mother always got stories to come out her way), "why, they never expected your Uncle Bo to be a builder. Leeland and your Grandaddy were going to build the houses and stores and office buildings, Lloyd was going to finance their venturing a little, you know Lloyd was in the wholesale food business, and then the plan called for your Uncle Bo to decorate and help furnish the interiors. Bo never understood that. That was Leeland's dream. All the rest, the camping out, the math problems, all of that was just to make him part of them. A kind of testing."

"Well," I said, "it was testing of the wrong kind." I had never known Lloyd and loved Leeland and my grandfather, but at least at the time she told me all this, my sympathies were with Bo.

Bo said Leeland wanted him to become some sort of mathematical wizard and that because he knew this, Bo who had no mathematical aptitude, had in the course of two semesters signed up for Calculus, Geometry and Advanced Trig. Just one of these courses, he said, made him want to quit the university and near the end of his freshman year he did. Bo's quitting broke Leeland's heart everyone said.

Leeland who had to go to work young and never finished his architecture degree had made a present of Bo's tuition money, had been saving it for years.

I never understood why, instead of quitting the university, Bo didn't just drop all his impossible courses; I always thought Bo should have just stood up to Leeland. If he had, I was sure Leeland and everyone else would have let him finish whatever he wanted to do.

On those nights on Ransom Island Bo went over his side of things. And again, years later, when he went over the Ransom Island nights with Jay.

On one Ransom Island night I heard him crying. I was awake because a norther had come up. All this was on one long ago early October morning during a blustery ferry ride in rain. Bo always had to be at least a little bit high before he would talk much about himself and smashed before he would get out all of what I came to think of as "his story."

Around Jay he always wanted to tell it.

I read somewhere that's how you can tell if you love someone, that if you want to tell him or her your story, you probably do.

Hollywood

Bo told Jay about what a drunk Leeland was or at least told when Aunty and my mother weren't around, and about how he, Bo, was never going to be. "I'll never be a drunk like my brother, Leeland, never act or talk like him." And he never did rant and rave, or swear, like Leeland. Oh, he would say "Shit" over and over sometimes, but that was about as bad as his language ever got. As spring came and Grandma's sickness worsened, he became, I noticed, more and more jittery and some evenings drank so many daiquiris he would slur and distort his words. "Shit" would become "Shut" for example. This was back in March.

One Sunday when he entertained one lady friend and her mother, Essie Burnhardt I'm almost sure now it was, he started making and drinking daiquiris early in the afternoon and went on like this, putting off 'til nearly dark making the supper he had invited them for. He had planned to do a batch of tacos, frying and folding each tortilla separately in a big thick skillet on the stove. His tacos were particularly good ones with piles of chopped green onions and green olives on top of shredded lettuce.

When he finally apologized for supper being late, after eight instead of at six-thirty, Old Lady Burnhardt said, and I'm sure now that's who it was, "That's all right, Bo. We know now that when you invite us to your house for dinner, we should eat before we come."

The Sunday after that he had them all there, everybody: Robin Lee, her hair falling loose around her shoulders instead of in double pony tails as it usually was, and Essie, taller and skinnier looking than ever, in four-inch heels and a black and white striped suit, her black hair shingled and finally Pauline Honish, of whom I've told you nothing about so far, a big raw-boned girl whose father, before he died, had made money in cotton farming, about all you need to know. And all of their mothers with them. And Aunt Rena was there, too.

Because everyone Bo knew was at our house and Aunt Rena never had her friends there, when the telephone rang, I knew it had to be for me.

Ben wanted to know if I would go for a ride with him. Down to The Bucket maybe.

Just as I was about to leave, I was in the bathroom fixing my face, Bo started. I heard him beginning on Robin Lee's mother and on Essie and Essie's mother, Grandma so sick that day that the nurse had on both sides locked the door and when Bo came out from seeing about her he said, "Mother is not up to visiting with anyone today," and poured himself a glass of straight rum.

Then after Essie's mother and Robin Lee and her mother had the sense to go out the back door and take chairs on the patio and in the yard, he started on Mrs. Honish.

"Do you still have that formal sofa?" I heard him ask. "You know that's not the right kind of sofa for a country house."

And I heard her laugh and say, "We're hoping to make it less country, Bo."

And him retort and God knows how much rum he had in him by this time, "That would be pretty hard to do."

"Well, you know," she said, "Mr. Honish was a plain man and liked what was around him to be plain, too." She sounded as if that included her and Pauline and that she was proud of it, but at the same time wasn't prepared for Bo to say, "Well, that certainly includes the two of you."

"Bo, I think you have had too much to drink," Mrs. Honish said then, "and that maybe Pauline and I better be going home."

As I emerged from the bathroom and saw Pauline slowly shifting, and she was slow in everything, and then sitting straight up in her chair, Bo said, loudly, "Do you know that old Mr. Honish always smelled like fertilizer?"

"Pauline," Mrs. Honish said, "honey, get up. We're going home."

"Go on," Bo yelled, then after a pause, shooting a mean look to the other side of the room, "You too, Essie."

Essie stood by the book case, cocktail glass in hand. "I'm enjoying it here," she said in her throaty voice, playing at being a short haired brunet Bacall. Her mother sat under the grape arbor on the patio just outside the room.

"Well," he said, "I am not enjoying you."

"Best bar in town," she told him, tilting her glass.

"You like bars, don't you, Essie? I remember Monterrey, how you liked bars there and," he paused, "bartenders." Bo later related how after he spurned her she took up with several.

"That'll do, Bo," she said, nodding toward the patio. "You see my mother is present."

"Well," he said, "she shouldn't still be here. She told me herself you both already had your supper. So why don't you and your conniving old mother go home?"

"I told you," she said, "I'm staying for the drinks."

"Come on, Pauline," Mrs. Honish said. But poor, overgrown Pauline seemed stuck to her chair. Bo turned toward Pauline then and said, "Your old Pa smelled like fertilizer." And then to Mrs. Honish. "Do you hear what I'm saying? Your whole family is a pile of shit."

"Bo!" Rena reprimanded as she poked her head in through the breakfast room door, then turned and came through the living room toward me. I'd had one eye on this and at the front door had been listening. But was waving to Ben who was about to get out of the car.

"You hear all that?" she asked me. "I think it's disgusting."

"I don't know why he had them all here," I whispered. "He's never had any use for the Honishes and Miz Burnhardt has always irritated him and for that matter Miz Walsh." I spell the Miz out here so that you won't imagine I, in those days, said Ms. Miz Walsh was Robin Lee's mother. I thought it amazing that he hadn't done in Miz Walsh before she and Robin Lee took their lawn chairs outside by the flower bed where they sat nursing their drinks.

"He's just becoming mean. Just like Leeland."

"Aunt Rena," I said, "I don't get it."

"Honey," she told me, "he's drunk."

"Was he drunk when he invited them?" I asked. "Did he bring them here to insult them? Why not leave them alone?"

"If you ask me, he's drunk quite a lot lately," she told me. Then grinned at Ben who was upon us. She had always liked him. "Why hello, sweetheart."

"Oh," I said to her, not to Ben, giving Ben no explanation, "I'm glad I'm going."

Ben smiled back at her. By this time we were hand in hand on the porch. He said we were just going for a drive and then for something to eat in one of the drive-ins.

We didn't go there, though, but drove all the way to Padre. Nothing on it then. No hotels. Not even a hamburger stand. I still think of it like that.

I hear it's not so nice now. A lady I met recently on a train trip I took to and from Texas told me in no uncertain terms as we crossed West Texas desert what she thought of the state. "Don't judge all of Texas by the west of it," I told her. "It's different on the Gulf. I grew up in Corpus Christi."

"Oh," she said, "I hear that's tacky." Then she told me she had also heard Padre was full of expensive tourist traps. "Well," I retorted, "isn't everywhere?"

Surely nothing on it then. Just sand, all the way to Mexico. More than a hundred miles of sand against dark, sometimes threatening water. "Ben," I asked as he tore along over it, "just where do you think you are going?"

"Off the deep end maybe."

"Well, please don't take me, too."

He threw on the brakes then. "Listen," he said as he took me to him and I felt his trembling and felt my trembling, too. "Listen, I've got years of school ahead of me and I don't know how I'll make it—"

"I know that," I said to him.

"I don't want you to see anymore of whatever his name is."

"Dan," I told him.

"OK, I don't want you to see any more of Dan. The one with the cars."

Then his mouth was on my face, my throat, his thick lashes tickling the tip of my ear. "I don't want you to see him, you hear? I'll take you to those dumb parties."

One of the reasons I went with Dan to the parties sometimes was that I knew Ben made fun of them.

"No," I said and it was so hard to get words out that all I could do was whisper. "Leave me alone, let me go, take me back, now."

But even as I told him that, I clung close and let him kiss my face and run his hands over me; I tried to be still as he did it, early tried to train myself in stillness, but something inside me broke and before I realized what I was doing, I was all over him, too. With my hands, up his back and across his shoulders, with my mouth and voice, my beautiful radio voice, God only knows what I said.

And then he stopped and pushed me a little way from him. "Listen," he said, "Do you know why I'm like this? I'm nineteen years old and I have years of school ahead of me."

"You said that before and I know that," I told him.

"I don't know how we can be together. If I can ever marry you." I saw that he was in such dead earnest.

I turned from him and faced, instead, the window on what had been my side of the car.

"Ben," I said, "we shouldn't be here." I thought I saw a wind coming up and I knew the bridge without a fence wasn't safe. I remembered my mother's story of her and Bo and Rena and Leeland and the time they had all had of it in their little boat, then saw Ben and me in that boat and it sinking. "It's dangerous to be here," I told him. But Ben pulled me back to him and we stayed, kissing and caressing until the rain began to fall and maybe it was only that, the rain, that stopped us.

It seems in retrospect that at least in love, completion and fulfillment was prevented by something in the very elements down where we grew up.

Ben's hands were inside my blouse, on my breasts, then one was under my skirt on my thigh and after on the mound inside my panties; one of mine was on the shaft that was him where he had grown so hard; I wanted it and all of him still closer, but the car, by this time, was rocking, the rain slashing down in sheets. So we had to stop, but didn't until I said, in a rush, a whisper, what I had never said to anyone before. "Oh, I want you."

And he said, "I know it, but we're going to have to go."

By the time we got back on the mainland the fierce rain that had seemed to threaten flood had, unbelievably, stopped. In fact, on our side of you, Corpus, the ground was dry. As he drove I still cradled into one of Ben's arms.

When I got home I found Aunt Rena washing dishes in the kitchen and Bo slumped in a corner chair slurping coffee. I knew the coffee was to help him sober up. Grandma had been sleeping for awhile he said; he finally got her out on a combination of morphine and creme de menthe. "Grasshoppers," he told me, "I made a big pitcher. I finally got her out on those. She never knew there was any alcohol in them. 'Why, these,' she said, 'are so green and pretty. Bo you should have one of these instead of what you are drinking. The church teaches us that drinking alcoholic beverages is a sin.'" He looked up at me and grinned and didn't seem to care a bit that I was getting in at 1 a.m.. "According to her preacher, that old frog faced bastard, anything that's any fun is a fucking sin."

We were both of us, Aunt Rena and I, taken back by the language.

"Bo, honey," Aunt Rena said, "why don't you just go on now to bed."

"I don't want to go to bed," Bo muttered, still leering at me. He didn't seem to care in the least where I had been.

Aunty sighed then and asked me if we had a nice ride and if in April I was going with Ben to the big senior dance at the Driscol.

I said we had driven all the way to Padre and back, I wanted to confess that much, and that just going and coming had taken a long time, but it was nice to do that once. I also said a wind with rain had come up over Padre, it scared me I said like I used to be scared by the thought of storm and being lost in the Gulf, floating, when we used to go to Ransom Island. I said, and I thought I was a convincing liar, that although we had planned to hunt for driftwood on Padre, we couldn't stay.

I also said I wasn't going to the dance at the Driscol in April, that by then I would have no time for dances.

"But, darlin'," Aunt Rena said, "you love dancing."

Later on in the Spring I told her that she was right and that I had changed my mind. But , still later, when it became clear to her that Dan, not Ben, was taking me, she said, "Yes, I see you are going, but would you tell me this? Why is it you are going with that radio boy instead of the good looking one with broad shoulders and wavy hair?"

And I said, "Ben talks of going steady and I don't want to get serious."

And she said, "Honey, if you go round with a boy who has shoulders like that, feel them against you, you'll never be serious, you'll just smile."

Part Two

Sayer, Oklahoma

I was remembering how Aunt Rena said that when I left Uncle Bo at the bus station this morning. I had to leave him there. I had been back in the middle of the country selling off things I'd had in storage ever since I worked for stations in Chicago and Omaha and later Kansas City, had possessions stored away in each of those cities, and was driving back now to the West coast.

Tulsa was as far as Bo could come with me. Standing straight and taller than he's ever been, like a sapling that grows upright only as it gets older, Bo is now nearly through his seventies, his dark drinking years long over. I've needed his help in getting west where life and work have finally taken me, just as I needed it to go east when I was eighteen.

Until I came along, the Bells had never gone east, from the beginning had been caught up in western movement, so that what I'm doing late in my life seems finally right, the completion of some ancestor's longing or in my genes.

My mother's family were all Bells, my father's McElroys; my father, who took off long ago, had relatives in Boston and New York, which may explain my early longing for those places and certainly explains my coloring; except for Bo everyone else in the family was pale. "Dark Scot" Bo always said of my dark blue eyes and ashy hair. Ben told me once that my eyes were the darkest blue eyes he had ever seen, but at another time he told me they were slate grey and at still another, he concluded that they changed color with my moods or the weather.

My father, Burton McElroy, who, I was told, also had dark blue eyes, walked out on my mother and me when I was just a baby, he had gone a little crazy my mother said. Just took off one day in his old Studebaker, headed toward town, this was up near Nacogdoches, and never came back. Town was south of where we lived in the country and he went right through it and just kept driving that way.

"Poor Burt," my mother said, "he hardly knew what he was doing. He had been out of work, the depression was on, you know, and your grandma had been at him. And besides that, he was grieving over the loss of his own people. Both his mother and father had died suddenly up north, within a few weeks of each other, and he didn't even have the fare to go back for their funerals. He'd had to live not only with, but off, the Bells, and Grandma, my mother said, began to make remarks about what he ate. So one day he just got in the Studebaker. "I don't think he really thought he was going much of anywhere."

And nobody knows how far he finally drove that car. In a dream I used to see him in the car and it in a body of water and fast sinking, waves breaking and water lapping against the windows. I always dreamed this dream at Aunt Rena's which was lucky because she was always there to hug and hold on to. "Oh, Aunt Rena," I would tell her, "I just had the most awful dream. Burton McElroy drove right off the coast of Texas. His car hadn't hugged the road right and was just swallowed up with him still in it by Corpus Christi Bay."

I think he must have died somewhere. He never wrote or sent money. After seven years my mother declared him dead in front of a lawyer who had helped her sign papers and then she married Bud whom she met when she first came to South Texas. Leeland, who was doing some building in Texas, wrote that the depression hadn't struck the Texas coast the way it had the rest of the country, that Texas had money, that every little town wanted a music teacher.

I was just a baby when my mother left me with Grandma and Grandaddy. For a while Aunt Rena stayed with us in Arkansas and East Texas, too. Her family were all Brocks from Louisiana and there was talk of her being part Cajun and part black Creole and maybe she was. God knows her hair was black enough and her skin dark, her nose broad, though her eyes were merry and blue.

I thought of them as Santa Claus eyes because of the way they crinkled at the corners and because of the broad, almost chubby face they were set in.

Her full-lipped white-toothed smile seemed to me like Santa Claus, too.

As I write this Aunt Rena is—can you believe it?—still living, ninety-seven or ninety-eight, none of us knows for sure. I just sent her a birthday card, late by a month. We all keep forgetting Aunt Rena's birthday because it doesn't seem right she should still be having one. One way or another we all said good-bye years ago.

Nearly twenty years have gone by since she left East Texas to go back to Louisiana where she lives in a little house near one of her nephews. My mother always says, "Why in the world The Higher Power keeps Rena with us is hard to say."

Except for Bo and my mother all my other kinfolk have departed. Now here I am in middle life, past my middle forties, leaving the country that nurtured all of us, that is, generally the southwestern middle of it, which includes a sprawl.

Tulsa this morning seemed to me such a plain, concrete city and, as it appeared downtown anyway, completely utilitarian, without flowering tree or bush. Maybe I noticed because of the contrast to the hilly and flowery streets of Los Angeles. Or, maybe it's just that August in the hot middle with prairie stretching out on every side spares so little.

When I'm in L. A. I miss the prairie; it steadied me to know that in every direction that I could see I faced a sweep of land. And to my surprise, when I first saw the Pacific sorrow welled up in me.

Bo certainly hadn't favored my trip toward it. He wanted me near, wanted me in some near city: Dallas, Houston, New Orleans. Even Tulsa seemed reachable enough. But when he finally understood that L. A. was the only city with a job I wanted, he helped. Helped me pack up the few pieces of light furniture I had decided to keep and to sell the rest. Now from Tulsa a Houston bound bus would take him through to Texarkana and then into the East Texas woods and home.

In the bus station he grumbled about the coffee. "It's like water," he said, "and in such an ugly mug."

"I don't think it's bad," I told him.

"I like good strong coffee. And in a china cup. I guess I shouldn't be in a bus station."

I felt bad that I didn't have the money to buy him a plane ticket. He was even paying his own bus fare. For years Bo worked in Insurance so he would have some, and I had never worked a job that didn't pay.

He told me then that his life hadn't come to much.

"Oh," I said, "you were a super salesman after you got out of that insurance job you hated." After his breakdown he got a job in Foley's department store, selling housewares at first and, later, designer dresses. Then I added, "And for all of us, you made so many houses home." Even more important I wanted to tell him, but didn't, he wove a magic web of fantasy through them, in room after room talking out with me and sometimes with my friends and with Old Spanish his and our dreams.

In spite of his white hair and light eyes and his timidity, plus what was in my mind, a cruel German-English way or two, Bo was the exotic of the family, his skin as dark as mine.

"Uncle Bo," I wanted to tell him, "we are black Scots together." I sometimes thought, of course, that my darkness came from my family's other side. The unknown side, swallowed in my dream by Corpus Christi Bay and the Gulf of Mexico. And that may be.

"You made so many houses home." Right after I said that he reminded me of the state asylum.

"I remember the morning they came and took me away and locked me up," he told me. "I remember Bud signing the papers that sent me to Austin." That his own family had locked him up, that was the part he couldn't get over. "Oh what did I do? What did I do? I wondered."

"Hey," I said, "that's over. You did a lot." I was sorry we had gotten off on all this and wanted to change the subject. "You gave all my friends such good times when they came to visit."

"Good old Uncle Bo makes a mean martini." He took a big gulp of coffee. "And drinks a bunch of them."

"Why don't you stop coming down on yourself?" I asked him.

He just went on slurping. "So this is Tulsa. What a dead town."

"It's six o'clock in the morning," I said. "I expect it will liven up."

"Well," he went on, "I don't think I did much. 'Not worth killing.' That's what my keeper said. Said I shook a knife at Bud or somebody, I don't remember. I couldn't have shaken a knife at your mother could I? Couldn't have shaken a knife at Leona?"

After a pause he said, "But a drunk will do anything. And doesn't know anything. Never recalls anything. I had been blind with blackout. I remember them saying I shook a knife at somebody. They talked about it just before they took me away. I seem to remember Leona saying, 'Officer, he didn't mean to do it. He didn't go to do it.' And I remember the fuss they had about me, Bud and your mother. I guess that fuss helped split them up. I remember your Aunt Rena saying, your good-for-nothing Aunt Rena, 'He hurts himself mostly.'"

I tried to tune him out. I hated this review, hated his self pity, most of all hated what he said about Aunt Rena. I could hear her saying, could hear her so clearly, "That's what we all do, hurt ourselves when we hurt each other. But we can't seem to help it and it just goes on and on."

Later

*J*ay had come to our house on Palm Drive one scorching afternoon when it was nearly a hundred degrees. And sticky. We had all stripped down to practically nothing, Bo just home from work, barefoot and shirtless in a pair of old paint pants, my mother in a gauzy skirt and halter top—she had a half dozen of them in neutral colors made every summer—me in tattered shorts and a bathing suit top, all of us dripping sweat.

Bo was embarrassed for us. "Well, here we all are nearly naked," he said. "When I got home I just stripped down."

In seersucker pants and sport shirt, his waiter's jacket with a tie in the pocket over one arm, Jay was obviously dressed for work. Not that he seemed to mind; he was grinning. Said, "I can take the bedroom. I told Frank I wanted it, that I needed my own place." Bo looked pleased and Jay couldn't hide his happiness. "Of course I'll pay you for it," he said. "Just like a regular roomer."

Then a surprising thing happened. In what I have come to think of as his "For the Public" voice and by this I guess I mean the less sincere one, the voice he puts on when he's trying to protect himself, Bo said, "Why, Jay, we'll be glad to have you and don't worry about any money." But he couldn't have sounded colder if he had told Jay never to darken our door.

Then Jay said again, but this time stammering, that he would pay.

The four of us stood in a circle there on the sunporch staring at one another, sweat dripping. In those days we didn't have air-conditioning, only fans. My mother and Bo and I all popped up from our seats when Jay first came in. Jay's pale shirt was ringed in front with sweat, exposing a nipple.

"Sit down with us," my mother said. "We have cold cuts and potato salad. Have you time for a bite of supper?"

"Oh, n-n no m-m-mam," Jay stuttered.

"Well, maybe you'd like some tea. Just before she left Rena made a big cold pitcher." Aunt Rena was once again at the movie, or so she said. I thought she was smart to so often opt for air-conditioning. In the last three weeks she claimed to have seen every show in town.

"She visits nasty old men in their rooming houses," I could hear my grandmother say. Grandma thought the whole human race was "nasty." But I felt sure Aunt Rena visited no one with whom she had not first gone to the movies or at least no one with whom she had not discussed going to the movies, on a bus or in one of the city parks.

"M'-m-maybe I w-w-ill—" Jay stopped there, just couldn't get it all out. "Maybe I will have some tea." But then, after a pause, said without a bit of trouble that he expected the restaurant to have quite a business since it was Friday night and a hot one, cooler at Las Hadas than in most people's houses. By this time he was grinning like a school kid at my mother. He told Bo then that the room was going to be good to do his work in and that he hoped it would be all right to bring his drawing board and little drawing table and maybe, even an easel. "I-l-l-ff I u-u-se o-o-oil p-p-paint I I I-'ll t-t-take th-th-them o-o-outside."

"It'll be fine for you to do anything you like in the room," Bo said in his phoney voice, smiling his false smile. "It'll be just fine," he said. But he looked uneasy.

Bo was, I knew, pleased that Jay was with us and had accepted his offer of the room. But I could also tell that it was not going to be all right for Jay to do anything he liked in it, and this did strike me as an odd turn of events, and possibly it was not going to be all right for him to be in it at all.

Was this because the room had been Grandma's I wondered or because Bo had begun to have certain fears?

"I think it will be nice to have Jay," I told Bo later. We were in the room adding splotches of color; at Litchenstein's we had bought a bedspread, tailored and navy blue, but with a small geometrical gold colored design.

"Do you think it's nice?" Bo seemed to want my honest opinion.

"I do," I told him. And I did. I looked forward to having someone near my age at home, someone like a big brother. I had felt that close to Jay from the start.

"Well, then," Bo said, "I do, too."

But by the next night when he came home from his office he didn't think so.

In the office he had blurted out his news to both Pauline Honish, who, in case I haven't told you, also worked there answering phones, and Essie Burnhardt and by the end of the day, his boss had called him in for a talk. From what I could make of what Bo said, the talk was about grief, about what happens to people when they grieve.

"'You, don't know what you are doing, Bo, you have just lost your mother. That's what the old bastard told me.

"'You don't know that boy really. Where does he come from? Who are his people?'

"'They live out west somewhere,' I told him. 'He still has a sister out there; his mother and father have both passed away.'

"'Well, the S.O.B. said, 'but—'

"'You think he is odd, why don't you say it? You think he's queer.' I used that word, just blurted it out; you should have seen his face, the old bastard. 'You think I'm queer?'"

"'Why no, I don't think you know what you are doing.'"

"I wish I could have told him off, wish I could have walked out right there."

Bo often said the happiest day of his life would be the day he could walk out of that office. But I don't think that's the way things turned out. His last day there was the one before Bud, who had been in town just a few days himself, took him off to Austin. So it wasn't so much that he walked out of the office as that he walked into a nuthouse and a jail.

But he put the Palm Drive house on the market shortly after the day when he came home upset and mad from the reprimands he had gotten at the office. I was sorry we wouldn't have Jay with us, but I knew there were better places to live in you, Corpus. And I could hardly stand our neighbors, Lana's family, although Lana had been my friend.

Still Later in Sayer

I had felt sorry for Lana; she hated the way she looked which explains why she bleached her hair and then combed it in that silly peek-a-boo style which hid her but blinded her, too. And I hated the neighborhood where we all lived. Lana also hated it, and I knew her family never helped her feel better about anything. I thought it was pathetic that, afraid as she was, she still tried so hard to be sexy.

One day a few weeks after Jay had started visiting, Lana's brother came over to ask me what kind of place we thought we were running; he said he wasn't sure he wanted his mother and sister living next door.

It has taken me forever to learn anything and I didn't get all the implications of his questions; I had only the vaguest notion about what caused him to ask them. Nevertheless, I felt something for him that I can only describe as being close to loathing and I said, "Get out. Get out of our yard."

"Don't you understand anything?" I asked as he bore a hole through me, by just looking. "I want you out of here so GET. And don't ever come back again." Then I added, "Tell your mother to stay out, too."

I stopped at that. I couldn't bring myself to exclude Lana who was one of my first Corpus Christi friends. She always aimed to please and she had been so lonely. I reasoned she couldn't help who she was related to.

Brad looked me up and down the way he had seen some actor in a grade B movie do, fixing his attention finally on the crotch of my lime green shorts. He said, "You know what you need, don't you?"

I couldn't answer, only stiffened and clinched my fist, ground my teeth, pressed my thumbs against the backside of my knuckles hard.

"That's Elizabeth McElroy," Gerry told me years later. "Like her mother, a teeth-grinding fist-maker." But I only remember making those gestures once, on that day I ordered Brad out of the yard.

Brad grinned at me and mumbled, "Maybe someone ought to give it to you."

"I get along all right by myself," I told him.

"You're the kind of nut it's best to stay away from," he said. "And you might as well know it now, no regular guy in town is ever going to go out with you."

His tone of voice let me know he would see to that. "You never even comb your hair," he said, looking this time at my cowlicks, "and you live with a—" He stopped. Then said, "You're always going to be stuck with some spic-queer—or a Jew."

I let go then and began to pound him, his chest and then his face, then with bare grass-stained feet kicked him in the shins and then the groin. I don't know what would have happened, how badly he might have hurt me, he had his hands on my throat, if Bo hadn't come out on the patio, slamming the door to the sunporch behind him. Brad let go of me fast then and ducked under the pink gate which I immediately locked.

"Nut," he yelled back over one shoulder. And then, and this was directed at Uncle Bo, "Queer."

Bo called the realtor that very afternoon. "Nice friends you have, Elizabeth," he told me.

"He's no friend of mine," I said, "he's just Lana's brother."

"Un huh, I see," Bo said, "nice boy."

When Jay came over later, bringing some of his things, Bo said he would have to make other arrangements, that he was sorry and that of course he should have told Jay he was going to do it, but he had just put the house on the market. "I'm sorry, but I can't stay here any longer. For now you'll have to go back to Frank's."

Jay stood on one foot, then the other and looked down at them. When he finally raised his head I saw his pain and I don't think I've ever again seen such a look of disappointment on anybody's face.

Betrayal, I was sure that was the word he would say.

But he didn't. He just stood without speaking on the front porch, still purple with bougainvillea, where Bo had made his pronouncement. I watched his whole body sink: knees, chest, shoulders.

Before this terrible sadness a knot in my own chest tightened. I still feel the weight of it from time to time. And without saying anything, all caved in like that, Jay turned to go.

And Bo didn't call after him.

As far as I know he never apologized or ever offered more in the way of explanation.

After Jay left, Bo high-tailed it to Robin Lee's.

And still later.

But didn't get there what he had counted on. Unconditional love. Or, at least, sympathy. Not the way he told it.

"What she said to me was, 'Bo, you might as well know this. I've heard some things about you. People think that Jay, that there's something the matter with him. Not just his stuttering. Something that maybe causes his stuttering. Now, you understand, I'm not saying this. I'm just telling you about people.' Can you believe she would say this to me? When I told her I had no idea what she was talking about she looked at me and said things that were even stranger."

"'Bo, I'm going to be thirty-four years old,'" she said. 'You're a lot older.'" Bo was forty-eight. "'I think some things between you and me should soon be settled.' 'What things?' I asked her. 'You know how I feel about you. Why, we're close. Close friends.'"

"Then she told me, 'I think you know what I'm saying.'"

"Listen, a lot has happened to me," I told her. "I have let a lot hit me, and a whole lot has been taken. Can't you see that? My life's just a blank now."

"She said it wouldn't have to be a blank, that it could be nice, that I could fill it."

He stopped for a second, then said, "What I'm trying to get across to you, Elizabeth, is that in the late fall—" He cleared his throat. "Around Thanksgiving I've agreed to marry Robin Lee."

Then, over just a couple of ice cubes, he filled a water glass to the top with bourbon.

"If you want to drink," he told me once, "and live to any age at all after you begin to do it, buy and drink only the highest quality bourbon. Scotch has a nasty foreign taste, so forget it. And never drink any kind of rot gut. Or vodka which rots holes in your brain and makes you crazy. Or killer gin."

Still in Sayer

*C*ertain times in life for certain places. I'm pointed west now though who knows if I'll stay or for how long. I'm not sure I'll see my Uncle Bo much more. He's talked for years about making a return to the Gulf coast although I don't know now that he can go. He says he hates the pine woods more than ever. He never liked them. He says, "I want out into open country. I hate living in all that dark."

"Maybe I'll go to Galveston," he told me just this morning. As I drove on and all the way across Oklahoma I remember him saying that. And here in this motel where I rest and write this and drink even more bad coffee, I watch on the TV that hangs over the counter the big hurricane Alicia wash over that town.

Wash over the old Galvez Hotel where we ate several holiday dinners and which has long lived on in my mind as a reminder of Bo and Grandma and all the family and what I sometimes falsely think of as gentler and better times.

They weren't, all things considered.

Now I see the Galvez is all but gone. And I know that when Bo sees the waves wash over it — he will by this time probably be home to see it on his own TV — his dreams about returning will be gone too.

Each year he has fantasized about returning to a different Gulf coast town, all but you, Corpus Christi—Rockport, Port Lavaca, Aransas Pass, Port Isabel. But, I suspect, Galveston was the town he thought he really might get to.

Once Uncle Bo drove my mother and Rena and Grandma and me to Galveston just so we could eat Thanksgiving dinner. I had been there for the first time with Uncle Leeland when he and his crew were building bridges, rode the bus from Livingston on a highway called "The Hug the Coast."

From where I lay stretched out on the back seat, the three grown-ups crammed together in front, I was only aware of fat clouds and blue sky. The road when I saw it was only a shiny little sliver of a thing, clean and empty. Oh, I often think, that was the time for traveling in Texas!

Because I got car sick I always had the backseat all to myself. Bo or my mother always spread a pallet for me there and put a bucket of cokes and ice and cut limes and a pan with a washrag in it, for me to throw up in, on the floor. The coke and lime never prevented my car sickness as everyone hoped it might. But that I got car sick also never stopped us from going anywhere. Or stopped me from wanting to.

Very early that Thanksgiving morning, and it was still years from the Thanksgiving that was first scheduled to be Bo's wedding day, Bo said he would drive us all to Galveston. Grandma and Aunty had been grumbling over coffee about making dressing and about the, for them, dismal prospects of cooking a turkey all day; they had already, at eight in the morning, set the pecan and pumpkin pies out to cool.

"I would rather go to the Galvez and have crab," Bo said, "and have those pies when we come home. Who needs turkey and dressing?"

"Well, I don't know about going all the way to Galveston," my mother said, nervous, expectant, laughing, dutifully pointing out that Galveston was two hundred miles away; everyone in the family expected my mother to be practical as if to compensate for Bo.

Bo said your hotels wouldn't serve crab, Corpus, that you were in your ways, if not in your population, too small-town. Anyway, he said we should have a change of scene.

"I like turkey," Aunt Rena said (Aunt Rena liked everything), "but it would be fun to go."

"Well, then," Grandma said, "I expect the Galvez has turkey, too."

I knew then we would get off.

On our way out of town we gave our uncooked turkey to the Gonzales family who lived on the corner and who often sent us homemade tamales at Easter and during Christmas time.

Now here I am in this sad looking little town, its houses sagging in the heat, just a few miles from the Texas Panhandle, not too far from Amarillo, before I leave my Motel 6 looking at Galveston in black and white in all that strange weather. Strange weather all over the world, the Doomsday folk tell us, as they always have. But we see it, shadowlike, in more places, see a big hurricane named Alicia now washing the old Galvez away.

"Maybe Galveston's too big," Bo said to me just this morning when he talked of wanting to get back to the coast. "And once in a while," he went on, "it freezes. If we moved south far enough we would never get cold. Port Isabel or even Port Lavaca might be better. Port Isabel is the southern most point in the United States."

Bo never mentions you, Corpus Christi. After he came back from the crazy-house, he had to live in you with shame.

By the time he had to face you, Jay had taken off and Robin Lee's mother had moved Robin Lee to her relatives who lived near San Antonio.

Bo broke their engagement the first time three days before Thanksgiving and broke it the second time, the following June, just hours before he was scheduled to show up at the First Methodist church.

Although Robin Lee finally came back to you, Corpus, people tell us she was never the same, was someone entirely different, much older, prettier, and surer of herself, but super serious and sick quite a lot.

As soon as he could, Bo left for Houston where Jay helped him get a job with Foley's; at first he handled designer clothes for women, after working in housewares for a time, and later became the buyer for designer clothes for both women and men.

And after my mother's marriage to Bud broke up, my mother joined him and began her own business, a music store. The two of them were in their own way, happy. What they knew about mostly was work and in those days Houston was a good town to work and work hard in. Bo said it was always against his better judgment and my mother's too, to retire near Aunt Rena in the pines.

"I may not be around too much longer," he said this morning when I put him on the bus. And I, thinking of Aunt Rena, way up in her nineties, was put out with him.

"Oh, you don't know," I told him. Bo is only seventy-five, not old in our family.

"I have premonitions," he told me. "God gives us premonitions."

Aunt Rena always called them signs.

Near New Mexico
Near Santa Rosa

*S*igns all right on old route 66, now Interstate 40, on the road to California. Near the end of Oklahoma, just the other side of Sayer where I last wrote, I pulled off early to stretch and have some coffee, hardly able to deal with contemplating the miles I have to go, then afterwards came straight across the Panhandle and into New Mexico on good, straight roads, the wind behind me and hours still ahead with light.

As I drove I cried for Bo. And also thought sadly of Aunt Rena. When I last talked to her on the phone her voice was so clear. Until just last spring she got around all right, every spring planted a flower garden and some beloved vegetables, too. She always cooked and ate a lot of them. But she can't navigate anymore and when she tries, just topples over. Seems cruel to me because Rena loved to travel, was off to Acapulco on Uncle Leeland's insurance money just a few days after he was in the ground. You can imagine what Grandma said. If she couldn't take a big trip, she would take a little one, if only on one of the city buses.

"Rena, where do you go on the bus?" Grandma always asked her.

"Why," she would answer, "to the picture shows. Or sometimes just downtown to bum through Kress's, you know I always did love to Kress a little, or sometimes," she laughed, "I'll just ride to the end of the line. I always meet somebody. Somebody who likes a good time." And Grandma's lip would curl up at Rena.

Later I would hear her talking about Aunt Rena as if she were a whore. And would see when I looked at Aunt Rena that she had been crying.

And sometimes I just let Grandma have it. "Talk that way about Aunt Rena if you want," I would tell her, "but don't let her hear you and hold your tongue in front of my friends."

When C.C. came over and heard some of the things Grandma said, I was embarrassed to be related. I was also mortified the night Grandma convinced my mother to have C.C. and I followed. They thought we were going somewhere to be with boys; we were just on our way out in the country to see Gerry when I caught sight, in our rear view mirror, and this was in T.J.'s car, of Mother and Bud behind us. C.C. had been telling me of her troubles with Travis and how she hoped he would get away, but to college, not to the army. Talk of war was all around us. "Oh," she said, "I hate it when he says he is going to enlist."

We were a family, and finally a town, of travelers.

How many places I had been with Uncle Bo.

Dear Uncle Bo, (I said on the card I just wrote.)

I have missed your company. We have taken a lot of trips together and today I have remembered them all.

Then I made a remark about the scenery and the weather, so much cooler than the weather we had been in back there, and then I wrote that I loved him. I had never done that before.

It seems right to me now that I think back on it that we left each other in the early morning hours, him going back on the bus to a place where the light is paler, me driving straight into it out of a hot wind.

"Here we are, two single people," Bo had said back in the bus station, just before he boarded. I thought maybe it was the last time we would see each other. In a flash then I saw Robin Lee and Jay, saw their faces, Robin Lee's wry smile, Jay's broad one and also saw for just a minute the faces of the two young men who had, for any period of time been in my life, both Easterners, the first of whom made me feel I ought to shuck my background, conceal my identity or change it. "Sometimes Elizabeth," he would often reprimand me, "I can't imagine where you grew up." He was an opera lover, what we had in common: a love for opera, a pale-skinned, blue-eyed Philadelphian, now an announcer for QXR. The other, a jazz fan more tolerant of my origins, but so different from me, had grown up in the Bronx. I hadn't lived under a roof with either of them. This doesn't seem the right place for me to tell you about them and, maybe, there is none. But Bo and I once had both considered sharing our lives with these others. I could hear Aunt Rena saying, "He could have lived with a person outside his family if he had wanted to."

Could he or I have done that? I remember asking Joe if happiness is important, I thought he surely had the answer to life's big questions, and I can still hear the resonance of his impassioned, "Yes."

"I was never afraid of work, hard work," I could hear Grandaddy saying. Well, none of his children were either, and certainly Grandma wasn't , though they were afraid of other things.

"Mother," Leeland always said to Grandma, "for God's sake hire some help. You're killing yourself with so much housework, cooking and canning on that wood stove, then sewing all afternoon into the night." And I can hear Grandma telling him, "Whoever I hired wouldn't clean to suit me, would just piddle around." Bo locked himself in the room with her that hot June day she died and wasn't sober for long periods after. I guess I have already told you a lot about that summer, how sometimes he would sober up for Jay or Robin Lee. But he didn't stay sober until after he was released from the asylum. He went berserk in the fall after he had taken me to college; after he was released he never drank again, but he also didn't laugh much or spin out his dreams.

Bo spent nearly a year in the state hospital and was visited often, or so he told me, by a beautiful girl from what was then the ward for "nymphs." He considered bringing her home he said, but she overdosed before they released her; he told me this story many times and told me other sad ones.

When asked, he assisted with shock treatments and lobotomies.

When he finally came home to the cream colored house where he had moved us—the house was close to the street and practically downtown, all of us sitting on the porch he had painted shrimp pink—the first person he talked to was Robin Lee.

I thought I had never seen her look so pretty. She was wearing, in complementary contrast to our loud porch, a sleeveless linen dress in robin's egg blue, the color that matched her name. Her hair, which when not in a pony tail or in pigtails usually hung limply around her shoulders, was done in a French roll. She seemed to me, and I expect to Bo, too, many years older. And so much calmer.

But then, how must he have seemed to her? To me he was almost a stranger; it had been so many years since I had been with him when he was really sober. He seemed all flattened out.

"You're looking well, Bo," she told him. His smile was faint; he took her hands and said, "You, too." (She died of bronchitis a few weeks after.)

She was all composure when she said, "I thought about you." He told her then in a matter of fact way that he had thought about her, too. I wondered if he had much. As he talked, my mother and I pumped on the porch swing.

"Everyone hopes you will come back to the office," she told him. Then she was quiet for a second; he didn't speak. "Maybe you have heard I have been out of town."

"People in my family," I told Joe Copeland, "people in my family don't just drink too much and then have genteel breakdowns from which they recover in fashionable sanitariums. And after that take crusies. They get locked up in jails or crazy houses. Or fall out of hospital windows." Uncle Leeland had almost done that when he was in the hospital to dry out, two big nurses and a nun pulled him from the ledge.

Later he claimed he was jumping because he had to get away from the nun. "Meanest woman," he told me, "God ever put breath in."

"Darling," Joe said, "we are alike. The people in my family, too."

Santa Monica

From my new apartment nearer the station.

*T*hat we were alike, of course, was exactly what I wanted him to tell me.

He told me stories of alcoholic uncles, desire-ridden aunts, explosive fathers, or shiftless ones, of mothers who were nagging and martyred or sex-starved and restless, of crazy people, mothers and fathers, uncles and aunts, who ran away from their children and each other and of all the children he knew who were abandoned or who died of horrible diseases or, worse sometimes, who lived on with broken hearts.

He laughed before he said, "I wanted to tell some good news. Something exciting. Wanted to play some music, put on some drama. Build a network. Something for us all."

We were alike and I had wanted him to tell me.

One way in which we weren't alike, he had married, had made a household, or rather, households, had apartments in London and New York, while I traveled precariously through the world, all my stars in air signs in spite of my New Year's birth.

Once again I was trying to relocate. No job with any station seemed to last. I wanted work in a place that would put on my dramas. That meant, with Joe's help, and I was grateful for it, National Public Radio and very little money. Probably even meant working another job.

I guess nobody talks anymore about making any move final, but I thought I might stay in Los Angeles three to five years. I had been grieving prematurely over Bo when I lost Joe. I see that now.

Like Leeland on the ledge, my people hang on even when there's not much to hang on to.

I had idolized Joe and followed his career since childhood. Seemed to me sometimes that I had always known him, that I had no life before him. I met him the year I graduated from you, C.C. I told you that, and in the fabric of my life that memory is one of the brightest colors. But we didn't meet again until just a few years ago at Dan's station, KSD in Dallas and later at WKY in Oklahoma City.

At first he barely remembered me. Wouldn't have if I hadn't been Leona Bell's daughter, oh, he remembered my mother!

He had, even then, a fatal illness. And I grieved for Bo. And slipped away when I wasn't looking, his heart just failed, as if he had planned it, as if being free of his body was what he wanted.

I read somewhere that you can hold people to their bodies, to relationships, to desire, by prayer. The piece quoted a dying man who asked his wife to stop praying so that he could get on with what he was doing.

"Damn you," it reported him saying, "stop your selfish praying," and that shocked her so that she stopped. And with the energy she transmitted through prayer gone, he took a last breath.

By the time I met him at Dan's station, Joe was in a body that no longer made a good home. Twice Joe gave me just the boost I needed, and was about to give me so much more, but he couldn't stick around.

And in that regard was like Julia Winter, my English teacher at Corpus Christi High School who along with our famous Miss V, oh, V for Victory, launched me on my creative life.

My religious life. With so much energy going out over the airways, radio did one of the jobs of prayer, connected my mother to Miss V and Miss Winter to me. Life to life to life.

Before I met Joe, before I won that contest, Miss Winter encouraged me to go east to college and late in September of 1952 Bo and I climbed in the DeSoto and took off.

Except for Miss V, Miss Winter was my most important teacher and edited my first scripts.

Miss Winters taught an honors course in dramatic writing which she had a chance to begin because we had one of the first radio stations in the state. I almost didn't take it because I couldn't take everything and I thought a course in shorthand might be of more practical use.

But I adored Miss Winter, as I later did Joe, and months before I broke down and took her course, asked her to edit my contest entry.

I still remember some of our conversations.

"You see," I remember saying to her and remember being surprised she didn't laugh, "you see, I hear voices." Miss V who had more professional savvy and who was much more worldly, would have made a joke. "I put down what they tell me," I went on, "and what they call out to each other. And when they stop, I stop, but sometimes, when I rearrange what they tell me, I have a radio play. I've written one the station here will put on and I think I might get it on in other places."

"And so you might," she said, "but I'll bet that's not the reason you wrote it."

I didn't answer.

C.C. told me once it was plain I loved Miss Winter, that Ben was the only other person at the high school she had seen me look at just that way. I wondered if it was the same way she looked at Travis, the way Bo looked at Jay. As often as not when I was outside her classroom talking to Miss Winter, I could see C.C. and Travis making out in front of the door to the art room which was just down at the end of the hall. Wherever they were they nibbled at each other. C.C. could draw better than anybody at the school, but Travis was almost as good and getting better and better.

Oh all this, this memory, is just a few weeks before Travis left, split from you and from C.C., Corpus, and with that other girl.

"Even if I can't produce the script, I mean commercially," I told Miss Winter, "it may help me get a radio job. CHSR is going to put it on." CHSR stood for Corpus Christi High School Radio.

In the kindest possible way Miss Winters told me she thought I should get a general education.

"Well," I said, "I don't know what I would do with that." A major in speech and communications would, I was sure, get me a job in radio, if not in writing and producing my own drama or in interviewing and reviewing, and even then, these possibilities seemed to me fanciful, in programming or instruction, in the business end.

"Have you thought of television?" Miss Winters asked me. "Does Miss Van DeMeyer encourage you in that?"

Miss V hadn't. I don't think she knew much about it. Who did? Until my first year in college no one I knew had a set.

But Miss V knew all right about radio, had been a programmer for several Texas stations, did broadcasting when she was in the navy.

She had also done some parachuting in the navy and her chute failed once in California, over a field at the edge of an orchard so that she came down in a Japanese pear tree. She still limped from the fall.

"That's what she gets," I heard, and she heard, people say, "for acting like a man." Even navy personnel, her superior and others, she told me once, had made remarks like that.

Although neither Miss V nor Miss Winter had been married, many seemed to believe that Miss Winter's single state went along with her being a school teacher, an occupation that she somehow had to adopt and a second best thing. Best, of course, would have been the occupations of wife and mother. Talk had it that her fiance was killed early in the war.

On the other hand, most people thought Miss V's singleness was unnatural and went along with some kind of perversion though nobody would explicitly say what. She could not have been accused of being thick with women for there were none, either old or young, around her. Her students revered and loved her but kept their distances and everyone knew were just her students, though some also became her friends.

Alone, into herself, unnatural, no wonder she limps, has a sickness. That was as much as I heard anybody whisper. Or, sometimes, just say.

"No," I said to Miss Winter. "I don't think she knows much about television. And I've hardly seen any. What I really care about is sound, working in sound. I think I could make a little money at it. Enough at least to live."

They laughed at me in Hollywood when I said all I wanted was to make a living. Except for the people at KCRW everyone I meet thinks I should learn to write for TV or the screen.

But I don't. I write to you about Miss Winter and Miss V.

Younger than Miss Winter, Miss V was blonde and scrubbed looking with pink cheeks and bright blue eyes, and like mine, fine, unruly hair. No one ever imagined a lover for her or connected her in any way with romance, though of the two women she had led by far the most dramatic life.

Tall and willowy, Miss Winter combed her hair away from her face and always wore a flower, often a red hibiscus or a bright rose behind one ear. Thin skinned and lightly freckled with a small overbite and slightly protruding teeth, she was sparkly-eyed, would have been beautiful, Lana said, if she had worn her hair loose around her shoulders.

"She brushes it back to show off her wit," I said, one could tell she had it, "so nothing will show but her mind."

But no matter what I said, her shiny brown hair was noticeable, maybe because she stuck those flowers in it, and C.C. said she thought Miss Winter meant it to be.

Back then, and this was before I met Joe, I thought Miss Winter had the answers to life's most important questions and I was in earnest when I asked what she thought I might do with a "general" education.

She said, "Why, learn from it, Elizabeth, and enjoy!"

"You don't understand," I told her. "Everyone in my family works. Always have." Even the married women, I wanted to tell her. What I had said was, I thought, the central truth about us. And that Julia Winter would surely understand.

Aunt Rena was, of course, outside blood-ties. Grandma always said Aunt Rena had no ambition, didn't care how poor she was. Once I heard a group of distant cousins, Grandma's nieces and great nieces whispering about Aunt Rena's origins. Was Aunt Rena of another race I wondered. And if she was, how did that make her different?

Were other races more inclined toward different ways of living? Were they more loving? I didn't know.

All I knew was that Aunt Rena had married into a family who worked and who respected work most when it brought in money. My grandmother whipped up dresses, my mother taught music and both were paid. No one thought much of Uncle Leeland when he just stayed home drinking and drawing up plans for buildings that no one had commissioned.

I also knew Aunt Rena had married into a family that had a streak of cruelty in it. We were, I knew, cruel to ourselves and sometimes to one another, perhaps because we repressed our impulses toward loving.

"A regular work house," Rena would often say. "It tires me out just to be around you people."

"Well, Elizabeth," I can still hear Julia Winter saying, "I'm going to place my hard earned money on what I'm going to tell you. And that is, that no matter what kind of education you get, general or otherwise, you will work, too."

Then she asked me if I wanted to live and be old and that surprised me and still does. She wasn't sick then. I said of course I did, yes.

"So do I," she told me, her eyes crinkling at the corners, a devilish glint in her crooked smile. "Oh I do, too."

On the Sunset Limited
Southern Pacific, Austin Bound

But she didn't live and I lost her. The following winter she got the flu, then bronchial pneumonia, then leukemia; she died during the first spring I was away in school.

Grieving goes on for so long. I think it was Julia Winter I was, when I last wrote, telling you about.

Who would have thought that nearly a year would pass between letters and that when I wrote again I would, with engagements in three cities, be bound for Texas's heart? We have just pulled out of El Paso, Phoenix and Tucson far behind. I have always liked crossing the country by train, and I like working on it, watching the landscape slowly change from one kind to a totally different other. And in this part of my life I seem fated to swing back and forth between the far west and the middle of the country, just as when I was young I did between the middle of the country and New York.

When people asked me where I was from I used to say "I'm a Texan." Now I say, "I have lived in a lot of places." And I'm always homesick and yet no matter how many times I return, never feel I have arrived at home.

Hell, I had told Travis, I want to get out of hell.

The chartered bus I rode to Dallas after I won the radio drama contest took me almost out. I had just turned sixteen. A bunch of students who wanted to tour the Big-D stations and meet important performers, announcers and programmers rode with me. We were all excited and it was March and spring.

The days had begun to turn warm in you, Corpus, leaves coming out on the trees in sticky green buds. And the Gulf had begun to sing. Far across town as we lived from it, I seemed to wake each morning to its singing.

The feel of the sun through the bus window told me that soon I would wear only cotton, that in another month I would be in sun dresses of soft colors. That year I favored lavender, maybe because it is a fantasy shade and that was a time for dreams. On the bus I saw shiny lavender cloth before me, smelled it, the polished cotton. I took such pleasure in smells and inhaled all the ones I had cared particularly for, all the new leaves and new cotton and linen and the straw of new hats.

I remembered a straw cloche with a bunch of cloth violets pinned to one side, a hat Grandma and I decorated together before the onset of her illness, her last healthy spring on earth and before she got so cranky, though she always had a little something critical to say. "It's a good thing this is a cloche and close fitting," she told me. "It may once and for all tame that wild head of hair your father gave you, stick those cowlicks down to your head."

Bumping over the Texas countryside on that bus I wore the prim grey suit she had made me. Slate grey, she called it. Ben said that in rainy weather or when I was sad it was the color of my eyes. Back then if we were really going somewhere, we dressed up, wouldn't have dreamed of arriving in jeans, jeans were for hayrides and Saturday mornings.

On the bus I was careful of the way I sat because I didn't want to wrinkle my skirt and through all the miles was expectant, excited, looking out the windows at the new grass and all that rolling country and at the delicate little field flowers that had appeared suddenly. Some, like the bluebonnet when we came on a whole expanse of them, took my breath; they made a flag of a field, a flag that stretched out as far as I could see.

"When you are really yourself, Elizabeth," Ben told me after giving me a bunch of bluebonnets he had picked in the vacant lot, "your eyes aren't grey at all, they're darkest blue." Just before I left on this trip I took the flowers out of the vase on my desk where I had stuck them and into the bathroom where I held them against my face as I looked into the mirror, the only one in the house except for those in Grandma's room, to see if what Ben said was true.

Which brings me to a thought. Some postures are, maybe, for each of us, characteristic. Here I am still traveling. Looking out a window. At a desert this time and in August, too.

Much farther east the fields are all burnt up, but in six or seven months will be green all over. The train takes me across the expanse of Texas, across the tough roots of all the wildflowers I remember. Year after year they come back, gay and sprightly, no matter how hard the freeze in winter or how bad the August burn.

After that trip I have been remembering, my life turned over.

Miss V put me in charge of the high school station; she was a pro and, some thought, a slave driver and although she favored me, or because she did, she was on me especially hard. Every day she would ask how the new script on which I was working was coming. "Oh," I would tell her, "it is."

"Like it was yesterday? When it was also coming? Do you want to be in charge?"

"I want to be in charge, Miss V." I wanted to be like her, victorious.

"Then learn how to meet a deadline and how to write a script that will play."

My radio play, A Basket of Flowers, was subtitled, A Drama of Spring. When I sent it off it had never been performed and only Marion Van DeMeyer and Julia Winter had seen the script.

I had written about three little girls, best friends until two of them begin to grow up faster than the other, and begin to wish to separate themselves from her, and from all childhood rituals and games.

The play opens on May Day in the school hall where the friends, after biking to school, are scheduled to meet, the metal baskets of their bicycles filled with small straw ones which hold spring flowers.

The narrator says that for the last several years the children have on the first of May met in the school hall in just this way and together delivered throughout the surrounding neighborhood many baskets of flowers.

The youngest girl has been standing in the hall waiting for her friends for sometime, waiting and looking out at the sky which is black with rain clouds and threatening. "I wonder when they are going to come," she says. "I hope it won't be raining."

Then we hear the giggling voices of her friends, named, the narrator tells us, April and June after those spring and summer months. After some preliminary conversation that establishes their ages, nearly thirteen, they tell their friend, little March who is still only eleven, that they are going to spend the day at the town's new teen club where this very morning a juke box is being installed. "Come with us," June says, though her tone is not really inviting. After a pause during which the listener hears only the wind blowing, the younger girl says she means to deliver the flowers.

Her friends tell her she's still a baby, that delivering flowers is boring and, they have realized, dumb, a dumb thing for little kids to do. Then they run off and we hear their scuffling steps, yelling back at her, "Oh, March, you're such a baby."

I long ago lost this script, but I remember the drama ending with March calling, "April! June! Come back."

And them retorting, "No, we don't like you anymore."

And then March crying, "Oh, the weather's so stormy." And the narrator telling the listening audience that for March it was a ruined spring.

I remember the wind machine going "Whooo, whooo, whoo" and the sound man throwing a Benny Goodman record on.

Then more giggling and shuffling and the wind machine again. And then the narrator saying the youngest child's flowers had been blown out of their baskets and into the school yard, were scattered in the dirt there and in the school building where some had also drifted across the cold stone floor.

Well, it was all a little heavy and too obviously symbolic. But in my adolescence I justified that by telling myself and others that life was.

Hadn't my two best friends from the grade school in the refinery town deserted me in just that way? Friends I had met before I met C.C. and now she was way ahead of me and going.

And hadn't other people's friends, in ways similar to the ones I dramatized, deserted them, too?

Didn't nature, time itself, separate people who loved one another?

I had wanted to tell about that, like the preacher in C.C.'s church wanted to "sing out the story."

More than that, in what I saw even then as a vain attempt, I wanted to make a metaphor for emotion and its passing. Wanted to name it, explain it, tell others. Especially the beloved.

You see, here we have it. This is what it was or is.

Joe, if I could only write to you.

West Texas

I would say: *A Flower of the Field*. That's what it was, all that feeling that sprang up between us.

That's what I've wanted to tell you, Joe, and looking out at all this dirt and sand reminded me. Six months ago fields to the east were covered with bluebonnets as they were thirty some years ago when I went to Dallas because I had won a contest with a five page script. Even then you were just in Texas for a visit.

You had stayed on in Europe where you had done so much broadcasting during the war. Were with us only for the spring, my charmed one, from France. The night after the broadcast, two hours of shows written and produced by high school and junior college students, you walked me out of the back of the big frame house which contained, more or less, the party for winners. The house, as I remember, was out of town, up toward Denton, off a red country road.

We faced a field alive with wildflowers and you stopped in mid-sentence and never got back to what you were going to tell me about writing radio plays.

"Those," you said, pointing. "I've missed them. They come back every year. I love those little flowers."

I still remember, as you spoke, your dark face and big, dark eyes shining and your hair, with only one little streak of white in it. I also remember thinking when I saw you years after, that it was odd, that solitary white streak, and even odder that you never got another.

"I love those little flowers."

Just last March you wrote me about them, after the train ride you had taken from Dallas to Austin and what I think of as rich-black-dirt country, though, mostly, its rolling and green. At the end of the paragraph, the first of your letter, you said, as you had back then, "I love Texas."

Well, you didn't live in it much.

Remember how you said, when we first met, "Don't tell me you are Leona Bell's daughter: She opened KTHS up in Arkansas where I put on an early radio play. When I first began I worked all the Southwestern states."

"Yes," I said, "Leona Bell is my mother."

"Well, then, Elizabeth," you were in those days always so formal with your 'Elizabeths,' "there's no help for you." You opened your arms as if to release the station to me. "All this is in your blood."

Later you told me I had learned my grit from my mother. Hardly news to me. "No woman has more grit than a Texas woman." That was what you said. I admired no one more than my mother. But her trouble terrified me. And sometimes I railed against her so I could break away.

On my last trip here I saw Dan Rodriguez in downtown Dallas. He was a programmer for KSD and had several announcing spots. Like me he has been pretty faithful to radio, has never done television much. He has opted for commercial radio and he makes good money at it, though not the kind I once thought he would go for. He took me out to lunch and we talked about those early days we worked together when I first met you, and afterward we browsed through Cokesbury bookstore where we ran into another high school friend, one I never spoke to you much about, a girl named Gerry. She has her own ad agency now and carries several important accounts. She and her mother were so poor back in Corpus, lived way out in the country in a dark, nearly windowless, frame house. Like me she hadn't any father. "My word," Gerry said, "I always did say to C.C. that you and Dan would finally wind up together."

"Oh it's only business, Gerry," I told her. And, of course, it was.

"Why are you going with that radio boy?" my Aunt Rena used to ask me and I didn't say, couldn't have then, "Aunt Rena, I'm in love with radio."

Dan wouldn't have wanted me or anybody in love with him. Even at sixteen he was too ambitious to lose work time.

From our high school class I think Dan and I are the only two people who have stayed single. Even Gerry had a try at marriage. In the early sixties I lost track of Ben. He married one of his young history teachers, then became a history teacher, a full professor at the University of Chicago now. Even in high school I knew he wasn't cut out to be a lawyer.

I never told you about Ben did I Joe? Or about any of these people. There's a whole lot I never told you. And I wanted to.

One day yet I may sit down and tell you all of our stories. Not that there's any sense of urgency.

When I first met you I felt you already knew.

Knew about Bo, and before him, Leeland. And Grandaddy and Aunt Rena. And understood about my mother whom you, you alone, just plain loved.

It was as if they were your kinfolk, too.

Later,
near Austin

You had told me about your family, how your mother's people were poor and struggling and some of them shiftless, but also about how they were a people of sense and more or less of stability. Oh yes, you had told me all about your mother's striving family and about your father's half crazed one, ambitious and gifted but tormented, drunken uncles and, more hushed, drunken aunts, and men and women who couldn't get jobs. All of them, like mine, had been woodsmen, builders, teachers. And one or two had inclinations toward art.

Oh, our families were just the same. "Our families," you told me once, "built Texas."

"One of these days Leona's going to burn up," I once heard Grandma say when she heard my mother yelling at Bud.

And I can still hear Aunt Rena saying, "Well, I'm not sure what's the matter with Leona."

"I know what's the matter," I would tell her. "She didn't get to finish what she started trying for. And stopping like that broke her heart."

Joe, you always said she was the kind to do things. It hurt her, Joe, to stop doing, and even more to have the man she stopped doing for drive right off the Texas coast. And when he was gone and she was alone for a long time it was hard supporting me.

Oh Grandma always said, "Leona was this wild dark-haired thing. I couldn't keep her in the house. She was always outside in the woods and in the fields with the men, and she rode Bob, that high-spirited horse, bareback right over the side of the mountain without asking permission and that was a scandal; we would have to take the razor strap to her. She wasn't even twelve years old."

"That was one trouble," Rena said, "they all tried to break her. When she was sixteen you know she had a kind of breakdown and before she went off herself to work and study music for awhile they had to take her out of school." And then Rena would laugh! "Oh, but, she was the only one who could break Bob and, honey, he was the craziest horse I've ever seen."

"They used to whip him," my mother said. "I never had to." She started the same way every time she told me. "One day when I saw Lloyd whipping him I said, 'You had better stop that. If you don't, one day I'm going to use that thing on you.' He stopped then because he knew I meant business."

And, Joe, she did, too. Everybody in the family stopped whipping and riding Bob soon after.

Corpus, why am I writing to Joe? He's gone. The past is gone, the world sinking and Texas in it. But why go on like this? You are there. And I'm not, and am never going to be, crazy. These letters are all, of course, to you.

Corpus, Joe thought my mother was a queen. "I'll tell you, Elizabeth," he always said to me, "she has got it. She's something royal. When I was just a teenager and told him, on that weekend I went to Dallas, a few of my troubles, he said I shouldn't fuss with my mother so much about wanting to go far away to study, that she would come around. "Why," he would say, "when she was your age she scrapped for what she wanted." Yes, I thought, but she also broke down, keeps having little breakdowns. But I knew he was right, of course.

Later when she met him, my mother really liked Joe; there weren't too many men with whom she hit it off.

"The Grand Old Guy," that's what Dan always called him; he would have hated that, the name, partially, my fault since I told Dan how Joe had been on hand for the opening of the radio stations in two neighboring states. Three if we counted New Mexico.

"Why the fuck wouldn't I count New Mexico?" Dan asked. He never talked that way when we were back in high school, but like the rest of us, tried to keep up to date.

"Well," I said and this was years ago, back in the sixties, "Why would anybody? It might as well be on the moon." In my mind the world stopped with Big Bend, coyotes and rattlers and stinging scorpions under the creosote bushes and Spanish dagger. All of that near Valentine, a town we passed not too long ago on the train.

It was through Dan that I met Joe. Met Joe for the second time I mean. I was past my middle forties. Before I went to the Midwest and National Public Radio I had worked for Dan at KSD in Dallas and, before that, in Ft. Worth. Dan had scheduled Joe for an interview at the Dallas station and I had never seen him, Dan, more nervous.

I was nervous too. I dreaded explaining that we had met when I was just a kid. I didn't think he would remember. But he did, dimly, and we just got on from the first. I can still remember telling Dan, "He's so nice."

Also, and this is what I didn't say to Dan, beautiful. Tall and thin, sinewy with nice shoulders, remarkable I thought then for a man in his sixties, his arms still shapely, his hair barely streaked with white. My own which, as you know, has had ashy spots since childhood is now half grey and I've given up trying to cover it all with color. Only once before, when I met Joe as a kid, had I come face to face with such vitality; it bubbled over. He had such plans for the station! He was there, you see, to help with programming and to do a few shows.

Joe was the first person I had met in radio, at least since Marion Van DeMeyer, our beloved Miss V, who made me feel I ought to work harder. I hadn't been around him ten minutes before I began to have some clear ideas on ways I might improve.

I told Joe I had met Floyd Tillman's wife once on the train, I was always a great train rider, and believed if I called her, I might get Floyd to the station to be interviewed and to play and sing a few songs. Floyd, as you may remember, was the father of country music. I added that Frances had told me that in the early days Floyd, along with Hank Williams and Eddie Arnold worked in radio a lot.

"He worked for both KTHS and KPRC," Joe said. "And he was fired from both for plugging his songs. Afterwards I think he may have gone to KLPR in Oklahoma City. But he is a real musician, never gave a damn about fame or money. Would have lived in a tent if he could have played and composed."

I told Joe I thought Frances was a singer but quit because she wanted all the limelight to be on Floyd. She said she had seen too many marriages go bust over double ambition. Right then I made a mental note never to marry. "Not that Floyd was really ambitious," she told me. "He is too much of an artist for that. But I just want him safe."

Not long after we talked about Tillmans, Joe disappeared to call Kate. "What's she like?" I asked him our first evening together at dinner and he said, "She's a singer."

I waited for more and he saw that. Of course I knew she was a singer, from Michigan, when Joe met her a Yank abroad; just his age or a year or two older or younger, she had been part of his first broadcasts for the BBC after the war. She had kept her voice, still did concerts.

He repeated, "She's a singer." He thought he had said it all, but to please me, he winked and added, "Elizabeth, Kate's show biz." Then he made a little gesture with his right hand. "Getting it all on. Getting on the eyeshadow, getting on the mascara." Winked again then in a theatrical way and tugged at his shiny tie. "It's everything to her," he told me, then cleared his throat and said, "Kate is strong."

I didn't know how to put all this together. Wasn't he important to her? I thought he surely was, yet there was something pejorative in that "It's everything" and in that "Kate is strong." Remembering an old country western song with the title "Prison Bars Are Strong," I almost asked, "Like prison bars are strong?"

But I didn't dare ask anything. I only told Joe that I couldn't really get a picture of Kate. I had, of course, read about her, who hadn't? For years the Texas papers were full of Joe Copeland in England and of his midwestern wife, and he ended the discussion by saying, "She's a voice."

That made me want to hear her, made me want to go out and dial her on the phone, but, of course, it wasn't a sensible idea and anyway, I couldn't.

I had to call Frances Tillman.

When I did she was just as friendly as I remembered and sweet with lots of spice; when I told her that, she made barbs about the name of the town that she and Floyd lived in, Spicewood. Of course she would talk to Floyd she said. He was out playing golf but when he came in she would have him call me. She thought he would be glad to do it.

And he was.

On the night of the broadcast Floyd wore an open throated striped shirt, Joe a white one with the usual elegant Italian silk tie. Joe was such a mix of homey and worldly, elegant and plain. Both Floyd and Joe were in a mellow mood and when Floyd sang some of his standards, "I Love You So Much It Hurts," "I Gotta Have My Baby Back" and the song he was most famous for, country western's first cheating song, "Slipping Around," I thought I had never heard him in more plaintive voice. Afterwards he talked about his beginnings in the 1930s and also about hard times as Joe in his warm and inimitably intimate voice continued the interview. Who wouldn't tell Joe anything I wondered.

After it was all over, two weeks of broadcasting, one of them devoted to Van Cliburn whom I also met, and all of this for rebroadcast on the BBC, Joe and I said our reluctant good-byes. For days after I felt as if I were floating.

Then he was doing a job for the BBC, taping material in a number of cities; he called me from Paris, he called me from Cairo.

Toward the end of our conversations he always said, "Send word to me here. I love to hear from you. Write or call." As if I had the money for trans-Atlantic dialing, or even always knew where he was.

When I did know I wrote him letters which sometimes he was slow to answer, but then he would and with lines that read, "Forgive my slow answers. Send more news. I'm here."

He told me once he carried my letters with him everywhere, put them all around him on the floor of his hotel rooms, that they fanned out from him like rays of light or spokes of a wheel.

"It's all right about your slow answers," I wrote, "for I know you are there. I'm very patient really." He quickly said that delighted him and that he felt on top of the world. "Oh, the world is large with so much in it!"

After that I didn't hear for months.

Then I had a postcard with spring flowers on it. "I'm glad you're patient," it said. "Happy Valentine." He had drawn a heart for February 14, the day he wrote. He must not have mailed the card until weeks later; it came to me in March.

I wrote him that his message made me happy. I didn't hear for a while after that.

After we began it was hard to say which of us was the most impulsive, which the most reticent.

But always we did more talking than writing as if as radio people we had to depend on voice. We talked about the shows we were doing and our schedules and also, oddly, with some real interest and seriousness about the weather. The Southwesterner in both of us maybe. Odd that Joe and I had early chosen to spend so much of our lives cooped up in radio stations, so often windowless and dark, because both of us were happiest out of doors.

We also talked about our birthdays which fell close together. Should I be depressed I asked now that I had passed my middle forties? He laughed. "Should I be depressed to have passed my middle sixties? Oh baby—" That was the first time he called me baby. "Oh baby, you are going into something gorgeous."

Well, it was another spring before I really was, March and spring in Texas. Months past our actual birthdays. But back in the fall we had promised each other that when we were next together we would split a cake.

The one we got, a plain white and the choice of both of us, was the best I ever ate.

"Darling," he said to me that afternoon, we had stopped at Safeway for the candles we had forgotten and picked up a number of packs, "I'm so happy to be here. So happy we are going to do this in all this open country."

Joe used endearments as if he had invented them and had never said them to anyone before but me, peppered his speech with "sweethearts" and "darlings" all that afternoon.

And I, I, each time astonished, Joe had always been so formal, as if for the first time in my life I had been given hearing, I asked, "Joe, is happiness important?"

He took some time to answer, but before he brought the car there by the side of the field to a gentle halt, and he was the slowest, the most careful of drivers, he took my hand and pressed it and uttered a resounding, "Yes."

"Jesus," Dan said to me when Joe was hospitalized for the first time, "emphysema, that's terrible. I didn't know Joe was a smoker."

"Three packs a day. Sometimes more. Or that's what he tells me. You didn't know because he never smokes at a station. He makes it up in other places; it's been impossible for him to give it up, but I think he is going to try now." Then I told Dan that of course Joe was going to get better.

Believe it or not, one of Grandma's old oilcloths was with us, a particularly durable red that throughout my life I had kept in the trunk of my cars and transferred to Joe's rented Buick and when we stopped I threw it on the ground first thing. "Sweetheart," Joe said, "this is certainly the spot."

For a while, before he came back, I tried ignoring his notes, his phone calls, tried to be suitably in the mood for renunciation. His marriage was a rock for him; I was even half-glad he had it. We had to keep clear, had to keep straight. I tried putting him out of my mind.

Silly as this sounds I went out and bought myself all white bed covers and a white nightgown and when I crawled in my nun's bed let go, surrendered, all I had been feeling. What I thought I wanted.

What I thought he had wanted too.

How many times had he told me, "What you know, Elizabeth, what I know, is work."

And yet here we were in this field north of Dallas, the past repeating itself, the landscape so familiar that I wondered if this was the same field we came to when I was just sixteen. I watched a flock of white birds sail around the cows crouching beneath its one live oak tree.

We dropped down beside the oilcloth laughing. Before us stretched acres and acres of grass and little blue and white flowers. I tried to be gentle with the cake.

He had told me, "Oh, I want to be with you in the country, want to breathe all that good air now that I can again."

We had potato salad and breast of chicken sandwiches in the basket Joe had carried and a thermos of Brazilian coffee from a coffee house in Dallas and, mostly for me—Joe couldn't have much, he had been under oxygen in the hospital—a sweet white wine. Joe was going to have to partake of our feast slowly, but it was always good being together. We always had such a good time.

When we were ready for the cake Joe said he had to load it with candles, that our combined years came to more than a hundred. "One hundred and twelve to be exact," he told me and then insisted, laughing, coughing just a little, that we get on all of that. "Well, it's time we get it all on," he said, looking at me and winking, "not that I can blow any of it out."

We made jokes about that. I thought our humor was becoming grotesque.

"There are too many of these to go out," I said as I stuck in a bunch of candles, "hardly matters if you and I are huffing and puffing over them or not." He held my left hand, he was a firm hand holder, his smile and eyes right on me as I lit them with my right. Then, just before we tried to blow the candles out, his expression changed.

"Well," he said, "if I called you more often, if we were together more often, it would never stop, but just go on and on."

"Oh," I whispered in that conflicted moment, "wouldn't that be fine?"

But he didn't answer. Only said, "Then we would both be crazy."

The implication seemed to be that he already was. "That first day I met you I missed lunch with the network president, missed afternoon drinks with the governor."

"Joe," I asked, "what are you talking about?"

He didn't answer, only grazed my cheeks with his lips. "Baby," was all he said.

Austin

Although there was that time when I stopped writing letters, so we could just stop, when Joe wrote me to send word, I sent it.

I no longer had a job with National Public Radio or any other kind.

After which he wrote me about a number of public stations he thought could use me in the west. He had been in and out of L.A. for more than a year; he had even bought a small Laurel Canyon house. I should come out right away he said; he wanted me near and for a while, before he had to go to Australia and New Zealand for BBC broadcasts he thought he could help me get started. We talked about it on the phone.

"Joe?" I asked right after I picked up the receiver. I don't know why; we hadn't talked in a while and, besides, I was staying with a friend so he shouldn't have known how to find me. But I knew it was Joe before I heard his voice.

"You are there," he said. "I just got this phone number from your Mama."

"You have just talked to my mother?" I wasn't sure how; I didn't think she was in any book. I remember that I had written him once on her business stationery from Nacogdoches.

"We just taught a piano lesson together, she had a student there. I told her what a fan I had been of hers. We just hit if off."

I had been chopping vegetables all that hot morning, my mind on Aunt Rena and how she loved them, parsley and green onion up to my elbows, all over my hands and arms.

Then Joe gave me names of directors at several stations. "Now wipe your hands," he said, "and go call them." How did he know, I wondered, that my hands needed wiping?

"To live out there," I asked, "doesn't it cost a lot of money?"

"Darling," he said, "you can live on sunshine and the sight of flowers." Then he told me about oranges and avocados because I had said, "Joe, you know how I love to eat."

But it didn't take me long to decide.

After I had, he said, "You make me so happy sweetheart."

One day back at KSD in Dallas, Joe, getting ready for a broadcast in his usual flurry, shuffling papers, polishing his glasses and then the mike with a trouser tissue, looked straight at me and from out of the blue, said, "We get it all mixed up, don't we, soul and body?"

And I, in my ungrown up, uncompromising way asked, "Wasn't it meant to be?"

He flinched a little at that. And sounded angry.

"Well, hell," he said, oh, Corpus, how well you taught us to say this, "we can work together. Hell, that's finally what it's all about. Day after day putting one foot in front of the other. When you get right down to it, the thing to say is that we are both workers. I can work with you."

I was glad he said that, but a little angry, too. I knew Kate was his refuge and never mind what else he had said about their marriage, the loss of desire, the loss of the body. He had married Kate late; when he met her had all but given up the idea of marrying. As had she. But they got along. "Oh," he told me, "both of us were ready!" Married they would have a plan, construct something. In London and New York they established and maintained households, built a life.

Just a few months before, at the Dallas station, I heard Joe talking to Dan about someone Dan had been seeing and about "lust."

Are you talking to Dan about what you feel for me, Joe? I had wanted to ask. I hate that split that severs spirit from body.

Did Joe worry that what he felt would split him off like that from me? Everyone I knew seemed hurt by that severing. Body from spirit, body from mind.

Dan had been talking about a topless dancer he met at one of the clubs. Someone he had been going to bed with or maybe I should say someone he had been screwing. Dan didn't go to bed for the night with anybody. Or so he confessed to me. After he had as much of a woman as he wanted, that is, when he took the time to actually meet one and take her home, he would help her get dressed and into a taxi and in the process, put a gold or silver bracelet on one of her wrists, or, around her neck, a necklace of semi-precious stones. He told me once he spent hundreds and hundreds of dollars every year on women's jewelry.

As I walked in on Joe's conversation with Dan, it was one that took place just before a show and as many thousand shows as Joe had done, he was always nervous, as I walked in on the conversation I said, "I'm going to look that word up in the dictionary."

"What word is that, darling?"

"Lust," I said.

I slapped the script that I had just been over down on the shiny table. "It is in the dictionary, isn't it?" Not just in the Bible? I almost asked that but bit my tongue. Your fucking Methodist Bible.

Joe had been brought up in Methodist and other protestant churches. I almost said—you read it often enough for one who is never in a church. He did read it, too, though he didn't take them literally, quoted scripture and verse.

I didn't say any of that, but might as well have, for he surmised my meaning. "Elizabeth," he said, "you're tired."

"No," I told him. "No, Joe, I'm not tired."

I picked up the dictionary then. There was one on the table at the far end of the room.

"Then what's wrong?"

"Nothing's wrong, Joe. I'm just trying to get an education, trying to discover meaning."

"You know what it finally means, honey," he interjected. "Craziness. And that won't quit. Torment, baby."

That began the first argument we had. We only had one other and it was toward the end in California and of a gentler kind.

It came just before he took off for Australia, the BBC taping there. I think even then I was angry at him for being sick and that, in spite of his hospitalizations and the difficulty we knew he often had in breathing, none of us acknowledged how serious the sickness was. I can't imagine why else I would have started anything, why under any other circumstances I would have said anything so awful.

We had been talking around something when I said, "I don't believe in the survival of personality." Said that quite suddenly.

Said that to Joe. And I knew deep down that he was dying.

He was even then beginning to lose his radio voice, the voice that was his life and dollar and that he was famous for. He looked at me fiercely, steadily and replied in a whisper, "I do."

I hated myself, hated my anger, my stupid blundering. And tried to make things better.

But made them worse.

"What I mean is, I don't believe we go on as we are here," I laughed nervously. "Radio people, brunets, Texans."

Family people, I wanted to add, flower-lovers, cake eaters.

So strange that I had said that; certainly I couldn't imagine Joe as anything but a radio person; if he was anything else, would he have meant anything to me?

"What I mean is," I went on, my voice getting weaker, I was sounding sillier and sillier even to myself, "what I mean is, I think we have to undergo some sort of drastic change. Become nothing before we do it. Nothing, or almost—"

Then Joe looked angry, too. He cleared his throat. "Well, then," he said and his voice had come back to him, "well then, I think that's going to be exciting. I would like to get on with that." For a minute I thought he might say that when he did he would do a broadcast.

"Damn it," I wanted to tell him, "it's too soon for you to want to get on with it."

We were in a parked car, another of the ones Joe had rented, as we talked like this; Joe had driven me home from the station to my tiny apartment here on 11th Street and sat straight behind the wheel.

I hated the rigid way he held his body, the way he looked absently out the window. Already he seemed far from me. I leaned toward him, touched his face, then kissed it and with one hand touched his beautiful dark hair. He gathered me to him then.

"Darling, there's nothing to do, there's no help for it." He held me close. I was sobbing and continued to sob as I clung onto him and pressed into him, my hands sliding across his shoulders, wishing as he kissed my neck, my ears, my hair, my face all over that we could both in this moment disappear. "We've waited so long to have this. We love each other," he said.

Los Angeles
January 6, Epiphany

His mouth brushed back and forth, one side to the other and again and again, across my mouth. "Breathe with me," he whispered; I parted my lips, was very still, gave him breath.

But we couldn't go on like that. We never had a weekend or even a whole night together; it was as if those waited in some far country in which we were both free and where there was no sickness. Often when Joe had to go home, or to the doctor, and I had to go back to the station we nuzzled each other in the car like two teenagers who hankered after some distant life.

He became too sick to work, to see me, often had a hard time speaking over the phone. When he did improve he packed a bag full of medicine, packed oxygen, and in spite of his doctor's warning, left for Australia. Before he left he came by the station once.

"We don't see each other anymore," I told him.

"We'll see each other when I get back. When I'm better." But he spoke without conviction.

He said, "I hope you get on here." Then said in a halting broken-hearted voice, "I love you."

He ran a hand across my back and kissed me on the mouth, lightly, but with great sweetness and quite publicly, several times.

Corpus, is your festival still held on Thursday, the first after Trinity Sunday? The Feast of Corpus Christi, Mexican children running through your streets turning their little musical wheels? I remember the ringing going on and on and now think of the celebration as something to hear, a cacophony of bells.

"We celebrate two thousand years of His living and dying," I still remember the priest saying, his mass reaching me through my shiny white radio, a graduation present from Bud. "And we celebrate this place. Corpus Christi. This cathedral consecrated to Corpus Christi and to all our living and dying."

He went on to say that the bay was named by Alonzo Alverez de Pineda, a Jamaican explorer who mapped the Texas coast line and brought the first white men to Texas and whose ship arrived on this very day.

Mexican people do celebrate dying. With dancing and skeletons and bread for the dead and laughter. And they believe the dead visit and partake.

Yesterday in East Los Angeles where little English is spoken I went to a service with a Mariachi band and glittering Aztec dancers who, barefoot in skin tight sequined costumes and enormous feathered head dresses, carried torches as they gyrated up and down the aisles. I sang half a dozen hymns in Spanish and embraced that many people at the Paz. And afterwards ate homemade tamales and drank Margaritas by the glassful and felt for a moment as if I knew again what birth and death, our own and Jesus Cristo's, are about.

Back in you, Corpus, we were Mexican and Anglo alike taught that the spirit goes on though we must give up the body. Dark skin over shapely shoulders, amber eyes, luminous hair.

It had been hard to get my life on the line. Joe finally put me on it, then slipped away.

After his trip to Australia and in, of all places, New Zealand.

The BBC, of course called Kate immediately and not long after, all the papers publicized her grief. But no one told me, no reason why Kate should have; I only met her once. I heard about it over the radio, a rival station of the two I worked for.

Corpus, I recently traveled fifteen hundred miles across the state of Texas and never even saw you. In memory I walk thirteen steps up your seawall, visit the old Nueces again where we held some dances. And, on the bluff, past the Driscol and the Plaza, then drift to the Cathedral where your festival was held.

Although I don't go often, go always feeling like a transient, and don't trust orthodoxy, I have once again taken to churches. You may remember my telling you about the one I like best here, the one that feeds the hungry, provides help for the addicted.

I'm in Hollywood to work at that church today.

Some days before Communion I think I see Uncle Leeland standing alongside my pew like an usher. At other times I see Grandaddy, as far as I knew he was never in an Episcopal church in his life, and just last Sunday in the pew in front of me I saw Miss V, her V-shaped wings, spread behind her, and Julia Winter. In that moment I knew she never had a fiance, that we made her fiance up. And at The Peace both turned to face me, smiling. Then, standing by Cecil B. DeMille's Ten Commandments, I saw Bud in the narthex. He and my mother split up just a year or two before he died and I never did know exactly what was the trouble. As I step out into the sunshine I think he may be speaking to me, but what I hear finally is another voice.

"Lady, I only have two cans of soup in the house and three little children. Can you give me something?"

"Not much," I tell her, pulling a dollar from my purse. "See the Father."

Just then a flock of Korean children run by me.

Earlier I told you the church had no children, and at that time, there were only one or two in the English speaking congregation. I am conscious of places without children since I have none.

What I haven't told you: the church has services in Korean every Sunday and a Korean-American congregation who have many children. And last week the sight of them as they passed me cheered my heart.

Later

 $\mathcal{W}$ hen I was young I never had a romance," Joe told me. "I was all absorbed in family. I was going to make things right for them, going to conquer the world." He told me he had missed love.

Finally that made him furious.

A generation apart, and a gender, we had such similar histories. Our difference? He had married. Late, but at least he had finally done it. I knew marriage was a relationship like no other, bonded, involved intimacies, like no other. He met Kate during the war and her career took off after she was in some of his overseas shows.

Also a difference: His greater calling and ambition. No dynamo, I had never really considered "conquering the world."

But I certainly did want to make things right for my family, accomplish for Uncle Leeland and Uncle Bo. And, yes, Grandma. And Lloyd and all the others I hadn't known. (Also a drinker, Lloyd died suddenly after a fall down a flight of warehouse stairs.) Call them back and extend what each of them had tried to begin. What my mother did begin. Most of all I wanted to make things right for her.

Corpus, you taught us that spirit goes on and love is lasting, though maybe not us who contain it and through which it passes. Who move, change, go.

Who knew what it was that after so many years finally broke my mother and Bud up?

When he was drunk Bo railed against Leona. And so did I that summer before I went to college, the college in a place much farther away than she thought I ought to go. Before Bud called the police and later signed the papers that committed him to the state hospital Bo had threatened my mother with a knife. Yet she always defended Bo to Bud. And it was Bud, not Bo, who she finally dismissed from her life.

I pondered their breakup a lot.

Bud held unsteady jobs; she never fulfilled her musical promise. They both had tempers and, I realized, heavy responsibility for me and, after his breakdown, for Uncle Bo, were tied to Uncle Bo. Nor would Bo, as much as he complained about the shackles of his family, let them go. Still, none of that seems enough.

In retrospect I see they both grew up in a country that blighted erotic feeling, and several other generating kinds, that removed it from spirit and made of it a sin.

Although they were still together the summer I graduated from high school, their relationship was stormy. One was forever lashing out against the other and at least twice they had fights in which they threw things, shoes, books, keys, cups and saucers. During the last of these, after Leona had thrown a cup of coffee, Bud socked her in the face and knocked her to the kitchen floor leaving on her cheek the impression of his Masonic ring.

I didn't see him do this and I wouldn't have believed it. But the design of the ring, which forever after I thought of as "Bud's mark," was there. That she had been knocked flat by it was hard for me to comprehend. I had always thought of my mother as so strong. Bud had been nice to me, if distant. But he threatened Uncle Bo.

"Hell," I heard Bud yell across the yard to the porch, one of those first hot nights before my graduation, the thick air potent with the smell of gas and gardenias, "hell's bells! You piss ant. Come down from there! I want it out with you. Let's you and me take a walk down to the vacant lot. I want you to fight with me like a man."

Bud had, I think, heard Bo talking about him to Grandma, this was just a few nights before she died, about how another one of Bud's jobs had ended and how Bud and my mother were back on him again, about how he would never be free of his sister or her child or her man. I believe this was the night right after my senior party. I can still smell the gardenias. To this day I associate their perfume with death, not to its sadness, but to the cleansing agent in it.

To the power that sweeps mercifully away.

Bud had for a long time been tired of being with our family and he knew it was Bo who tied him and my mother to us. If he thought Bud's job was OK, Bo was always on the phone begging, "Come back to me!" And if he knew Bud's job had played out, he was on it saying, "I have secure work; I'm here to come back to."

What Bud said must have scared Bo half to death. He ran like a rabbit from the challenge, ran into the house and through it and onto the back patio and into the yard and through the bright gate to the driveway where Bo hopped in the car. He didn't come back until all the lights were out in the house and the garage apartment; after mid-night I heard the sound of the tires against the gravel drive.

For me it was such a strange summer, strange to be out of high school, my glorious career there over, to be out in the work-a-day, working-class world. For Bo it must have been even stranger. Strange to be without his mother, have his house on the market, be engaged to a girl he was afraid to marry and in love with and estranged from a beautiful young man. He had the courage for none of this nor even enough to answer my step-father's accusations.

He decided at the last minute to drive me east to college and that he could pay for it; he really couldn't and the pressure of trying to pay so many bills contributed to his crack up. I had decided at the last minute that east was the direction in which I had to go.

Travis had left you, Corpus, and C.C. couldn't share her grief, rage or sorrow. But I didn't know that then; I thought she didn't want to see much of me. That summer I saw little of my high school friends.

Except Bartola. From July on he was around. And I felt a kinship.

One reason maybe: My job was awful.

I had always, all my life, when I went to bed at night looked forward to the morning. But I didn't anymore. And I wondered if Bartola also dreaded each day.

He was a mystery to me, but there was something in him, something reckless and wild, some loveliness, that I responded to. That plus the torment that I could tell was in him. The torment that I and all my family knew.

Although at school we had conversations, I didn't really get to know Bartola until both of us went to work. We met here and there, in front of a movie house or down by the seawall, and once or twice in his store. Bartola worked that summer selling cheap costume jewelry, bracelets and earrings and rings, as a clerk at Kress's. Every time I saw him at Kress's he tried to convince me to buy a birthstone ring.

"But my birthstone's a garnet," I told him. "They don't cost much. If I save I can get a real one someday; in fact, I plan to."

He didn't seem to know what to say.

"You going to college, Elizabeth?" he asked me. His voice, hoarse and high at once and the same time, was barely a whisper, his eyes, framed by the thick, long lashes, almost closed.

"Yes," I told him. "I guess so."

I told him I didn't know exactly what I wanted to do, that I had been lost since graduation. I said I hated my job at Litchenstein's where I worked in accounting, typing numbers all day. I said that as soon as I got off at night I started dreading the morning.

Bartola opened his eyes wide then and shrugged his silky, hot pink shoulders. "Well, honey, look at me. I even have to work Saturdays." He sighed and picked through the rings, held up a gold one with an insert of lavender glass. "You like this? Isn't it pretty? I'll bet it would almost fit you."

I shook my head.

"Aw, come on, Elizabeth, some of this stuff isn't so bad. Maybe one of the green ones. Baby, real emeralds are expensive. What time do you get your lunch? How do you like this for $2.95?" He held up a large chunk of electric green.

He knew I wasn't going to buy it. I told him I had to go, but before I did we agreed to meet early in the week at the seawall and eat sack lunches there while looking at the lucky people who had their freedom and could sail boats in the bay. We surely couldn't linger; neither of us had a full hour for lunch.

The next Tuesday was, as things turned out, one of overpowering brightness. I wore a black sundress which I thought of as defense. A white one would have been cooler.

Bartola winked when he saw me, slowly closing one of his gorgeous golden eyes. If I had gone looking for his black eyelashes at Kress's or even at Litchenstein's, I couldn't have found them. "You look so sophisticated, Elizabeth. You ought to travel. You ought to use your college money to go to the south of France or to Spain.

I told Bartola there wasn't any college money, only the Installment Plan and Bo's labor. None of my teachers talked scholarship, or even loan, to me. They thought Bo had money. Scholarships were for kids who lived in a couple of rented rooms with a single parent or for those with many brothers and sisters. Not that any of us needed a bundle. Most of us applied only to inexpensive state schools.

"Probably just as well," I said, "considering the trouble I have with language." After three years of high school French, neither Bartola or I had learned much. More disturbing to me: I knew almost no Spanish, the language that three-quarters of our population read and spoke. And during the Christmas and Easter seasons we had hundreds of additional Mexican visitors who came to you, Corpus, because of your name.

But when I told Bartola that he said I shouldn't worry, that no one in Corpus did much better. "They speak Tex-Mex here," he told me, "not Spanish." He claimed his Spanish was better than most since his grandfather was from Mexico City. I doubted that his grandfather was, but, if he liked it, wanted Bartola to keep this fantasy.

And, anyway, I thought, who was I to say?

Certainly Bartola's mother, a small town and yet worldly looking woman, might have grown up anywhere. Voluptuous but slender, Mrs. Perra was sexy. No wonder, I thought, when I talked to Bartola, that sex was the uppermost subject on his mind. "She's been attached to a few men," he told me, "but they have never given her money and she has to live in these low down clubs." She waited tables and, sometimes, was a singer. Bartola said his father left too long ago to be remembered. But, he insisted that Perra was a legal name, that his father was an Italian-born-Italian and that his father and mother had been married in the Cathedral on the bluff.

Anybody who had five minutes acquaintance with either Bartola or his mother would know how easily either of them might have made this story up. Or how easily it might be true.

"Do you believe in love?" Bartola asked as we sat on the top step of the seawall that first afternoon we were together. On the way there we passed the blind man I had seen walking the waterfront all winter, a big sign around his neck that read "Alms for the Blind." Ever since I have thought of the seawall as "Blind Man's Bluff."

"Do you believe in love?" He asked me that question before he took the warm cheese sandwiches, grilled at the Kress's counter, out of his brown paper sack. He had insisted on bringing both our lunches. "Kress's cheese sandwiches aren't bad," he told me. "They use pimento-cheese."

In addition to the sandwiches, Bartola also brought lemon cokes from the Kress's fountain, two small bags of popcorn and Hershey Bars with almonds. We gave most of our popcorn to the gulls "I mean love like in the movies," Bartola said, "a picture with Clark Gable or Tyrone Power."

I said, and I didn't know what to say, I didn't think I had seen any love like what he talked about. But as I spoke an image of Ben flashed through my mind as well as one of Travis and C.C. In my mind Ben was behind the wheel of the car we sat in on Padre Island. I said my mother had told me once that she had been in love with my father, but I thought she might have imagined that after he went away. And that I didn't think she had been in love like this with Bud. I said I thought Aunt Rena might have been with Uncle Leeland. But then I remembered the women Uncle Leeland saw at the Elks Club. I said I thought Aunt Rena and Uncle Leeland were confused about it. "I think we are all confused about it." That's what I finally said.

"Baby," Bartola told me, "I believe in love. I'm going to have it. Going to get away from this town and maybe work in the movies. Going to California. Going to the coast."

He jangled a bunch of bracelets, pulled out of his hip pocket every color in the rainbow, then slid one over my arm. "You like one of these?" he asked.

I wrinkled my nose. "I don't wear bracelets," I told him.

These are special for a dollar fifty-nine. If you don't want them, I'll take them."

He shook the bracelets in his hand, then slipped them over one of his bare brown arms. He said, "Right here in Corpus I play parts already."

"Bartola," I told him, "you don't belong here. You ought to go to California soon. You ought to get away."

"Baby, I am," he told me.

And later on that noon he said, jangling the bracelets, "I'm going to have love. Going to have money. And when I have those I'll also be able to buy some really nice things."

"Oh, I'm sure you will, Bartola," I told him.

Again he jangled the bracelets. "I'm going to have LOVE," he sang as he began to dance around. Then he stopped and said quite solemnly, and softly, "You're going to have love."

"I don't think about love, Bartola," I lied, whispering. Then raising my voice I said, "And I don't care about money which is funny because I have to make some. I just want to be myself. And to work in radio. How I miss the station!" As I spoke I hated Dan Gonzales, and I had always liked Dan, whom I hadn't seen since he took the KRIS job. Next year I told myself I would apply, instead, at KEYS.

A family of gulls landed at our feet then, the bay before us still as a lake and sparkling, in spite of the heat, not blue, but brown. I gave them several handfuls of popcorn and the last of my sandwich. "Oh, Bartola," I said, "do you suppose we'll be disillusioned?"

He didn't answer and then I realized he had no idea what "disillusioned" meant. I didn't want to embarrass him. The last thing in the world he needed was more shame. "I mean," I said, "do you suppose we'll be disappointed?

So disappointed that we become bitter or crooked or mean? I mean when things don't turn out?"

"Baby, everything is going to turn out," he said.

The gulls were by this time ready for the rest of my popcorn, but I didn't want to give it up. I looked beyond them to the water. "Come on, let's wade," I said to Bartola, taking his hand.

And then we were down the steps, free of shoes and even of our popcorn bags which we had dumped on the way. Bartola rolled up his sailor pants and hand in hand, we entered the hot, sticky bay. I loved the feel of it, always had, even tolerated a nip from a jelly fish or two. I was not one of those people who when they came out made a B-line for some shower. "Oh, Bartola," I asked, "won't you miss the bay?"

"After I have seen the Pacific?" He raised one of those Tyrone Power brows. It was the one feature they had in common. "Oh, Baby, no."

"They say it's a gorgeous ocean," I told him. "My Uncle Bo's friend, Jay, always says it's gorgeous, but wild, too, he says, and cold."

"If it gets too wild or cold for me," Bartola said swinging one of my hands, "I'll just hop a plane back down here. I'll have so much money hat will be easy; I can come back to this bay any time I like."

On our way back we picked up our popcorn sacks from the steps and tossed them in the waste container just across the street from the seawall on the corner with the stop light, when an orange Thunderbird swerved around it and almost up onto the sidewalk where we were. The boy who was driving, and for just a second I thought I knew him, thought he was Lana's or somebody else's brother, yelled, "Hey faggot!" And then, "Hey, fag hag!"

Bartola didn't even startle. "Corpus has so many crude people," he told me. "That's why I am going to leave it. They think they're so hot. They think they have all the answers. And they're just crude and dull." Then after a pause, he added, "All the same, if they could, they would run over you."

"Bartola," I asked, and I was shy with this question, "what's a fag-hag?"

He dropped his lashes and his brown face reddened. "Someone who hangs around people like me. A woman who does that." I had never before seen him blush. "A woman who hangs around queers."

I was quiet for awhile. Then I said, "You're my friend, Bartola. I like you for being proud of who you are. A lot of people here don't know who they are and don't want to find out."

"If they did," he said, "they wouldn't be able to stand it. But they wouldn't admit to nothing."

"Well, why think about them?" I asked.

"They're brutal, baby. You have to think about them when they nearly run over you in a fancy car."

He had to watch out for them he told me, then added that I had better watch out, too. "But I think you do watch out, Elizabeth," he went on, "though maybe you don't know that you do. That's why you won't think about love. You might find out it belonged to one of them."

I knew then why I was with him. Never mind that he didn't understand the word "disillusion"; he understood something more and in a way no one else had, not Uncle Bo or Aunt Rena or my mother or even Julia Winter, something that until that moment, and even then I only got a glimmering, I didn't understand myself.

Hollywood

C. C. married during my second year of college. The shock of her announcement was so great that nothing since has much surprised me. She had a baby in the first year and another in the second and two more before many more years had passed. She sent me all their pictures, all girls with smooth brown hair like hers, and two had her sky blue eyes, and sweet, smiling faces. And she wrote letters which, while detailing some of the struggles, made child bearing and rearing sound like the most natural process in the world.

And for her I think it was.

My placid, smooth-haired, home-based friend, my opposite in many ways and yet also an alter-ego, was gentle with herself and with her children. And had married a gentle man, a hill country lawyer, from a ranching family, who finally didn't like to practice, who took to breeding dogs, herding dogs mostly, simply because he liked them; bought and ran a kennel. And who, after a few years in Corpus where he tried to live for awhile because T.J. couldn't stand to lose her, moved back to that rolling green flowery country in the center of the state.

C.C.'s story always seemed to me to have a genuinely "happily ever after" ending for her youth, and I sometimes imagined mine. An ending which she came to quickly, even abruptly, and one I often wanted to claim.

Unlike so many fictional heroines she never seemed betrayed. But I know there is much I don't see because I view all this obliquely and at such a distance. C.C. was the first to admit that none of her children had been planned for, that they had all been born before she had a chance to comprehend what had happened to her and that she didn't know how to deal with it when she did. She wrote me once that she had been nearly overwhelmed when they were all pre-schoolers and again when they were in middle childhood, and that for a time she had seen a counselor.

And I do remember that the news of Travis's death shook her. She had been married for some years when she wrote me about him, explaining that although he learned draftsmanship in the service, he seldom used it, that he had practically become a professional soldier, had fought in several wars. She wasn't clear about which war took him, but I believe it was Vietnam. He had died of some tropical fever. Only a few days before they shipped him in a box back to you, Corpus, the State Department let his father know.

The Assembly of God members from that little church near where he had lived held a memorial service. C.C. read about it in the papers. She supposed his wife was there, his wife had come back to you, Corpus, or so C.C. said, as soon as Travis flew for the final time overseas; they didn't have any children. The Caller Times said burial was in the graveyard next to the church. C.C. speculated that Travis's father had probably done the lettering on the stone.

"It already seems so long ago," C.C. told me in her letter. "I was another person." She documented what had happened as if she was relating to the plot of a film.

After she married I kept in touch with C.C. only by card and occasional letter and, as time went on, more and more infrequently. Seven or eight years passed before we had a visit. That was my last to you, Corpus.

I have always been baffled by children, never known what to do or say around kids, anybody's, and I surely didn't around hers. I could see that the job of caring for them and of running the little house they all lived in was a hard one, but at least at the time I visited, C.C. seemed to take it in stride. Her secret, I thought, was that she always did a lot of what she liked and wouldn't take on anything she really hated. She had never learned to sew and wouldn't and she and Will hadn't been married long when she refused to give dinner parties for people who were less than friends.

Part of what she liked to do was read, to herself and also aloud to the children. When I visited she asked me to read to them, too. "Oh, please, Elizabeth," she said when I protested. "They know you're on the radio. Oh, they've heard so much about you." And so I did, although I felt awkward. Lined up in a row, little to big against the bedroom wall in their rose, green and blue flowered nightgowns, they made a picture. How silly I felt when I dropped down on the floor beside them. And so I read them something silly. ("They went to sea in a sieve," I read. "In a sieve they went to sea.") after telling them very short stories that I had made up about your keys, Corpus, Port Aransas and Mustang Islands.

C.C. had taken to framing art prints from the Impressionist and Post Impressionist period, and when my reading was through and the children were in bed, she showed me her collection. She would always love best, she said, works from the late nineteenth century. Although she still drew, and would eventually finish her degree in art and maybe even someday teach it, her own drawing didn't satisfy her and she didn't know that it ever would. More than anything else, working with these prints transported her at times when she needed transporting. "When it comes to art, I guess I am mostly a receiver," she told me. The central hall of her ranch house was lined with Renoirs and Cassatts and near the end, by the door, with Gaugins, the painter who she said best expressed her hidden yearnings. When she spoke of what she felt for these last pictures I realized she was also speaking of what she had once felt for Travis, and still felt for me.

126

Later

*T*wo years went by before I saw Bartola again by the seawall, although during that first summer we were together I continued to visit him at the Kress's counter over grilled cheese sandwiches and lemon cokes.

Winters and springs and another summer sped by quickly. And during that second summer that I was back in you, Corpus, I spied Bartola when on a late lunch hour I was walking the seawall by myself. The old blind man walked it too and later in the afternoon we put quarters in his cup.

My job that July was with the Nueces and although I still didn't like typing for a living, I tolerated my place of employment a little better because at least it was with an old hotel.

Dan still had the only summer job at KRIS, but he never contacted me and I couldn't get a job at KEYS. In the winter time Dan worked on a degree in communications at UT. I hadn't seen Ben since I graduated, but had received some letters, which, of course I answered. Pre-law, he had gone to Northwestern on a scholarship, was working on a history degree.

The news of C.C.'s engagement during the previous winter had depressed me. It came when we were off to college just half a year when I was far away in the east and the wide world just opening to me.

I reasoned we could still be friends if she was marrying Travis. Travis was familiar or at least I had certainly heard enough of his banter at the drive-ins and on the bluff overlooking the shrimp boats and had seen his tow head bobbing up and down often enough in the front seat of the car.

But C.C. was not marrying Travis; she was marrying a stranger who lived in far away Kerrville. Had, in fact, already married him and moved there. (Although, as things turned out, she didn't stay, but came back for awhile to you, Corpus.) And not a boy either, but a man.

For me New York was exciting, but also difficult and often, a puzzle. I was beginning not to know what to think about life.

So it was that on that hot summer day when I was walking the seawall the sight of Bartola cheered me. No mistake about it; it was Bartola in his silky magenta shirt and white sailor pants.

"What are you doing here?" I asked, hugging him. I had run straight into his arms. "Are you working?" I asked. I had imagined him so many times out west.

"Oh, Baby," he told me, "would you believe it? I'm still at Kress's."

"No, I don't believe it," I said, but the moment after I was sorry. He looked so ashamed.

"The only reason I stayed," he told me, "is because I was promoted. I manage a whole section now, cosmetics and jewelry and what we have now is better. We even sell, behind the counter, some semi-precious stones. Anyway, I'm saving my money."

"But I'm so glad you're here now," I told him. "I'm so glad to see you."

"Oh, Baby, I'm glad to see you. When did you get in?"

"Weeks ago," I said. "I have a typing job at the Nueces."

"And you haven't come to see me? I'm hurt."

I told him I hadn't known he was in town. He said now that he had seen me he wouldn't take no for an answer, I was spending the evening with him.

And I did. At North Beach Bartola bought me all the corn on the cob I could eat, more than a half dozen ears as I remember, and took me on several Ferris wheel rides. And on the Ferris wheel, on the last go round, we agreed to meet for lunch at the seawall the very next day. Bartola said he would bring the lunches.

"I won't have to worry about being fired if I'm away for awhile this time," he told me. "Now they give me a whole hour." He looked so proud when he said that. Kress's had given him just twenty-five minutes before. Then he asked me, and he seemed embarrassed to be so late with the question, "They give you an hour, don't they?"

"Yes," I said.

He said, "We'll have lots of time. I'll take care of the food, don't you worry. This summer Kress's has a good turkey sandwich special. I'll bring something else, too, something extra." He winked. "A surprise."

In spite of the heat which would, of course, have melted it, I think I imagined some gooey ice cream extravaganza.

But the next day after we had eaten our sandwiches and drained our tall paper glasses of coke and iced tea, after we had fed the birds our crusts and half our popcorn, nothing else from Bartola's sack seemed forthcoming. I thought maybe he had brought homemade pralines or some especially beautiful Mexican cookies, iced maybe in yellow or pink.

"Bartola," I asked finally, "where's my surprise? It's time you told me."

He looked pleased. He said, "You remembered."

"Well," I said, "of course. I never forget a surprise. Do you?"

"I've been saving it," he said. He smiled broadly. "Give me your hand." "No, no," he told me moments later when I extended my left hand. "I can't marry you. Now give me your other hand."

As I held out my right hand, palm skyward, I thought he would pull some sort of delectable candy from his pocket, or a party whistle maybe, or silken streamers in purple and gold, CCHS colors. Or sparklers maybe. We both loved those.

He slipped it on then; I still have it and from time to time remove it from my jewelry box and squeeze it on a finger.

"Open your eyes now," Bartola commanded.

What I saw took my breath, a big square cut garnet set in gold filigree. "This is the new line we carry," Bartola told me. "It's real."

I wanted to tell him that I had never met anyone like him and that I loved him, as, if only in this moment, I did. But I couldn't.

No one before had ever given me a ring.

Part Three

Los Angeles

$\mathcal{A}$nd no one since.

Bartola's ring my one and only. The garnet, I'm told is associated with all that is Victorian, antique.

"I've missed love," I told Aunt Rena. She's gone finally. I just got word about it.

"Well," she said the first day I saw her after more than twenty years of being away. We sat in lawn chairs in front of her tiny house in Shreveport, a house that was nearly on the street; she lived alone but her nephews looked after her. "Well, you never did marry and I guess you won't now. Some people marry for the first time when they are past forty, but not many. Not many marry then for the first time."

"It's too bad, " I said, "but I wasn't grown up enough for it when I grew up." I laughed. "I mean when I was through school and was, maybe twenty. I grew up, did that finally, just a year or two ago."

Joe always told me that in the region we came from people didn't grow up. Or at least not, if they did at all, until late in life. He grew up he said only after he had lived for years in Europe as a broadcaster; he met Kate during a broadcast, years after the end of World War II.

Aunt Rena looked at me the way one looks at a stranger. And I couldn't blame her. But in my whole life I had only seen her look at anyone like that but once or twice.

"Tell me about it," she said. "Tell me what happened, honey. I never thought you would stay single like all those others in your family. I guess even your Mama finally wound up single."

"I think, Aunt Rena," I told her, "I wound up even more single than any of them."

She smiled, her eyes still like Santa's, still bearers of gifts. She said, "You know when you were a girl I thought you were crazy about that little Jewish boy who came to Corpus Christi." She made him sound like the only Jewish boy who ever had. "What ever happened to him?"

I told her Ben had become a college teacher, a professor, and had married someone who was also a teacher and had children, a boy and a girl, who became teachers, or I thought one of them had become a teacher and the other maybe was a lawyer, I forget, and who, like everyone else I knew, or almost everybody, either got a divorce or talked of getting a divorce, what everyone does at forty. I said I had lost track but that we had exchanged Christmas cards for years.

"That doesn't sound natural, " she told me.

I had always considered Aunt Rena an authority on what was natural in life.

Which leads me back in memory to the mystery. To the spring.

A literal one and hidden deep in an Arkansas thicket where in my early childhood we went, and almost in secret for I never told anybody, to swim.

A Thousand Drippings. That's what the spring was called. The drippings came out of the mountainside. A Thousand Drippings Spring. I still see Rena there so clearly. Rena in the nude, overweight even then by the standards of that day by many pounds. Rena laughing, oblivious to the water moccasins curled against the rocks to the far side.

Uncle Leeland liked the spring as much as Aunt Rena and was as much of a skinny dipper, and he often brought me. When I came along I would step out of my shorts soon enough, (I never in the hot summertime wore a top or shoes) and naked as the day Leona had me, join them. I was scared of the moccasins curled up on the rocks on the spring's far side and yes, they were always there. But Aunt Rena would reassure me.

"They haven't any interest in you," she would say. "They haven't any interest in me. They don't notice much; they are shut up in their skin. But we mustn't scare them. We want them to stay where they are, cool and dreaming. If you keep a good distance and swim quietly by they won't even know you are here."

"Oh, Aunt Rena," I would whisper, "I am such a quiet swimmer."

As I think back on us I realize we were all three of us quiet swimmers. I always went quietly to the spring's deep bottom first thing. The snakes, too, when they slid off the rocks swam quietly, and never for us, though we got out of the water when we saw them getting in. It was a way for all of us to be together, of and with each other in a place near where each of us was born. In no real danger though within sight of it. And sensual without sin.

"I always did think it was all right, his being Jewish," Aunt Rena said to me. "You probably were the right girl for him and I expect he might have made you happy. He was, even back then, different. And you were, too."

"He was only half Jewish," I told her, "and no one in his family practiced the Jewish religion or any other kind."

She told me that we should have probably just run away.

I said, and at that moment at least I thought I was speaking truthfully, that we probably should have. "I was crazy about him," I said, "but we were just children."

"You were seventeen," she said. "I had been married a year when I was seventeen and I had a baby." Then she thought about what she had said; she didn't want me to feel I had taken all the wrong turns or to get discouraged. "Oh, but you have lived in such places," she told me. "All over the country and in Europe and New York. You must have known interesting men, and—"she added after a pause, "cared for some of them."

"I never lived in Europe," I told her. I haven't even done much traveling there." I had, in fact, toured once or twice. "But you are right about this country. I have certainly gotten around."

"And now," Aunt Rena said, "you are way out in Los Angeles. What's it like?"

"Like everything," I told her. "Los Angeles is a country. It has hills and flatlands and desert and ocean." I said although I first lived in the hills I had recently moved to the flats. "It has sunshine and, in the mountains, snow. And many different temperatures. And every kind of tree and person and flower. Oh, Aunt Rena, the oleanders are so thick in August! It would be beautiful," I went on, "If so many hadn't defaced it. And, "I laughed, "If it weren't for all the cars."

I didn't know why I was going into this or what anything I said about Los Angeles could possibly mean to Aunt Rena. But to myself I thought: There are so many possibilities for life in the West, if the big quake doesn't get us or we're not nuked.

"Well," she said, "you must have a lot of fun there."

"It's a work town for me," I told her. "Work is what I know there, what there is to do."

"But you must have a good time, go to the beach, go to shows, go visiting."

I remembered that in four years I hadn't gone to the beach four times or to the theatre or even the movies, at least not just for fun, many more. "Not much," I told her, "not as much as I would do here. What I do there isn't personal."

She just blinked at me. I knew she couldn't comprehend that. "You know," I went on, "all the time I was growing up I was just crazy about radio. I don't know why. Don't ask me why, but all I could think of was that I wanted to work in sound. Well, that's what I do there."

She smiled her sweet, cracked one-hundred-year-old smile which was not very different from her fifty-year-old smile and would be, I decided, not very different from the smile of her invisible ghost. "You like it, though, don't you?"

"It's lonesome, Aunt Rena," I said, "and hard, but yes, I like it."

Then Aunt Rena wanted to know about love, if I had ever been in it. I told her I had been finally. I had not wanted to talk about this at all. But once I got started I knew I had to, for at least a little while, go on. "He was older than I was," I told her, "and, of course, married. Even—" And this was painful for me, "even well married." I stopped. "Whatever that means. Whatever, he was, more or less, I guess. And then," I said, "he got sick and we all lost him, he was an international broadcaster so he belonged to many." Then I stopped. Joe Copeland, I almost said, I'm sure you remember his shows. But I didn't. Aunt Rena wouldn't have listened to Joe's shows much. She didn't say anything. "You see, it wasn't intended." I couldn't go on after that.

"But he cared for you?"

"Yes," I said. "Very much. Very deeply."

I wanted to add, on the deepest level of existence, because I knew that was central and that it was true.

But I couldn't and so, instead, I turned the subject. "Aunt Rena, we might as well face it. An old bachelor brought up an old maid. Not that I blame Uncle Bo. It's hardly his fault."

"Why, honey, you mustn't think that way, people don't think that way anymore." Aunt Rena had always prided herself on keeping up and even at nearly a hundred she knew that anymore no one said "old maid."

"Well," I said, "I just mean that I don't think I was meant to be married or to even live with anyone. Except for you and Uncle Leeland, no one in our family was."

It was her turn to change the subject. "Stay overnight with your Aunt Rena," she said. "Like when you were a little girl and slept with me in the bed. Do you remember how you did that?"

"Oh yes, of course I remember," I told her, "how could I forget?" I always slept with Aunt Rena when Uncle Leeland was away and sometimes when he was home. "It was a feather bed," I told her; "it felt so good and I loved to lie in it and be half asleep in it, just half, I fought sleep because I didn't want to lose awareness of the pleasure."

She laughed. "It did feel good. I haven't had a bed that felt so good since that one."

"I can't stay, Aunt Rena," I told her. "I have to get back to Houston. I have a show to do."

Well, she said she was sorry, then went on to tell me a little of hers and Leeland's story and something more about Lloyd whom I never knew, and more about my mother, Leona. This was the last time I saw Aunt Rena. But I don't know that it's important to give any of that to you.

Right now I have to tell you about Bartola. I just found out while going through an old newspaper file in the UCLA library where I have been researching for a show.

Bartola did finally come to California, lived for awhile in Hollywood, just off Franklin, not far from my first apartment, where not so long ago he was shot through the heart. The shooting disrupted a movie premier; he fell on the walk of fame in front of Mann's Chinese Theatre. The news story I read in the Times talked about the victim being identified as "Bartola Perra" about fifty years old, born in Texas, formerly of San Diego. Although no drugs were found on the body, police believed the victim to be a dealer. He had a history of arrests for performing sexual acts in public. Those interviewed who knew him thought he had lived in California for about five years. I hadn't seen him in more than thirty.

Odd how I thought there could be no truth to a similar report when it was just a rumor back home. Now the only part of the story that strikes me as strange is the brevity of Bartola's life in California. I wondered if he had simply moved from naval base to naval base or spent all his time in you, C.C.

I guessed Bartola had hustled for awhile on the bases, then finally drifted on up to L.A. and made a meager living off Santa Monica Blvd., but I hoped found truer lovers, in Venice, maybe, or even Griffith Park.

Sometimes I think of Hollywood as a place for innocents, for adult children. Full of fantasies. So that when it isn't sheer terror, it's all high school fun.

Near Nacogdoches

I'm back here to visit my mother and my Uncle Bo. Bo is tied to a wheel chair now, having survived, though just barely, a massive coronary and a series of strokes. His doctor says he may live for years.

"He can take a lot," my mother told me. "He's sturdy." But he slumps in his chair and he can't talk much, his bow string seems broken; now sometimes I have to be his speaker. Though on the days when he starts, he still goes on.

"Everything I say may not be true," he tells me. "I hallucinate."

Uncle Bo, I want to tell him, you always did. "You always did," my mother says. Then to me, laughing, as if he isn't there, "He was always telling something."

"Bo," she tells him, "you talk in riddles."

"Well," he says, "you like it."

"His bow is broken," she tells me later. "No song." She considers. "So I guess," she says, "it's up to me to tell you. I am, of the family here, the last." In her eighties, she not only takes care of Bo, but teaches piano to half of the county, has had more students win college scholarships than any of its other teachers, might have helped me win one if I hadn't given up practicing for listening to the radio in eighth grade. "It was Grandaddy's dream, your Grandaddy's, that we come to Texas. 'If you all go to Texas and stay there,' he told me, 'you'll be all right.' And he, he and Leeland, blazed a trail for us. He knew how to do that, had a lot of adventure in him, came to Arkansas from Southern Illinois and to Illinois from Indiana in the 1880s when he was still nearly a boy. His stepmother had taken him out of school and put him in the fields so he had to teach himself and had to travel, had to come south and west for all the country to the south and west needed building. He was born to build, your Grandaddy, and a natural woodsman, and also a natural student and teacher; he was his own teacher, taught himself mathematics and how to read and read a lot, read Poe and Twain and the Bible and he loved newspapers. He loved Arkansas, too, the look of it, though it gave him economic trouble. But, because of all of us, for all of us, Texas gave him ease. 'Honey,' he said, 'you'll be all right, you and Elizabeth and all of you, if you stay in Texas. And I know you're tough enough to stand it.' What he was talking about didn't have a damn thing to do with the oil here, and not much even with making money; he was talking about the effect the country had on people. He knew it was hard on them, would be hard on us: the storms that came out of nowhere, hurricanes some of them, those and the crudity of some of the towns, why the streets in Ingleside weren't even paved when I went there, and the heat, he knew that for six months of the year his children and grandchildren (though you, Elizabeth, turned out to be the only one of these) would have to face that and, God knows, the crudity of some of the people. But he also knew that we all could take it and that taking it would help us continue."

Los Angeles

his brings me to Aunt Rena and maybe to the place where I shouldn't write to you anymore, though it has helped a lot over these last years to be able to.

I began, if you remember, in a cold New York town. There I stayed in a room with a world globe that had a light in it, all the brightness near the center; much of it seemed to come from you, Corpus. So that you appeared to me, not only as the place of my beginning, but as the world's heart.

Then I wrote that first letter and have just rattled on. And it's been good to do that, to know that people like me, wanderers, exiles, drifters, don't have to be homesick always. There is a way to go home.

If "home" means an emotionally charged relationship to only one person, living or dead, and that person is connected to a place, then I think this is still a relevant question. Radio is a way to go back. All the voices come back, all those ever close.

"When I put on those radio plays," I told C.C. "especially when I read a part, I think: Hey, this is for C.C.; she'll be listening." Of course I seldom do them on stations she can pick up.

Did I tell you that on my last trip to Texas I visited C.C. in Kerrville and liked her? And liked her husband who gave me a tour of his kennel. And the room, filled with television monitors and computers, from which he runs it, a charming incongruity: C.C.'s Degas dancers in gilt frames on the walls. And visited with and liked their daughters, a lawyer, an accountant, an elementary school teacher, a young businesswoman and mother of several young children, all of whom live no further away than Austin. And admired a grandchild or two. And several canine friends, Ingrid Bergman, Gary Cooper, named after those radiant presences from our childhood. And the sense of humor that seems to be in the family as well as the kindness and grace.

People can come back together. Those who say something different may not know it.

We all have to ask.

Have to begin by writing a letter. By talking about anything, about the color of the grass where you are from, or the lack of color. Or by asking after the color of the grass you are writing to and miss.

About Aunt Rena: One of her nephews wrote me. In her last year she moved out of her house and in with him and his family. You remember how she spoke of both her nephews as her "little boys."

> *I am so sorry to inform you about our Aunty. She passed away on Jan 1, at 12:30 p.m. and is at peace and out of pain. Her heart just quit. All at once stopped.*
>
> *We put her away very nice as she asked us to. And me and my brother and our wives have spaces next to hers. And all our children in an adjoining plot.*
>
> *So sorry to bear this news. We all loved her so much.*

It was signed, "I remain in sorrow, Searcy." That is his name, Searcy. I laughed aloud at the sound of it and when I read that Aunt Rena had asked to be put away "nice." Then I wrote to say I hoped to soon visit Louisiana. I said I hoped I could come to Aunt Rena's grave with a picnic lunch on a pretty spring day, that I wanted to get to know him and his wife and his brother and wife and all their children, or at least to get to know them a little, although I didn't say this, for as little as a weekend or a day. And that I was sorry that over all the years I never had. "Why, you must remember Searcy," I now recall Aunt Rena saying once, and I didn't, "When you were little he carried you out back to the creek and once all the way to the spring."

Maybe when I make this trip I'll also drop down to see you, Corpus, and never mind what that woman said to me about you on the train. I hear you're still very pretty, some say prettier than ever and more fun, a jazz festival in the summer, a Bayfest in the fall, new hotels on your shoreline.

I hope to stay in one soon. Next year, maybe. In March, maybe; I'm scheduled to travel then. Yes, it will be March when I leave for Texas. The very next time I go.

Rena, A Late Journey

The author wishes to thank:
Susan Bright for editing;
Stel DeLeón for transcription;
Roberta Kanefsky and Sharron Kollmeyer
for special assistance; and, as always,
her daughter, Bethel Eve,
for her love and encouragement
and for her creative spirit.

In memory of my Aunt Bo,
Leola Merritt Davitt,
and of all beloved departed.
With grateful acknowledgement (once again) to
The Corporation of Yaddo

"As a blind man lifting a curtain knows it is morning,
I know this change:
On one side of silence there is no smile;
But when I breathe with the birds,
The spirit of wrath becomes the spirit of blessing,
And the dead begin from their dark to sing in my sleep."

Theodore Roethke

The Last Dime Store

*D*on't tell me Kress's is still here? Why, it must be the last dime store! And here I am seeing it in my last days."

That's what I said when I got off the bus for the last time there in Corpus Christi.

Now I don't have to be transported by bus. Like one of those gulls on the bay front, I just hover.

At that time, late in one of the last decades of the century, I was into my nineties, in good health, but a little unsteady. My nephew, Searcy, who lived in Nacogdoches and has always been nearby, argued with me about taking the bus trip from the Houston terminal. He didn't even seem to understand why I had to go.

I had to go because Leeland, my husband who wrote "I love you" on a pad for me to see just before he died (with cancer of the throat, he couldn't speak, honey), had come in a dream and told me, "Rena, go back to Corpus Christi one last time while you can still go fishing, while you can still get around. You'll enjoy it and maybe go on to something new there, something you need to find."

Then I asked, "What is it?" And wouldn't you know it? Once again he was mute.

But I knew I should listen to my dream. All my life dreams had been taking me places. I got into trouble when I didn't listen, didn't go.

When I was just seventeen and pregnant for my first and only time, I didn't go to see my mama who we called Mammy or my little sister, Lucy, who up until the time she died, was a healer (she couldn't heal herself, honey!) and that caused me to lose my baby. My dream told me to go back to Mammy and to try and find Lucy so the baby who I called Juliette — because she was beautiful as a girl in a play — would be safe. But I didn't; the husband I was with then made fun of me, said I was dumb like all women and superstitious like all Creoles, like all my family. Can you imagine that? When I was just a child, I married a man like that, stayed with a man like that? Oh, but not for long, darlin'.

This was years before I met Leeland, but even then I wasn't crazy.

After that when I dreamed, I tried to pay attention. If a dream told me to take a trip, not long after I was on the bus, on a train! And from childhood, right up until the last months of my life, was as blessed with health, with only a little tendency in my nineties to lose my balance and topple over. Even then I usually did all right on my three-pronged cane.

But in Corpus Christi I had forgotten about the wind which had a force and a character unlike any other. You would be wrong not to address it, not to speak to it as you would an entity, not to give it a proper name.

"You're one of the things I've forgotten," I told it out there on the street corner. "I would do all right in Corpus Christi if I hadn't forgotten you." I didn't believe there was anywhere on earth where the wind could blow like it does in South Texas there on the Coastal Bend.

Blows a constant gale that rocked the bus I was on as it drove along on that long, gray road, cotton fields stretched out either side on flat-flat land, telephone poles stringing out to the sky.

We followed the same two-lane highway we took years ago on that flat lowland —and oh, it was way low down, below sea level, scrubby green country covered with a big gray sky, green leaves from the cotton fields rippling. Green as they were because of a summer of unusual rain. Miles of black-eyed Susans alongside, all the way to a town called Beeville where no bee or anything else ever seemed to be buzzing, to the bleak towns of Sinton and Taft which seemed mostly concrete, mostly highway, and finally after miles more of flatland, low moving clouds over it, into a little crossroads of a town called Gregory which should have been named World's End — for there the end of the world seemed called for — and beyond it, Portland, overcast, but which did transport, for from it, coming down a little grade (some called it a hill, low down as we were), we could see some of the Gulf, then Corpus' little bay and above it, an ocean of sky, and just below that, the city.

High-rises right on the bay front shocked me. Years ago, only hotels on the bluff rose more than four or five stories. When I first came, Corpus Christi was only a few thousand people and seemed the sweetest little town sitting there on its bay so quietly. Well, now it's like everywhere. Oh, honey, the world is overbuilt and close to breaking.

When we made it over the Causeway and past North Beach on the bay side of us and the sign of *The Caller Times* building on the other, and what I used to think of as town, the first marked building I spotted was Kress's. (Oh, what a landscape I had been traveling over, telephone wires running messages and newspapers calling out the times!)

"Why, is Kress's still here?" I asked the bus driver. I had spent many hours of my lifetime in Kress's. And since the wind nearly knocked me over as soon as I stepped out of the bus station — leaning on my cane with all I had in me — I was happy to once again see that Kress's store!

I told myself I could buy a scarf in it and have a bite to eat and a cup of coffee if the lunch counter was still there, ask directions and get my balance. What had I meant coming without a scarf? I could consider that. Get all my thoughts together.

Nobody was on the street when I crossed, leaning into the wind on my cane without too much trouble. I had all I'd brought with me, medicines, a nightgown, cold cream and two changes of clothing, in a Foley's shopping bag I carried over one arm. I never believed in carrying much with me, talked Searcy out of using his valise.

Once I was inside Kress's, I found the scarves on a rack not far down the center aisle right away. Though red was always my color (and I liked a bright one with some gold shot through it), I had on a dark blue cotton — the red just too hot to look at the day I left so I stuck it in my Foley's bag — and I picked out a blue scarf to match, and also, for a change, a black one, the color some of my hair still was, to go with my pocketbook and shoes.

A Mexican boy with long eyelashes, wearing a shirt bright as cotton leaf, left the jewelry counter to sell it to me. "With a wind like you have in Corpus Christi," I told him, "These must be a popular item. All the tourists must buy them."

The boy said Corpus didn't have too many tourists and that because of the lack of jobs, his one sister, a few of his brothers and almost all of his cousins had left the county.

"Honey," I told him as I picked a loud pink scarf that caught my eye off the rack and handed him another two dollars, "if you have brothers and sisters who don't have jobs, sell them a bunch of these and send them out to get twice the price for them on the street corners."

The boy said he didn't think Corpus had too many buyers anywhere. "The wind," he said, waving an arm, "blows everybody and all the money right out of town." Then from the tag he was wearing on his shirt, I found out his name, RENATO, and it startled me, for I saw the first of my name in it. (I found out later he was part Italian on his mother's side.)

He reminded me of a boy, also Mexican Italian, I used to see with Elizabeth, Leeland's niece who I helped raise after her father took off and her mother went to work in another town. But that was years and years before. Maybe forty years had passed since I saw her talking with that boy right in Kress's. People said he went off to North Beach with sailors who bought him things. Now that boy would be a man.

"Renato," I asked, "Do you have an older relative who used to work here?"

"At one time or another all my relatives have worked here," he told me, "But the pay is so bad that finally they all take off."

Not much I could do with that so I changed the subject. "Do they still make strawberry sundaes over at the lunch counter? With those good frozen berries? I always liked any kind of berry."

"Sure do," he said in a velvety voice, "And with whipped cream and a large cherry on top."

"What counties did your brothers and one sister leave for, honey?"

"Webb and Maverick and Zavala, Uvalde and Medina, counties all over South and Central Texas," he told me. "My twin brother, Reynaldo, left before he finished high school after our mother passed away. And then my sister, Mara, got married and moved to San Antonio. But Jesus has not left yet and he is the oldest, and my baby brother, Julio, is still here. We have cousins who have moved everywhere, I'll bet you all over Texas and all over the United States. Some to cold places like Kansas City. But we don't hear from nobody so I don't know how they are doing or even where most of them are."

"You have a large family," I told him, "So it's easy to lose track." I had tied the black scarf around the back of my head the way the nuns taught me when I was a girl in their school in Louisiana, and I dropped my other scarves in a shopping bag. When I caught my reflection in the lunch counter mirror a little later, I saw the scarf made me look like an old nun.

"Scattered to the winds now," he said and pointed to the street which I knew had no one much on it.

For I had just walked a ghost street, no longer the main drag. Chaparral only ran three or four blocks, the Central movie house across from Lichtenstein's Department Store which I had been told was closed (and later its windows all boarded up) on one end of it, and the Ritz, where the Bells saw all those Bette Davis shows they liked so much on the other.

When I crossed that street I noticed Kress's was on one of the few streets still open for business. And for all I knew, the wind that was still blowing a gale would one day blow poor jobless Renato right out of town as it had done the rest of his kin. I saw when I crossed Chaparral that the Ritz had a sign that said CLOSED FOREVER on the front door, the criss-crossed plastic strips on the marquee broken and peeling and flapping in the wind.

I remembered Ellen Bell, Leeland's mother, saying, "People in Corpus Christi walk around with their heads tied up in rags." A good thing I had bought several. Oh, on that day I was glad to have the scarves from Renato! I would try to get a city bus to the Ramada Inn which was only a few blocks away. Not that it was my idea of a place to stay. Still a room would be comfortable there, I supposed, and in this new Corpus Christi, as good as any other.

My first idea when I talked about taking this trip with Searcy was to rent a room in the big old-fashioned rooming house that used to stand on the edge of the park just the other side of the Ritz picture show where Leeland and I once lived and were happy. Of course, it's no longer there.

I could still hear Leeland saying, "Rena, bring me my specks, I want to read you something." Then he picked the Bible up from the bridge table where he worked on plans for some buildings no one wanted to commission or construct.

What did he read that day? I think maybe it was just once again from the Easter story, the last of the book of Mark that he read so often. Outside I watched the azalea and the first canna blooming. I don't remember exactly where he began, only him reading about how Jesus, after he had risen from the dead, appeared first to Mary Magdalene. And how it was Mary M., as I always called her, — the M. for the fishing village where she had been born — who spread the news about seeing him. Seeing him and talking with him on the road, Leeland always emphasized that, that Jesus came to Mary M. on a road, like one in Texas he and his Daddy had helped turn into a highway. In the 30s they even worked on the one that swooped down from Portland to the Causeway and then C.C. Mary M. was the first of God's new messengers put on a road to spread heavenly news, a woman of the road, Leeland said, in a time when women didn't travel.

How in the Springtime, every Springtime, Leeland loved to read or tell that story — the only others he read us for fun in the evening, spy stories or Ellery Queen.

How much pleasure we enjoyed in that little room in the rooming house with the park on one side. A place where we had nothing. Not even a refrigerator or a stove, only a hot plate and a window cooler to keep snacks in. I kept the colored eggs there that I boiled and dyed every spring, bought the dye for them at Kress's. We ate them, one by one, and gobbled them down along with all that mystery of spring. (Darling, Spring is the mystery season.) Our own home communion! We didn't need a church.

Leeland kept his strong cheeses in our cooler and I saved the pot liquor from the vegetables I boiled in a pot on the hot plate every noon. Oh, I always liked a good boiled lunch. We relied on that cooler to keep food fresh for us and trusted the Gulf gale to blow the stench from it away.

We rented the room which came furnished, so poor that we didn't even own the bed we slept and loved each other on. But we were happy. And often had a neighbor or two in, Myrna Teague who lived just below us, a widow, who liked to drink beer with us and smoke cigarettes and talk with Leeland — honey, they both died speechless, Leeland with a malignant tumor of the throat — and quilt sometimes with me. And the boy, Billy, who cleaned the park, picked up trash with a spiked stick, weak of mind and leg, but full of laughter — he couldn't remember his name, but I called him Billy Park — sometimes he came to visit, too.

And sometimes Leeland would read the paper to him, or maybe even some Bible stories about the miracles. He liked to dwell on those. Raising Lazarus was his favorite and he would read it over and over.

"Why did he do that? Raise Lazarus who had been dead four days and had begun to smell?"

Myrna and I didn't know and Billy looked baffled enough and just twitched.

"Why, because he loved him!" When it came to quizzing us on the reading, it seemed Leeland always asked and answered his own questions. "When Jesus came to Mary and Martha's and found his friend gone four days, he cried, suffered from human grief. And raised Lazarus because he wanted him alive. Not in the next world, but in this one, where he could be with him some more. And he wanted to tell us, too, to get our minds on life in the here and now. Not life in some place which for all we know may come with some of the same old problems. He was telling us that our concerns here were not with 'afterlife.' But just with life, that it's all of a piece for us to weave and with help, maybe into something good."

Standing in Kress's in my ninety something or another year, I remembered Leeland saying all that, heard it, though the rooming house where we had lived and the park next to it, was gone, was memory. Was a parking lot! Just concrete like so much else that used to be green or blue or multi-colored (at Eastertime all flowered all over). Some greedy thief would have paved over water for a dollar!

"Well," I said to Renato who was rearranging the scarves, and I don't know how long I had been standing in front of him as all this came back to me, "Your relatives are not the only ones who have gone, looks to me like everything and everybody I ever knew in Corpus Christi has been blown away. Tell me, though, do the city buses still run?"

Maybe the buses were memory, too! If they weren't, I wanted, after I got settled, to take one up the hill, behind the stores on Chaparral Street and inland down Leopard to Palm Drive, never the best side of town and probably gone down further, which even in my time had precious few palms on it — and I had heard more had died of blight — where the Bells and all of us used to live. Palm had boasted some pretty yards for a neighborhood of working people and the Bells always had the prettiest because of Leeland's baby brother, Bo's love of gardening. And it was with Bo with whom Mother and Daddy Bell and I and Bo's niece, Elizabeth (his sister's child), came to live.

"The buses run every twenty minutes," Renato said, "And every which way."

"Do they still go out Leopard?"

He nodded that they did.

I was glad of that. I didn't have enough money with me to spend much on taxis which I told Renato. But since I didn't feel up to walking much more, I thought I might take one this evening and I also asked him if I could get a taxi over to my motel on Shoreline Drive.

Renato told me that city buses only came as far as Chaparral and the Kress's store, that it was the end of the line. But he said I didn't need one. He said that after I had my sundae, he would walk me to the corner where I could get a trolley. He would be off soon, he told me, and trolleys which only cost a nickel ran from Chapparal up and down Shoreline all day.

"That's good, honey," I told him. "Tomorrow I want to go over on the seawall and find a good empty spot to do some fishing. And if you sell them, before I leave Kress's, I'll pick out a rod and reel. I need a real good fishing pole."

I thought maybe it was to catch a big fish that Leeland told me to come to Corpus Christi for.

From the End of the Line

Or was it to meet Renato, who got off work right after I had my sundae and walked me to a tackle store where we picked out my rod and reel? (A red one, honey.) Held me under the arm and guided me like a grandson.

The truth is: from our first conversation I felt as if I had known him all my life, as if he was in the Kress's store waiting for us to pick up from where we had left off in some long ago time. When I first met Leeland I felt like that, too.

One thing I knew the boy understood: fishing lines, told me right away he didn't think Kress's had anything I could use, walked me up the street to a tackle store — he didn't seem to mind going slow — and tested three different rods before he found one on sale he thought would do for the thirty dollars I had to spend and after I paid the store keeper, saw me to the trolley which rolled right down Shoreline just like he said it would and I waved good-bye to him as it pulled away.

"I'll come to see you," I told him. "Maybe I'll have something good to tell." Though the town I remembered was gone, the new Shoreline just a place for those passing through, Renato and I connected. I felt close to the boy all of a sudden, glad to have him in Corpus Christi. In my life story he had become an important person. I was more than at the age to consider my life story, the mystery of it, had been considering it for some time, but had none to think about it on the trolley as I had to get off just a little while after I got on. Inside the Ramada I found dust in the corners and the molding peeling. Considering what Searcy was paying, the place should have been better kept. I called him right away to say everything was all right, and then ate a simple scrambled egg supper in the plainest of dining rooms. Not a flower on a table or a vegetable on the menu. Just meat and potatoes and South Texas drab brown. I considered looking for some paper flowers the next time I was in Kress's to fix it up.

After supper I sat in the hot, sticky air by the swimming pool, my back to the bay front and the tourists on their trolleys, my back to the wind. And the trellis behind me protected me from it. This was July, darlin', one of the last before my heart just quit (back in East Texas on a January 1).

I just sat staring at the block in front of the one I was on and at what used to be the old Nueces and what was now the Nueva Nueces, the hotel still as pink as that scarf I bought, but part of it also aquamarine, and at the block in front of that, the top of Kress's, the letters K R E S S across the front in red, a couple of gulls swooping down toward them from the big gray clouds that covered the sky.

The sky had been gray and clouded all through this day when I had been traveling and the streets here were gray and the water when I turned my head to view it, and except for a couple which were brown, all the tall buildings. And my spirits more or less. Renato and his scarves and the bright cotton leaves and the flowers of the field had been the day's only colors. Renato had part of my name; that struck me as strange as I sat thinking of him. Already he had entered the past.

I shut my eyes then so I could also enter and be in the town as I used to know it when I lived with the Bells at mid-century.

Once or twice a week in the 1950s I rode a city bus to the end of its line, then transferred and began all over. And for a few hours got away from those people in that family which through Leeland, though he was gone from us all, had become mine. I had always liked riding buses, used to ride them when I was a child in southern Louisiana near Vermilion Bay to get away from my mother who we called Mammy and my brother, Johnny, and my little sister, Lucy. And we were all close. But, you know, to live with family, even those in it you care for most, can be to live with tyranny. Time came when I just had to be by myself and free.

"Rena, where do you go when you ride the bus?" Leeland's mother always asked me.

"Why, to the picture show," I told her, "Or sometimes just downtown to walk through Kress's." In those days I bought myself a new picture puzzle to work on (how I learned patience, darlin') or a new shade of rouge. Or I talked to the birds in their cages.

Ellen Bell, you know, once loved a canary; sometimes I thought that bird was all besides her sewing she had any feeling for. She talked sweet to him sometimes, the way she never talked to people. But a yard cat got him one day when she put his cage on the front porch for sun. And she just said to Elizabeth, "Go find me a cigar box, and then go outside and in the back of the flower bed, dig a deep hole." The loss must have hurt her, though she never let on. Oh, she seemed a block of wood, darlin'.

But I often asked myself how she got that way. Was it from, as a child maybe, an excess of grief? Seems like people who feel too much, and get a bad hurt early, forever after can't feel at all.

Sometimes I looked at the canaries in Kress's thinking I would get Ellen Bell one. But finally decided against it and spent what money I had on cosmetics and puzzles and berries with frozen cream.

And whether I was at the lunch counter at Kress's or at a show or just on a bus looking out at houses and yards or seawall and water, I always met somebody who liked to laugh and have a good time, somebody I could enjoy. Speaking to people always came naturally to me, and I liked being spoken to.

"Mother Bell," I used to say to Ellen Bell, for that's what everyone called her, "Whenever I go out on an excursion I almost always meet somebody." Oh, her lip curled up at that! "Well, now, what's wrong?" I asked her. "What's the matter with a little conversation?"

One of my favorite rides was to Six Points — buses from there shot out in six directions — where I transferred to a bus that went out Ocean Drive all the way to the Naval Air Station. I enjoyed good conversation for the better part of the day, and as often as not, wound up with someone for supper. Oh, I talked with all kinds, men and women, teen-agers and old folk, Mexicans and plain white people and sometimes, when I sat near the back of the bus, some colored. You know, Mammy was part black, had been born in Cajun country where some slaves had first gone free and where black and white spoke French to each other and went to Mass together. Mammy spoke some French and a little Spanish, but seldom to us children, so not much from those languages passed to me.

But I always loved riding the buses with all the people! Lord, you have to get out of your own skin once in awhile, break free from your own kind, your own family, before it turns you against everything and everybody who is different from you.

Elizabeth agreed, but thought sometimes I went too far. Sometimes she warned me. Said, "Aunt Rena, you have to be careful, have to be a little careful sometimes of strangers." (This was forty years ago, what would she say about the world today?) Then she reminded me of the stranger I married right after Leeland died, that man I met at the track who took me for a rich widow. God knows that insurance money I put on the horse was all Leeland left me, all I had. (And right after Leeland died, I felt so bad I spent some of it on a trip to Acapulco.)

Before Jack Dubuffet took me to the bank, he took me to the nightclubs — and was a beautiful dancer. But I should have quit him on the dance floor. Leeland drank too much when he got discouraged and said things that hurt sometimes — and what I said back and his drinking sometimes took him to other women. But he never hit me, darlin'.

"You don't need to worry," I told Elizabeth, "I'm never going out with the likes of that man again. Don't trouble your head over your Aunt Rena."

Elizabeth worried more than any of them in that workhouse and in that family that I stayed in even after Leeland died because I loved him and because, through him, it had become mine. She was an only child, an only grandchild and they counted on her too much. I saw her life slipping away.

I would say to her, "Honey, life can't be all work and no play. And there's no proof at all it's serious. Now your school this week is over, so why don't you go on down to the waterfront with a friend?"

And she would say, shaking her black hair already shot through with gray and she was just fifteen, darlin', "Oh, Aunt Rena, I can't go by myself. Some boy has to take me. I know that's dumb, but that's the way it is."

"Well," I would tell her, "It's Friday afternoon and the buses are running and your Aunt Rena is going for a ride."

Some Fridays I took the bus up Leopard and met Bill Powers, a friend of mine, who ate in the cafeteria on the hill, just behind the Driscol Hotel where the movie star with a similar last name stayed.

When I first came back to Corpus to live with the Bells, and this was after Leeland died and after I was in and out of legal ties with that no good Dubuffet, I got off the bus there at the cafeteria because I wanted a good vegetable dinner. I had always loved vegetables. (When I was just a little girl I tended our vegetable garden, and before I was in my teens planted one of my own.) And that cafeteria had every kind: okra, fried or with tomatoes, turnips in a sweet white sauce, and white onion rings in vinegar, kale with bacon, and Texas slaw, and every kind of green.

One evening when I was there after I returned to Corpus, I started a conversation with the fellow at the table next to me. I had noticed him there before and observed that all he ever ate was pie, coconut cream and blackberry cobbler (how I once loved to pick berries to make that. Met Leeland in a blackberry thicket.) And pecan. And chocolate banana. Ever hear of that? Two or three kinds on the same tray! Oh, maybe he would also have a chicken leg sometimes or mashed potatoes. But never anything green. Or yellow. Or any healthy color.

"Honey, I said as I passed him, just before I sat down at a neighboring table with my tray, "honey, you are going to get sick this way."

"Well," he said, sticking his fork in a piece of chocolate pie and pushing it toward me, "I sure don't want to do that, so why don't you eat a piece of this for me?"

I sat next to him because he looked so lonely. Something about his expression reminded me of Leeland. Leeland, near the end, after he had stopped drinking, all but lived on pie. And Bill was lanky like Leeland, too, who no matter how much pie he ate, never gained any weight. Also like Leeland, he was with women at first a little bit shy. I could tell by the way he turned color when he spoke.

"Maybe I will," I said, "I've forgotten my dessert. I'll exchange these mustard greens for it." When he shook his head I said, "Eat them, now, they're good for you." And so he tried them. And began to talk, in between bites and making ugly faces.

Before I knew it, he had in his shy way, told me some of his life story. Like Leeland, he was also a veteran of the first war. His giving up the bottle and craving sweets after was like Leeland, too. His wife died of a sun stroke the year before when she made an August visit to her sister in Dallas; she just keeled over on a city sidewalk one hundred degree Saturday afternoon when they had gone shopping and she never came to. Their only child, a naval air pilot, was shot down in the South Pacific, Corregidor, in War II. I told Bill then that I was a person who understood about the terrible loss of children. I told him about Juliette, my baby who died all those years ago and about Searcy's little boy who I took care of years later, being run over by a bus. And I told him about meeting Leeland years after Juliette died and about my life with him and about the man I met and married, though it was no real marriage, after. I thought I made it, I told him, as an escape from grief. After it was over I escaped some more by running off to Mexico as I had years ago after my baby died, and I told him about that, too. And about coming back to live with the Bells after.

By the time I was through telling, all the pie had disappeared. "Do you like to play cards?" I asked him. "I have a deck in my pocket." I had bought it just the week before at Kress's. "We could have a game or two at one of the tables down in the park next to the picture show."

He had come to the cafeteria on foot because he lived in an old house on Tancuhua or Carancahua, I forget which — two streets in Corpus have those Indian names — and when I slept in that house as I did later I heard the Indians singing in the trees, songs of young Indians, real Corpus natives, who seemed to have risen from the very ground.

Next thing I knew we were walking down the bluff toward the Ritz and by dusk playing pitch — the game Leeland and Daddy and I most liked to play — at the table nearest the rooming house where Leeland and I once lived and we talked about meeting there the next afternoon for a show. Matinees were cheap and air-conditioned, a good way to beat the heat and pass the time.

"We could play horseshoes here after," I suggested, "Or take a bus to Shoreline and play miniature golf."

After that I saw him now and then, but not every Saturday. And months passed after I first talked to him until the time I went to his old Tancuhua house. I think it was Tancuhua and not Carancahua that the house was on. I don't recall which, but I do remember it was a pretty place, built in the early part of the century with these great big rooms and twelve-foot ceilings and at night young Indian spirits whispering and singing and telling stories out in the biggest live oak trees. Oh, it's gone now, trees and all. The freeway's come right through the place where it was standing whichever street it was on. So the spirits had to move on. But I wondered where to. Where did spirits go when they lost their quiet places along with their trees and ground?

Through my life I asked that question many times and had no answer. Anyway, before that place where those spirits liked to talk and sing (where I could hear them, darlin') was paved over with concrete, my friend, Bill Powers, one sticky summer evening gave a neighborhood party, threw a barbecue in his backyard and opened his house, all those big, old downstairs rooms, for dancing. I made a fruit salad and a slaw, but he tended to all the rest, meat and toast and pinto beans.

At first just youngsters took to the dancing — Bill Powers had cleared the great big dining room for it — then some of us older ones joined them. I enjoyed the party so much I stayed on for a long time after supper, went on dancing with Bill before I helped him clean up the kitchen, then remembered that was how I got started with that no good Dubuffet.

Then when Bill Powers first ran a hand down my back as I was washing the dishes, I turned against him and said, "You sure do feel good, darlin', but I want you to know I don't get in situations like this often." Before I even came to his house I let him know that although I had been legally tied to three partners, two bad men I didn't really care about, one when I was too young and the other when I was too old to know any better, and one good one I loved, as far as I was concerned, I had only been married one time. And one time was all I wanted. "I haven't had casual relations with many," I told him. I knew the Bells thought differently. "And never mind my age."

Then he leaned real near — all this, you understand, was at the kitchen sink full of dirty dishes. "God knows I can't compete with the sainted dead," he whispered (he didn't know how soon he was going to join them), "with that man you'll always be married to, so maybe it's time to start."

Fishing

From the Seawall: One

How jealous would that have made Leeland? That's the question I asked that morning at the seawall after I first threw in my line. Asked the wind how jealous did it make him?

Bill Powers was a nice man to be with, but he wasn't Leeland, who I couldn't be near, let alone touch, who was gone, darlin'. I reasoned that since Leeland was in a country without flesh, or at least that's the way I understood it then, whatever I did with Bill Powers while I was still in mine, might be ok.

My body gave me pleasure, but also pleasure's opposite — doesn't everybody's? —and on lots of days, I thought I would be just as glad to leave it. But not during that long summer when the heat in Corpus, to say nothing of between Bill Powers and me, stretched into October which was the month he died. Maybe joined his wife or some other person in that other region.

I found him slumped over the kitchen table one hundred degree Friday when I dropped by for a cold supper: boiled shrimp on beds of lettuce over ice, that's what he said when he called, and when I got to his house, that's what I found in the refrigerator. "We'll go to a show," he had told me, "If you know a good one that is playing, maybe an old mystery."

Instead, after calling the coroner, I spent the evening at the funeral home across from the park. And when Billy Park saw me, he came leaping across the street making back of the throat noises, trying so hard to cry out when he saw Bill Powers stretched out on a slab inside. (Honey, because of the heat, when the coroner found Bill had an insurance policy and I knew just where that was, he got him straight to the funeral parlor so they could go to work on him right away.)

"Don't cry, Billy," I said and put an arm around the poor boy's shoulders because he was wailing so hard.

He pointed to Bill Powers' chest and toward mine, touched the breast above my heart. Awful sounds came out of his mouth, came from way in the back of it. "You" and "Friend" or "Your Friend." Those were the words I think he was trying to say.

"Billy, honey," I said, "He was your friend. He was just plain friendly." And lonesome, I thought, as I sometimes was, and I knew Billy, too. "We'll miss him." I wanted to add that he got through death fast and expecting something pleasant. A cold shrimp dinner and a cheerful mystery in the air-conditioned picture show.

Because I had so much to do comforting Billy, I pushed my own feelings about the loss of Bill Powers down. "If it feels good," I told Billy, contradicting what I had said earlier, "Just bawl."

The funeral director, when he heard Billy, had little patience and made signs to me to take him out. Since I couldn't answer many of the questions he asked about Bill's relatives, anyway — I only knew about his dead son and wife — I saw Billy across the street quick as I could and into Myrna's where Myrna and I drank a little beer and Billy kept crying and crying while guzzlin' Seven Up. Myrna wept some, too. I didn't. I expect I was still in shock, but somehow I was also happy for Bill, that he had accomplished what most dread so easily and with so little fuss.

Myrna, Billy and I were the only ones at the private service at the funeral home on Sunday morning. (I arranged it, darlin'.) In connection with Bill's death I got my name in the Saturday paper which reported that "a friend, Rena Bell Dubuffet," found the corpse. (You can imagine what the Bells said about that.) The movie Bill and I missed was "Charley Chan in Rio," which I had seen anyway five or six years before, part of a Charlie Chan festival the Ritz was putting on that October and a re-release.

Rena Bell Dubuffet. As I sat by the seawall I used to say my name out loud like that. But while the name rang out, even with the wind blowing, I stayed curled up inside myself separate from it.

But ready to break out. Ready to break through, darlin'.

Used to say my name. And Leeland's. And my runaway brother, Johnny's, who long ago disappeared into Mexico. Half believed if I said it often enough I'd summon him near. And the names, Searcy and Johnny Two (after his lost uncle), children of my little sister, Lucy — I called her "Clarity" because her name meant light (I found this out from a naming book Mammy was always reading) — who slipped away from us into water, whose sweet face I saw rising that morning over Corpus Christi Bay.

When we were children we set up an altar to the Sun Queen in our front yard where it was most of the year so hot and bright that we were sure a queen from the sun ruled over it. We pulled one of the yard benches to the center of our grass front and set fruit jars filled with water from the porch spigot on it and stuck oleander or canna or sunflowers, or just whatever, besides weeds, happened to be growing there.

And we knelt down before our altar and threw our heads back, and we looked up toward the sun and spread our hands in front of our faces, opening our fingers so that pieces of broken colored light spilled through them and over us. When Clarity, as I called her, slipped away from us and into Vermilion Bay as she did years later, I said the Sun Queen must have seen her do it and dipped down after to take her off.

And sure enough, her face rose before me there over the water. She always looked pretty, but this time, troubled, too. Was she just there to greet me? I wondered. Was there something she wanted to say?

In my mind I called to her. And said: Lucy, I've missed you. But I've enjoyed your children. Looked after them after you drowned.

They were sweet boys and became good men, caring and steady. We lost your only grandchild, Searcy's son. Your Johnny couldn't have children and never did adopt any; his business and his wife, Maurine, became his life. I didn't know if our brother, Johnny, ever had any.

I went searching for him in Mexico after my baby, Juliette, died and I broke away from my first husband. And I went looking for Johnny again a long time later, after your Johnny Two and Searcy were grown up and Leeland was dead and I had married and then left Jack Dubuffet whose name I still carry.

Somehow I didn't think to look on my trip to Acapulco right after Leeland's passing — I was crazed with grief. But all the times I traveled there, I found a lot in that country and across it. Monterrey to Veracruz to Jalisco. A lot that stirred my heart, and clarified my thinking the way you used to do when we were little. Remember how you did that for me?

Remember the day I learned I failed Algebra, and almost failed Latin, brought home an F and a D on my report card, and lay down on one side of my own little garden, the one I had planted and started digging, trying to plant myself maybe, trying to make more of me, digging and thrashing, making myself a pit in the ground, digging myself into a hole?

(Never mind that you were younger. You explained things so that they would come clear when I was all mixed up and had thrown some fit.)

That day I felt such a failure in my own garden — lettuce and tomato plants on the other side of me, and all kinds of flowers. (I had just scattered some mixed seeds in between the vegetable rows.) I might have dug a grave for myself, sure enough, if I hadn't heard your voice, felt your hand on one shoulder.

"Ree-nee, Ree-nee" (what you always called me), "Look around you. What do you care about some old school subjects?"

I raised my head to better catch the sound, and when I did I saw through the dirt a stream of light and the colors breaking in it that seemed to come from you, and the vegetables that had given us such good big salads (and fresh buttered carrots and the best red tomatoes for chicken stew) and the sprightly flowers. (I had never done a thing but water and pull a few weeds.) And I crawled out of the earth instead of going farther in it. I'd let the dirt fall in on me; dirt was what I thought I wanted instead of air.

Mexico in some way said to me: who you are is ok (even a help) — the way you did, Lucy, when we were growing up.

But I never did find our brother. And he never presents himself. Nor none of the rest. Since you had special powers here, I expect you also have them where you are now, and that's why I can see you.

That was a lot to tell the wind and Lucy, even if I didn't do the telling out loud, but only sent a message with my mind. And on my very first day back in Corpus Christi!

But her face, darlin', and her presence was on that morning, just as it had been when we grew up together, so clear. Made me want to put down my rod and reel and reach out to touch it. And would have if it had been a little closer instead of way out over some waves.

When I lived with the Bells in the 1950s and took the bus down to the seawall, Lucy's face sometimes rose like that, too. And though I was glad to see her, I was never startled.

In those days the buses ran the whole way, so when I didn't stop to see Myrna Teague who stayed on in the rooming house where I had lived with Leeland or to visit Billy Park, I would come right on down to the seawall.

As I guess I've told you, Billy's mind was bent a little, like one of his legs, and he didn't hear or speak much — read lips to understand. But he leaped around the park like a forest creature on the leg that was good and on a cane. And he kept the park clean. Sometimes Myrna and I helped him do it and had a good time, Billy, a real cut-up who, except for that day when he walked in on the corpse of Bill Powers, always seemed happy. He told jokes in signs.

Bill Powers especially liked to have fun with Billy; he'd hop around the picnic tables with him, picking up plastic forks and an occasional beer can that didn't make the garbage, or paper plates — shaking his fist at the imagined litter bug responsible, sometimes even pretending to be a police officer. Watching him and Billy play-act was good entertainment and cheaper than the picture show. Billy always skipped ahead right on out to the sidewalk in front of the Ritz if he saw Bill Powers and me coming and it was Bill he hugged — no wonder Billy cried so when he saw he couldn't do that anymore! He was too shy to hug me, though I always got a big smile.

In the years gone before Billy was shy around Leeland, who always shook his hand when he saw him in the park; Billy never touched Leeland that I remember except to take his extended hand in the good, strong handshake Leeland was known for, and often looked down when Leeland spoke. But they say Billy went on his first, and as far as anyone knows, his only bender when he heard that Leeland died. This was what Myrna told me when I came back to town. Billy, as I remember him, was a teetotaler.

On nights when Myrna and Billy Park weren't around or when I just wanted to be solitary — and as much as I took to people, there were lots of times like that, I would come here, to the seawall, to talk to the wind and for some fishing. Unless the fish were nice and small, the size I could pan fry for Myrna or Billy — the Bells didn't like fish much (Ellen Bell couldn't stand the smell) — I always threw back whatever tugged on my line. What I liked was not so much the fishing — to tell the truth, it always hurt me to see anything die, even the flounder which was so delicious. What I liked was talking, talking in my head or right out loud, that and just looking into the water and the sky.

Sitting on the seawall with a good line like the one Renato had picked out for me, that's when I brought up memory after I cast deep down.

From the Seawall: Two

*R*ena Bell Dubuffet, *who are you?*

Seemed almost as if that was the question the wind was always asking.

And only I was there to answer. Well, as far as children are concerned, an aunt seemed to be the role I was meant to play. My baby girl, Juliette, tore me all up when she was born, and afterwards I developed an infection, so that before I was twenty I had to have a hysterectomy.

Juliette's father called me a "dumb Creole" and sometimes a "dumb nigger," and had no respect for me or for much of anything living. Why did I, Rena Brock, who was brought up in an ordinary family, a mostly loving family, marry a man like that? And why did Mammy let me? By the time I did it, our big brother, Johnny, was in Texas and Papa J — that's what we called our daddy — was gone.

Because we were ignorant, darling. Because we didn't know.

In those days everyone thought a young girl should marry, should be "protected." If she did, everyone called her "safe." And when the man first asked Mammy for me, she thought he would be a good husband. He came from people who were well known in our parish and he had a little money.

Mammy was, I know now, flattered that he had asked, and believed he could give me more than what I had. Our farm had never done much more than feed us if the weather was right. And with Johnny and Papa J gone, it was hard for us to care for more than a few chickens and a garden. Mammy thought I should have a man who was a little older. He was thirty-two and so good looking. Green eyes and black hair. I didn't know much about what men and women did together — and he was sure no one to teach me — but I liked his looks, had a yen for him, so I thought marriage would be fine.

But he wasn't tender, darlin'. The man wasn't tender. From the beginning that's the way I thought of it, that I had left a tender family to cast my lot with some other kind. What sort, I asked then (and still do), was it?

I never found out completely. All I know is that after our wedding, a small candlelight service in the Catholic church, instead of driving to New Orleans like he promised, he stopped at a cheap hotel in the next town and before I had even taken off my traveling clothes just held me down on the bed. And hurt me, darlin'. Body and heart. Why did he want me? It took me some time to learn why, but I finally did. Because my blood was mixed.

What did he want me for? To have someone to hurt and not get arrested for it. And to have someone to treat like a whore.

This took me awhile to realize because he had put on such a show with Mammy and me before we married and went to N.O. to live. (Yes, in the Quarter, darlin'; he played cards for money there.) But when I was pretty sure I was pregnant, a dark-skinned girl who looked like Lucy came to me in a dream and told me to watch out. And not long after, that man took off with another woman, someone he met in the Quarter (and to tell you the truth I was glad of it) and when he came back to our rooms to get his things, he hit me across the face when I said I wanted to leave, too. After he struck me, he held me down on the bed, like he had the first night we were married and rammed me hard and after he was finished (and I lay curled up in a ball, hurt and sobbing), he slapped some bills down on the bedside table and called me "nigger" and some other bad names, darlin'. (I don't want to repeat them here.) And then said I was legally his to do with as he liked and that he expected me to stay there and wait for him to maybe come back when he had a mind to. Someone would be in to check on me, he said.

"You are just a woman," he told me, "And inferior." (Yes, he said that, darlin'.) "When my friend comes round to see about you, I want you to open the door" — He locked it when he stepped out — "and do for him whatever he asks."

Well, there was no way I was going to let myself in for his friend, darlin'. I took the money he left and after throwing a valise that held most of my clothes out of a window, lifted myself through it and then slid down the drain pipe at the side of the building and went to live up the country with our cousins, all dark brown or blue black — they had that much more black blood than Mammy. I hadn't visited them since I was a child, but that dream gave me directions, and the route it marked out took me right there.

I didn't tell them, or anybody about the baby. Didn't tell a living soul. But, of course, Juliette finally showed and I could feel her and began to love her even though she was his — after all, she couldn't help who she was related to and I reasoned even he wasn't born perverted and mean. (I found out he grew up with cruelty, darlin'.) I began to think I should go back to Mammy and Lucy who I thought I needed for the baby to be OK But though I longed for them, I didn't go.

My cousins didn't taunt me about my condition — I never told them I was married, I was ashamed to have married — and I was grateful they took me in without asking questions and that they let me alone.

But they didn't know a doctor to get me to after I fell from running when I thought I saw that man coming after me. Saw his shadow everywhere. (Seems from the time I was very young I was always seeing shadows.) I imagined that, darlin', afraid as I was all the time. Yet out of panic I ran on.

Ran and ran. But finally tripped over a tree limb fallen in the road and had to turn around and drag myself home. And Juliette came early and just tore me apart. (The midwife didn't know the right things to do, and I got an infection and later on, after I got back to Mammy but was still having trouble, had my uterus out.)

Juliette was a pretty child, but sickly. Colicky and prone to rashes and the croup. Then she contracted scarlet fever. And after awhile she died. I didn't go home right away to Mammy and Lucy — I was too ashamed — and they didn't know how to find me. For a time with the last of the money that man left me, the hundreds he had slapped down on the table by our bed, I ran off to Mexico, a crazy girl who didn't know where she was going, or what she would run into. And I'll tell you about that sometime, honey.

Leeland married me knowing I could never again have a child, and he said, not caring. After a long time together we were given his sister's child, Elizabeth, to care for. At least for awhile. Elizabeth lost her daddy, and for a time, her mother who during the depression years went to work in South Texas (the only place where there was any) while Mother and Daddy Bell and Leeland and I stayed in Hot Springs.

Elizabeth and I seemed destined for one another.

Before I met Leeland, awhile after I lost the baby, I did go home where I told Mammy and Lucy, too, my troubles. They were glad to see me, darlin', had all but given up on me. That man I married had been to see them, told them some awful story about me and that I had run off. Mammy hadn't thought about me being with her cousins who we hadn't seen since I was a little child. I don't know how I remembered them, darlin'. Only through the dream, I guess.

By this time Lucy had married and had two little boys just a year apart, Searcy and Johnny, the second, who I called Johnny Two. (Maybe he should have been Johnny Three since our father's name was John.) But her husband who she met because she was a healer — he was tubercular, honey — crashed his pick-up into an oak when he slid off the road. He had been in the woods to pick up a Christmas tree and everybody thought he had been drinking a little. Some people in our family went all of a sudden. Something to do with the stream of energy we got born in — falling off places in it — that's what Mammy believed and told me.

172

A few years later when Lucy couldn't heal herself of typhoid fever — oh, people died young of awful diseases! — it affected her brain so that she took to getting up from her sick bed and wandering away and once to swimming — I reasoned she wandered to the river because she was burning hot — and was caught in a whirly place and just went down in the water.

And now rises over it. Has maybe been rising over it somewhere ever since. Brown-skinned like Mammy and light-eyed like our papa. A shine on her face even after dark.

Oh, who was she, darlin'? Besides my sister and Searcy's Mama, and Johnny Two's. Who was she and where is she now? And where is our brother, Johnny? He seemed my other half, me almost, but a different side.

I see you before me, Johnny, hear you calling, "Come on." See you darting through the trees, Lucy and me after you, jars in our hands to capture fireflies.

I always saw you before me whenever I struck out, took a chance.

Searcy stared and stared at that face in the pictures we had kept of Lucy. Of her two boys, he took the loss of her hardest. Asked me to tell him all I could remember about her. And I told him how she had prevented me from burying myself in our flower and vegetable garden — he laughed when he heard how I had tried to do that — and how when she was just a baby she straightened an old man's legs just by wrapping herself around them. Some say he had been depressed and needed someone, anyone, even a baby, to take an interest in him. But never mind how she did it, after she wrapped herself around that old man's legs and crawled up onto his lap, giggling, he ever afterward walked straight. And came to visit her with candy and presents every day.

I went through all the pictures I had kept of Lucy in an old shoe box and found one of her with this man holding her, him standing up on his legs straight as you please. And then I showed him a head shot of Lucy and in color when she was pink checked and radiant, taken just before he was born.

And later when I began to see her in the world — as I did that morning in Corpus Christi — I told Searcy, sometimes, about it.

All of us are different in our needs. Honey, from the beginning this boy needed me, needed to hear about my visions, needed my storytelling in a way that his brother, Johnny Two, did not.

From the Seawall: Three

*B*eautiful. Lucy's face was, like always. But this time I thought I also saw some trouble in it. Her lips moved, but no sound came from them. I needed Billy Park with me to know what she was trying to say.

Back in "Bell Family Time," the 50s, I also saw Lucy rising over the waves of Corpus Christi Bay, also saw her dark skin shining and her mess of auburn hair. She looked just the same back then — except for the worried expression — arms open, beckoning, lips parted. (But her lips didn't move, only looked as if they were about to.) Which raised this question. Is an instant of eternal time like fifty years in time I then knew? Maybe so, though I still don't have a sure answer, darlin'.

Both times she rose while all that teeming stuff teemed on underwater. If you dive far down, like I used to when I was a girl in Louisiana, you see that life for the creatures of the deep is violent and terrible and that they spend their whole time chasing after and away from another, killing and consuming as they can (though way far down are places where they sometimes sleep), just living out a horror story. Even back in "Bell Family Time," I saw Lucy rising over that.

Back then I asked Elizabeth who was just a teen-ager, "What did she want of me? What was she about to say?"

And Elizabeth answered, "She was about to say, 'Rena, take me out of this hateful bay where every creature feeds on every other and I have to dart between fish hooks besides!'" (Oh, darlin', to think my hook was one of them.) Later Elizabeth told me that if there turned out to be such a thing as reincarnation — and this in spite of all the Christians in the world who said there wasn't — she hoped she would be spared a new life, however short, as a creature of the sea — then as an after thought, added, she supposed jungles and woods weren't much safer.

"No," I told her, "And in some places, or so I've heard, not even city streets." I was thinking of parts of New Orleans and what I had heard about Chicago and New York City. (And of the whole world, or at least a whole lot of it, during World War II.)

Sometimes when Elizabeth involved me in these conversations I considered the fish-terror at the heart of life a force that we're all driven by. But, honey, it'll drive you crazy if you think about that too much, and most of the time when Elizabeth got on that subject, I tried to change it.

Up in Arkansas where Leeland and I lived for a long time after we first married, Elizabeth was like my very own child. Even when she was little more than a baby, she toddled from Ellen Bell's house to mine, which sat next to Ellen's, came right up to my front door. I tended her most of the time when she was little before she went down to South Texas to live with her mama who was teaching music in the schools. Knew all the time that finally I would hand her over to her mama and to others, but that's what all caretakers of children do or ought to whether they are the natural parents or relatives of the natural parents or not.

Elizabeth was a teen-ager by the time I came back to the Bells and when she asked why I liked to take off so much on buses, I said, "Honey, I just have to get out of this place where they all stay too much with each other, and you should get out, too." I told her I always urged my nephews, Lucy's boys, Searcy and Johnny, to get out in the world and make friends, although of course I didn't want them running so far off I could never be with them — like Johnny had — didn't want them running all the way out of this country and through Mexico

Unless, of course, they were called to go.

Johnny Two and Searcy I took care of before I married Leeland, and they were good children who grew up to be good, steady men. But to tell you the truth, I always thought they were a little too somber. Johnny Two, especially, who made such a success in business, maybe because he didn't want to be a runaway Texas wildcatter or crazed silver miner or just a no good drunken drifter like many said the uncle he was named after was. (I never believed those people, honey.) Searcy liked doing ordinary jobs, was more like me that way.

I was happy working in a department store as an alteration lady, taking up hems that were too long, or taking out seams on pants that were too tight. And I never minded the job I had as a receptionist with the telephone company in Shreveport, could talk to a lot of different people in the course of a day — though that's where I was the morning Searcy's little boy was killed, run over by a city bus because the woman I paid to look after him wasn't. I felt responsible all the same.

Is there something in me, I asked, that works to kill children? First Juliette. And then little Newt, Searcy's son.

I had come back to Louisiana to be with Searcy and his boy when Leeland was on a job way up north somewhere — I believe some place near Chicago. I was put out with him because of his hard drinking and what I thought he might be doing with the women he met when he left Elizabeth at Sunday school and disappeared into a nearby drinking club (a place where he could bring his own bottle). I had never liked cold weather, and I believed a short separation — maybe just through the winter — might do us good.

Searcy thought I could help him and little Newt out, but I knew in order for us all to make it, I had to work part time. Little Newt's mama died when he was born. She had him at home without good help, the way a lot of women did, and she got a fever and it went too high.

But I'm leaping ahead in time. Maybe you'll get used to me leaping ahead like Billy Park and then hopping backward like Billy did sometimes, too. Whatever happened to Billy? I wonder if he lived on much longer. I can still see him leaping for Bill Powers when he saw him, right into his arms!

All this I now tell you was years after I lost Juliette, my own baby. I lived a long time, nearly eleven years, without a steady man before I met Leeland.

I hadn't known Leeland a week when I knew clear through me that he was it, my natural connection, and though I didn't know why and never found out, he did turn out to be. Just who was he? (Besides Mother and Daddy Bell's son, I mean.) That remains mysterious, darlin', as you will see.

When we lived together in Arkansas and Texas, we were poor and he dreamed too much — I never knew why, or what that ambition was that fired through and tormented him — drew up too many plans for buildings no one commissioned or even wanted. Once after a week of hard drinking — and, honey, he could put away a fifth of whiskey in an afternoon — he went into that place he called his "office," just a narrow hallway where we kept the ice box and where the iceman came twice a week to drop a big block in — that ran off the kitchen of our two-room pine board house (the one Leeland put up as a place to camp till we could do better after the bigger house we had burned down) and drew up plans for buildings in an underground city. He said the top of the world wouldn't be a fit place for people and that they would have to live in holes without natural air or light. (Sometimes when I looked around in some neighborhoods in the new Corpus Christi, I thought he might have been right and not just drunk or hungover.)

Drunk or sober, Leeland was always good to my family and glad to see Johnny, Jr. and Searcy when they came visiting and before she died, he put Mammy up for whole winters and summers at a time.

When I was growing up with her and my daddy, we were just an ordinary family. Our daddy, Papa J as we called him, had a small farm that fed us, but that's about all it did, we saw little profit from it, darlin'. And Mammy was happy just to do cooking and to make our clothes and to teach Lucy and me what she knew. She took a nap every afternoon after we had our dinner, which she had colored help in fixing, the big meal always being near the middle of the day when it was hot and not good for much but eating or sleeping. Papa J and our brother, Johnny — as I may have told you, Papa J's first name was Johnny, too — if he wasn't in school, who had come in from the field for dinner would sleep a little while after, too.

When Mammy got up, she sat on the porch and rocked and talked to us children or the neighbors, and sometimes as she spoke, she sewed scraps of material together. (Prepared me for the work I did later for those alteration places.) Following Mammy's lead, I got into the habit of talking then, of telling all I knew. And I learned piece work on that porch, pieced material, learning to work a needle and thread, and sometimes if I was tired of sewing, or there wasn't any, pieced together one of Mammy's jigsaw puzzles. (She bought one after another.) And, honey, I learned to put the pieces of lives together, too.

After the sun went down and Papa J came in, Johnny with him in the summertime when he wasn't in school, we made our supper mostly from leftovers in the cooler, and then we sometimes played a game of cards as Leeland and I came to do. Because it stayed light late, Johnny sometimes took me and Lucy to comb the woods in back of our house for wild greens and berries, and sometimes we trapped fireflies in jars. And Johnny liked to play hide and seek — always that streak of adventure in him! He'd run far from us.

Sometimes I thought it was only Mammy's calling that brought him back to us.

"Lucy! Rena! Johnny!" (Maybe that's when I learned to call out the names of those I missed, wanted to learn more about or wanted to see.) "Come in this house now."

It was getting dark. When Johnny heard our mother's voice, he would run straight to us.

"Come on. You heard. You want pie?"

If we came when she called, Mammy would serve us cobbler and milk before she heard prayers at bedtime. But if we lingered, we had to jump in bed and close our eyes at once, and take our chances on sleep without that comfort or, as far as we knew, blessing from either God or our mother.

But we didn't always have to get up early, never did on Sundays though someone had to gather eggs. (Us children took turns and sometimes fussed about who.) Papa J said he couldn't see getting up and then having nothing to do. During the week he worked the field early to miss the worst heat. He wasn't church going except for a few times a year and then he went to the Presbyterian where he had been raised. Mammy went to Mass every week, to the last one in the morning and often took at least one of us children, Johnny or me or Lucy, with her, though we never did study Catechism, not even when I went to Catholic school one year, and never were confirmed or made a First Communion in the Church. And we went on this way until just before I got married.

Then Johnny moved to get work. He was fed up with subsistence farming, he said, and wanted something good to do. Moved far from us, way down the Texas coast where he became an oil rigger and then a wildcatter, wrote letters to us from towns with names like Port Lavaca and Port Isabel. Finally, he drifted across the border (we heard from Matamoris; he said he would send money), then, I guess, all the way down into Mexico. We never heard after that.

But I couldn't believe he was gone from life like so many others.

(He was running drugs, honey, and I guess got himself into bad trouble, though I couldn't know that then.)

Papa J died and then my baby and then our darling Lucy. And many years later Searcy's wife died, too. Finally leaving just Searcy and me and for awhile, Mammy, to console each other, Johnny Two being all wrapped up in his wife, Maurine, and his farm machinery.

With our full lips and dark hair, Johnny and I looked something like our Mammy, but my round face, fair skin and blue eyes (blue-grey, darlin') I got from Papa J. Johnny was thin-faced and his eyes as brown and murky as the gravy on one of Papa J's stews. (Mammy taught me to make stew red from the tomatoes we grew and picked and put up in the summer, and to use fresh vegetables — green onion, bell pepper. I gave up eating red meat young, darlin', half a century before it came into fashion. Wrung the neck of many a chicken when I was a young woman — tried not to dwell on the killing I was doing — and kept a garden until the year before I died.)

Oh, people knew how to live when I was a girl in Louisiana. In Arkansas and Texas where I moved with Leeland, times grew hard, though before he began to drink so much, Leeland and I enjoyed being together and always had a good time, no matter how bad things were. I never really knew, honey, why he cared so much for me, just knew he did, was always astonished by that. I thought it too good to be true. Except when he was drinking, and what torment that came out of I never understood either, the time I spent with Leeland was prime.

But it always wore me out to be around his people. Ellen Bell ran a work house, sunup till sundown and suffered through the whole of every day, never seemed to enjoy a thing, not even listening to the radio or the victrola in the evening when Leeland's daddy or Elizabeth liked to put records on. Just wore her grim face and talked about the neighbors, how she thought the people across the street drank beer in the evening and that the woman next door had strange looking callers.

"What do you care?" Elizabeth always asked. "What do you care who anybody sees or what they do?"

Well, she left the world like all the others and as everyone does. (All of us, honey.) All from the family are gone now except Elizabeth who works a radio job somewhere in the west (western United States is what I'm referring to). Elizabeth is the last of the Bells — and I thought of her as a Bell, though her father wasn't. (He never figured in her life, darlin', he left before she was two.) When she was just a teen-ager I encouraged her to break away a little from them, to join herself to the human family. That, as things turned out, was what had always been in her to do. A good thing because she didn't marry.

In my oldest days when I moved to East Texas and lived near Searcy, I didn't hear from any of the Bells much, though Bo and Leona in their old age moved up to East Texas, too, and lived in a nearby town.

Of all the remaining family, at nearly a hundred I was the oldest. Leeland who died forty years before me had been Ellen's oldest child, the "Lee" in his name after General Lee — that's why they kept two "e"s in it — and never mind that Ellen Bell's own father fought in the Union army. Though some of the North was still in them and the West beckoned, Ellen and Daddy Bell named their first child after the Southland they had moved into.

Ellen Bell began in Southern Illinois, the youngest of twelve children and the only one who never had to work in the fields though she made clothes for the whole family. She married Leeland's Daddy who came to her county from southern Indiana with its Reb sympathies and took her down into southwestern Arkansas, and later to Texas. She said all her children were accidents: childbirth for her was never easy and the woman hated sex. She might have been abused when she was little by someone in her family. (That would explain a lot.) I never really knew.

But you would have thought that she would have at least welcomed her firstborn when he came into the world no matter what she had to go through to have him. Though she fed and clothed Leeland — and I guess in her own way loved him (loved him somehow in her head) — she kept herself distant from him. And I believe may have been relieved when he left home. Though Ellen Bell didn't like me, she never tried to lure Leeland from me, either. Leeland was his daddy's boy from the start. I was lucky that way, lucky I never had to put up with a mother-in-law who tried to snatch her son. Leeland looked to me for tenderness from a woman. (The women he met in those drinking places weren't real to him, darlin'.) Ellen Bell always said she would make Bo, her youngest child, born accidentally like the others but when she was facing menopause, a pleasure, train him to serve her, care for her in age. And oh, honey, he did. And ruined his life. Bo, you know, never married. Outside the family never formed deep attachments.

I told myself that maybe all the Bells would relax a little when the time came for them to pass over. I hoped they would so as to have an easier time with the letting go they were going to have to do. And to maybe finally become more loving.

"Aunt Rena," Elizabeth asked me once, "Are other races more loving?"

Well, what could I answer? We were meant for each other, Elizabeth and me, linked somehow (But I guess one way or another, all of us interconnect, darlin', more likeness between us than difference, no matter where we come from or what our blood.) People remarked on our physical resemblance, never realizing that my black hair was from my Creole mother and Elizabeth's from a black Scot daddy who, because he disappeared when she was a baby, she never knew.

Never realizing we were of different racial lines.

I knew Elizabeth had heard Ellen Bell talking about me saying I was part colored and then saying nasty things about the colored. But I also knew Elizabeth didn't put stock in what her grandmother said, that, in fact, if her grandmother told her something was so, she was likely to think the opposite true. Part of that was because her grandmother seldom showed her any sign of affection, or even much in the way of respect, though when she brought home her grades or evidence of some honor awarded to her, Ellen sometimes bestowed a smile or two.

So when Elizabeth asked if other races were more loving, what could I answer? I told her I thought loving might be more than we could ask most to do, but maybe we could ask that we treat each other decently. I said maybe if we did, the worst of the suffering would stop.

From the Seawall: Four

*J*ust as I was thinking about this, I saw Renato coming to check on what I had caught. Only memory I would have to tell him, not another thing! Or maybe he was coming to check on the rod and reel, to see how it was working.

I stood up and waved. "Renato," I called, glad to be wearing the black head scarf he had sold me which was flapping in the wind. "Come sit down by me, honey," I said as he came nearer, and was all at once right there, smiling at me.

"I'm on my lunch hour," he told me. "I took the trolley. How do you like the fishing line?"

"Oh, honey, it's a good one." I reeled my line in to show him. "Nice and light and just suits me. But so far, it hasn't caught a thing."

He took it from me gently, then whipped it around, reminding me of my lost brother, Johnny, who used to fish just outside of Delcambre, Louisiana on the Vermilion River that fed into Vermilion Bay. I don't know that you could get there now.

Most of Mammy's family were fisher people or shrimpers who loved fishing and pulling in a good catch, and were happy and fun loving — Papa J's were more serious — who danced all night and sometimes to Cajun music or played cards for money on a big table in front of a wood stove where Mammy or one of the others — men and women — got up now and then to stir the fricassee, usually garden vegetables and shrimp or chicken in a stew.

Seems like Renato no more than had the line in the water when something was a-tugging and before you knew it, he had brought out this little wiggling snapper, shaking salt water.

"This rod and reel is OK," he said before throwing the fish back in the bay.

If I had still lived down in my old rooming house near Myrna Teague we could have kept it and I could have Renato and Myrna Teague and Billy for dinner. That is, if we caught more fish to go with this one and if I shopped for a green and made corn bread or a biscuit or two.

But when he turned to face me, I saw Renato looked so serious. I touched his shoulder.

"Renato," I asked, "What is the matter?"

He didn't look like a boy ought to look on his lunch hour. He told me then he was worried about his little brother, Julio.

"Julio didn't get a job this summer like he did last year for the newspaper." Then he paused. "He seems different."

"How is that, honey?"

He just shrugged, then said, "I hope he's not mixed up with the wrong people for easy money. He's just fifteen. Our father left a long time ago and our mother died. She never had a strong heart, like her parents before her. When she died they were already gone, and her relatives scattered in San Antonio and Houston and other places. (I guess just about all over Texas.) So Jesus and I have had to be mother and father, brother and sister since all of those are gone."

That was a lot for him to tell me, but I knew I had his trust from the hour when he walked me to the tackle store and then to the trolley. He said his family had lost people to cocaine dealers — and worse, crack — and to using, too. Some they knew the particulars on and some they didn't, but they mourned them all, even those they didn't like. He thought most had not been members of gangs.

"Julio has Jesus and me, so they won't get him. God only knows what happened to half of the family, to those who have moved away, uncles and cousins."

When he said this, looking right at me, I understood our connection — we needed each other. I needed a guide in the late twentieth century Corpus Christi. And he needed someone from a simpler time who would understand to tell this to.

"Honey," I said, "You are a worry wart. No reason to think just because Julio acts a little peculiar that Julio is in bad trouble."

"No," he said, handing my rod and reel back to me, "And I don't want him to be." Corpus Christi, he said, had some people who promised easy money. Maybe South Texas towns always had: after all, drug running took our Johnny.

"Darlin'," I told him, "The world is split right through. Poor people on the biggest part of it and greedy ones on the little strips that make up the other and Old Man Cruelty crossing over." I was about to mention what Leeland always said about this, when a car that I took for a very old Caddy with Julio in it came down the street and pulled into the T-head parking area where a few tourists were milling. I knew it was Julio because Renato called out his name. A few minutes later a boy who was stockier than Renato and shorter, but not much younger-looking, came toward us.

Wanted to know if he could borrow money.

"Just twenty dollars," he said. "I've got a hot tip on the dog races."

I had heard Corpus Christi had a big greyhound track not too far from the Bells' old neighborhood on the road to San Antonio in the back part of town.

Renato said, "I don't stand on my feet all day so you can gamble away my twenties."

"Honey," I asked after Renato had introduced me, "What is the dog's name?"

But Julio, who seemed a sullen boy, mad at the world about his condition, just shook his head and wouldn't tell me.

So I spoke again, "I might bet on a lucky dog," I told him. I knew from the way Renato looked at me it was the wrong thing to say.

God knew I should stay away from gambling. All a track ever brought me was a no good man and the wrong last name.

"I'm not going to lose," Julio said. "This tip is hot. I won't lose your twenty."

Oh, life is loss, honey! Something urged me to tell him. But I kept my mouth shut. Just loss. Loss. No matter what happens to that money. That's what I wanted to say.

Renato, who had drawn in the fishing line, slipped his hand in his pocket and took out his wallet. "I want this back," he said as he took out a twenty.

And Julio took it from him and said, "I promise you, you'll have your money." Then ran, without even giving me a nod, back to his long, black car.

Renato whipped the fishing line back into the water, mad at himself, I could see, for giving in to his baby brother.

"You probably did the right thing," I told him (but in my heart, I didn't think so). "He may really win something with that money."

Renato pulled the line in then and gave the rod back to me. Shrugged, gave me a pat on the arm and a smile.

"Keep in touch," he said. "You know where to find me."

A few moments later I heard him call, "Good luck to you with the fishing!" and I watched him step on a trolley and wave as it took off.

From the Seawall: Five

Poor Renato! He wanted a comfortable life for his baby brother, a life with no pain. Whether we like it or not, suffering goes on though, of course, we must try to stop it. Stop the worst of it. That's what I wanted to tell him. And that most of us aren't improved by it. We're not like the saints, or Jesus. We aren't improved one whit.

Anyway, that's my opinion and it was sometimes Elizabeth's, too. Elizabeth said her grandmother was a good example of a person who was not improved by suffering and that there were other outstanding examples in the family. Made most of them mean, she said, just as it did some sick people and most prisoners and so many outcasts and underdogs.

"But, once in a while," she told me, "Some people become more compassionate as a result of having suffered, or at least learn more than most how to get through it." She wanted to know what I thought about that.

I said I couldn't say anything about whole groups of people, only particular cases.

"Well," she said, "Let's talk about you, Aunt Rena. You lost your sister, Lucy, and your brother, Johnny, and your baby, Juliette, and years after that, Searcy's little boy who you looked after. And before you even grew up you married a man who was bad to you, and afterwards your baby died and you couldn't have another. And after you married Uncle Leeland who drank too much because, or so everyone says, he couldn't fulfill his dreams of building, and came to live with his not so happy family, you lost him, too. But you most always have a good time. If you can only talk about particular cases, tell me about you. Tell me, how do you stay happy?"

"Where do you want me to start?" I asked her. I didn't know what to say. As bad as I felt when I lost those people and as much as I missed them, Leeland most of all, happiness was just in me, like trees and grass and oceans and rivers are in the world.

"Start with your first big loss," she told me, "With your baby's death and then your little sister, Lucy's. Tell me how you got through that and then through Johnny's running away. And about the loss of Mammy and your daddy."

"Everyone loses her parents," I told Elizabeth, "And I was grown up before Papa J's death came, so while I grieved for a time, and I grieved for Mammy as much as for me, I got through it, and I believe we all did, by telling as much as any of us could remember about Papa J, about the time he cussed out the elders of the Presbyterian church when they stopped by the house to scold him for his poor church attendance — and to ask for money! Papa J was a quiet man who lived a quiet life, so we didn't have many dramatic stories."

But help came from telling any kind. About the way he plowed his field, following a tape line to keep the furrow straight. Can you imagine that? That way of plowing was particular to him. I never knew anyone else who did it. Or about the time we saw him break out in tears when he heard about a typhoid epidemic in a nearby parish on the radio news. He had lost a sister to typhoid, and although he wouldn't live to know it here, he would lose Lucy to typhoid, too.

Talking about the way Papa J was and what we liked in him, and even what we didn't, helped. (He was too quiet, honey, kept too much to himself, was distant from us.)

But Lucy! Lucy! For a long time I couldn't talk about her. (And words mean so much, darling.) In the beginning was The Word. Lucy, like her name, had the power to heal through the word that ran through her. From the time she was very small, those who were sick felt better when they just came near her, and some claimed to be healed by her touch, and maybe so, but even more I think were healed by what she said. And what was that?

"Do you know you are good with flowers? Do you know you help things grow? What do you care about those old school subjects?"

Honey, Lucy healed through The Word. What she gave was praise!

But she gave honest praise. Praised people for what they truly were or could do.

After she left us I couldn't much speak. Couldn't talk about Lucy, who died before she was twenty, pulled down into water and darkness — honey, for a long time I couldn't speak of her, or anything much. I sank into darkness, too.

But then I began to see her sometimes, and told myself that she would come back, that she wouldn't just go off and leave us without her forever.

"I will not leave you comfortless." Mammy always quoted Jesus saying that, but not until after Lucy died and then appeared many times before us, did I realize that the comforter he was talking about was not separate from us, but in us, in our power from all creation and in our connection to that.

And as time went on, I began to see that loss is part of living, though as often as not, unexpected. But that unexpected gifts, even after those who bring them are gone, arrive sometimes, too.

After awhile I saw how parts of life fit together the way I do when I work my puzzles, looking for certain pieces that turn up sometimes only after I have been really still, really patient.

After maybe sitting at the table and staring at it, twisting a piece of my hair, all but memorizing the shapes of the pieces before me for maybe half a day. After I all but give up — look away from the mess before me and out the window at a jay sitting on an oak branch — just the right part will leap up at me, give me more of the picture, let me know it was worth it to sit in my chair by the table all day.

The one that turns up, I guess, is never the one we were expecting. I wasn't expecting Leeland. Or love. Or a child.

The last thing I thought when I married Leeland was that I would know the pleasure of caring for a child, have the friendship of a child, through him. But companionship and a lot of friendship from the little one I looked after came with her, along with some education, for Elizabeth taught me (even as I was teaching her), as children so often do.

From the Seawall: Six

As a grown person, I first learned from Searcy who showed me his need. Over and over he asked me to tell him about his mother and to get out the shoe box that held her pictures. So that one day I said to him, "I tell you what — why don't we do something with these pictures besides keep them in this box. Why don't we go to town and pick out a nice photo album to put them in? You can pick it out."

When we got to Kress's, Searcy spied a gold album more expensive than the rest. Though I don't know that he went to it because of its color, he picked it up first thing and asked, "Can we buy this one, Aunt Rena?" And though money was short, I decided that we could.

What a radiant boy he was by the time we got home! He never looked more like his mother, glowed all over, just shone. And going through the shoe box to select pictures for each page in the album absorbed him, took up the time when before he had moped or sulked around on rainy Saturday afternoons.

One or two of the pictures were bigger and more beautiful than the rest. In one, Lucy, in a blue dress, looking like the Mother of God, held Searcy in her arms, and in another Searcy and Johnny Two in their Sunday suits, sat either side of her. These pictures, we decided, needed featuring in the album. One in the front, maybe. One in the back. We couldn't decide where.

"I'll tell you what." I said, "Why don't we just leave these two out."

"Leave them out?" Searcy asked.

"Yes," I told him. "We need to make another trip to Kress's. This time to look for frames."

As things turned out, one was all we needed. A double. And like our album, also gold.

The next I can remember learning from another person, who also happened to be a child I had cared for, was when Elizabeth made it clear that she was going to be away for a long time, away from me as well as the rest of her family. Maybe for the rest of her life. And that I might not get to be with her during much of any of it.

And where did that happen? Would you believe it? In Kress's! I can be specific about the time and place, because one summer afternoon when I walked into Kress's and saw Elizabeth talking to her friend at the jewelry counter — he was a gay boy she went to school with, darlin', a Mexican Italian boy, as I may have mentioned, that times being what they were then, very few in Elizabeth's class had anything to do with or could accept. But in a different way, Elizabeth was also outside the status quo, and her Uncle Bo, too, so she and the boy, Bartola, as they called him, could talk about that. (I thought of him first thing when I came back to Corpus Christi and went into Kress's and saw Renato selling scarves.) On this particular day, I viewed Elizabeth in an entirely new way. I don't know exactly what made me see this — Elizabeth had been home all summer, working a typing job at the old Nueces Hotel and living with us to save a little money (oh, she planned to go back East, all right) after being in New York for a couple of years, and was nearly twenty and I was used to seeing her. I saw her every day — but when I first spied her with her friend on this day I saw her all at once as a grown woman, not our little girl anymore, and I saw that when she left this time it would be for good.

Did you ever do that, darlin'? Realize something important in a flash? And just know that it's right? I've done that once or twice and this was surely one of those times.

When I came close to Elizabeth I saw she had been crying, her eyes a little red and her pancake make-up streaked with tears. Then she held up her right hand, illuminated by all the colors of the rainbow under the fluorescent lights, and I saw her birthstone, a big garnet — I knew she had always wanted one, though she usually spent her savings on something else. Plane tickets, typewriters. Tape recorders and books.

"Look, Aunt Rena!" she said. "Look what Bartola has given me."

This was the first time I had met the boy, though she had told me some about him, about how she admired him for being himself and not trying to hide who he was.

"Bartola, this is my Aunt Rena."

"Do you like Elizabeth's ring?" he asked me. "It's from a special line we now carry."

"Why, darlin'," I said, "It's beautiful."

And I told the truth about that square cut dark red stone set in a gold filigree. "It looks Victorian."

"Do you think so?" Bartola asked, his voice both husky and high. "Like an antique?"

"Just like that," I said. "But it's bold."

The boy had given her a bold emblem of herself, that was clear to me immediately, though I wouldn't have said anything about it then. The message seemed to be: claim your life. (Just the way I had always encouraged her.) Go wherever you have to go.

She was gone for good shortly after that, darlin'.

When we got back to the house that night, Elizabeth told me that Bartola had plans of leaving for California.

"Pretty soon," I said, "We'll have no young people here. I sure hope you can get back for the holidays and to celebrate your birthday." (She didn't and I didn't see her again for twenty-five years.) I always liked to bake a cake on New Year's Eve for Elizabeth. As I may have mentioned, she was born on the same date I departed the world, one minute after midnight, on a January 1.

No, Elizabeth didn't get home that year for Christmas or her birthday and somehow I even lost track of where she was. She traveled, darlin'. But I knew I would always be a part of her life, no matter where it took her, just as she was of mine.

When she was a grown woman, she wrote me a letter that said, "Aunt Rena, the final condition of my childhood which turned out to be the foundation that supports and sustains me, rested on you."

All my life, even after I stopped hearing very much from Elizabeth, who became a wanderer, I kept that letter, and I asked Searcy to keep it after me with the idea of giving it to her maybe if she ever showed up for a visit or if one of us found out where she had finally gone.

I heard she had gone west, but not until she came to see me years later in Shreveport, a middle-aged woman, darlin', did I realize that "west" meant California, which had always seemed to me beyond the west, the other side of the west (or, at any rate, surely the last of it). Whether she stayed there or not, I don't know. What happened to her after that last time that I saw her, I don't know.

Elizabeth was a questioner and a seeker, always quoted Jesus on that, and made me realize that, by nature I was, too. Maybe Johnny had encouraged me to be, and maybe reaching out, even when it wasn't safe, was just in our blood, mine and Johnny's — in some ways Johnny always seemed an older me, a male me, and a guide. But when I was young I didn't think about this much (just knew it somewhere deep inside).

From the Seawall: Seven

When Elizabeth was a very little girl, she used to tickle me by looking right at me and asking, "Aunt Rena, who are you?" Just as the wind asks me here.

"Elizabeth," I would tell her, "Once I was just Rena Brock from Louisiana, the southern part near Vermilion Bay. Once I was a round-faced blue-eyed girl with curly black hair I never had to fix much — a blessing, darling — though I pulled it off my face when I grew old. For a long time, though, it curled all around it. Once I was no older than you!" She would laugh and laugh when I said that.

I went on to say our mama told stories to us when we were children, but then grew quieter and farther from us. That's what life does, takes us away from the very ones we gave life to. Took Mammy away from us children finally. But we knew she loved us: she never whipped any of us, never scolded. Smiled at us all the time, the Louisiana sun in her and even more of it in Lucy who healed some of the arthritic, crippled people she came near. Wrapped herself around the legs of an old crippled man who brought her peppermint when she was only two. And when she let go, his legs straightened and he walked as good as any of us.

Johnny, our big brother, brought sunshine, too. Never mind that we found out he was running drugs across the border. Where did he go? That was the question I asked after he slipped into Mexico.

The Bells weren't sunny. The Bells are another story. When I married Leeland I saw how they were different, how they weren't a family who laughed much or who touched one another, funny people, I thought, that way.

Lord, you have to hold your children! Tell them how beautiful they are.

Although I knew Ellen Bell didn't like me (but that it was nothing personal), and that she had hurt her own children, I tried to feel affection for her because she was Leeland's mother, and I came to. She said cutting things about people. Hard on them! But a lot of the time she was just silent and fretted, working her brow to and fro, I expect hard on herself, too. I could see the worry in her and it was easier to care for her then. Her family had been stern with her and with her brothers and sisters as she was with her own children. Hard on them, cruel even (part of that came out of the religion), the same way. Leeland from the beginning grew closer to his daddy than to his mother, pretty young separated himself from her.

Hard on children! What a thing for any of us to be.

Give children tenderness and they'll grow up tender. Childhood for Lucy and Johnny and me was happy. Later on, Papa J died (but his death came quick and brought no pain.) Then Johnny ran away and into Mexico. So life got sadder. Never sadder than when I married that first time except later on when I lost my baby and then a long time later in life lost Searcy's little boy. And finally lost Leeland. But I had to find him first! So I knew joy. Became one of the lucky ones who knew joy, too.

I met Leeland in a blackberry thicket one steaming summer day. He and Daddy Bell were in Louisiana building bridges, one of them across the Texas-Louisiana line. I hadn't spoken with him for more than a few minutes when I knew he would be the one for years and years. But why was that? And how did I know it? Oh, I wonder, darling.

I had been picking berries on a day like this one, July and sweltering, had a bucket full when I remembered the tributary to the river that ran nearby. Then I put my bucket down and slipped out of the berry thicket and at the riverbank out of my cotton dress, and wearing only a chemise and panties, slipped into the water, cool because it was flowing, and shaded by big trees. I swam down deep and stayed under, eyes open, looking at the pretty pebbles of blue and grey and rose, and when I came up I saw a tall, thin man bent over the bank smiling at me.

I ducked under again right away and swam back to the bank I had left. In swimming I lost myself, found release. But I had to do it alone. I heard the splash he made into the water and I swam fast for my dress on shore, but when I came up for air not too far from it, this long white man with freckled arms and sweet thin lips (they always seemed to be smiling, darlin') swam beside me.

"Fine swimmin' hole, ain't it?" he said.

The "ain't" I could tell was put on.

"I have to get out," I told him. "I've left off blackberry picking."

As I touched the bank, he asked, "What's your name?"

"Rena," I said it plainly. Stood all but nude before him, oddly glad of it, dripping wet, happy, my chemise sticking to my breasts. Then, all at once shy, I threw my dress over my head and ran dripping into the thicket, thrashing through the berries, the trees just loaded with them, their shapes making patterns on my light frock, staining the gauzy fabric on it so that I could never wear it again except to scrub a floor or to can or cook in. But I knew I would never throw it away.

And when I came to the place where I had been picking those overripe berries, plump, glossy (oh, so sweet, darlin'), Leeland soon stood beside me, telling that he didn't mean any disrespect, but that he wanted to get to know me.

"What makes you think you do?" I asked him.

He blushed and grinned. Later he told me he could see I took pleasure where I found it.

"I like a woman who is at home in the out of doors, isn't embarrassed to jump in some water when she's hot." He added that he was a builder and outside all the time. Then he looked down at my full bucket. "I see you've a mess of blackberries."

A serious aspect to Leeland. He meant what he said. Wasn't just being fresh or smart.

"Well," I said, "Do you like a blackberry cobbler?"

I wanted to be with him all the time from the start, and invited him and his daddy — after I learned his daddy was with him and that both of them camped near the bridge site — to our house for the Fourth of July. Although I had not until that moment once ever thought about it, I said we planned to have catfish and gumbo fillet with blackberry cobbler for dessert.

And, darlin', it was a good party. After we said hello, he introduced his daddy, who was, I could tell right away, a person who liked to laugh some. Though he had a serious aspect and some darkness was in him — and in us all, darlin' — sunshine shot through him, too.

We had our fish and our gumbo and after supper, Leeland pulled out a bunch of plans out of a cracked leather valise he had with him, said he wanted me to see them if I wouldn't mind looking and right after, spread them all out on the floor. And when he did I saw everything come over him, excitement and pain — passion, honey, with all the torment — and all the sweetness — that can be in that. I didn't know anything about architecture, or about building, but as I sat there beside Leeland that night as he pointed out the difference in the design of two big bridges, and to the rooms of a ranch style church he meant to put up for the Catholics near Nacogdoches (my funeral service was conducted in it, honey), I knew I would learn something about it because it consumed this man. And after he died I spent weeks poring over his plans trying to see the way he had made them. And, if truth be known, darlin', trying to find him in one of his rooms.

When he had been gone awhile and I still couldn't, I took off for Acapulco and when that trip was over, and after I took up with, then got rid of that no good Dubuffet, I traveled in Mexico some more. I don't know, maybe I was still looking for Johnny. Or maybe I was deranged and thought I might find Leeland. Whatever the reason, I drove my old car, a De Soto Leeland bought one time after his old Studebaker would no longer go, drove it out of Arkansas down the South Texas coast and into Mexico where I had gone by train when I was a girl. Maybe I thought I would enter another dimension if I just drove on.

To tell you the truth, Leeland often seemed so near that I think I believed that the place where he was overlapped whatever place I was in.

Anyway, after he died, the next world seemed just over the Texas state line — if it was that far. And I didn't expect it to be much different. (Mexico never seemed much of a foreign country.) On the other side of Laredo I followed the winding road into the mountains all the way to Monterrey, and after I spent some weeks there, Myrna Teague joined me as I had called and asked her (she used some of her insurance money and took a plane on down) and the two of us followed another road to the city where Bo Bell once wanted to live. Tampico. (I don't know why Bo was stuck on that — he just wanted to live in a place where he felt freer — and think maybe he had just looked on a map down the coast of Mexico and picked out a name.)

When I traveled in Mexico, I felt a little better driving the roads with Myrna along, though driving in the Mexican countryside is not really safe for even two women together to do. Finally, we turned west into the interior. Looking back, I see we took some awful chances. Not that I ever considered Mexico romantic. Not even when I was young, and I ran off into it in that wild way after my baby died. I expected something different, darlin'. But I always knew it was a poor country and hard to live in, that it was easy to get sick, or I had heard, attacked by bandits or (if you were a young girl), sold into prostitution, or even to get thrown into prison for something you didn't do. I had heard all the stories, darlin', and knew some of them were true. But I also knew Johnny had gone there, and I thought maybe even after all the years that had passed since he fled, I would hear something of him or even find some trace.

In the evening in the *zocalos* when I watched the boys and girls promenade past one another, I more than ever, remembered Johnny and Lucy as children. And after Myrna joined me, thought I saw each of them once or twice — first in Veracruz, then in Jalisco (I'll tell you about that soon).

After Myrna left me — she had a round trip ticket — I headed back, drove all the way back up into Texas and Corpus Christi where Myrna was and where Elizabeth was, by this time, living with Daddy and Ellen Bell and with her mama's and Leeland's baby brother, her uncle Bo. I figured I would just drop in. I would surprise them, and stay for the afternoon and maybe, through supper, or even, if they had room and I felt welcome, for a day or two. I pulled into the driveway in the back of the house, right in front of the garage apartment, early on a sultry Sunday morning. Elizabeth, who was cutting roses, all those dark ones Bo grew (they were nearly black, darlin'), was the first to see me. Dropped the scissors and came running for the gate, all arms and legs, a gangly thing. And threw her arms around me still clutching the roses. I knew when I saw her that, if I could, I would stay until she finished high school. She seemed almost my child.

A few minutes later Bo seemed happy to see me and later on in the morning said he would be glad to have me stay on the property with the family, said I could live in the garage apartment while Elizabeth's mama and stepfather, who was on a traveling job for Tennessee Gas, were away, and in the spare room next to Ellen's if they came back for a visit.

Two or three years later after Elizabeth graduated from high school and was on her way into her own troubled life (nobody's is trouble-free, darlin'), I didn't know just where I should go.

Searcy often wrote and told me to come back to Louisiana, and I did that for awhile, lived in Shreveport where Searcy moved after he remarried, and to please him, in a little house in town. But finally all of Louisiana seemed strange to me. I had been in my late twenties when I married Leeland and left it.

One day in the early spring of Elizabeth's graduation year when I saw the first wild flowers, primroses and bluets (those deep blues!) just cropping up in the grass, I knew that what I should do if I followed my heart, was go back to the country Leeland liked so much in east Texas, the other side of Nacogdoches. Leeland loved that country, best of all the Texas country because of its trees which reminded him of the Ouachita woods in his native Arkansas. I knew I would be happy living in a place he loved. And at the same time I would be close enough to Searcy to visit when I liked (he had remarried, darlin', a quiet girl I wanted to get to know) and set my foot back on childhood's home.

And, of course, finally, that's what I did. Left Shreveport where Elizabeth as a middle-aged woman visited me once, the very last time I saw her. Just moved into a little house near Nacogdoches and planted a garden. I hadn't been there long when Searcy and his wife left Louisiana, not to return for a year or two, and moved nearby.

Finally, I had to live with them. (Searcy took me to Louisiana for burial after my funeral in the Catholic church that Leeland built.) But we stayed in East Texas until I died.

But when Elizabeth was in high school, I knew it wasn't time to leave Corpus Christi, so I just went on there, and as much as I could, tried to help Bo out in the house and yard. Paid my way, too, bought a lot of groceries for us out of my Social Security.

Daddy was still living when I first came and I saw him through his last sickness, and Mother Bell through hers. Both died of cancer, darlin', he of the face, she of the colon and in agony, went out screaming with the pain.

Daddy, though, was at peace toward the end, hugged Elizabeth and kissed Ellen and told her good-bye. And asked all of us if we saw Leeland who he said was sitting on the foot of the bed.

Before he found that peace and that reunion with his oldest son, he had done some suffering, I can tell you, and he sunk into a long coma toward the end. For two days before he died we could all hear the death rattle from as far away as the street. Daddy had lain on his bed on the sun porch through most of the days and nights since the beginning of his sickness, the cancer daily growing bigger and spread all across his face. He asked Elizabeth to paint it with the green medicine the doctor left and told the rest of us that he wanted only her to do it because she had the gentlest touch.

Through it all, he was a good patient, seldom complained, and darlin', I know he hurt. He never asked for extra attention. Was interested in Elizabeth's progress at school and in her friends and comings and goings. And when she came in from dates and parties — often through the back door, honey, and his bed was there in the back room, back on the sun porch — he would call out to her and sit up in his bed and talk to her and ask her if she had a good time.

Sometimes when that boy Elizabeth liked so much brought her home — he was a new boy in town, from out of state, Kansas and half Jewish, somebody said — I would hear him and her whispering out on the porch under or near the bougainvillea vine, could hear him say, "Think about it, Elizabeth." (For months he had been asking her to go steady.) And could hear her breathin', "I will, Ben." Seems I could all but hear her hands sliding up the silky material of whatever shirt he was wearing, the little kisses he planted all over her face. (Maybe I was just remembering Leeland and me together.) And then would hear her tip toe into the house — hear Daddy softly calling to her to ask her if she had been to a dance or party and if she had had a good time. And she would always say, "Yes, I did, Grandaddy. How are you feeling?" And he would always say, "I'm just fine."

Oh, but his sore got bigger and bigger and spread across his face and down across his throat — no medicine the doctor gave him could stop it. And one afternoon he asked for us to wire Elizabeth's mama who was off with her husband, Bud, on one of his jobs, to come home if they could. He wanted to see her, he said, and believed his time to do that was growing short. (He hadn't been able to eat in a long time — just a little soup from a spoon.) And so Elizabeth wrote out the wire and took it to the Western Union.

Daddy sank back on his bed as soon as he knew she had done it. And the death rattle began right after.

Have you ever heard a death rattle?

Honey, I'm telling you, it's a fierce sound, deeper than the reptile kind — and Daddy's was loud; no stop, no pause to it. Made an awful music, and I expect fell into the big whirring noise of the universe, maybe even came out of and finally fit back into the hideous roar of that. (Why "hideous?" Oh, I don't know. I guess most of us just aren't up to hearing it. I wish I could tell you, darlin'.) At any rate, for more than thirty-six hours, it just went on and on.

Made me nervous sure enough. We were all of us all that day pacing around, walking out into the yard on any excuse. I said I was going to pull weeds from the flower beds (a job that in heat I hated) or to edge grass. In the evening I went out to water — and that was more pleasant, and to cut roses and gardenias so we would have cut flowers in the house when the doctor came. The doctor said he could hear the death rattle over the phone when Bo called and said he didn't believe the end could be too far.

And we all agreed it would be a blessing.

But the doctor was wrong. The rattle went on all through the long, hot night. A steady whir, a persistent drumming I thought of as African. Whirra, whirra, whirra and then, Ram! Ram! Ram! I kept getting up to go out for some air. Even though there wasn't any. Or very little. And what there was, hot, and smelled of gas.

I slept a little toward morning, but of course, woke up feeling sick and groggy. Although it was only May I could tell we were going into more heat and another brutal day.

And the death rattle went on through it until Elizabeth's Mama got there.

Stopped as soon as she walked into the room. Daddy pulled himself up on the bed, sat bolt upright and looked around as normal as you please.

And said then, "Thank God," as he hugged his only girl, and Bud, and Elizabeth, and finally, Bo and me. And then called out for Ellen, crying, "Ellen, you see what faith can do." And kissed her on the cheek.

And then he asked us if we could see Leeland. (And, of course, we couldn't.) Told us positively that Leeland was right there with us.

"Do you see Leeland there?"

I looked toward what I hoped would be him, or at least for some something luminous around the place that should be him, for at least a circle of light.

No one answered. Not one of us saw him. Or anything.

Then Daddy said, "Well, he's right here." He pointed toward the folded quilt that covered his feet. "I don't know why you don't see him." Daddy sounded annoyed with all of us. "He's sitting right on the foot of the bed."

I was jealous then of Daddy Bell's dying (could have put up with terrible suffering and all if that's what it took to do it), of his positive belief that Leeland was with him. Honey, my faith wasn't strong.

All during this time I watched Elizabeth grow into herself and when she had time at home, I enjoyed her company. And as you know, I enjoyed riding the buses. And visiting with my friend Myrna Teague who liked to talk about our Mexican travels, and Billy Park, and yes, Bill Powers. And talking to various ones. To whoever would hear me or just to the wind, or just to myself and to nobody else at all.

Churches

Churches

*R*enato caught the morning's only fish. I caught memory and a glimpse just before I left, of Lucy's face rising above the water, her dark face shining, and her mouth open, lips moving — oh, I thought she would speak! — as if she had something to say.

And I asked aloud: "Are you here to announce some news?"

But heard nothing.

And I left the seawall after that.

Turned once to wave to Lucy. But when I did, she was gone. So I walked to the trolley which took me back to the Ramada Inn and, from there, took a city bus to the Catholic church on top of the bluff which had a sign that said:

COME IN STOP REST PRAY

The door was locked or, honey, I would have done it. So I decided to walk on. The heat was bad; this was July and it was near a hundred. So I went very slow. I even took a chance and walked across a freeway that hadn't been there thirty years before, and surprised me. Although when I started out it hadn't a car on it, I worried I wouldn't make it all the way across without being run down by something that might come from out of the blue.

But it was a day on which not much was moving. So I made it, lifting my skirt, to step over the railing in the middle, and went on. I walked all the way to the Presbyterian. Oh, I was slow, honey. It was a longer walk than I had remembered and took a long time and the heat was terrible. Because the churches were so far back from the bay and the seawall, the bluff raised over that, they got less wind. Wind would have cooled me, darlin', but it also might have toppled me over.

On my way I passed the YW where I stayed once years ago and where I thought I might stay again the next time I came to Corpus Christi. (I wasn't thinking then that the next time I came I wouldn't need a room.) Maybe I could have a hot plate so that if I caught a good fish I could cook and eat it. By the time I got to the church the sweat was dripping off of me, running down my legs and I could feel my old heart beating. Could hardly get my breath.

Now, as I told you, because Mammy was Catholic and Papa J Presbyterian, I went to church both places when I was growing up, though not every

Sunday, and I never learned much about the differences and never cared. Prayer is prayer, honey, no matter where you do it, and no matter who you are, it finds its way. In my last years in Nacogdoches when I went to church at all I went to the Catholic — there was only one small one for the whole county — and never mind that I was a divorced woman, several times a divorced woman. (Wonder why I kept the name of that no good man, Dubuffet?) People in that church looked more like the ones I knew when I was a girl in Louisiana, didn't wear as many sober expressions as they did in the Presbyterian, and anyway, I had always loved the Mass.

But here in Corpus Christi the Presbyterian looked so pretty, friendly even, that I wanted to go in it. Oh, the Presbyterian seemed fine! But would you believe it was also locked, honey? What kind of world do we live in when we can't even get in the churches? I didn't know, but since I couldn't, I just stood by the door and got my breath and said a prayer and sat down on the steps for awhile until my heart stopped beating so hard. (You know your heart is beating too hard when you can feel it.)

And when I got up, I walked down the long block some more — this was the longest walk I had just about ever taken, and I was past ninety, darlin'. If a car had passed by I would have called out to it. But on that ghost street no car came.

Then I neared The Good Shepherd, an Episcopal church that looked Catholic because of the Spanish architecture and what had been cream colored stucco, gray now in places and in need of a good cleaning — where I all at once remembered Elizabeth when she was in high school used to go. The church back then had been new and pretty. Though they had been brought up Methodist, Elizabeth took her mother and Bo to The Good Shepherd — she loved the Episcopal church partly because it was the one where Leeland took her when she was small (he left her in a Sunday school there two doors from a club where he could drink if he brought his own bottle) — and I believe both were confirmed Episcopalians though neither went often. Except for Ellen, none of the Bells were faithful churchgoers, and I always thought Ellen went mostly so she could dress up.

Anyway, when I found myself in front of The Good Shepherd I was dizzy, sure enough, faint. I told myself that after I rested on the steps, I would try to find someone in the rectory — I saw it across the street — and use the phone to call a taxi to take me back to my motel on Shoreline. And never mind what the driver charged! But, to my surprise, I found that when I tried the door to the church, it was open, and that made me so happy that I just stepped inside.

I sat down in one of the pews in back and it felt so good to do that, to be in air conditioning and out from under the broiling sun, that I hardly noticed what was going on. I didn't sink down into the wine-colored cushion meant for kneeling — couldn't, honey — but just bowed my head for a minute. I knew God and all the angels would forgive me for not kneeling and that so would most of the people who stared.

When I entered, a young man who I guessed was an usher whispered, "Take that place there, Mother," and nodded at the empty space at the last pew's end.

Why had he called me "Mother?" Just because of my age, I guessed. (To my disappointment, a mother was something I hadn't been for long.) I didn't know, just smiled at him and sat. And that felt so good I was afraid I might never get up.

The church was packed and I had taken one of the few empty places. As I sat there, sweat pouring down my back and over the sag of my breasts, and down my legs, my dress sticking to me — and this with the air-conditioning on (and that sure felt good, honey!), I thought it was odd, a little peculiar, that so many people had turned out at noon on a Thursday to take Communion and pray. I thought it must be a saint's day, but I never knew saints were so popular with Episcopalians. I tried to remember what the saints' days for July were but, except for Mary Magdalene, I couldn't think of one.

As I sat there wondering and cooling down, the minister took the pulpit and spoke of this being another kind of Easter service. What did he mean? I felt sorry for Mary Magdalene then, for her grief.

Poor Mary M. Had the church decided to give her Easter, her own Easter in July? I imagined her as small. I thought of her rolling away the heavy stone, maybe in terrible heat. I knew Jesus loved her. Easter, this is like another Easter, the minister had said. Hot, for Easter, I thought. Even for a different kind. Maybe I had walked in on a sermon which would teach me something, open a window on a new world.

Then it hit me.

I had come to someone's funeral.

I was glad I still had on the big black scarf that Renato had sold me tied around the back of my head, glad I was still wearing the dark blue dress which I had rinsed out in the sink the night before (filthy from the bus ride, honey), and not the red one, the other dress I had with me, but which on account of the heat and Searcy's lecturing me against wearing such a color, I had almost left at home. Most people, I noticed, were in black though a few around me wore white or gray. But some were just in dark colors. (I always thought white was nice for a funeral and wanted to wear it when Leeland died, but Ellen Bell discouraged me.)

The person who died was named Joe. I remembered that Elizabeth when she was in middle life, in the last year I saw her, had cared for a man named Joe. And that he had died. He was someone she had worked with or for, an old broadcaster she admired. He was married — "well married," I remember she had said that — so that they could only be friends, with some thread of romance maybe between them. And she had said also something profound. I never knew what — maybe some inkling of eternity, darlin'; I had the idea from listening to her that it had to do with intuitions about whatever it is in us that lasts. But I wasn't straight on that (who is?), only clearly knew that the friendship meant a lot to Elizabeth who never really connected to anybody in flesh. She never married, never even lived with anybody outside her family. Like her Uncle Bo that way, and a sadness to her, darlin'. And to me for her. Ellen Bell's legacy. In some ways she was like my child. Who would have thought she would have a life like that?

I said a prayer for Joe whose funeral I attended as if he was Elizabeth's friend. Or my own beloved.

"Joe's family is happy now," the minister said. "They know he is well taken care of and in the best place."

Please welcome Joe, I said in my prayer. Please treat him right. Make him feel at home and forgive any meanness he was into or did here. (All of us sometimes have meanness in our hearts.) Lies he told. Betrayals. Ease his people's grief.

"Joe's family," he went on, "Should be happy now for he's all right!"

When you lose someone you love, it's damn hard to be happy. And I doubt that Joe's family was.

I remember when Ellen Bell's Methodist minister talked about Leeland "going to glory." When he said that, I wept bitter tears. Were they just selfish? Was Leeland better off all that long way from me?

"Ease their grief," I said that again. Aloud. Just as if Joe were my very own family. And in a sense I guess he was.

As the service went on, I thought maybe a lot of people ought to take up attending the funerals of strangers. Had Leeland sent me back to Corpus Christi so I could pray for Joe? Oh, honey, the dead need mourners! And the Bible tells us Jesus said, "Blessed are those who mourn." Well, Mary Magdalene was there for him. Bless her heart.

Maybe, I considered, Leeland had sent me to Corpus Christi so I would forever be a part of the power of Communion that joins us to everything and to one another. ("Galaxies," the prayer book said — I couldn't see the words, honey, but heard those around me say them — "suns, the planets in their courses, and this fragile earth, our home." During this service the minister stumbled over, then repeated this part.) Maybe when I went back to East Texas I would attend more funerals. Joe of Corpus Christi had a lot of friends or at least a lot of connections for the church was full! But back where I had come from I knew some people died with only a handful of mourners. Or none at all. That was probably true, I told myself, in Corpus Christi, too.

Leeland hadn't had many. Because he drank, the masons wouldn't attend. He once aspired to belong to them, even to attain the 32nd degree, whatever that was, and I don't think he knew. If he had, might have hated whatever it was — he just wanted to belong to some order that he believed stood for right. To tell you the truth, at his funeral even I couldn't send any good word up to or for him. I just wanted him back, just wanted him there beside me. I didn't hear what the minister said.

I was numb, honey.

And I hurt so after. I was in pain, darlin'.

Pain, anyway, is the only word we have for what I was in, so I guess that's what I have to call it. I never remember feeling like that. Some asked me why I didn't cry. I couldn't have answered them. But now I know. Because it was too deep a hurt to let go of. So, for a long time I didn't.

Then one day I woke up and stood up and held onto a wall and tore a fingernail trying to pull that wall down around me. And then I heard an unearthly noise — and it was coming from me, darlin'. I didn't know what to make of it, but the neighbors told me I keened.

But then after a long time, months and months I think it was, I slept through a whole night and well into the morning and I woke up hungry. And this after a hundred days of hardly eating and nights when I barely slept at all, and oh, people said I looked thin and haggard. I can't tell you how I looked because I never saw myself, not even when I stood before a mirror. Darlin', I ghosted out in front of the glass.

But that morning I woke to the prophecy in my name come true: I was reborn. (When I was little, Mammy told me she named me Rena so I would never have to die.)

And so I dressed myself and walked to the nearest cafe and ordered grits and eggs and my old favorite, blackberry cobbler. And then I left the cafe and walked to the cafeteria and picked up bowls of slaw and fried eggplant and black-eyed peas and several kinds of greens. And sat down and ate them all. And then went back for strawberry shortcake. I should have been sick. But I wasn't. For months I hadn't been able to keep anything down. As they say, I could hardly swallow water. But when I woke up on this morning I was so hungry that I just ate my way through the whole day, tasted everything as if it was for the first time, devoured it. And it was all so good.

And when I looked at the world, it was as if I was seeing it for the first time — trees so green, sky so blue. Oh, yes, it was summer, darlin'! July and hot, wet with humidity, but also with sparkling. And I loved it.

"Thank you," I said out loud while walking down the street, "Thank you for the morning." I addressed the air — and who knows? — maybe in it the Holy Ghost.

"Hot," people said to me.

And I said, "Yes, I love it."

I wanted to go dancing that night.

Leeland loved to dance. No matter what he said about dancing, he loved it.

"The mouth is the instrument of mendacity." Leeland himself said that. "But the body doesn't lie."

When he and I were first married he and I would go to dances and sometimes danced all night. Did that, instead of, like some couples, going to picture shows. Leeland didn't think much of shows. And he got mad at me for liking some of them and sneaking off to matinees.

Most of the time we were too poor to go anywhere so we just stayed home and listened to the radio — no wonder Elizabeth wanted to write radio shows, she saw us around it so much listening to those sounds, as if the radio was magic. And, of course, it was. And is.

And the telegraph and telephone. And the way I can now talk to you! (Even though I have returned to what I think of as "dream time," or that is what I suppose.)

Sometimes we read stories aloud to one another. We read some of the good, exciting ones from the Bible like Esther's and Joseph's and the one in Matthew that told all the miracles that Jesus did. And we read some stories from a book of fables Leeland had. And some from mystery magazines. Leeland read all those to me, and oh, darlin', he was the mystery, who he was and why my life was entwined with his. (When I asked, he would say there was no reason, it just was.) Or we would play cards, Black Jack or Pitch

— Daddy used to join us — and we had some good times doing that.

And in the night we made love, held each other and with so much longing and so many small kisses (and a few deep ones, darlin'), and wet all over and aching slipped into each other just right.

Then came the long year of Leeland's dying and that was hard to take. He wrote, just before he died, "I love you" on a piece of paper and I knew it was true. But, at the same time, it astonished me, always had, why it should be, why it ever was — that was the real mystery story. One day, I told myself, I have to find out. Then he wrote, "If I could only have a cup of coffee." I guess I told you he had cancer of the throat. Maybe from rolling and smoking all that Bull Durham and mixing it with so much whiskey. He couldn't speak.

After I came back to myself — and yet also to a new person — I just wanted to go out, to the nightclubs, go dancing. Shake old death away, shake, rattle and roll old death away.

I had a little money saved up from Leeland's insurance and winnings from the races and I bought some burgundy satin clothes. Oh, red was my color, honey. And the dark reds went with night!

When Jack Dubuffet saw me he thought I was a woman whose husband had left her money. He was thirty-nine and I was nearly fifty and ought to have known better, but he seemed sincere. Like an old time gentleman, that you read about in books (and maybe that's the only place they were). He was so pretty. And he could dance.

And I thought, oh, Lord, this is what I need in these years left to me. I've had all I want of what weighs heavy. Poverty and relations — and yes, love, too — and all that long dying. My life with Leeland was heavy with all of that. Jack Dubuffet might just like dancing.

Oh, I found out different.

I left him knowing for all the time left me, knowing for always, that I had been foolish to think I was going to have some lighthearted dancing years with a pretty man. When he found out I didn't have anything but a little Social Security and what was left of Leeland's insurance money — I lost most of it on the horse — he struck me with the back of his hand. And then with his fists, honey. And when that happened I knew that when he stopped I would dance alone or go to each dance for the rest of my dancing time, with a different fella. And that for awhile I wouldn't be going anywhere. (I couldn't dance, honey, could hardly get around.)

After I left him I didn't know what to do, as I guess I've told you — oh, darlin', I know I may get tiresome. Forgive me, but don't we all repeat ourselves? Repeat, and repeat? So I just struck out for Mexico — by that time, it had become a habit — drove down the Texas coast right around Corpus Christi, didn't think to even ask Myrna if she wanted to come along until I was all the way to Monterrey. I guess, as I've said, deep inside, I thought maybe I would at last find Johnny. Or who knows? Maybe Leeland's ghost. And when I went as far into Mexico as I could and still didn't find either, not really, not even with my friend Myrna Teague along, I turned back and traveled the other way.

You were Rena Bell, I told myself. And are still Rena Bell even if you now at the end of your name also have a Dubuffet. So go back and live with the Bells who are still your people.

Oh, I knew Ellen Bell didn't like me, and Bo only some of the time. (Sometimes he was influenced by his mother.) Still, I thought that Leeland's family was the place for me, that I could help out with all the dying and that by taking me in to do that, Ellen and Daddy Bell would also help me. And that Elizabeth and I could be together for a little while before she packed her bags for college.

Plain to see she was going to go, and I knew I had encouraged her to get out of the house where there was so much sickness and anger, where they all just worked all the time and stuck to one another, where they would never let in anyone new.

"Life is too short," I told her, "For you to stay here. Get out and find yourself some friends. Oh, there are a lot of nice people. You can hardly take a bus ride without meeting them. Just introduce yourself and begin. You know how. I see you do it. You aren't like the Bells who cut themselves off.

"A long time ago something caught hold of them — oh, I don't know what it was, and kept them away from life. "But it hasn't got you, yet. You've learned something else. And everything you are takes you the other way. Honey, go out beyond this family. Then you can return when and if you want to."

"Aunt Rena," she said, "You went deep into Mexico."

And I told her, "Yes, but it never seemed to me a foreign country, but like an extension of Texas, only going farther in."

For a long time so much of the country looked the same. Miles and miles of plains, barren places, plenty of mesquite. But I did go far in. And I came on mountains — you could only imagine mountains in our part of Texas — and trees and flowers the likes of which I had never seen. Women with baskets of roses — towers of roses! — on their heads in Oaxaca. And, for someone who had been a long time in Texas, other odd sights.

Myrna and I arrived in Oaxaca on a Friday and after we checked into our hotel just off the central plaza and washed up, we went right away into the big church on one side of that square, dark clouds banked all around it (though they never brought rain), and saw a man standing in front of the altar there in one of the side chapels for one of the saints, masturbating. His member out of his pants and his hand right on it, moving up and down.

Well, darlin', out of respect for whatever moment he was having, the love affair he was in — and, oh, that's what it was, in an instant I could see that — I tried to look away.

But Myrna whispered, "Do you see that?"

And I had to look back at him!

Later Myrna asked, "How could he desecrate the church that way?"

And I told her I didn't think he meant it as a desecration.

"I think maybe," I told her, "He is in an ecstasy."

I saw how communication with a saint could lead on to that. But Myrna didn't get this when I tried to tell her and she said it was a wonder to her he wasn't reported and arrested, not that she personally cared what anybody did.

She said, "I personally don't care what anybody does, but I don't think we should have to see this."

I agreed it was too bad he was on view. I thought maybe he ought to be able to pull a curtain. I thought I understood how he wanted to be transported, or nearly was — that he wanted out of himself, that he wanted union. We often want that when we pray, don't we? If we prayed with our whole selves, if we didn't just put our prayers in a separate chamber from the rest of us, if we didn't just keep them mental, maybe we'd all want to take our bodies with us when we made them (and in a way wanting to get out of those bodies that trap us into our separateness, too). What he was after seemed to me natural. But us looking at the way he had to do that was another thing! So I had to agree with Myrna about his exposure.

"Let's move on," I told her. "Let's just go on the other way."

Myrna told me once that although she cared for Mr. Teague, she never thought much of sex, not that she disliked it exactly, and didn't see why people made so much fuss.

"I don't see what all the fuss is about," she told me, "At least not for women. That's something men want to do much more than women."

(When she spoke, I could almost hear Ellen Bell whisper, "the nasty things!") I guess Myrna couldn't help not knowing about the pleasure and release. (Or maybe she did and, even though she was a straight shooter about most things, thought it would shame her to admit it.) Or Ellen either, who I expect had been brainwashed and maybe, even abused as a child. How many women did? And why was I so lucky? Because I grew up swimming rivers? Because in our family we all cared for each other with touch? Because, though they took me to Communion, I never went to Confession and until just a few days before I was married when I had to be instructed (and then most of it I didn't understand) no one in my family spoke to me about sin or any rules that went with church?

I enjoyed Myrna's company and she was modern in a lot of ways, what I called modern. After all, Mr. Teague left her nothing except life insurance and she took care of herself, clerking in stores and sometimes sewing for people, after he died. And, there was a streak of adventure in her; she liked having a good time with friends. Who else would have gone with me to Mexico? So I didn't make a case for the man we had seen playing with his member right there in the chapel of that big church. (Darlin', I believe it was a cathedral.) Not even when Myrna talked about him as if he was some kind of freak.

"Let's move on," I said, and we did.

But later in the afternoon in the place we had come to after wandering through many streets and seeing Indian women with long pigtails — down to their knees, darlin' — dancing in long, red and gold striped dresses and Indian children wearing capes embroidered with pictures of the Virgin chasing each other and playing tag, and many more in plain worn out clothes begging around tables where tourists were eating and drinking, we saw an old man, all in white, white shirt and pants, straw sandals and a big, natural colored sombrero — he was maybe seventy — at the side of another church in front of one of the statues and he was also exposed, erect and whacking. And moving his lips with an "Our Father. *Padre Nuestro, que estas en el cielo.*" I noticed he had stained his pants with urine or semen.

I couldn't help but say then, "If that man we saw this morning was a freak, this town must sure be full of them!"

That old man didn't wait for death to feel at least a moment's release from his body to be with God! But no, honey, we didn't watch it. And though Myrna gave up on criticizing, she said as long as she stayed in Mexico she never wanted to go near any more churches. (I knew there were so many that would be hard to do.)

The next day we went to Monte Albán where all we saw was a bunch of hikers, and a lot of black pottery, and a blue sky, a pure true blue. *Cielo.* The same as the word for Heaven. (We did seem near.)

I never did tell Elizabeth this story. She was too young for me to tell her. I would have told her if I could have seen her when she was thirty or thirty-five. But she left my life — that is, my life of seeing her — before that. She was always in my heart.

What then, did I tell her? Only that there were people everywhere who were friendly and nice and fun to be with.

"Don't listen to the Bells," I told her, "Who are just suspicious."

Once in awhile, I'll admit, I got in trouble by not being suspicious enough. Mammy didn't bring me up to be any judge of men. She told me nothing. And Papa J wasn't much around. And when he was, as silent on this subject as on all others, a steady father to us and let us know he cared, hugged us all a lot (strange, I learned, for a Presbyterian), but a silent man.

"Aunt Rena," Elizabeth said, "You get into trouble by being too friendly."

"You will have better sense than your Aunt Rena," I told her. "All the same, she knows some things. So listen to what she's now telling you."

I said all this the Christmas the Bells had the big ruckus. Just after Ellen sickened with the cancer with Bo drinking hard. After Daddy had died. Elizabeth's mother and her husband, Bud, were home for Christmas, so I let them have the garage apartment and took the little empty half room on the other side of Ellen's and could hear her constant moaning. (I believe it had been a dressing room, not much in it, but it had a day bed.)

Bud thought his job was in jeopardy — I heard him talking about it to Bo out in the yard — so he was drinking hard, too.

And he began screaming at Elizabeth's mother who had nagged him about not looking for other work, so that I thought that he might hit her — he did that once later on, darlin', hit her hard and his Masonic ring left a mark on her cheek. And then Bo said bad things to him.

Bo said, "You never really have supported my sister."

So that Bud swung at Bo and raised his fist.

"You sissy pissant," he shouted, "Come outside and I'll let you have it."

This was Christmas Eve and we were all of us — Ellen (who was just beginning to sicken with her cancer), Bo, Bud, Leona (Elizabeth's mother), Elizabeth and me — out on the sun porch sitting around the still undecorated Christmas tree. Bo always did wait until the last minute to buy one; he was a fastidious housekeeper and hated the mess. At Elizabeth's bidding we had gathered to string the tree with lights and put the ornaments on. But Bo and Bud had been drinking since mid-afternoon and Bud and Leona quarreling, so for tree decorating, it was not the best time.

Bo didn't answer Bud when he challenged him, not at first. Only trembled. But then he said, "You're uncouth."

And Bud doubled his fist again and said, "Come outside, Buster," jerking his head in the direction of the back door. "Let's see what you're made of away from all these women."

And Bo said, "I think you better get out of my house."

And Leona jumped between them, ready I think to slap either or both. (She had a temper, honey, and was never scared of — in fact, welcomed — a fight.) Elizabeth sat at the foot of the Christmas tree, a silent onlooker, as she so often was (but I could hear her crying in the night, darlin'), and from her easy chair Ellen Bell held her stomach and moaned.

"Everybody, stop it," I said. "We've come here to trim the tree and I think we had better get to it. You men have had too much to drink."

Bud brought his fists down on the flimsy card table, piled high with tinsel and boxes of shiny glass balls, most of which spilled over on the floor, but which by some miracle didn't break, and then he walked out the door. (The next day he called in drunk from some bar and told Leona he had found a woman to be with who liked him the way he was and didn't have a family.) You can imagine what a nice time everyone had trimming the tree after that!

And what a happy Christmas dinner, with Ellen moaning from the bedroom, Leona red-eyed and silent, and Bo, Elizabeth and I pretty quiet, too. Though I tried for Elizabeth's sake to make some cheerful conversation — it seemed to me none of the full adults had behaved very well — and suggested that after dinner we all go for a ride.

"I'll bet the water front is pretty today." We had beautiful weather. 75 degrees, blue-skied and sunny. "And they say at night the yachts down in the basin are all strung with lights. Has anyone seen them yet?"

Elizabeth said she had, but that she would like to see them again. No one else answered.

"Well, honey," I continued, "After we've eaten our fruitcake, and done the dishes, why don't we just get in the car and go. Before you know it, the sun will be going down."

That was the evening that Elizabeth told me that she couldn't wait to finish high school and go on to college.

"When that time comes," she said, "I can finally leave this house."

She would leave more than that, of course, and would be gone for good. I knew I was going to miss her (though I didn't realize it fully until I saw her a few years later in Kress's, a red birthstone on her finger, with her friend, Bartola, illuminated in an eerie way under the fluorescent lights). But I also knew she would remember her Aunt Rena.

I thought about Elizabeth as I sat there at a stranger's funeral. (Well, he had been a stranger when I came in. Now he was just Joe.) Suddenly, I was so homesick for her I missed our conversations. I hadn't seen her in years. I didn't think she had ever married. In high school as I have told you, she liked a little dark-haired boy, but wouldn't much go out with him even though he seemed crazy about her. That was the problem, I think — the intensity of it scared her. She thought she might never get out of Texas and, honey, although I believe she liked Corpus Christi in lots of ways, she was ready to go.

That day in The Good Shepherd, nearly forty years after the time I remembered, my thoughts drifted like this and on and on. I don't know what went on much toward the end of the service. But I saw the people lined up to go to the altar rail and take Communion. I had cooled off and didn't anymore hear my own heart beating. Air conditioning and the flood of memories helped me. (Since early morning at the Seawall I had reviewed my life.) This stopping place had restored me and given me direction. I would walk with the others up to the altar and take wafer and wine, and then exit. Just make my way through the side door. I knew when I left the church I would somehow find my way to the old house out on Palm Drive.

The Cut

Palm Drive

*A*fter I took the sacrament, I made my way out a side door, then walked to the corner and crossed the street to the vestry, not yet crowded since the service was still going on, and used the phone to call a taxi to take me back over to Leopard where I thought I could get a bus that would take me to the back of town where we all used to live on Palm Drive.

When I left the church that same boy who first sat me down in The Good Shepherd took my arm to help me down the steps and said, "Good afternoon to you, Mother. Glad you could come."

I realized then he thought I was a nun. I just smiled and said, "Sure enough, honey." (I didn't see a reason why I should tell him any different. He was just a baby, only twelve or thirteen.)

But I never set out to be an impostor, and I hoped the taxi would come to get me out of the sight of any who had the wrong impression, and out of the heat.

On Palm Drive it would be even hotter. The street ran through a place where you couldn't hear the lapping of bay water and where, unless the town was struck by hurricane, and it was sometimes, the wind seldom blew. Ellen Bell, when she lived there, dipped sheets in ice water and strung them on a clothesline which she ran wall to wall in a back room in front of four or five big fans, kept all the fans running and the double doors to the dining room open so that the cool would blow right through.

When the taxi came and I told the driver where I wanted to go after getting a bus at Leopard, he said he didn't think I could because "The Cut" went through it.

"Well, what is that?" I asked him.

"The freeway," he said, "The interstate to San Antonio. What was the number of the house you wanted?"

Well, darlin', I didn't know the number. But if I remembered right, it was in the twelve hundred block. Or the thirteen. Which is what I told him.

"I used to get off the city bus at Leopard and Palm," I said, "And after I walked a block or two I was at the right house."

When he asked how long ago this was, I was embarrassed to tell him. He said the only way I could get to that house on this day was over the freeway pass after climbing up a bunch of stairs.

"Honey," I told him, "I don't think I could do that on a cool afternoon, let alone on this one. So maybe you had better take me and let me off at Noakes."

I remember Noakes as being lined with pin oaks, the street Elizabeth came home on after returning from a day in school. I always admired the yards on it when I walked to meet her or walked to the IGA store to get vegetables for Ellen Bell's lunch. I thought I might like to walk to the house from that store before I realized the place was probably gone.

As I was considering this, the driver asked me if I was visiting someone. I said no, that I was just sightseeing.

That gave him a good laugh. By this time we were ready to turn onto Palm Drive. "Here?" he asked. "You want to sight see here?"

"I used to live here," I told him. I saw right away that anymore the neighborhood wasn't nice.

When he asked me how I was going to get back, I said I would call him, that I would use somebody's phone.

"Do you know anyone here?"

"Not yet," I told him. "But, honey, I'm going to knock on some doors, so I'm sure to know someone soon."

Then he said he thought I should be careful. "This neighborhood is not a good place to stay long in," he told me. He went on to say "The Cut" began here.

"And what is that?" I asked him. "I thought you said it referred to the freeway."

"More like the territory the freeway gets into," he told me. "The world is not what it was."

"Well," I said, "Change is natural."

"Ma'am," he said, "This place is risky."

"Why, this street looks all right to me," I told him. But when I looked out the window I could see it was really poor, run down. Some of the windows of the houses were boarded up and others just smashed through.

After the taxi driver let me out and his car pulled away, I saw other houses had bars on the windows. And a chill went through me even though it was a broiling day. I had told the taxi man to go on, that I would call him.

Maybe I shouldn't have. Maybe this was the place where the world divided.

"Why," I said aloud and seemingly to no one, for the place was deserted. "It must not be safe here." (I was always slow to get things, darlin'.) I could hear Elizabeth lecturing me then.

Although some of the houses were vacant, their yards grown up in weeds, Noakes itself was familiar. Elizabeth had come to and from school on it, running as often as not, running and singing, all the young life rising in her. When I looked down the street I seemed to see her running, the ghost of the girl she was shimmering in the two o'clock heat. (Sure enough, when I looked at my watch, that was the time.) Elizabeth, the girl child I was close to on earth, a gift from my husband's family, my Juliette being gone.

But when I looked away from that phantom, I saw all the broken windows and vacant houses and yards grown up in weeds, beer cans and bottles in the grass.

Then when I got on toward the corner, I saw the back of what I was sure must have been the old Bell house where Bo tended the chinaberry tree and the pretty willow (both gone now, honey, though I thought the stump I saw by the side of the house belonged to the chinaberry tree) and the bed of banana trees and roses where he had painted gates and porches in a bright rose shade — just a little darker than the scarf I bought at Kress's. Oh, the first spring I lived there, I bought some material that color and made myself a dress. Now there were no trees or flowers or gates or even porches.

A big, ugly box-shaped room had been tacked onto the back of the house where the old porches had been, where the glassed-in sun porch had been and an outdoor patio covered over with a grape arbor Bo had constructed and planted. The big, ugly box-shaped room covered all in my memory.

When I came round to the front of the house, I saw the lattice work over the front porch was gone, too — Bo's bougainvillea had climbed and fallen over it — and the whole house was a kind of dirty yellow, although it hadn't in years been painted any color, trimmed in an ugly brown.

Bo used to sing a song about brown and yellow. A tisket, a tasket, a brown and yellow basket. Oh, I can hear him singing it still. But if he could have seen his old house the way I saw it, he would stop singing. He had stopped by the time he got out of the house back in his day. He lost several people he cared about — a young man he cared for (but couldn't live with the way the world was then) — while he was in it and his mother and father to cancer. Enough to stop anyone's song. (Bo went to pieces after his mother died, drank himself crazy and into the state asylum. Bud signed the papers and told them to keep him there until he dried out.) I heard the people who bought the house from Bo died of cancer, too, and I wondered if the disease was in the walls.

I hesitated before I walked up the sidewalk of that bleak yard where the grass was dead and no pecan tree or gardenia bushes grow. In that awful heat with my blue dress sticking to me I could still smell the gardenia bushes from forty years before. Elizabeth said she associated their perfume with death, not to its sadness, but to the cleansing agent in it. I could still remember her saying that. "Oh, there's a cleansing agent in death, Aunt Rena."

I wondered who lived in the house now and what they knew about the neighbors or those who had been there before. But when I rang the bell no one answered. The name Cortizar — and I guess it was the name of the people who lived in the house — was on the door. Some way it made me think of the word for heart, *corazón*, and I wished I could have taken the association as a warning, read it as a sign! But I didn't and I had lost interest in finding out much about the people or going in the house. The heat was getting to me, honey. I felt dizzy. I didn't think I wanted to stay on Palm Drive long.

And I wondered why in the world had I wanted to come here?

I saw the fat, stubby palms that had lined the street were chopped down, only stubs left. (I learned later that was because of too much water during a flood, that they had grown sick from all the water, that the very elements that nourish us also kill.)

I wished then I had just stayed back on the seawall fishing. I must have been crazy to leave the waterfront where the fish were nibbling or beginning to, the breeze blowing and where Renato, that sweet boy I met at Kress's had dropped by. I wished for him. People always said Gulf breezes cooled you in Corpus Christi. Well, I can tell you they didn't reach those here.

Why had Leeland wanted me to come to Corpus Christi? For a few minutes when I was in the church I thought I knew. But I didn't anymore. What was it Leeland thought I would find?

As I turned my back on the front door and walked back down the broken sidewalk (yellow weeds in the cracks) across the burnt up front yard to the street, I saw a big, black car, a long Caddy, round the corner at the end of the block through waves of heat. I watched it come slowly closer and closer, a door bashed in and paint chipped off the back bumper. Then I saw Julio inside!

Why, how does that boy get around all over town in that great big car with no money? (I almost asked aloud.) And him hardly old enough to drive!

The dog track wasn't far away, I suddenly realized. The taxi driver had said it was just the other side of the freeway. Maybe Julio was in this neighborhood to pick someone up.

"Julio!" I called out, but the car was going past me. "Julio! It's Renato's friend, Rena!"

But the car had passed me by.

The heat beat down, down. And I knew would get worse. I was sick from it, darlin', and from being in a place that no one seemed to care for. And from the stench of gas from the nearby oil refinery. I didn't care who lived in the house or anything about the neighbors. I just wanted Renato's little brother, or somebody, to take me out of there.

"Julio!" I called again. But the car was gone.

Then a few minutes later when I rounded the corner, I saw it on Noakes Street going the other way.

Going really slow, crawling. I thought it was peculiar for a car to crawl like that. I asked myself if I was having hallucinations in the heat. Heat itself has a presence, honey. You can just about see it come at you in waves.

Scared me a little. It's only Julio, I told myself, Renato's little brother. And I should be glad I've found him. No reason at all not to flag him down. And I kept walking toward the car.

It looked like it might stop. And when I could look its driver in the eye and see that it was Julio, I spoke.

"Julio, do you remember me? Rena? Renato's friend."

He didn't have the manners Renato did, never answered me, only asked, "What are you doing out here, Mrs.?" And although he had stopped the car, he didn't invite me in.

"I used to live out here," I said. "Forty years ago with my husband's people."

He looked disbelieving, so I turned around and pointed.

"In that house right there," I said.

I wanted to add that in its way it had been beautiful then.

"The people who live there now don't seem to be at home."

When he didn't respond I said, "I'm tired, honey, and need a ride. If you could take me over to Leopard, I could get a bus from there."

He said, "I have to wait here. I have to meet somebody."

I wondered if he had been to the dog track and if with Renato's hard-earned twenty he had won any money, but I didn't bring that up. Instead,

I asked, "Well, do you know anyone in the neighborhood who would let me use a phone?"

"I might," he said, and pulled what looked like a tiny telephone out of his pocket (it might have been a real phone's baby).

I had never seen anything like that before.

"Do you have a message for me?"

All at once I wondered if the dog track was what he wanted Renato's twenty for; maybe he had just needed it to gas up this big old car. Why would he ask me if I had a message?

"No, honey," I said, "Should I have one?"

My own question made me wonder if Renato had told me something I had forgotten, if there was something I was supposed to pass on.

"Did Renato say I would have something to tell you?"

Julio just looked at me, disgusted.

"I shouldn't have come out here," I said to him. "I forget sometimes I'm an old lady. Is that a phone you have there, honey? A real phone? If it is" (and he had nodded that it was), "I'd be much obliged if you would use it to call a taxi."

When I said that, Julio revved the engine which made me think he was going to take off.

"Wait, Julio," I said. I couldn't believe that he was leaving. "Julio," I continued, "Don't go."

I wondered if maybe he was going to let me in. I didn't have time to wonder long when I saw its side door fly open — Julio must have pushed a button for its release. And I had just taken a seat inside, mumbling, "Thank you, honey," so relieved I can't tell you that the boy had obliged me and that I was out of the worst heat, when I heard the shots. And I knew that's what they were even though the sound wasn't "bang-bang" like in old shows, but "pop-pop," and almost pretty, a soft cracking noise of the kind you hear when opening a string of shiny red and green crackers on Christmas morn.

Crack-Cocaine: One

The bullet cracked the front and then the back window glass, and whizzed, or I guessed it did, past me. I saw that Julio's shirt was torn at the top of his right shoulder and that he was bleeding. (Oh, honey, the blood oozed through Julio's cotton shirt, and he was just a child!)

Then a second bullet broke the glass.

I don't know where those bullets came from. To this day I couldn't tell you. The street was empty, deserted. Not a soul stirring or anything, not a leaf, not a blade of grass (and most of the grass was dead), no one to see. Nothing in the houses or on the porches or in the yards. Mid-afternoon and the world, darlin', was empty, mean Old Sol a-blazing (the beautiful Sun Queen that Lucy and I loved as children, dead or asleep). And yet, those shots rang through.

"Julio!" I yelled, "Darlin'."

Julio gave me no answer as the car swerved around the block.

"Julio," I called again, touching his shoulder near the place where the blood oozed, "Stop the car. We have to get someone for you." Still no answer. "Julio, stop." I said again, "Let me drive, honey." I really thought I could do it. Never mind I didn't have a license. (Julio didn't have one either.) A highway patrolman in East Texas had given me a ticket the day I ran into a pick-up at the crossroads that took it away. "Julio," I yelled, "are you hurt?"

Of course he was! But still driving, the car careening this way and that, a good thing that at first there was no traffic. But the next thing I knew we were on the freeway. Going at a terrible speed and rocking this way and that, telephone wires strung out on either side of us all I could see. (The world seemed all sky.)

"Julio, where are we going?" I shouted.

What a question for me to ask him! I don't think he ever knew.

And it didn't matter because I soon saw that even if he had a destination in mind, we weren't going to get there. We hadn't been on the freeway long when I heard the sirens and I knew we would be stopped by police.

And I should have been thankful because the way Julio was driving, he would have soon killed us both. But I wasn't thankful because I knew when the police got to us, Julio would be in deep trouble. And all I could think of was that he was hurting, and just a baby who needed help, that I was being driven by a wounded child.

Corazón! I felt my own heart pounding.

Julio didn't try to out drive the police car, couldn't, darlin', just pulled over to one side and stopped. And then fell straight over on the wheel.

Blood stained the front seat, honey.

"This boy's been shot," I told the officer who didn't need me to tell him. "Call an ambulance."

As I spoke, I noticed a big grey cloud cross and cover the sun, and although we were on a freeway, nobody else much was on it and I guessed hadn't been (that was a blessing, darlin') and the world seemed still.

And the patrolman did that, called the paramedics who arrived in an ambulance, but before it came, he asked me a lot of questions about Julio, who he was, what had happened, most of which I couldn't answer. He didn't seem to understand a bit how Julio and I were connected and I didn't want to say much about Renato. At first I pretended I didn't remember his name.

"He is just a boy I know slightly," I told them. "I'm a visitor to Corpus Christi. I met his brother at one of the stores downtown."

I said I couldn't remember which one. I had come by taxi to visit the neighborhood where I once lived, I said, and I became overheated and the boy when he came along, gave me a ride.

The shots at the car came out of nowhere, I told them. We hadn't seen a soul on the street or in any of the houses. As I spoke, I saw the sky was getting darker though it was still in the middle of the afternoon. There was no wind at all — very unusual for Corpus Christi — but I wondered if it was going to rain. Changing the subject might have brought relief. And I almost asked the officer, "Do you think it will rain?"

After the paramedics had Julio on the stretcher and were ready to take him away, the officer said he had to drive me down to the police station for further questioning. Honey, he was very polite. But I knew he would get in touch with Renato, that some identification Julio had on him would tell the police where he lived. And, anyway, Renato would have to know, would want to know.

"Renato," I said suddenly, "That's his brother's name."

At the police station I saw Renato was already there. He told me the hospital reported that Julio had been hit, not once, as I had believed, but twice, the second time on his left side, but that neither wound was critical. Julio might have to have a blood transfusion, Renato said, and that he was worried because like his mother and many in her family, from childhood Julio had a weak heart.

When the officers asked, Renato said he didn't know why Julio was on Palm Drive, but that he knew he was going to play a horse at the nearby dog track. (Later a hospital nurse found a racing ticket in his pants pocket, along with a note about it, and we learned the dog Julio bet on had come in third from last.) He said he didn't know of any drug involvement. The police suspected Julio of dealing, thought maybe he was meeting a contact. I remembered how he had asked me if I had a message for him, but I didn't say anything about that. Later I found out he was trying to get out of a promise he'd made about dealing, that he had called someone on his phone before he went to the track.

Anyway, after the police found out I didn't know much, they drove me back to the Ramada, but said they might call on me again. I saw the sky had gone black — by this time it was late afternoon — saw dark clouds over the water near the seawall and that the bay was still. I wanted to ask the officers, "Where is the wind?"

But it was one of the officers who asked me. I had been quiet and I expect he was just making conversation.

"Where in the world is the wind?" he asked. "Do you think it is going to rain?"

Crack Cocaine: Two

*B*efore I left the police station, I had given Renato a hug. I felt like I'd known him always, and told him to stay in touch. I said I would like to visit Julio when I could in the hospital.

Once inside my room in the Ramada, I lay down on my bed right away, though it was only late afternoon. And except to get up once to get out of my clothes and go to the bathroom, I stayed in that bed, darlin', done in. And in the night dreamed of sirens, of red lights flashing and saw some out my window when I woke up, and looked out into the dark.

And it came to me that I was in a strange world, like the one that back in Nacogdoches I saw on television and that I had believed came only from the big cities like Houston and Dallas and, of course, New Orleans, and from up in Chicago or far out in California where they long ago made all the movies I like so much that took us through the Depression and the war. A world like the one I saw on TV news or read about — I could still read a little — in the paper. Guns firing out of nowhere, people hit on quiet streets! Deserted streets. Cars going crazily down the highways followed by ambulances and fire trucks and police.

All at once I was frightened. For I knew all this was not just in the big cities, and not just far away — but right here in Corpus Christi, right on the Body of Christ (which is all the world and all of us in it, darlin'), and which is not anymore just a sweet small place, a refuge sitting quietly on the water, a peaceful little town.

When I first saw it, the population came to 17,000. And back then, we all thought that for where it was in the world, that was quite a lot.

Oh, I thought it was the sweetest little town. And so did Elizabeth's mother.

"Oh, Rena, aren't you glad work brought us here?" she always asked me. Leeland and Daddy were building bridges and buildings and she was teaching music. "Isn't this the sweetest place? So quiet and pretty. Aren't you glad we came?"

And I was!

And I am when I remember.

But that night in my room at the Ramada Inn, I realized once and for all that the town was gone. And that the world I remembered was everywhere gone.

And when I saw those red lights flashing through my motel window, then heard the sirens, when they took me out of sleep, I asked myself: when Leeland sent me to Corpus Christi, was it just a dangerous world — more than ever a dangerous world, a violent world — he wanted me to find?

I turned on the television then, expecting to hear all about Julio, and maybe even about others in the same kind of trouble like him, and heard a hurricane warning instead. Angeline, the first of the season, the weather caster said. I remembered how black the sky had looked after Julio and I had careened down the highway and had been stopped by police and when a half hour later I had driven to the station with them, how dark it had been over the water and when I first looked at it, before I fell asleep on the bed, through the window. (To tell you the truth, I wasn't sure if it was really that dark or if it just seemed dark because of my frame of mind.) I remembered it being unusually still — the fierce wind seemed to have temporarily stopped blowing — and how the officer asked if I thought it was going to rain.

"Do you suppose that would cool us off?" he had asked finally, "Or leave us just steaming?"

I said I thought it had to bring some relief.

But the next morning and for two mornings to come, we had no rain although the sky was still darkened. And we still had heat.

Time seemed almost to have stopped and as it did, Renato came to see me and told me that Julio's heart had failed, and that he had died.

Churches

Renato's family held the funeral in the Catholic Church, the cathedral on top of the hill; this time its doors were open and I had no trouble getting inside. (A big place, darlin', regal with its tall ceiling and scrolled chairs with velvet kneelers. To be with Julio's family, I had to walk down the central aisle a long way.) But it was a stormy morning with a fierce wind blowing, some rain already falling and a report from the taxi driver's radio that hurricane Angeline which everyone hoped would play itself out in the Gulf, and had been hundreds of miles from us, was gathering momentum and heading directly for our coast. I guessed that news of the storm had delayed Searcy on his way to Corpus Christi and I hoped that he was safe.

I had called Searcy right after Renato visited and told him most of what had happened, and darlin', he was upset, told me he had always thought the trip back to Corpus Christi on the bus was a crazy idea, that I had no business being there alone and that he was coming to get me. I asked him to hold off for a day or two.

"Honey," I said, "If you insist on making the drive, I'll be delighted to see you. (I would be fine on a bus, I had told him.) But you need to wait until after the funeral." (I also thought that might be after the storm.) I said I had no idea why I had come to Corpus Christi in the first place, but I had become friendly with Renato who had helped me and who I liked, and I felt obliged to stay for the funeral of his baby brother.

One thing seemed sure — this trip featured funerals. And for this one, storm warning or no, Renato's relatives had come from far and near. If there was anything good about Julio being shot — and, darlin', I have learned that most suffering, bad as it is, brings some blessing — those who came together may have been it. The death of this boy brought his family back together; his sister and her children and even many cousins, once and twice removed, children of Renato's dead parents' brothers and sisters. Everybody, or almost (at least those who lived in Texas) except Reynaldo, and nobody knew where he was. The priest told all of us who were there that the church was that morning honoring the wish of family members to say something about and for Julio since most had just arrived and hadn't been at the wake, to begin. So before the Mass proper, each member who wished to say something ascended the steps to the pulpit and spoke.

And from that pulpit which, high up as it was, seemed made for kings and queens, Jesus, as head of the family, introduced each one. Only one brother, he said, was missing, Renato's twin.

"If anyone here knows anything of our brother, Reynaldo," Jesus said, "Please tell one of us. He left us years ago after our mother passed away. He grieved for her, as we all did, and maybe believed in a young man's way, that he would somehow find her again in another place. Or at least lose his grief."

(I thought then of how I had gone looking for Johnny after my baby died and I was trying to get over that and over losing Lucy. Johnny was the one person I thought I could talk to.)

This was the first time I had seen Jesus, the brother who had worked his way through teacher's college and become a teacher of little children. And he was, like I had always imagined the man he was named after, craggy faced — I often think of Mexicans as having smooth faces but, of course, not all do and besides, Jesus was half Italian — with a furrowed brow and fierce eyes (a passion burning through them, honey), but soft-spoken. In an odd way, a beautiful man. A serenity about him although he burned with life.

"And he may have lost that sorrow, or some of it, but he left us with more. And now that our youngest brother is with God, we call for word of Reynaldo again, and pray for both our brothers and offer thanksgiving for their lives."

That put me back on the train I rode into Mexico when I went off, down the coast on a bus and then onto that train at Laredo when I was only nineteen years old and already a mourner. I had spent almost every penny my cousins gave me, and some more I earned in a dress shop, on train fare, didn't stay anywhere, just spent weeks riding all over Mexico on a rickety train. I remembered someone at the Laredo station had called the one I took to Monterrey "The Silver Bullet." The first class trains were all called "bullets" because they were supposed to move with the speed of gunfire.

But this one hardly did, was slow and ugly, scarred paint on the cars inside and out.

My cousins back in Louisiana had spoken about Mexico as "a different world," and with my face pressed to the glass, I kept looking for it. Disappointed to see the same world, the same old world, with nothing different at all. The train was hot and noisy with babies crying, and everybody speaking fast, all that Tex-Mex Spanish ("Spic," Ellen called it). That was the same as in South Texas, but there, you heard some English, too. Maybe, I considered, I was, after all, going into a foreign place and that I would see it was foreign further on.

At the first little town where it stopped, I decided to get off since the ticket taker who did speak a little English indicated to me we would be there for awhile and I was curious about what was for sale. Through the window I could see a half dozen vendors holding up their wares, an old man with sacks of what I found out were peanuts, several women with plates of food (fried chicken and fish), another with flowers and there were little children, too, holding up sticks of gum and candy.

When I got off and stepped to the ground, an old woman came toward me with herbs and another with a blanket. Maybe they thought I looked cold or sick. Or maybe they just thought I looked like a person with enough money to be a buyer. I could see they were poor, darlin', and I thought if I bought a few things I might help them a little though I was poor enough myself. I told myself I should get something like one of the handmade necklaces one of the women showed me that would last awhile and bring pleasure to someone. I thought about Mammy then. She liked jewelry. I knew she worried about me. I gave the woman the pesos she asked for and took a necklace from her with blue stones. I would mail it from Monterrey along with a card.

When I got back on the train and began to study it, the vendors came on selling food, sugar cane, tequila and fruit, but, hungry as I was and thirsty, I was afraid it might make me sick and I also thought I should, for awhile, hang on to my money. But then a light-skinned, sandy-haired man got on and offered me a tin of juice, pink grapefruit, he said, and sweet, from the Texas valley and I took it and thanked him, grateful to have my thirst quenched and for his presence (I needed someone to speak to, darlin'), as the train rattled along and he sat next to me. I had not learned Spanish, honey, and when I got on this train it hit me that unless I saw more Anglos, I might never be able to speak.

Right away I introduced myself, explaining that I was traveling in Mexico for the first time.

"All by yourself?" he asked.

Yes, I said, but added that I hoped to find my brother in Monterrey. My brother had left Louisiana for South Texas, I explained, and South Texas for Mexico where he had gone in the interior. I hoped I would have news of him at one of the hotels in Monterrey.

"What is his name?" the man asked, interested.

"Johnny," I said, "Johnny Brock."

He pulled a wallet out of his pocket then, and took a card out of it and handed it to me.

"Ask about him there," he said, pointing to the name on the card. "Tell them Ray sent you. And good luck."

Then he put his face into the Laredo newspaper and didn't take it out until just before he got off at a little place where when I looked out the window I saw more vendors. After I realized we were going to be there for awhile, I got off the train to buy some candy from ragged children (I was starvin, darlin', but afraid to eat a piece of their mother's fish) but by the time I did, Ray had disappeared up the road.

CLUB FANTASTICO was what the card he had given me said, a spectacular nightclub I was told when I arrived in Monterrey, with tropical birds and trained zoo animals.

I didn't get there until the next day because our train broke down that night, stranding us in a desert-like place under a bright dome, a whole big sky full of stars. As I looked out the window, I thought of Mary M.

Earth Mother, I thought. Star Mother.

Before this, the silence of the night had come to me through the window even though the wheels on the rails were making a lot of noise. Everything was dark except for the big moon centered in the window and circling it, or seeming to, the stars.

I drifted into sleep with a sense of peace, honey, and I guess it was hours later when the big bang woke me up. I was scared until I realized the noise came from the brake. Why were we stopping in the middle of the desert? We never found out, but a few hours later we were going again.

During this time everyone was awake and told stories of their lives, and I thought of Johnny and how he used to introduce Lucy and me.

"Lucy who stays at home and helps us all so much, and Rena who gallivants and visits with all the people."

Then to make me feel better he would grin and say, "She's like me that way, I guess."

While we talked of our lives and laughing and joking (that made us less afraid), a man took out his guitar and we all sang "*Cielito Lindo.*" I was singing as the sun came up and I never forgot the colors I saw in the sky or the green land, for we were in, by that time, a green place.

Jesus spoke of Julio's childhood, how Julio seemed to lose his speech after their mother died.

"We all grieved, but he who was her baby, especially. We hope he is with her now."

Renato got up then and said he had discovered his brother had written a note asking someone to count him out of a transaction that was to take place near the corner of Noakes and Palm Drive, that he had a good tip on a dog, a 20 to 1 shot, and he had saved and collected more than a hundred dollars to bet. (Honey, the dog's name was Angie — can you believe that? — nearly the same name as the hurricane whirling toward us from out in the Gulf.) The note Renato found in Julio's pocket said he had called and left a message, but he thought he had better also write to explain "why I don't anymore need this job."

Of course, he never mailed it — Renato couldn't find any envelope or address — but the telephone call got his message across. Renato's voice was close to breaking.

"He had never been mixed up in anything bad," Renato explained. "He was never a gang member. I don't believe he even knew much about gangs. If he had, he would have behaved differently. He would have been scared.

"He was a naive boy. If he wanted fast money, it was to help his family, for he worried for all of us, and if he got mixed up with gangs near his end, it was because he was so discouraged. He had been like that — more discouraged than the rest of us — since our mother's death."

Tears streamed down my face as he spoke. Johnny had wanted fast money, not just for himself, but I felt sure, to help his family, too. Before he left he often said he wanted to help us all. He had been running drugs, darlin' (though in those days, it was mostly marijuana).

All this came back to me as I heard about how Julio thought he would win big money on a dog. Renato said someone who hung out at the track and wanted to sell him a ticket probably made up this story. And that Julio thought he could use this money to help put food on the table and to pay his own way through the summer. When it came to spending money, sometimes he made errors in judgment. What fifteen-year-old doesn't?

Before he talked with anyone else in the family, he had lied about his age and agreed in writing to pay off a gas-eating old car (Jesus and Renato had just found out) and a cellular phone to go with it, and he hadn't had his learner's permit to drive long.

In the past years he had always had a job at the CALLER TIMES. This year the paper cut its staff, even cut those who worked in circulation. Julio hadn't known where else to get a job — he had never been good with fixing cars — if he had more sense about him, he would never have bought the one he drove — and he couldn't make anything much by working in yards (too many people were doing their own yard work or letting them go) and none of the stores were hiring, so he thought of the track as a place to make some fast money. Even if it had been, he thought of it too late. For he also had an idea about something else before (something more dangerous) or, more likely, met someone somewhere who had an idea about it for him. But he had no history of being mixed up in gangs or drugs, had been a home loving boy, and a happy little boy who liked to play ball and sing songs. Only after their mother had died — and she, too, had been taken from them because of a weak heart — had he become unhappy.

When Renato sat down, Mara rose to say that after they lost their mother, she had tried to be the mother of the family, and that she had felt responsible for Julio, especially, but taken special pleasure in him, too.

"He was a happy boy who enjoyed life!" She told everyone how he enjoyed his meals (he was a chunky boy, darlin') and how she liked to cook for him though she was just fourteen and not much more than a child herself, and how he liked to sing songs when Jesus, who was musical, played the guitar. And how he enjoyed the neighbor children and played ball, kicked around a ball with a bunch of Mexican boys who lived nearby, after supper.

But not too long after her *Quinceanera*, which her brothers gave her, although it cost their hard earned money, she met a young man who courted her and before she was seventeen, left the family and Corpus Christi for San Antonio to begin a family herself. And now she was a mother with her own children. They sat beside her, darlin', three pretty little girls no more than a few years apart, the youngest just a toddler, in fancy black net dresses, and pieces of black net pinned to their dark heads. (Mara wore black, too, with a black lace shawl over her head.)

As she spoke, I remembered from Mammy's naming book and also from Leeland's readings from the Bible that Mara's name meant "bitter." But she was not bitter though she had every reason to be. Something saving in her kept her this side of rancor, kept her speaking sweet.

That speaking somehow brought back Monterrey and the nightspot where I got the only news I ever had of Johnny after he ran away into Mexico and left the rest of us without any word.

And outside I could hear the wind blowing. The first thing the priest had said after we entered the church was that reports indicated Corpus

Christi might have gale force winds by noon, and for the safety of all of us mourners, the speakers would keep their remarks, and he the rest of the service, brief. And Jesus, when he rose, said he would speak for only a short time about his beloved little brother. That Julio would have wanted all of us who mourned him safe.

Then I thought again of Searcy and hoped he was all right. I knew he hoped to take me to the church. He said he would try to arrive in Corpus Christi before mid-morning. But he hadn't showed up, darlin', so I left a message for him at the Ramada Inn and took a taxi to the church. I thought we would probably have to head inland after he got here, maybe drive all the way to San Antone. Outside the cathedral, the wind made an eerie sound.

When I remembered Club Fantastico, I knew what Mara was feeling for her brother. For it was there in that strange supper club that I learned our own beloved Johnny had become a runner for drugs. (I somehow thought that might be true when I heard whispered talk about marijuana "pick ups" back in the Laredo station.) Although I had not been to a nightclub anywhere when I arrived there, the Fantastico was not like any I had imagined. In the first place, only a little of it was indoors — most of the place was garden, walled in, with monkeys and jungle birds in cages, and some other birds, along with a group of peacocks, just wandering or flying around.

When I entered the front door of that place and walked for the first time across the bar room that opened onto the fantastic park with its animals and even what looked like a couple of trapeze performers walking around in costume, I can tell you I heard my heart beat. My mouth went dry when I entered and it was hard for me to speak.

But when a waiter came over to me and asked me if I was meeting someone (he spoke in English when he saw I couldn't answer in Spanish), I shook my head no, then handed him the card the man had given me on the train. Then I told him, "The man who gave me this said you might have news here of my brother, Johnny Brock."

The waiter left me then and returned with a sandy-haired man, who looked and spoke like a Texan, and who guided me through the room and out the glass doors to the full expanse of lawn and seated me at a table.

He said, "What can I do for you, honey?"

I told him the man, Ray, who I met on the train, had said someone in the Fantastico might have news of my brother, Johnny Brock, who had disappeared several years ago.

Yes, he said, he knew Ray. Ray had been an employee of the club, but he didn't know Johnny.

"I'm sorry, hon, but I don't know anything about your brother. I'm afraid Ray sent you to the wrong place."

When I showed him letters Johnny had written to me, he just shook his head.

"I'm sorry, sweetheart," he said.

Then he asked me if I was also looking for a job. No, I told him, only for my brother.

"I'm sorry," he said, "I don't know what happened to your brother."

But something about the way he said it, or maybe it was just his expression, made me think he did. Then he asked if my husband was with me, and I said I had no husband. (No, darlin', it wasn't a smart thing to say.)

"Oh, then, is your mother or father with you?" And I shook my head.

He walked me down the hill then and seated me at a table, and told me he would bring me a menu and that he wanted me to order anything I liked and that my dinner would be on the house.

He said, "Honey, after your long trip you must be starved."

Then he disappeared and in a few minutes, a waiter brought me a large gold menu with *Club Fantastico* scrawled across the front, and another man, a good looking Mexican, sat down beside me, and made some smooth conversation, telling me I looked like I should be on the American stage — this was before the movies had taken hold — then moved his chair in closer and closer to mine, and asked the orchestra which was nearby to play what I can only say was a wild song and the next thing I knew that man's hand cupped my breast.

And all through this time, the peacocks were screaming and an aerial artist was running back and forth on the high wire which had been set up down the hill. And I was getting dizzy from watching him and from a foamy drink! And I supposed I had, after all, found what people I had talked to said they came to Mexico for: a different world.

But it was chaos, darling. Behind the pretty name of that nightclub spangled across the front of it in gold letters, I found myself in a place of chaos where nothing made any sense.

All this came back to me in an instant as Mara told about her love for her baby brother, and as I heard the eerie wind whistling outside.

And then the priest say:

"*Padre Nuestro, que estas en el cielo, santicifado sea tu nombre.*"

In no time at all I was once again taking wafer and wine, for as we listened to the wind, the priest hurried through the Mass.

And I left the church that stormy day in Corpus Christi, grateful for my escape through a garden wall from Club Fantastico sixty years before. As I ran I heard that pimp screaming at me that my brother had been a drug runner. "He was a no good runner. I expect he's dead by now."

All that long time ago I had been lucky to make my way back to the train and to ride all the way to Veracruz where I thought I saw Johnny making his way down a hill to the sea.

Later after riding a long ways on a train that traveled west, in Guadalajara where I got off for a day or two, I saw a flower seller somehow wear his face. And then in Manzanillo, a mask-maker who wanted to sell me one of his creations picked a mask up from his counter and held it in front of him and I screamed because for just a minute, the face I saw was Johnny's! I decided then I might be a little crazy and that I should go home. (I would have had to anyway for I had only enough pesos to ride the train back across the country and into Texas, where I hoped to get another train up the coast into Louisiana with the ten dollar bill still left in my bag.)

And I did, darlin', and Mammy, when she saw me, wept and wept.

"You are so skinny," she said over and over as she brimmed my plate with garden vegetables and chicken fricassee, and later, wearing the necklace with blue stones I had sent her, spooned up a bowl full of berry cobbler for my dessert. She thought that not just Johnny and Lucy, but that all of her children might be dead. And to tell you the truth, I felt like I very nearly was. I had hardly eaten in weeks.

All this came back and yet was leaving me as I moved toward the center aisle in that cathedral in Corpus Christi where I attended Julio's funeral and took the Sacrament at the end of a High Mass.

I bumped into Renato then and felt his arm go round me. He brought me back to myself and felt so good to me, darlin'. And I knew why I was there. This boy and I were linked.

I didn't understand the reason for it — could hear Leeland saying, when I asked why he and I were together, "There's no reason, it just is." — or why.

I guess life's not what they call a linear equation or maybe any other kind — I was never good at mathematics, darlin', or in translating languages, or even learning them. Or in science class. I didn't know why — and maybe there was no why — but he might have been my own child, or Lucy's or Johnny's. I felt as close to him also as I always had to Searcy who long ago came into my life. And who I hoped was still safe.

I wondered where Searcy was.

But didn't wonder long for we had no sooner walked through the cathedral's big front doors when I saw him at the bottom of the steps.

"Searcy," I called as I stepped into the wind — and rain, too, darlin', for it had begun to fall — still holding onto Renato.

"Searcy," I called again and saw him wave.

In a parked car I also saw the stranger (a handkerchief tied around his face, and yet the part that showed eyes and forehead looked familiar), but I hadn't any time to think who this was. The idea that something was not right about me seeing that man in the car did go through my head, but mostly I was concentrating on telling Searcy that we had to get out of Corpus Christi, and I was going to ask Renato if he or any in his family needed a ride. (Oh, but darlin', they still had the cemetery to get to.) But I didn't get the question out. I saw that the man in the car somehow made the same shape as Renato, for all the world looked like Renato, could have been Renato if Renato had not been right beside me, holding me under one arm.

And then in an instant I heard the pop through the weird sound the wind was making, and the splashing sound the rain was making, the pop through all of that, through the wet plopping and the whooo, whooo, whooo.

And in that same instant felt myself falling (into some terrible pain, darlin'.) Was Renato falling, too?

Oh, it's hard to tell you how it was.

But fantastic as it sounds — in my life this church had become a Club Fantastico Number Two — the wind finally had me. And sucked me into its vortex, a dark funnel.

The Causeway to Portland

The Causeway to Portland

*W*as it my own death? Was that what Leeland had sent me to find? If he had, I didn't recognize it.

Just fell into the wind (and for awhile into pain, darlin'), then mostly into the SOUND the wind was making, a hmmmmm, hmmmmm, hmmmmm, at first, then more distinct: an au ooo mm; then louder, AU OOO MM, AU OOO MM, a grimness to that grinding noise. And that scared me.

(But once I got past it — or, maybe just into it, through to its center — dying wasn't bad.)

Oh, what is happening to me, I wondered. I didn't see Searcy anymore or the car or the street or Renato, didn't know anymore if Renato was beside me. I was lost in the awful noise and in blackness.

And I had no idea where, or even who, I was.

Rena Bell Dubuffet. Who are you? That was the question The Wind had always been asking.

And now I asked it, too. (Or asked most of it. I couldn't remember my name.)

And had no answer. Only again the question over and over again.

And then though I was still lost in blackness and the relentless grinding noise (that would not stop) and into what seemed like some terrible disorder, I sensed — don't ask me how — that I was on or near the Harbor Bridge over the ship basin that connected the Causeway to Portland and that soon I would be able to see just where.

On the bridge, darlin'. Crossing over. Was it still a drawbridge? (I didn't think so.) How many times when I lived in Corpus Christi had we been caught on one side or the other with the bridge up and boats passing under, waiting for whole half hour stretches and feeling our lives slipping away, in un-airconditioned cars?

I looked down through the sheets of rain that were gusting across the place where I stood, and which were whipping me hard, at the ships being rocked in their basin and then up toward the Causeway on the other side. And to one side of it the shiny building with all the Texas fishes who I guessed must be still chasing and calling to one another and some eating one another, but who at least didn't have to worry about the dark, who (were either equipped to see in it if they had to or didn't need sight) and all this wind and rain.

I had a hard time making my way to that highway, along the railing nearest North Beach and Corpus Christi bay, and past the gleaming house with the Gulf fishes — and no, darlin', no cars and no one was a comin' — I would have welcomed them if they had! — feeling for all the world like Mary M. fighting the fierce wind and the rain. And after a long time of walking — oh, my walk of a few days before past all the churches on the hill had been short by comparison (but good practice), seeing someone who looked like Jesus (the Jesus in the Bible, darlin') or the way I thought of Him, before me, smiling at me, and more and more resembling Renato's older brother, then fading away into the storm. No sign that would stop; the rain was really coming down. And big waves kept breaking right over the road.

And I thought, why, after all, heaven may be lateral. And our world, even those parts below sea level, God's body, not a way station that we just pass through on our way somewhere — our world all broken and bruised and scarred from abuse, but not just a stop on our route, not a place we can wreck and abandon.

But our eternal home.

It came to me then that with all the suffering in the world God must suffer most, that whatever happens to us must happen to God, too. (God, a word, darling and, yes, The Word, but part of us and living — A He-She-It — we are never separated from.)

As I found myself on that highway with rain pounding and the wind whipping me (but me somehow being able to stand it), I thought, why Heaven is not some distant place but right here. No more foreign than Mexico had been to me when I went there as a girl (looking for another world and, except for Club Fantastico, finding the same old one).

I worried I might never get down that highway. I walked and walked, all bent over, holding onto the railing and soaked clear through and didn't seem to get very far. And wondered how I was able to move at all. I didn't know what had happened, or where I was walking or what for.

It was a hard passage, honey. And to tell you the truth, I was about ready to give up on it and maybe would have if I had known how to do that but I saw, or thought I saw, through the gusts of rain and wind a shed of some kind a little way down the road and way beyond that I seemed to see a light.

(I thought then of Johnny, of Lucy and I running after him and of the fireflies we all wanted to trap in our jars.)

And I told myself, well, maybe I can reach that, the shed anyway, which would give me some shelter and would maybe even have a bench in it where I could for awhile sit down. If I could rest myself for a time and dry out a little, I might then be able to think of what next to do.

I hadn't considered this long when I seemed to see Bo Bell coming toward me, crossing over toward me from the other side, the Nueces Bay side of the road, waving and calling and, honey, he was the last person in all the world (or beyond it) that I was looking for.

Bo had died, I knew some years before, for Searcy told me he had a letter from Leona — Elizabeth's mother, Bo's sister — who had cared for him during his last years of heart attack and stroke, and who lived nearby — in a town nearby — though we never visited. (And I wonder now why not.)

Anyway, I thought I saw Bo — waving and crossing the Causeway, and through all the wind and rain walking straight toward me — who wanted to speak of his life.

Bo had cared for a shy young woman who everybody thought he might one day marry — and who he even planned to marry but never did though they once had a date set at the Methodist church. He liked her, darlin', loved her in his way, and would have liked to have had his own home with a wife and children like other people. But he couldn't go through with the wedding ceremony.

As I may have told you, he cared for a young man, too. A person who brought light to his life and a kind of magic and was the one he most wanted. But couldn't have in that time and place. (Not and be accepted by his family. Not and keep his job.) And after Ellen Bell died he just went to pieces, drank himself into a state institution — the insane asylum, darlin'. Bud and Leona put him there after he one time in a drunken rage threatened one or the other of them (and I now forget which one) with a kitchen knife.

Leona first called the Corpus Christi police who took Bo off to the city jail and after he sobered up, he requested a place to dry out. But never thought that place would be the state hospital for the mentally ill in Austin which at that time was a true crazy house. And never mind that they said he would be in the alcoholics ward, they just threw him in a room with all those poor, deranged people, and some of them had drunk too much I guess, and some were just nuts. But none of them, those who had drunk so much they had fried their brains or those whose brains were fried for other reasons, were getting any help.

By the time Bo got out, it was too late for him to do anything much except live with his sister — by then her husband, Bud, was gone. And, of course, Elizabeth, too — Elizabeth worked on her radio shows and for this station and that for National Public Radio (which none of us much heard) in many places across the country.

Well, anyway, it seemed that on the Causeway to Portland which was taking me forever to get across, in all that rain and gusting wind with waves crashing over the road nearly knocking me over and causing me, while fighting the spray from the water, to hang on hard, to the rail, I saw Bo Bell who wanted to tell me something. And as he came closer, I seemed to know what it was.

Rena, I had a sad life, he seemed to want to say. Except when I was drinking, I never had any fun. And only in the early days of that, because drinking became my torture even though that wasn't what I was after. I wanted to enjoy my life. The way you seemed to.

I wanted to tell him then there was plenty of hurt in my life, hurt and loss, loss, honey. But I couldn't seem to speak to him somehow.

Through all that storm, I saw him and was close. And yet, wasn't.

Nothing made any sense.

(Oh, God, I wanted to cry out. Oh, our Father-Mother. Is it You and not Bo that I should be addressing? Or are You, somehow, one and the same?)

But for what seemed a long time, I couldn't speak at all. I was in paralysis, honey, a paralysis of the throat.

"Bo," I managed to say, finally — he had reached me and I held onto one of his arms — "Hold on to this railing with me. (Oh, honey, the wind was beating us, we were both drenched.) Tell me why it is we can withstand this and why we are here together and where we may be going?"

But he didn't answer. And that was because (I felt sure) he didn't know.

"Well, then," I told him. "What is it you want to say? Just tell me what you can."

"Rena," he said into the salt spray, into the wet dark, "I want to tell you about what I wanted. I want to talk about desire."

"Well, hold on to me, honey," I told him, "And maybe you can do it."

I pointed up the highway toward the little road side shed — yes, darlin', it was still there! "Maybe if we sit down up there, you can tell me. We can make it if we walk together. This storm may be dying down."

I made that up to comfort him and me, too, but as I spoke, the wind did seem to be subsiding some.

Walking with our arms around each other, holding each other up, so to speak, after a time we reached the shelter and yes, it had a roof and a little bench inside and cold and wet as we were (why cold I don't know because we had made our way through hot rain), it felt so good to sit there and to rest. But we hadn't done that long when Bo began his story.

(I believe we sat at a bus stop, darling, though I don't remember seeing it when I made my bus trip down from Nacogdoches and cross the Causeway into C.C.)

"I met him in San Diego when I was in the navy," Bo said. "And there, another person in my outfit was also from Corpus Christi, a man named Frank, who ran the Mexican restaurant we all went to before and after War II. Jay was a beautiful person — beautiful in almost every way, and just by being near, brought a shine to my life I never thought really existed.

"But I was too timid to get to know him well, and didn't see him again until I came back to Corpus Christi. Saw him when we went to the restaurant, Las Hadas, one Friday night to eat our dinner. Hard to believe, but there he was, working with his paints in the hall — painting a mural. And the sight of him took my breath. I came to a dead stop there in that entry way, Mother who was in her 80s on my arm.

"Do you remember me?" I thought maybe I blushed when I asked him. Though I probably didn't, Rena. Not with this olive skin.

"'Sure I do, Bo,'" he told me and stepped down from his step ladder and took my hand. And when he did a shock surged through me. But that shock was sweet.

"He usually stuttered, you know, was a stutterer, but that day when he talked to me, didn't, not at all.

"He was living here with Frank, he said, their rooms on an upper floor. He asked if I knew Frank and I said not well. Everybody in Corpus Christi knew that Frank was queer. I couldn't very well have had anything to do with him, he was a laughing stock, the same as a freak — worse, a blight on the town! Most people whispered about him. Or pretended he didn't exist. Only the brazen laughed. Men mostly. Ha! Big men.

"I couldn't have anything to do with Frank.

"Not that I ever really wanted to. He didn't interest me much even though we had been in the navy together in San Diego where we both knew Jay.

"No, I told him. I had never really gotten to know Frank, though I liked eating at his place. Then I asked Jay to come out to the house sometime, and he said he would, and as you remember, did. What else happened during that evening I don't remember, how Mother and I got through our dinner or went home. (I was in a trance.) After we spoke Jay disappeared. But I do know from then until a long time after, life took on color and meaning and had a shape, so that I couldn't wait to get up in the mornings. And when I looked out the back windows from my bed on the sun porch at the grape arbor and the willow tree and on the other side of the walk at the flower bed with the banana trees and black roses, I saw that they all shimmered, were surrounded by a glow.

"And saw that it came from them. And when I put out my hand before me, I saw that a glow came from it, too. Saw for the first time, though I was in my forties, that the world was living. And that I was alive, too.

"I began to eat my lunch at Las Hadas every Monday. And would have gone more often if I hadn't known that would create talk.

"Do you remember, Rena? At this time the girl — Robin Lee — was in my life, a shy sad-looking mousey thing. But she cared for me and we had a good time together. And one time she surprised me by being bold. She asked me to make her my wife. And I said yes before I knew what I was doing. And I might have gone through with it. But couldn't after I met Jay and couldn't keep seeing him either. The town had begun to talk. The old bastard I worked for put me on the carpet. 'Who are his people? Where does he come from? You don't know that boy, really. I don't think you know what you are doing.'

"So, Rena, I drank myself into the insane asylum. And when I got out except for Leona — who became my keeper — I was all alone. And then lost my health.

"And now I'm here."

"Well, me too, darlin'," I said, "And if we ever warm up and get our strength here, and if this storm ever really passes we can just go on." Maybe it was because I was in the shed, but I did think the storm was dying down.

"But," he said, "I didn't finish the other part."

"Well, I guess you did," I said, "In your way."

I thought of Elizabeth then and wondered what she would tell me, or someone, when her life was over. I remembered the boy, Ben, she had cared so much for. And her friend, Bartola, whom I had met at Kress's.

Once when I lived back in East Texas and was remembering Elizabeth I thought I heard her say:

"Aunt Rena, maybe I missed love. Do you think Uncle Bo and I have that in common?"

I could hear her asking that. Hear her saying, "Uncle Bo fell in love with that young man. Jay, wasn't that his name?

"When I was in high school you know how I felt about Ben. Oh, I don't know that it was love exactly, but it was a powerful yearning. I think Uncle Bo felt that, too. Not that he ever said so, but you know when someone close to you experiences something powerful the same as, and at the same time as, you.

"Maybe I couldn't have known love until much later when it was too late, but I did have that yearning early, and who knows what it would have become? You always thought Ben and I should have just run off together.

"But I was afraid. Afraid I'd lose myself. Finally I paid a high price not to do that. Was it worth it?

"Even now I don't know. All I know is I never wanted Uncle Bo's fate. Poor Uncle Bo! A human sacrifice! For all of us. And then lost love and himself, too. I never wanted to be a martyr, didn't think in the long run I could help anyone by being a martyr. I wanted to be bold as Bartola, but couldn't be.

"And being bold like Bartola finally might not have been such a good thing. But I wish I had been a little more open, more receptive. I wish I had been more like you."

When I lived in East Texas I imagined she said all that to me.

And standing there on the Causeway I remembered hearing her with Ben one hot May night on Bo's porch, and seeing the silhouette of both of them, the scent of natural gas and gardenia in the air. And the whole porch illuminated by the bright moon, a full moon, darlin'. But because they were there together, clinging, I turned my face away, wanting to leave them to their privacy like I wanted to leave that old man in Oaxaca to his. I was in the living room where I had just turned out a light, just the other side of the front door screen. Darlin', it didn't seem right to look. I watched her hands, small but strong and agile, run up his arms, across his wide shoulders, rumple his silky blue shirt.

"Ben, Ben," I heard her moaning, and it was a sound to break the heart. And then heard him whispering something, and both of them sighing. And her crying. I think she was crying.

Hearing their sighs, and then her crying, as she pulled away and reached for the door, broke my heart. She was my child, was like my own child, anyway, and I couldn't help her.

"I have to go in now, Ben," I heard her say. "And I can't see you as often. Maybe I shouldn't see you any more."

She wasn't far from me, was just out the porch through the door — the two of them were caught in a circle of light — but even if I walked through it and went to her, I couldn't help her wrestle with her life's dilemma, couldn't help her handle the pain.

That hurt me, darlin'.

And then standing there on that bridge, my own life mostly behind me, in my mind's eye I saw Elizabeth from a distance from the seawall where she was with Bartola — a blazing August noon. She was always flooded with light, whether I remembered her in a night scene like the one I saw on the porch with Ben or on a scorching summer day. Maybe that was because what I learned from her brought me her truth: that taking what we want always has a high price. (I wanted Leeland, but look what all came with him!)

The day I saw her with Bartola was the last summer either of us was in Corpus Christi and one of the last memories I have of her when she was young. They were holding hands, swinging along the seawall together, behind them the sun burning a hole through all the world it seemed, surely through our bodies and brains as well as through the August sky. Searing heat, darlin'. Searing light. And in it I knew something.

Elizabeth, like her Uncle Bo, would be forever single. When I saw her later in the dime store (under bright fluorescent lights) talking to Bartola, who I met for the first and last time, she showed me the garnet Bartola had given her after their lunch together, from a new line Kress's carried of semi-precious stones. And when she lifted her hand for me to see it — and with the fluorescence bounding off the gem stone, it was circled with red light! I was both glad for her and filled with sorrow.

For in that artificial brightness who she was, and her fate — some now say "Karma," darlin' — was revealed.

Ellen Bell stood in front of us then — where did she come from, I wondered. I guess for a long time I didn't know because I had been looking straight at Bo who rose to scoop her in from out of the wind — which had subsided, yes, but was still blowin', darling — and draw her into our shelter and after she was inside, kept his arm around her, something, as much as he cared for her in life, he rarely did. Even odder: she put her arm around him.

"Rena, I was a block of wood," she said, looking straight at me. She looked up at Bo then. (Darlin', he was very tall — his head all but bumped the shed ceiling — and she was a little thing.) "Do you know they called us 'The Odd Couple?'"

Then Bo said, "They called Leona and me that, too."

I knew that what he was telling me was that the town thought the attachment between them, Bo and his mother, Ellen, and Bo and his sister, Leona, was too strong, un-natural, even. Incestuous was the word nobody would say. (Given the close conditions under which the Bells lived, the way in which they shut the door on others, the assumption some made wasn't hard to understand.)

I got up then so they could sit down and I walked to the edge of the shed and looked out on the Causeway, still covered with water. But the waves weren't anymore breaking over it. I looked toward Portland and I thought I saw Jesus again. Jesus from the Bible, looking for all the world like Renato's school teacher brother, but He vanished and instead I saw Lucy, just as I had for many years, and then she vanished and near the little light way up the road — oh, I was sure of it though they were just small figures — Mammy and Papa J, waving and calling to me, but then they disappeared, too — oh, darlin', this was a strange highway! — and I was wondering if I would soon see Johnny, when Julio stood before me.

Right there on the Causeway real as life. And he said, "Thank you for coming to my funeral and tell my brothers Jesus and Renato and my sister, Mara, not to grieve anymore, that I'm OK."

And I said, without asking him a single question about where he had come from or how it was he suddenly appeared, "I will if I can, darlin'. But it looks as if I won't be able to; we are on the other side of the channel from them now — see back there."

I turned toward Harbor Bridge as I spoke.

"The bridge is behind us and we are moving the other way."

(In the olden days the drawbridge would have been up.) Then I introduced Bo and Ellen Bell.

"I guess," I told him, "We were all meant to walk to Portland together."

I pointed. And as I did, I thought once again I saw my mother and father and little sister (Clarity), near the light down that way.

Scared me, darlin', somehow scared me to see them. I had seen Lucy, of course, here and there for years, but it was different seeing her here. So I turned all the way around.

I thought no matter what I had just said, I might get away from all these people (the Bells and Julio and my family up the road) who, after all, must be just thoughts or shadows. For as long as I could remember I had been fooled by shadows. Or maybe we were all just in a fantasy together, some sort of fantastic illusion that had come in a dream at the end of my life and sucked me in it and given me my own part to play.

For a minute I considered walking back toward Harbor Bridge to see if I couldn't get across some way back to where my life was, to the Cathedral steps where I had last been and to the heart of Corpus Christi.

I looked across at the beach then, and a long way back to North Beach — and I thought I could see even in this wet, wild night, the Ferris wheel lighted and going round, and from one of the seats rocking on the very top, some people who were waving. Were they really there? It was a long way back.

How could they be? How could a Ferris wheel be running so soon after a big storm? But maybe, I reflected, it was really early in the evening, not the middle of some dark night — after all, it had still been morning when I was in the cathedral and maybe now that the worst of the storm was over, businesses had started up again and life was, as usual just going on. I would walk back to the bridge to find out, though it was far.

I wasn't sure I could make it. I had come a long way, and without Bo's help might never have reached the little shed. Even with the storm dying down I might never go all the way back again. Just thinking about it, darlin', somehow felt like defeat.

First, I decided, before I did anything else, I would go back to the shed and say good-bye to Bo and Ellen Bell.

And when I turned to do that, I looked at a young woman with my face, darlin', or anyway with a face that had some of my features.

She just smiled at me and then a bus arrived at the shed where Bo and Ellen had been sitting and without saying a word or even thinking about it, we all, Bo, Ellen, Juliette and me (yes, darlin') all got on. When we did I saw that Myrna was the driver — I was sure I was in a dream then — and her assistant, a person who asked us our names and then spoke them into a tape recorder (we gave our names instead of money to pay for passage, darlin'), was none other than Billy Park! Both of them when they saw me started laughing. (Juliette and I sat right up front near them and Bo and Ellen went farther in.)

"Why," I said, "Where have you been? And what brings you here?"

And asked myself, Oh! What kind of dream, what sort of strange dream, a Club Fantastico am I in?

"I always wanted to be in the driver's seat," Myrna told me, "Ever since you and I went traveling together. Remember how I drove in Mexico? And now I, once again, am. Honey, I died in an automobile accident. If I had been driving I would have lived on!"

She just whooped with laughter then, and Billy, too. (They said that just a little while before they had been riding the Ferris wheel at North Beach.)

Billy told me that his death had also been connected to a mode of transportation. He had been hit by a car while crossing the street to get to the funeral parlor (to meet his mother who was making arrangements for a "family plan") and the doctors had to take off his bad leg, and during the operation he hemorrhaged and never came to.

"I guess nobody ever expected me to live long," he said.

Then he looked at me and asked, "What happened to you?"

And I told him what I suddenly knew, that I was shot by Renato's brother, Reynaldo Santos, who may have been aiming for Renato instead, who maybe thought Renato wanted his territory or had used Julio to find him so he could squeal on him to the police. One or the other. (And poor Renato didn't even know where his brother was!)

I said, "Renato was a boy I met in Kress's whose family was in trouble."

All at once I wondered what had happened to Julio, if he had got on the bus before us. I turned my head to look around.

And waved to Ellen and Bo who I could see sitting near the middle. I wondered who else was on this bus. I didn't see anybody much. But then in the back it was dark.

Juliette, who sat beside me, just smiled, and shy as I was with her, I reached over and touched her hand. I was so glad she was with me! Then when I looked out the front window, I saw way up the road, near the grade that swooped just a little way up to Portland, little figures that somehow seemed to me to be Mammy and Papa J and Lucy, and what looked like — I didn't dare even think the name — (oh, could it be?) — All of them smiling and waving.

I was glad the bus had come (even if everything was happening too fast). Bless Myrna's heart! She had always helped me out. And I was glad to see poor Billy Park. Mostly I was glad I hadn't quit, hadn't turned back. And I relaxed a little and grew silent as we sped along.

As she drove, Myrna talked some. Told me all about those we both knew that she had recently seen, or transported. Not long ago she said she picked up an old friend of Bill Powers, a buddy from world War II, and had a good time visiting with him as they traveled across and then enjoyed catching up with Bill who helped him with his bags when he got off the bus at Portland. She thought some of Bill's family, maybe his wife, was with him and there to help, too.

"Sure enough!" I said. "I wonder if I'll get to run into him at all."

But when I looked ahead, I wondered if I was really seeing what I thought: Mammy and Papa J and Lucy — and someone else — way up the road. Maybe I was hallucinating or it was some other people. I supposed I would soon find out.

But the Causeway seemed endless, the way it never had in life, and our trip took quite awhile. When I looked out the window I saw the rain had really stopped. I guessed the wind was still blowing (didn't it always?) since our bus rocked. I seemed to see over the water bursts of sparks. (Lightning? Was it from lightning?) Then a flame that drew me into it or seemed to. I drowsed off, darlin'. Was I sleeping within the dream? Dreaming within the dream? Oh, darlin', even now I wouldn't say.

And when I woke I looked out at a sky full of white moonlight, then — was it sunlight? Or that flame again? — into the color orange. The Sun Queen? I asked myself. Lucy's old friend and mine, had she awakened? Was it morning? Was I looking straight into the Sun Queen's light?

Or was it just Lucy's? Or were Lucy and the Sun Queen one and the same?

I didn't know, darlin'. I only knew the bus had stopped and that Myrna was shaking me to — gently shaking me to — and that before I knew it, I had disembarked.

And that Papa J was hugging me and Mammy. And then Lucy, who was not any more a vision, but real. ("Renee, before you know it we will together plant a garden!") And that we were all standing near a depot at the top of a hill. And that when I looked down it I saw the Causeway and Corpus Christi's shining, tall steel and glass buildings near the waterfront, on the other side. And that all the rest of wherever we were seemed to be sky. A feeling of boundlessness about it.

"Why," I said, "We are all in Portland. And I have never stopped here before. And I don't know a thing about this town."

And they all said I would get to know it (and that I would like it) before going farther on.

And, oh, I was so happy to be with them (and happy to see the morning) — Mammy and Papa J and Lucy, and Juliette who was still with me. Myrna, who waved to me, turned the bus around. But I saw all the others, except Billy Park (Julio and Bo and Ellen) had gotten off and walked away from where we were, in different directions, leaving me with blood kin, Mammy and Papa J and Lucy, and Juliette, who I didn't yet even know, though she was my very own child.

And then we all entered a bleak little cafe that sold coffee and doughnuts but was so depressing, darlin', with its down and out, or just very sleepy looking customers and its plain gray linoleum floor and stark white walls. Well, I thought, maybe it doesn't matter for, after all, we are in Portland. And as soon as we got seated at a couple of small tables, I looked up and for a moment thought I saw someone else. My brother.

But when I came close, he was gone. Why, it must have been just a shadow, I told myself. I must have only seen a shadow. One of those shadows I was always seeing. My own maybe? (I considered that.) Maybe I only saw my own shadow, I told myself. And it seemed almost funny, that kind of illusion.

I had grown excited over a phantom. But I had wanted to see Johnny standing there.

And I sat there in the cafe, blue, thinking of what he had meant to me, my brother, and dreaming of what he would say to me if he were really there. Oh, I wondered, why wasn't it Johnny I had seen instead of some illusion? Why could I never find Johnny? Even at the portals of eternity couldn't find him, but only air?

As I sat there I fell into dreaming. Saw him before me, darting through the trees, running straight into the darkness. Lucy and me behind after him and the fireflies with our open jars.

I hardly saw those around me. My family, I think, had exited, each trekking off in a different direction, though Juliette, I seem to remember, had lingered for a little while. "I'll be with you soon, honey," I think I had told her.

The cafe we were in, darlin', was the kind of place where many in poor little towns start their day — oh, just after sun-up, honey — as early maybe as 4:30; this one sold mostly doughnuts and coffee, but some in the town I had come from and like many of the towns Leeland and I had lived in, featured eggs and grits and biscuits and gravy.

Myrna told me she and Mr. Teague had once owned and run a little doughnut shop, but it drove her crazy. She had to get up at 3 and open the place to make the batter for the doughnuts and get them in the oven by 3:30, and that by the time she was ready to enjoy her own supper in the evening and maybe a beer or two, she had all but already passed out. Now what kind of life is that, I ask you?

She told me she finally said to Mr. Teague, "I don't care if we are making money, we are never awake to spend it and we haven't got any children." So they sold the business.

A big barrel-chested, dark-haired fellow and a skinny tow-headed girl had charge of the Portland place. I wasn't hungry at all, though God knows after what I had been through I ought to have been (I think I'd been through too much, darlin'), but ordered coffee and a box of doughnuts to split with the family if I ever again saw them, though coffee was mostly what I had. And even before it came, I fell to dreaming. And later as I sat there drinking it, the shadow that had been Johnny appeared in front of me and then fleshed out and finally began to speak of its life.

He had been a runner for marijuana, it said. But that was it. He never dealt at all in anything harder. He thought he would just do it for awhile to get some money together so he could buy himself a little business — maybe farm machinery.

"That's what Lucy's boy, your namesake does," I told him. "He's made it his life. The boy I call Johnny Two."

"That a fact?" This shade of Johnny asked.

"Well, I thought I might get enough money together to try it, and that maybe I could send some to all of you."

But he said he was one time in Laredo apprehended and had to flee the Texas and later some of the Mexican police. And that afterwards he worked for a club in Monterrey where he thought he might be safe until he found out how bad it was. And the ways in which they had plans to use him and that after that he just took off after the place shut down one night and went far into the interior, then after some time had passed came north again, but no further than Cuernavaca and finally settled in a crude house near the village of Tepoztlán, where he sometimes acted as a tour guide for hikers. (By this time he could speak pretty well in Spanish.) The soil, he said, was too rocky to grow anything much. But he didn't mind, he said, since he had never been in love with farming as he was sure I knew and maybe wouldn't have even liked selling farm machinery.

He did miss the water. He had always liked to fish and he missed the Gulf.

He got along, he said, though he didn't have much and after some years passed he no longer worried that he would be found by police and then he married a village girl he liked to be with and had three children, two girls and a boy, who as far as he knew, all still lived there.

By the time he was this far along in the conversation, I realized everyone had left the cafe but Johnny and me and that although I couldn't see it outside our window, I knew the sun had risen in the sky.

"I lived peacefully, Rena," the shade of Johnny told me. "I never made money like I planned and I couldn't help any of you and had to live apart." He said that was his sorrow, but in Tepoztlán, he didn't have a bad life. Everyone treated him all right and after awhile he realized he liked living there. He said he had beautiful children, the youngest a girl named Rena. "After my stories of you." Then one night, he told me, his heart stopped beating.

In my dream, as Johnny talked, I seemed to see the brilliant sky outside the little cafe and I felt such a peace coming over me — I think I may have been awake by then — and when I looked out the window saw Mammy and Papa J and the biggest surprise of all, my Juliette, returning. Though her questions broke my heart.

"Oh, Mother," she asked me later (yes, darlin', she called me "Mother"), "What did I miss? Would it have been good?"

What could I tell her? Do you suppose I was still dreaming? That I had dreams within my dreams, maybe?

And I saw the sky outside going all white, bathing all of us in it.

And when I rose and headed for the door (Johnny, or my dream of him, by this time seemed long gone) and opened it so that I could join the others, there he was. Leeland. There he stood before me. Grinning like he used to. Shy as he had always been.

"I'm glad you got here," he said.

I couldn't say a thing — but I had my arms around him — for I had begun to bawl.

Now, you may ask, was all of this a dream? All of what I have told you? Not just the part about Johnny? What was in the wind — that terrible wind and where did the terror and chaos in the wind come from? And why wasn't it all chaos and terror? Because it wasn't, darlin', awful as that terrible wind was, crazy as it was, and — eerie — there was way deep inside it, a weird sense. And something that forced us to use all of ourselves to be able to stand in it.

You may ask, what did it bring me? Or you may even ask, Rena, where are you now? Are you real, or are you just a voice in my head? You may even ask if I am your own voice maybe.

Oh, darlin', you think I have the answer to so many questions!

And I might ask you some of the very same ones. Who, you who hears me, who are you? Are you a friend or relation, or some stranger (but somebody I may like to meet)? Could one of you be Johnny? The brother I followed with an open heart? Or you, Searcy? Or Elizabeth, the second child I lost?

In Between

No, darlin', I didn't die then and couldn't from Portland go away with Leeland. But seeing him, and all the others on the road, prepared me for my actual death, which was very easy — when it came, my heart just stopped. And the life I had left, sweet, or mostly. Maybe I just don't remember the pain.

I don't know why I never did see Johnny. And still haven't, darlin'. But he lives inside of me and maybe that's the most important thing.

Maybe some of our outward connections really do get lost forever. And that we just have to accept that. Anyway, it surely seems to me that — though we have to go on looking, even in eternity some people we love, close to us as parts of ourselves and who are part of us, really, we may never be able to find.

What life was left to me I used to be with Searcy who I saw still needed me and wanted me to be near him and to get to know his new wife. She was a sensible girl, darlin', but didn't take life too seriously (together we laughed a lot), so we got along just fine.

But sweet as most of this time was, and as much as I used it to enjoy being with the only earthly family I had (I never saw Johnny Two and I didn't know where Elizabeth was), only half of me was in it. The other half even then was gone.

Had permanently crossed that Causeway, asking questions. Who am I? (Always asking, honey, always asking.) Who is Leeland? What is between us? Between me and this man I'm not finished with, who is somehow at my center, without my knowing why or being able to understand, a part of my being I need and must find.

But to get back to where I was and what I was telling you:

No sooner did my arms go round Leeland — the instant I saw his face, heard his voice — when I began to bawl. And then heard something besides my own crying: the sound that brought me to the Causeway and Portland in the first place. And I was overcome by the humming, the awful buzzing, the monotonous, singing sound which numbed me and held me prisoner.

And seemed to me louder, and with it the question: Rena Bell Dubuffet, who are you? (Was I or was the wind asking?) And then, why don't you finish what you start? And though Leeland's face had just been in front of me, the world suddenly went black and the question that seemed almost to come out of my own voice, carried me back into the sound, by then a kind of roaring, louder and more ongoing (not nice at all, darlin,) than any other I had ever known.

So that for just a moment I understood that all the world outside me that I even in blackness remembered — the bay and the Gulf beyond it, and all the fishes and the wind, and yes, all the people — Renato Santos and all his family; Julio and the drug runners; all those who laughed and cried over Julio and prayed together for him, as well as the one who had shot him, and all those who shot each other; and all those who fish and hunt as well as those who dart past the hooks and flee from hunters — I understood that all, all of these are the same, fish and fisherman, hunter and hunted, all all the same. And also the same as what is inside of me.

In that moment I understood, saw them move through and become each other. For just an instant before I became whatever I am now.

(And you tell me, darlin': What am I? What are any of us? What are you?) I understood this. But some way, it seemed all too big and too scary to keep in front of me and so I came back to whoever I am — the self I walked about in all those years, surely just a fragment caught up in everything else. (What do you see, darlin'?) Came back to my own voice, too — all I am now maybe. But that could be a lot.

Maybe my voice is in your head now so that part of it is you.

Is that right, Searcy?

Is that right, Elizabeth?

To whoever hears me: You who may also hear the wind... The wind singing and singing, singing all the way through me, all the way through you, through us as we are separate, and then again each other. (That's what spring meant to me every year in Corpus Christi, the sound of the wind, seeming to be all of us, singing through me and everybody and through the Gulf and Corpus Christi Bay and onto the shore.)

Coming To

$\mathcal{I}$ hadn't time to answer these questions or even to think about them much (and maybe I'll just leave them to you) because before I knew it, I opened my eyes and saw that I was in a white room that had to be in a hospital somewhere, and that Searcy was sitting beside me.

Was I glad, darlin'? Yes and no. I was glad to see him and glad not to be so confused about everything — just dizzy and floating through too much that was new and too many changes — glad to feel the solidity of the bed beneath me and the table beside it and to see the chips in the paint near the door, and even the ugly greyish liquid in the bottle to one side of me that I guess was going into the rubber tube that dangled from it and was attached to my arm.

But then an awful sense of loss came back to me. And Leeland's face. Oh, where was it? And Leeland? Oh, where, oh, where had he — and all my family — Lucy and Juliette who was so new — where had Leeland and all of them gone?

Although they had vanished and although I was now not sure I had ever had a solid sense of them, they and the place I had come from were more real than this hospital room. And never mind that I had been dizzy and floating for weeks and weeks; they remained more real to me than anyone or anywhere else. For a long while, darlin', the world was a shadow, though I couldn't let on.

"Aunt Rena," I heard Searcy say and saw him smiling down at me, "Aunt Rena, it's Searcy."

I had to laugh at that. "I know it's you, honey," I said, "Sure enough. But tell me, what has been going on?"

"Something good, I reckon, since you are coming to."

He told me then that I had been wounded in the shoulder and though the wound was superficial, the shock from the injury and loss of blood during the surgery had strained my heart. He said they weren't sure I was going to make it. He grinned wide then.

"Since you can speak to me I guess you have." Since he was a little boy he depended on my speaking to him, he said. "You told me the first I ever knew about my family. You explained the world."

"Oh, honey," I said, "I don't know that I can explain anything anymore. But I sure do have a lot more to tell you. And when I rest a bit I will. Seems like — for just a little while — I saw your mama."

He said he was sorry he ever got into the comfort he took from my speaking, that I probably shouldn't say any more, but just lie quietly. We saw then that the nurse was coming.

And when she said, "Why, look who is awake. How are you feeling?" I said, "A little weak, darlin'." Then I asked her the time and after she told me it was nearly noon I felt myself getting hungry and asked her if she thought I could have a little broth for lunch.

And before I knew it, the boy was there with a tray with a bowl of clear soup in it. Plain broth but I couldn't remember anything ever tasting so good.

That evening the same boy brought in a supper of toast and poached egg and the next morning a full breakfast and by afternoon I had the news that I could go home. And before I knew it Searcy drove us both through the streets and down Ocean Drive and Shoreline to the Ramada motel.

And, darlin', I saw telephone lines down and Corpus Christi as a soggy mess, so many trees broken with limbs still in some of the streets. And the place I had come from, Portland as well as the Causeway to it, seemed more real than what I saw before me in the world.

All the same, Searcy said Angeline hit Port Isabel, sparing Corpus the worst. He said he had stayed right with me in the hospital on a cot the night after my surgery, told me he had removed our things from the Ramada since it was evacuated and shut down.

Had just reopened the afternoon we arrived back there and you can believe they asked us plenty of questions — the boy at the desk and the one who walked us to our rooms — since they saw my shoulder was all bandaged and my arm in a sling. The Ramada had its own troubles; all the broken glass out front had not been cleaned up, some windows were still boarded up and most of the carpet in the lobby was water stained and some was still soaked.

On our ride in, I also noticed broken glass outside Water Street Market with its oyster bar and seafood cafe, and I figured most of the places on Shoreline were a mess. Still I saw the seafood cafe was open.

"Searcy," I said as we passed it, "Do you know what I'd like before I leave this town? Some seafood, maybe even oysters. I don't believe I've had any seafood in years."

"Well," Searcy said, "I guess seafood wouldn't hurt either of us, if that's what you want. But I don't know about oysters. They may be too rich and I don't believe they are in season. But we can see how you feel this evening and ask at the Water Street Cafe if you would like to go over there for dinner."

I told him maybe I couldn't eat much, probably not oysters even if the cafe had them, that maybe this yearning was mostly in my mind, but that I would like to go.

"Do you know what else I would like?" I asked him. "I would like to ask Renato and Jesus and whoever might still be around from the Santos family to come, too."

Searcy had told me first thing that Renato was all right, that I had received the bullet that had been intended for him and that the second bullet struck the church wall — fired as the gunman (Renato's own brother, darlin') was taking off.

"Well, we can call them," Searcy said, "If they would like to come that would be all right."

"I think it would be nice," I said, "If we made a little party."

When I said that I knew just why it was I had brought along my red dress, and bought to go with it, a loud pink scarf.

The Water Street Cafe

enato said he would be pleased to eat fish or shrimp or maybe even oysters with us at the Water Street Cafe. I told him if he could to also bring Jesus and his sister Mara and the little girls along, and anyone else he would like.

"Searcy wants to treat us," I told him when he mentioned expense, "and he has plenty of money."

Searcy groaned when he heard this, but I knew that though he wasn't a man of much means, he had enough with him to do this evening up with a little style.

Searcy and I seated ourselves by the front windows of the cafe and waited for the Santoses quite a while before the sun set over the water that last evening of my life in Corpus Christi.

Renato, when he did come in, grinned when he saw me, something he hadn't done, I don't believe, in days, brokenhearted as he was about both his brothers. The only good thing was that as far as we knew, Reynaldo hadn't killed anybody, only tried, so that if he wound up in Huntsville, it wouldn't be for life.

The three of us had not been at the long table near the front of the cafe where we could look out at the water more than just a few minutes when Mara came in with the three little girls who seemed to make a rainbow (no longer in black, but in pretty colors: pink and violet and green). And with her was her brother, Jesus, and all of them embraced Searcy and me, even two of the little girls, one — the older girl in green — who was shy, and the baby in pink who was bold. And Searcy ordered cokes for the children, and for the rest of us beers and iced tea. And a platter of French fries for the children and shrimp cocktails for the grown people, and when none of us objected to this order, told the waitress after we studied the menu we would continue on from there.

Although the world still seemed to me unreal, and I watched it turn into a pastel, a tinted shadow, I was at that time glad to be more or less in it.

"To all the Santos," Searcy said, lifting his frosted mug to Jesus and Renato and Mara after the drinks came, and then to me, adding, "And to my Aunt Rena whom we almost lost."

"To Julio," I said, looking at each one of them in turn and lifting my glass of tea.

Everyone drank then; even the little girls drank their coca cola. For Julio. And maybe also for me.

"It was a sweet service," I told them. "It sent him off in good standing." Then to Searcy I said, "When my time comes I want something like it. I have a little policy that should cover a plain coffin. I don't care about music or flowers or anything fancy, just that people I care about be there. You and Johnny Two if you can get him to come, and Maurine and your Bea. (That was his wife's name, "Bea.") And Elizabeth, if you can find her."

Searcy smiled and said, "We'll put you away nice."

Everyone laughed after that.

After I ate all I could of my shrimp cocktail, I decided I wanted to try the flounder which the menu said was the catch of the day.

"Nothing like fresh Texas flounder," I told them. "A sweet-Jesus fish, I always call it." (Jesus Himself seemed in it.)

Then the Jesus who was with us ordered flounder and so did Mara and Renato. Searcy ordered fried oysters which may not have been in season, but when they came he said tasted fine. As we got into our eating, we grew quiet as if we had been through a lifetime of suppers together.

From the time I had called Renato and asked him and his family to eat with us, a temporary calm fell over the world. But as we ate and I looked out the window, I saw the palm trees were once again blowing — the Santoses and all of us were quiet, so I was aware of the sipping sound from glasses and the clicking of spoons. And, all of a sudden, I seemed to hear the wind once again singing. The sound of it seemed to come right through the glass.

And I knew I was back to where I had always been and might always be, and that it was a place of perpetual beginnings.

Through the glass I heard the whooo, whooo, whooo all over again.

Rena Bell Dubuffet, the wind seemed to be singing.

Who am I? I had always wanted to ask the wind that and then to be able to answer the question. And then to ask and have an answer to: Who are you?

Who are all of you who hear me?

Is one of you Searcy? (Can you hear me, Searcy?)

Is one of you Elizabeth? (What do you have to tell me?)

And, Johnny, where ever did you go?

Oh, I keep listening, listening.

And sometimes it seems I can almost hear you and some one of you soon will tell me, that I will have another answer even as I am delivering my own. For part of you is me, and me you. Darlin', we are each other. And I can almost hear you. The wind keeps singing and singing.

I can almost hear your voice.

Looking For Johnny

For All Who Seek

"...we are all a part of one nature and from each other we learn how to live."

Matsu in Gail Tsukiyama's *The Samurai's Garden*

Acknowlegments

Thanks to my students at Los Angeles City College who have read and written about *Rena, A Late Journey*, for their many questions, as well as their interest in Johnny's story and for encouraging me to write it.

Thanks also to Susan Bright and Plain View Press for supporting my work through the decades.

Thanks to Valerie Garrett Miller for so generously giving of her time and talent to proofread this manuscript and for cheering me on during the publishing process.

For special assistance and proofreading, thanks to Mary McFadden Rosetto, in a city of angels, one of the brightest and best.

And thanks to John and Carolyn King Waller and all in their large Texas family, especially to Mike and Laura DeLaRosa for inspiring landscapes — with apologies for the liberties I've taken with their inviting home in Liberty Hill.

Many thanks to the talented Neil Potter for his invaluable technical assistance.

And, as always, thanks to my daughter, Bethel, for her loving support (and for making me so much luckier than my fictional heroine, Elizabeth McElroy) — and to the Corporation of Yaddo, where the first of my "Corpus Christi Novels" was conceived, for my writing life.

*Johnny and all his kin
are fictitious characters
and any resemblance to
living persons
is purely coincidental.*

The Only Home We'll Ever Have

*M*emory is the only home we'll ever have." And then on the heels of that, a voice whispering, "All memory is fiction."

Near the end of the 20th Century, Elizabeth McElroy —still mostly dark haired and scrappy —in her 67th year, daydreams working overtime in her just as they had when she was a girl, heard that somewhere and in one of the radio dramas she wrote for National Public Radio in Los Angeles that season, claimed the first declaration as her own.

Didn't want to admit to hearing the second; to shake it off, tried to pretend she hadn't. For the sake of making her radio play, said what the first voice spoke to her aloud. "Memory is the only home we'll ever have."

And yet, in her tiny apartment —all too near the freeway —she kept looking at maps of Texas where she had grown up. Kept imagining that she might one day buy a piece of land there, put a little something on it (never mind the heat or the politics), a small house or cabin, or even a simple shed which would give her shelter when she visited afternoons while at night she read or watched the tube in a not-too-far-away motel.

She hadn't become a sporadically paid radio dramatist because she was always sensible or stayed put —or cared about security as much as she ought —had she? Some restlessness had taken her toward risk and farther and farther away from whatever was familiar. Now she wanted to stop it, to go back the other way, back to some field where maybe, she told herself, she could rest, could for at least part of the year (a week or so in spring or fall, perhaps), settle.

It's all in your head, Elizabeth, she then countered, a fantasy.

But damn it, why was a retreat somewhere far fetched? As much as she liked writing and performing in her radio plays, as much, for that matter, as she often liked living in Southern California, she was tired of working ten hour days, tired of forever driving freeways, dodging trucks and other oversized machines (all of which looked as if they belonged on a battle field), tired of what sometimes felt like exile, wanted to STOP, to find a place that at least seemed hers.

She knew no one really owned land, but also knew that it was possible to belong to it, be one with it, and she wanted that, wanted to stretch out for a while in a place where she connected and just look at the sky.

If she knew how she could reach her Aunt Rena, departed this life for more than a decade, she would ask her how to do it. Aunt Rena had certainly conducted a few searches of her own —mostly for her older brother, Johnny who went off from Louisiana to Texas when he was just a boy to make money for the family and got lost somewhere. Rena crossed and recrossed Texas and then, Mexico —and got into some real scrapes — hoping to find him.

Except through prayer, or her notebooks (which were prayers, maybe, written down) Elizabeth didn't know how to reach Aunt Rena. Rena's nephew, Searcy, now in his eighties, was still living on a place somewhere near Nacogdoches —he had written to her when Rena died —but he wouldn't know anymore than she.

More immediate, more practical to ask her old friend, C. C., who lived in the Hill Country and who had children who had recently bought property in a place called Liberty Hill. That had a ring, didn't it? She would call C. C. and as soon as she could arrange it and manage time away, go to visit her. Maybe also, while she was in Texas, rent a car and take a side trip up to the piney woods to visit Searcy.

As things turned out, she went in the fall, not the spring as she often liked to do. In early November the radio station in Los Angeles where she worked unexpectedly gave her release time from her shows. Rumor had it that in seasons to come National Pubic Radio would no longer use dramas, and that she might be forced into interviewing or reporting (the demand seemed to be for more and more talk), and perhaps into semi retirement with a small pension from the Writers Guild.

All her life she had loved radio. Just as a medium she loved it. She would continue, at least on a part time basis, to do what her station requested. But. writing and performing dramas, that's where her heart was and where —what? (Beauty was the only word that came to her) — could be found.

Beauty. Beauty in the Texas countryside broke through mostly in the spring.

She was making this trip in the wrong season. But it did seem destined for her to use this time to go. The heat had broken, she and C. C. could take walks, recall old times when they both lived in Corpus Christi and went to high school, but reminisce about more than that. She remembered C. C.'s father and grandmother and, as far as she knew, C. C. was the only person on earth who remembered Aunt Rena, her mother and her own grandmother, and other relatives.

They would tell stories of these people as they picked up pecans fallen to the ground from the trees. Then in the evenings they would watch old movies and afterwards, in the upstairs bedroom of C. C.'s spacious house, she could speak to whomever she pleased in her notebooks and before consulting realtors or C.C.'s children, fall into hopeful dreams.

270

One: A Piece of Land

*W*ild as *The African Queen!*" (the movie they had seen on the first night of her visit), that's what C. C.'s middle child Louellen, visiting from Austin, told her about the land she and her husband had just bought as they sat in C. C.'s living room sipping from tall glasses of iced tea. C.C. made up half a dozen glasses of tea each morning, January through December of every year, covered them with plastic bags and filled them with ice later in the day. "But we're going to clear a portion of it —it's where we'll retire one day." Louellen pointed to a spot on the map she held in her hand and with her well manicured index finger, circled the words "Liberty Hill."

This young woman can't be more than a year or two over forty, Elizabeth noted, and yet she already has a future that most people her age don't like to think about literally in her hand. When I was her age all my energy went toward making my radio plays and getting connected to stations —no matter how small — that would broadcast them. I never thought of anything else, never gave a moment's consideration to, of all the out of the question things —retirement, something I never wanted to do. She still didn't, just wanted to slow down, take life a little easier, find a place somewhere to do that.

November or not, when she got off the plane the day before in Austin, Texas looked so green. So green —a reminder that she lived in a desert —and for all she read in the L. A. and *New York Times* (and she subscribed to both) about pollution in Texas, the sky, with a rose ball going down in it, was a clear, deep blue. Of course they were nowhere near a big city. As they climbed into the gentle hills with C. C. at the wheel of her Land Rover Elizabeth hadn't been able to take her eyes off of it. "It's so pretty here," she said, "so green, still. And the sky so clear and blue."

C. C. had nodded and said they had nice days in fall and spring and then reminded Elizabeth that the summer, just a few weeks or so gone by, had been one of the worst on record, weeks on end of more than 100 degree heat. "Everything was all burnt up, but then we got heavy rains, and they just stopped a day or so ago. God must have said, 'Enough!'"

"That explains the green, I guess," Elizabeth had said. If it were spring, late March or the first week or two in April —the fields would be covered in wildflowers, primroses and buttercups and then long expanses of bluebonnets, some Indian paints among them, maybe. Even now she longed to see them. She had just returned after a three year absence and she knew already that when this trip was over she would have to come back again soon. Traveling back and forth. For many years that had been her pattern.

Best friends since high school, Elizabeth and C.C. were in many ways, opposites. Elizabeth hadn't married, had never even lived with a man (although she had loved one or two), but had roamed the country and seen a little of the world. C. C. had married at nineteen, had four children in six or seven years and now had a flock of grandchildren, even one or two great grandchildren; rooted in Texas, marriage and family had been her life.

C. C. often told Elizabeth about a story she read over and over to her newest little ones about four kittens who had to decide what kind of cats they were going to grow up to be. They could be alley cats and free, but they would have to scrounge for a living; they could be farm cats, comfortable, part of an enterprise that sustained many and, in catching mice and insects, helpful in maintaining it; they could be ship cats, have adventures and see the world (though they would have to weather storms and run the risk of getting homesick for land) or they could be house cats, their impulse to wander curtailed, but loved and pampered with security guaranteed. C. C. said she was a farm cat, Elizabeth a ship cat. The story took hold of Elizabeth's imagination.

"We are only going to clear the front of it, " Louellen said as she sipped tea from her glass and looked out the big window at her mother's grassy back yard. "Clear the trees with oak wilt, leave the healthy oaks on the slope behind them. We can put up a shed for not much over $4,000, one with a loft in the back of it where we can sleep when we camp there, and with electricity.

"What's oak wilt?" Elizabeth asked.

"A disease of the root," Louellen told her. "It spreads from the root of one tree to another. But we can clear the trees that have it. Nick even likes clearing them, likes working hard out of doors instead of in the office. And the boys and I like helping him do it."

Elizabeth grew excited as this self possessed young woman spoke. What a project! C. C. had told her Louellen's husband was as enthusiastic as Louellen —their two boys who were bound to enjoy camping there —a great thing for a young family, and after the boys were grown, the place would be there for all of them, perhaps with a house on it by that time. "Oh, I want to see it!" she told Louellen. "Would you mind taking me along the next time I visit? I hope to come back in the spring." In a day or two she knew she would leave the Hill Country to drive to Searcy's place in East Texas near Nacogdoches.

"Of course," Louellen said. She had C. C.'s sky blue eyes, but in other respects resembled neither of her parents, a slender natural blonde with a radiant smile in a heart shaped face, glamorous as a film star, she looked younger than she was which to Elizabeth made her self assurance even more remarkable.

"How many acres did you say you had?" Elizabeth asked.

Louellen smiled. "Forty."

"Oh my," Elizabeth said, "And I'd like just one. Or even a half. Do you suppose somewhere I could find just half an acre?" She knew Louellen was humoring her, her mother's eccentric old friend, when she said she was sure she could.

Two: Hello, Aunt Rena

*I*t's me. *Elizabeth. Can you hear me?*

That's what she wrote in her journal when she was upstairs in what she had long thought of as "her room." It wasn't, of course; it was just the large spare bedroom where C.C.'s grandchildren spent over nights, where one of her daughters had lived for a time after she separated from her husband, and where C.C.'s brothers and sisters stayed when they came to see her. When C. C. commented on her big extended family she often told Elizabeth to consider herself a part of it. And this was also the room where Elizabeth had stayed when over the last twenty years she visited from California and she looked forward to her alone time in it. It was her habit to keep "journals of address." She had once, now long ago, even written to her hometown, Corpus Christi, the city where she had lived when she and C. C. were girls. The last few had been to her mother's oldest brother's wife who had looked after her when she was a small child and her mother had to take a faraway-job, and who also often advised her during the time she lived with the family in Corpus Christi when Elizabeth was in high school. No matter that she was now a senior citizen, she wrote to Aunt Rena often, as if she were still a teenager —her aunt Rena's "little girl."

> *Here I am*, she wrote, *once again back in Texas and in C. C.'s upstairs bedroom, here this time to look for a piece of land somewhere, (and, yes, Aunt Rena, to pay a call on Searcy.)*
>
> *We are both of us seekers. You were, as I remember, always looking for your brother, Johnny. You lost him as I lost my father, Burton McElroy who one day just left what was then our house and drove up or down —or who knows? —maybe off —the Hug the Coast. As you know, I gave up long ago the thought of finding Burton. And I learned (maybe) how to father myself. But you never gave up looking for Johnny did you? Your big brother I expect fathered you some in showy ways (he was dramatic and your daddy, taciturn.) I'm not sure what he meant to you. You always said he was like a strong, good part of yourself.*
>
> *When you were looking for him, for a while, Searcy helped you. Well, Aunt Rena, in a few days, after I leave C.C.'s —but before I leave the state —I'm going to drive into East Texas to see him. I called a day or so ago and he is still there and his voice —though God knows, he must be up in his eighties —still sounded strong.*

Three: Visiting Searcy

When she saw him he was still plump, as her aunt Rena had been. Blue eyed, his wavy hair, like Rena's in her old age, still had dark streaks through the silver. He wobbled a little when he walked, but looked a decade younger than he was. Elizabeth was glad he wasn't all gray-headed and bent over and that he still had his husky voice. She remembered it from the one time he had come to visit Aunt Rena and Uncle Leeland when she was still a small child. She had only seen him a few times since then.

Aunt Rena who brought him up after his mother died once told her that it was Searcy who first took her to the Ouachita mountain spring (A Thousand Drippings Spring, that was the name of it) where they liked to swim. She didn't remember, but she had long thought of Searcy as a person who needed to take others close to the source of things. He had been with Aunt Rena at the end of her life journey, and after she departed, he wrote to Elizabeth. They had corresponded at least once or twice a year ever since and Elizabeth had also visited him, once in Louisiana and once after he moved to East Texas. (He had moved back and forth across the Texas Louisiana line for years, for a time owned property in both states.)

Elizabeth thought of Searcy as a family member although they were not blood kin. For that matter, Aunt Rena, her mother's brother's wife, had not been blood kin, but few people in her life had been closer. Aunt Rena had brought her through her early Arkansas childhood after Burton McElroy disappeared and her working mother, hired to teach music in a Texas school, had to be in that state. Rena cared for Elizabeth, just as years before she had Searcy, her dead sister's child and in Elizabeth's mind that made him a kind of older foster brother (who was in many ways, nevertheless, a stranger), one for whom she now felt oddly responsible.

They sat under one of those big shade trees, dark and leafy like so many Elizabeth remembered they had in that part of the country, at a little white table in Searcy's front yard. Hollyhocks, in rose and pink, lined his sidewalk. Hollyhocks always brought Elizabeth back to her Depression Era childhood because Aunt Rena had grown them, too. Maybe it would be nice to own a little place near Searcy's —the realtor she had contacted in Austin about Hill Country property had only talked about rising prices —it was on the tip of her tongue to ask him if anything was for sale. But first she would let him work through whatever it was that he wanted so much to tell her. Over the phone he had said that he had something important on his mind.

"I know you two were close, Elizabeth," he said as he sipped his coffee. He had filled two large mugs with it from an old percolator on the back of the kitchen stove, near a big window through which Elizabeth could see the backyard where squirrels scampered beneath two graceful pecan trees. Both Searcy and Elizabeth took their coffee black and walked with their full cups out of the kitchen in the back of the house, through the tiny living room, dominated by the large photo of Searcy's beloved wife Bea over the mantle of the gas fireplace, and out to the front yard where Searcy said he liked to sit so he could watch for the post lady and look up and down the street to see what else was going on.

"Close as you were, she would want you to know what happened to her brother." From a sweat stained pocket he gave her the card of an investigator with an agency in Houston. The man was a relative of a neighbor he said. The day was humid and unusually warm for November. Searcy used his napkin to wipe his face.

Elizabeth asked, "Why is it important that we find out?" Johnny had been older than Rena (if Rena were alive she would be well up in her hundreds); he had no doubt died years and years ago. She didn't want to disappoint Searcy or hurt his feelings —except for his memories, he was alone now, becoming fragile —but on this trip, or any other, looking for the long lost Johnny was the last thing she wanted to do.

"It would rest my mind," Searcy said. " He was my mother's brother as well as Aunt Rena's. And I think they would both want us to find out. I'm beyond driving." He paused and then added, "I might get to Houston on the bus."

Well, she would humor him. She shooed a fly, finished her coffee and said, "No, Searcy, I won't have you do that." She put the card of the private investigator in the back pocket of her purse. "I'll go there for you," she said, "maybe do some shopping. I'll let you know what I find out."

Four: Meeting John Shearer

*T*he man in the agency wasn't at all encouraging, said that he thought she and Searcy would be engaging in a crazy, probably futile search, one that would cost them a good deal of money, (though Searcy had told her he was willing to spend part of what he got out of the sale of his deceased brother's business.) Certainly, it was one she didn't want to do. But she didn't tell Searcy that, told him, instead, that she had to go back to California for work she couldn't turn down, but that she would return to Texas as soon as it was over and revisit the investigator who by that time might have given serious thought to where Johnny might have gone.

The trip to Houston had depressed her. On the warm side and humid, but that wasn't the worst of it. The smog stung her eyes. "It's worse than the smog in L. A. when I went there in the 80s" she told the investigator who (oddly, she thought) wore western boots, and didn't seem to want to hear what she had to say. "You live out there in that strange state, do you?" She thought he might add "little lady" but he didn't, only looked as if he wanted to. Even in Texas she guessed a professional man couldn't get away with that any more. (She remembered the men in her childhood and young adulthood who called her "little lady" even though she was fairly tall and had always thought of herself as a middle sized person.) This was, after all, a new century! She was glad about that, glad, of course, that Houston had wonderful new museums and theaters (a whole arts complex) and at the same time, sorry that much of the old Houston she remembered seemed gone.

The old Houston was mostly —besides her family's pleasant neighborhood, to the north side of the bayou on the Galveston side of town —Downtown. The department stores, Sakowitz and Foleys (both now nonexistent), the movie houses, the Rice Hotel. The Rice was still there, and so were some of the movie houses, but now, she supposed, people mostly shopped and went to the movies in malls near their suburban neighborhoods; that was true all over the country, she told herself which didn't make her like the idea any better or give her greater tolerance for the foul stuff that stung her eyes.

The headlines of *The Houston Post*, the paper she read while she waited to be admitted into the investigator's office, carried a front page story about a man who was to be put to death that night by lethal injection. This was why the blue sky and rosy sunset had been such a sweet surprise to her when she got off the plane in Austin. The media everywhere, apparently even in Houston, had made the state of her girlhood famous for more than oil money, (and from it a president or two), the lust for more, and the corruption that can bring. One way or another, and a good deal of the time lawfully, it was now also the state that killed. Had it killed her aunt's beloved older brother? Was he maybe charged with some awful crime? Drug running, if that was what he had done, even all those years ago, was a dangerous business. He would have been pursued and more likely than not been caught up in violence of one sort or another. Perhaps he shot someone or was himself shot. She saw him as the shooter, then as bleeding on a deserted street, and as she put her paper down, being taken away by police. He was part black (Aunt Rena was half Creole), out of work, poor, he wouldn't get a decent lawyer, a fair trial.

She knew her imagination was running away with her when she was called into the office. All the same she took an instant dislike to the man in a dark business suit and western boots she saw before her (a large diamond glittering on one of his fingers.) What was his name? Shine? No, the ring had just made her think that. Shearer or Shawn. She couldn't remember. (The card with his name and address on it —and she had at least found the place —was in her purse.) She wondered how he was related to Searcy's neighbor. She had to forgotten to ask and was sorry now. Before she spoke with this man she needed a connection, but in front of him couldn't say anything.

As if to protect herself, she tugged at the ends of the loud pink scarf she had flung around her neck when she dressed and took off for Houston from Nacogdoches that morning. The scarf Aunt Rena would have wanted her to have Searcy said when back in the 80s he sent it to her along with a clipping about the funeral, and she had worn it a few times a year ever since. Aunt Rena had probably bought it in a dime store —Woolworth's or Kress's where she loved to spend her free afternoons —but the sheer cloth held up all the same and so did the cheery color. A pink so bright it was nearly red.

"Ms. McElroy?" Mr. Shearer —she believed that was his name —addressed her from his open office door.

She nodded.

"Please come in." He turned and she followed feeling herself to be a character in a play.

"Now tell me," he continued after she had taken a seat in the office that faced a desk with one curious word —LIBERTY —spelled out in a red, white and blue carving that sat along one side of it, "why do you and Mr. Brock want to find out what happened to his uncle, this man —Johnny Brock." He shuffled the papers of the report he held in his hand. "Good Lord. Disappeared seventy or more years ago —nearly a century! Do you think he hid money away somewhere, or owned property? Taxes would have eaten the worth."

"No," she told him, "we just want to find out what happened to him because our aunt who helped raise us both cared for him so. Searcy was her sister Lucy's child. Lucy died when Searcy was a baby."

Mr. Shearer leaned across his desk, palms down on it, his diamond catching the light from the window behind him. He was a big man, she noted. Big John. Big John Shine. That was the name she gave him. She might use it in a radio play. "You're many years younger than Mr. Pugh," he told her. "How is it that your aunt raised the two of you?"

"My mother was her husband's sister," Elizabeth said. "My mother when I was small had to go away on a job. She left me with her family —her parents, who were old then and Aunt Rena and Uncle Leeland who lived next door and who were young enough to still have the energy to care for children."

He looked to her as if he comprehended none of what she said and she realized her story was confusing. She remembered then the way the man had looked who was the only other investigator of missing persons she had ever been to.

When she was a school child and reunited with her mother, her mother had taken her to talk to a man who might possibly look for her father, Burton McElroy, missing for at least five years. (The depression broke him, her mother said. "He lost his business and went a little crazy after that.") It had been in this very city —in a walk-in trailer on the sidewalk in front of a parking lot on Fannin with a big sign on the front that said, "Come in. FIND THAT MISSING PERSON!" Across the street she saw Sakowitz, her mother's favorite department store where they shopped for patterns and fabric (all the women in her family sewed) and sometimes even splurged on a tea room lunch.

The man had been gruff and insulting, his big belly hanging over his belt with its tacky brass buckle. She had wanted her mother to take her out of his make shift office and across the street and into the pretty store.

The man in front of her now in his well appointed South Main office, expensive suit and boots, was smoother, but she had the same sense of foreboding in his presence.

"Why would you want to find him?" that long ago con man had asked her mother who nodded toward Elizabeth. Elizabeth had clutched the sleeve of her mother's khaki jacket (like so many during World War II, of a military design) and looked at the trailer floor. "For her," her mother had said.

"Give it up, lady," the burley guy had barked in the most insulting way. "Give it up. That's my advice." Then accepted her mother's hard earned five dollar bill. (They would not eat in the Sakowitz tea room this day.) PRIVATE INVESTIGATOR WILL ADVISE, ONLY FIVE $ the largest sign on his trailer said.

"Aunt Rena cared a lot about her big brother," Elizabeth told the man in front of her now, "tried several times to find him. He went away when he was young to try to make money to send back to her and her mother and her sister Lucy's children, Searcy and his brother, who we called Johnny Two . But the loss of her brother Johnny is something neither she nor Searcy really got over. I'd like to find out now just for Searcy's sake and even though she's gone, finally for Aunt Rena, too."

The man looked baffled. "What do you think happened?"

She shifted in her chair, wished all at once she had never come and took little comfort from the red, white and blue letters on John Shearer's desk —that was the name on the card in her purse she remembered. "Well," she began, "Aunt Rena said she found out he was running into Mexico for marijuana, or just picking it up at the border. She thought something might have happened to him there." As she spoke Mr. Shearer looked directly at her, his icy blue eyes glittering like his big diamond ring. "I guess I'd like to think he came out all right —made a life for himself, somehow, had a family."

"Do you have pictures of him, letters? A birth certificate? Jewelry or old items of clothing?"

She shifted uncomfortably. "I'm not sure. I can find out maybe."

Mr. Shearer stood up —he was a tall man —leaned over his desk, over his curious carving. Said, "Nothing I can do until I have more to go on. Bring in what you have."

As he extended his hand and she rose to take it, she said, "Searcy told me you are related to one of his neighbors, I'm not sure who." He looked uncomprehending. Then she blurted out, "What is that —the word there?"

"Liberty is truth," he said. "Or rather, truth is liberty —that's the way I'll arrange it." He laughed out loud, friendly for the first time. "All the letters are not yet made."

Five: The Missing Word

*T*ruth was the word that was missing.

Well, Elizabeth thought after she left, these folks all seem to believe they know what truth, what THE truth is. John Shearer, Big John Shine. Arbiter of truth. Was she really going to try to track down the truth about Rena's long lost brother? She who since childhood had never considered trying to find out the truth about what happened to her father, her flesh and blood? And if she wasn't, what would she say to Searcy?

The office visit alone had cost a hundred dollars. She hadn't been there for more than twenty minutes, had been told to come back with whatever she could find that had belonged to Johnny. She didn't think Searcy had anything. But if he did and she came back, John Shine would charge her more —and if a real search got underway, God only knew what it would cost. It seemed stupid to go on. Big John Shine probably couldn't find anything anyway and if even if he did, it still wouldn't bring back this man who disappeared all that long time ago or ease his family's anguish. Not that it mattered —except for Searcy, everyone in the family was dead. She would tell Searcy this as nicely as she could.

Still, she didn't want to completely discourage him. She saw that the possibility of conducting this search gave him HOPE —something to go on for. He had been so lost after his wife Bea died; his little house was still filled with his memory of her —the big photo over the mantle in his living room, the room he never anymore sat in, kept dark. In daylight hours he stayed in the kitchen or the yard. Elizabeth noticed he didn't speak of Bea. He had responded in monosyllables when she brought up her name.

She hadn't planned to, but she went back to Nacogdoches to see Searcy the very next day. She had planned only to telephone, then write —tell him what he needed to do to go forward and that she would be back to help after Christmas or in the spring. By spring she believed he would have forgotten about it.

When she entered Searcy's little white house she realized she was caught up in this in a way she hadn't counted on. Searcy told her about Bea this time as they sat at his kitchen table , once again with coffee, told her in a reverential tone —after he started went on and on, and not wanting to break his remembrance, she sat silent and just let him talk.

Searcy's Story

She got cold, Elizabeth. Went out in a Blue Norther without even a sweater on —and never got warm again.

"She hadn't realized that the weather had changed overnight when she left the house that morning. You know how it does in Texas, how the temperature can drop all at once fifty degrees when something —who knows from where? —just blows in. She went on the bus to see one of her ailing cousins in Louisiana, came back later the same day a shiverin' though she had borrowed a jacket from her relations. Well, I reckon the jacket wasn't all the woman gave her. She went right to bed and never got up. I could hear her wheezing and sucking in her breath all night. You know she had TB as a teenager; her lungs were never strong. I got up early and went to the kitchen. When I brought her coffee to her with half a grapefruit from a box sent up to me from the valley —I order every Christmas —she was gone. I've never used our bedroom since, but I want you to take it tonight. I sleep right here in the kitchen, over there on the daybed next to the window where in the summertime I can look out and see the morning glories on the vine she planted that grows all over the backyard fence and up the garage wall. Some hate a vine like that. You can't get rid of it even if you want to —it just takes over. But I like it. I like waking up to see those dark blue flowers. Brings her back to me somehow. She came to me you know years and years after my first wife and little son died.

"We married late, too late for children, though we hoped for a while. But it was good just to be together, and all the time she was with me Bea seemed as tough as that morning glory vine. I always thought she'd outlive me. It was hard to believe that she could come in out of a Norther sick and just lie down and leave this life.

"My brother, Johnny, who Rena, as you know always called Johnny Two, and his wife, Maurine, passed away within days of each other a little while after. They were on the road back from California, the first vacation they'd had in years and the only long road trip I ever knew them to take when a pickup coming down the highway the wrong way ran right into them. Some drunk kid driving. They say Maurine never knew what hit her. Johnny was injured internally and his car wrecked beyond repair. But when police and paramedics came they got him to Dallas on a helicopter and a week later he passed away in the hospital there. We brought him back for burial in the plot with Aunt Rena in it. We bought a double plot so there would be room for the children; the remains of my little son and his mama were there.

"Johnny and Maurine had no children, that is, none they could keep or enjoy. They did have one, but as you probably know, she was stillborn. They couldn't have any others. The business come to me, but I was never a business man, Elizabeth, so I sold it. Put the money in the bank and haven't used it. Only used enough to buy a little land —I never knew how to invest in anything else —just a few acres with a creek on it. I'd like to show it to you sometime."

He looked across the kitchen table at her, saw that she was staring out into his backyard. She seemed in another place; he supposed she was anxious to go back to California, to whatever life she had there (he had never understood what was in it exactly), but he was glad anyway that she listened —he thought she really had —glad at the moment for her presence, glad she'd let him talk. "How much," he asked, "does Mr. Shearer want?"

"Well, Searcy," she said, turning to face him, "he says it could run as high as a hundred dollars a day."

He looked past her, out the window toward the pecan trees. "Well," —he paused — "We'll see. When can you come back?"

"After Christmas —in the spring probably —late March, early April. I'd really like to see the land you bought." She didn't tell him she was thinking of buying land somewhere in Texas. "By then, for sure."

But after she returned to California the months just slid by. She did write to Searcy and sent him a bowl with a nutcracker she had bought in Houston for his pecans for Christmas. (She remembered him cracking them on the kitchen counter with a hammer.) By spring she was over her head with work on several new shows NPR wanted her to do. She was glad to have assignments. She had been told her NPR station would soon not be using much in the way of dramas. She might have to write a totally different kind of show. Soon she might truly want to retire, to quit working for radio. Finding a refuge in Texas seemed more and more important. But because she had to finish the play she was working on she couldn't go right away to look for it. She saw she was going to have to put off her trip.

Six: A Question of Justice

*I*n February she called both C. C. and Searcy to tell them not to give up on her, that she would come back to Texas, but that she just didn't know when.

She had wanted to give Searcy enough time to go through the old family cedar chest he kept out in his store house, an enclosed shed with flooring and a single electric light, on one side of his yard. By summer she realized she had given him more than enough time and that she hadn't contacted him in months.

He showed her the shed before she left the previous fall, and together they went through some of what was inside —his mother's picture that Aunt Rena had framed for him (Lucy, "the healer," as she was known, a radiant girl), Aunt Rena's favorite quilt, one she had put together from scraps of dress material, the pieces worked together to make stars. Maybe if they had looked long enough something of Johnny's would have shown up, cuff links or a ring. Maybe Searcy would find something yet. She would encourage him when she next phoned to keep looking. In the meantime, she would write to the Louisiana state capitol at Baton Rouge and ask for a birth certificate. Searcy thought Johnny's birthday was the fourth of July. Funny, Elizabeth thought, that Aunt Rena had never told her this.

She was no flag waver, but once she had liked to think about living in a country that had been established just a little more than a hundred years before her aunt's brother Johnny was born with a Bill of Rights, with a Declaration of Independence that proclaimed "Liberty and justice for all." Liberty. There was that word again. Then she thought about Johnny —how he, if he had been caught running marijuana, or for something worse, might not have received justice —or how he might have tried to escape from whoever pursued him because he knew he would not receive it. She saw before her his likeness, or the likeness as she imagined it — for she had never seen a picture of him —on a poster lettered WANTED.

"It should read HUNTED," she said aloud. She was alone in her Los Angeles apartment so there was no one to hear. "Yes, I just may commit to finding out what happened to him, to my aunt's older brother all that long time ago." And in the meantime, she thought, I'm going to start a radio play that brings up the question of justice, something that may let people know what can happen in this country that was founded on the principle of justice for all. What does happen to the poor. If the station isn't going to broadcast drama anymore it may be a swan's song.

A QUESTION OF JUSTICE.

She wrote those words on her new yellow pad.

She had been poor enough herself, she thought, poor enough, God knows, though she had never lived on the street or in squalor, never been treated unfairly because of her color —because of her gender, yes, she remembered, many times. She had never been as poor as the poorest, those who were homeless or who lived with many others in one or two sad rooms in dangerous neighborhoods. But she had been poor enough to empathize; she knew what it was to live from Monday to Friday, or Thursday to Monday on potatoes and carrots, or pintos and slaw. She even knew what it was to roll pennies so she would have a few dollars in the bank and what it was to be poor enough not to have a car, (in a city where it was hard to get to a job without one.) After all, when she first came to L. A. she had been a bus rider for a full year.

And, of course, she knew about going to a strange part of the country to work because there was no work to be had in the part of the country that was familiar. She had been poor in a lesser way than Johnny, in a way that was less dangerous and terrible. But she had been poor enough to feel for him! And to want to present his drama to a radio audience. Maybe soon there wouldn't be a radio audience anywhere for dramas. Who knew? Maybe this was reason enough to look for him. She could consider her future dealings with John Shearer, if she had them, research. But she put off contacting him or Searcy.

Instead, she put these thoughts into a journal, then into some notes she made for a new radio play —and into a letter she wrote (again in a journal) to Aunt Rena. "Aunt Rena," it began, "what do you think happened to Johnny?" And then laughed out loud at herself and her imaginings. "I'm nuts," she said. "Maybe I could do some kind of radio play, yes, but it would be ridiculous to go in serious pursuit of this long lost man."

Nevertheless, by June she considered re-contacting John Shearer when the letter, written in a shaky hand, from Searcy came.

Seven: Dealing With Mail

*I*n late March, when he had hoped she could visit, he had collapsed with a stroke, and suffered a partial paralysis of his right side, but he had therapy in a convalescent hospital all spring, had learned to eat and even write a little, as she could see, with his left hand, and with the aid of a walker, might someday walk again. His speech was not affected much. Therapists still came to the house and he had other help at home, a visiting nurse, and a man who gave showers, from the county, and ladies from the church who did shopping for him and brought some meals. (Good of them he thought since he wasn't much of a church goer.) At other times he managed to heat some things in the microwave himself. Yes, he had one now and he had even retired his old percolator for a plug in coffee maker. That was hard, he said —saying good-bye to his old coffee pot, (not that coffee, no matter what it was made in, tasted like much of anything anymore.) His neighbor, Miss Lily, came by nearly every morning with homemade biscuits and items from the store. Miss Lily was related to Mr. Shearer he said. Mr. Shearer's father had been her older sister's child.

Everybody told him how good he was at getting around; he could wheel almost anywhere with his chair, and had no trouble making transfer all by himself to the toilet or his bed. He would call her, but he had never been any good at talking on the phone. He hoped she would come back to Texas like she said. And he hoped that one way or another they could figure out how to go about finding out what had happened to Aunt Rena's brother, Johnny.

Searcy's letter came in the same mail with one from C. C. who also said she hoped Elizabeth would visit before too much time had passed. No matter when she came, they would take a side trip to visit Louellen's land.

Elizabeth answered both letters that very afternoon. She wished she was closer so she could drop in on Searcy often, she said in her letter to him and meant it, but she was glad that he at least had good help and a neighbor who came by. (Help or no help, she worried about Searcy living in his little house all alone.) Yes, they would talk about how to search for Johnny. Had he looked anymore in the cedar chest? They would together have to go through that again. Maybe she could come in the fall, or surely by the following spring. She didn't want to commit herself to a time.

○

Aunt Rena came to her in a flood of moonlight from one of those gigantic moons that in Southern California sometimes take over and whiten the late summer night sky. Elizabeth could hardly hear what Rena said, but in her long, bright pink dress, she was oh, so visible. (Like the scarf Elizabeth had from her, so pink it was almost red.)

"Honey, you're in a new place, aren't you?" she seemed almost to whisper so that Elizabeth wanted to ask what was wrong with the sound.

"A turning place —and you don't know maybe in what direction?" That's what Elizabeth thought she said.

"You like where you are. And you can be thankful your health is good. But you are getting older and you are tired. And soon you may not even be able to do your same work which you love. You want to look at Searcy's land. And at Louellen's. Well, look, honey, it can't hurt. And, finally, you'll know what to do."

Somehow the dream had a grip on her that left her paralyzed and speechless. But Rena didn't seem to notice, or, anyway, didn't seem to mind even if she did. "About Johnny," she said, "it's sweet of you to want to help Searcy. Searcy is going to need more help than ever now. Sweet of you to set out to look."

"Oh, Aunt Rena!" Elizabeth at last heard herself say aloud. "Oh, Aunt Rena, what do you think —" She broke off her question to catch her breath, for the apparition that had been her Aunt Rena vanished as quickly as it had appeared. "What do you think," she had wanted to ask, wanted to have an answer to, "about Big John Shine?"

Eight: Put Your Hand Upon Me

*S*he didn't wait for spring or even for the cool that might come to Texas in November. Shortly after she got the definitive news that NPR might be doing away with radio drama at the end of the next season, in late August heat she flew to Houston, rented a car, drove to Nacogdoches and found Searcy —not looking terribly altered (thinner, yes, and paler, one side of his mouth twisted a little) —in the kitchen looking out into the pecan trees. His hands shook gently when she took them. He was glad to see her, glad she came. Although, as he had said in his letter he had all but lost his taste for coffee, people still made it for him in the new coffee maker. He thought there was some in the pot. His county worker had just gone home. He wanted Elizabeth to help herself.

"Is there anything I can get you?" she asked. "What do you have in the icebox? Juice, or a Coke?"

"Nothing now," he said. Elizabeth saw that the church women —or Miss Lily —had left a bowl of tomatoes, probably from a nearby garden, and what appeared to be Searcy's supper on the stove.

"You do manage here all right by yourself, don't you?" For a man who at well past eighty had been through a major stroke he looked to her wonderfully capable.

He said he did. As he'd told her in his letter, he could always make transfer from his chair to the bed or to the toilet which was just down the hall, and he could get what he needed from the refrigerator and cups and plates that had been put in a lower shelf along side. But he did have trouble getting outside. Someone had to push him out the back door. He missed sitting in the yard, and for the longest time he had wanted to look again through the cedar chest in the storehouse.

"I'll take you out," Elizabeth said. "While I'm here you can sit in the yard all day if you want to."

Searcy pointed to the three pronged cane at the end of the daybed. "I can walk a little on that," he said. "I had good therapy in the convalescent hospital. It wasn't a bad place at all. Though I was glad to get home. A therapist still comes twice a week. Sees that I get around the kitchen. Sometimes takes me outside." But it wasn't enough, he said. Like all of his family he was an outdoor person. While the sun was up he didn't want to be sitting around in a room. And he'd had such an itch to get out to the storehouse.

Elizabeth washed her cup and put it in the sink. "Come on," she said, "let's make that trip."

In the cedar chest they found a World War I uniform, old report cards, a Masonic ring (maybe Papa J's, the name Aunt Rena gave her daddy, Searcy's grandfather), a china doll, several envelopes full of yellowed photos —none, as far as they could tell of Johnny, marbles, gourds to drink water from when out of doors at a well or spring. They fondled every item and told stories about it, and then Elizabeth saw Searcy tire, the lines deepen around his eyes, his hands tremble when he reached out for a new object, his body shake. "Well, I think we've had enough for one day," she told him. "I'll take you in now. Maybe you'd like a nap."

Only after he was asleep in his daybed did she return to the storehouse to put what they had been through carefully away, wrapping each item in the crumpled tissue they had found it in.

She found the prayer when she was about to close the chest. (She thought it odd that she'd read a newspaper article about this very prayer just before she left California. Discover something new, she told herself, remembering what Aunt Rena one time told her, and before you know it, you see it everywhere.) She couldn't close the chest on first try because a piece of parchment paper rolled into a scroll was caught through a crevice on one side, interfering with the work of the hinge. She tugged and tugged to get it through, and then as she held it in her hands, the paper unfurled and the letters printed at the top alongside a faded photo of a dark haired, dark skinned young man were unmistakable. They read:

Request By Johnny Brock

Oh Lord,
Bless me, indeed.
Enlarge and map out my territory.
Put your hand upon me and
Protect me from Evil
That I may not cause pain.

The date at the bottom: 9/1/15.

September. The month, Rena's stories had it, that Johnny left for Texas to work as an oil rigger so he could send money home.

Nine: A Neighbor's Call

*M*iss Lily startled her by rattling the door. "Mr. Pugh said I could find you here. I'm Lily. I live up the street and look in on him sometimes. You're Elizabeth aren't you?"

Elizabeth came back to herself and extended her hand. "I'm glad you're here, Lillian." She didn't know why she used the formal name. Maybe because Miss Lily had called Searcy "Mr. Pugh." She gestured toward the only chair in the room, a wooden rocker.

"Just Lily," the woman said, as she settled into the chair. "The youngest in a family of girls. My big sisters were twelve and thirteen when I was born. And one sister, Iris, was five years older than that. My mother named us all after flowers."

"A lot of hardy ones grow here," Elizabeth said, remembering the hollyhocks in Searcy's front yard. " Your mother, undoubtedly, grew flowers."

"A yard full," Lily said, tapping the floor to move the rocker. (Elizabeth noticed she wore orthopedic shoes, and that her left foot turned in a little.) "Everybody in the family gardened, but me. Though I set out tomatoes every year. Left Mr. Pugh some this morning. When I was younger I didn't have the time for a flower garden. Too busy teaching school, always had papers to grade."

"Oh," Elizabeth murmured, inexplicably spellbound before this small woman, "a teacher."

"English," Lily said. "Forty years. Several schools. But all in this county." She bent forward and motioned toward the piece of paper Elizabeth was holding. "I see you've been going through that old chest."

Elizabeth sighed. "Yes, looking for things that might have belonged to Searcy's long lost Uncle Johnny. It seems a little silly, but in recent years he's been obsessed with trying to find out what happened to him."

"He told me some," Lily said. Her good foot had stilled the rocking chair. "People become agitated when they lose their history. I thought it might help if he really looked for it. I tried to look a little myself on the net, but didn't come up with much. So I quit and gave Searcy the card of a great nephew, a private investigator who has an agency in Houston."

Elizabeth sucked in her breath. "You mean Mr." —she paused — "Shearer?"

(She had almost said, "Shine.") She had forgotten what Searcy had told her about John Shearer's father being Lily's relation. "Why, I went to see him last fall, almost a year ago —he's your nephew?"

"Great nephew," Lily said. "The grandson of my oldest sister Rose's boy."

"Oh," Elizabeth said, "I wish I'd known you when I saw him. If I could have explained Searcy's connection my visit might have meant more to him. I don't think he took it seriously."

"Well," Lily said, "he has a lot of clients, I guess. Honey, he's making money hand over fist. All rich on that side of the family. He can do and charge what he likes. Rose married into oil."

"I'll probably see him again," Elizabeth told her, then pointed to the paper in her hand before giving it to Lily. "Look at what I've found. Does this mean anything to you?"

Lily read the prayer slowly. "No ma'm," she said. "It's a mystery."

Elizabeth sat down on the cedar chest, it's lid now closed. Then she told Miss Lily that she had read in the *L. A. Times* that this prayer, known as the "Prayer of Jabez" had recently become a magnet for marketing, that thousands had been buying a book about it.

"Lily, this *L. A. Times* article reported that thousands of people have been saying this prayer hoping to get rich! Who knows, maybe some still are. And not just rich like you and I probably think of that either —but greedy rich, King Midas rich, so rich that they want everything they touch to turn to gold. I don't know why exactly —I guess because of the poverty that causes such misery in the world —but I like to think that Searcy's Uncle Johnny said this prayer —if he did, that is —just hoping to do meaningful work of some kind and to make a good living with enough left over to send something to his family."

Searcy hoped Elizabeth would stay a while this time. That afternoon after his nap, while she and Miss Lily were talking about what she had found in the cedar chest, he told the county worker this and asked if she wouldn't get his old bedroom, the one he shared with Bea, ready.

At supper time he said to Elizabeth, "I don't want you in the spare room. It's no bigger than a big box. Take the big bedroom. The new worker got it ready for you while you were talking to Miss Lily. It'll be good to have a woman in it again."

"I'll be honored to take it, Searcy," Elizabeth said. Then as she spooned onto his plate a large dollop of the casserole the church ladies had left next to the thick slices of Miss Lily's homegrown tomatoes, she asked, "How did you know Miss Lily was here?"

"Heard her footsteps on the gravel. Lily's a little crippled, you know. Nobody else's shoes make the music hers do. I know it's Lily coming through the back gate even if I'm in the front of the house."

One of her feet had been twisted since birth he said. It made her self conscious as a child. "She was the runt of the family, she told me. 'Maybe I wasn't meant to be at all,' she once said. Her mama had her when she was way up into her forties. Her grown up sisters, Violet and Rose, were both tall beauties. Iris, too, I think. No one's too clear on Iris. She married and moved up north a long time ago. But Lily told me she felt worse than just short and scrawny because of the high top shoes she had to wear to help correct a weak ankle and a twisted foot. 'I felt really homely, Searcy,' she said. When she was growing up she stayed away from people who either made too much fuss or weren't considerate at all. She just made friends with books, always had her nose in one she said." He spoke with affection, then cautiously spooned chicken and noodles into his mouth. "She's like you, Elizabeth, a woman who has made her living by using her mind."

Elizabeth noticed the casserole dish was store bought. She remembered her grandmother's homemade chicken and dumplings, each dumpling carefully rolled out and floured and hung over a kitchen rack to "dry." She wondered if any of Searcy's church ladies made dumplings like that any more.

Later that night on soft cotton sheets in the bed Searcy had shared with his beloved wife, the air conditioner going full blast, Elizabeth slept like a blessed person —deeply, only toward morning visited by the sweetest of dreams. Great waves of blue green water, one after another carrying her —that dream, one she had several times during her life —brought both excitement and peace, and when she woke she asked herself, "Why do I want to buy land when it is water that brings me bliss?" She knew that part of the reason she had managed twenty years in California was because she could live not far from the coast.

She didn't want to leave the bed that brought pleasure. But she rose and dressed and then joined Searcy and the county worker for Miss Lily's biscuits topped with spoonfuls of sweet potato butter. (Never mind that Searcy's casserole had come from the supermarket. One of the best things about visiting Texas was still the food.) Afterwards she called John Shearer's Houston office and set up an appointment, explaining that when she came she would have something of Johnny Brock's with her. She also let the secretary know that she had been referred through his great aunt. Lily arrived in Searcy's kitchen as she spoke.

By mid morning they talked for a second time in the storehouse as Elizabeth once again rummaged through the cedar chest. She didn't know what else she expected to find, but she had a hunch something more was there. She hoped for something Johnny wore. Of course, he had been a poor boy. What would his family have saved? A cap, maybe, or a shirt he wore to church, or a class ring.

"Now that I know you've an appointment I'll send John an e-mail," Miss Lily told her. "I don't mean much to him, Elizabeth. I'm, after all, only a great aunt —but I am of his family, so maybe this time when you see him he'll pay you more mind."

Ten: Truth Is Liberty

All the letters of John Shine's sign, Elizabeth noted, had been made and were by the time she arrived in his office, lined up in front of each other on his desk.

He smiled at her this time. Pointing to his sign he said, "Too many of my clients don't realize this. They come to me, yes, but truth is seldom what they want to find." Elizabeth smiled back at him. "Isn't it?" she asked.

"No. What they really want is a confirmation of their fantasies."

Elizabeth fingered an edge of the pink scarf she had once again worn for this encounter. "It's human nature, I guess," she said.

"An obstacle to well being," John Shearer countered, his diamond still glittering as he rose, walked around his desk, lifted the word "Truth" from the front of it and held it before Elizabeth. "Facing THIS. That's what too many are afraid to do."

She flinched. "I guess it's really hard sometimes."

"Will it be hard for you? For your aunt's nephew?"

"I'm pretty far removed from all of this," Elizabeth told him. "Whatever happened happened before I was even born. I never knew my aunt's brother, and for that matter, Searcy didn't either —but he lost his mother young and Johnny Brock was his mother's brother, too. That makes a difference."

"And how would he take it now if he found out the worst about Johnny Brock —that he was a criminal, maybe even a killer? We already know that if he ran drugs, as you have indicated he might have, he was engaged in criminal activity."

Elizabeth considered. "I don't know. But from the stories Aunt Rena told us about Johnny it would be hard for me to believe that he could have killed anyone —except, perhaps, in self defense —or engaged, for that matter, in any serious crime."

"Isn't all crime serious?" John Shearer asked, setting "Truth" back down on his desk before "Is Liberty." "Isn't drug running serious?"

"Well, as I understand it," Elizabeth said, "if he did engage in anything illegal —and we don't really know that he did, I mean we have nothing factual to go on, only what Aunt Rena had heard —it was in driving from somewhere in South Texas across the border at Laredo into Matamoros to pick up marijuana. For a fee, a substantial fee. He hoped to send money home to help out his mother, Aunt Rena and Searcy's mother, Lucy. They had hardly enough to live."

"Marijuana is a drug, Ms. McElroy," Mr. Shearer said, "and dealing in it a criminal offense. If this man was driving it across the border and the authorities discovered he did, he could have been arrested and sent to prison."

Elizabeth had risen from her chair and rearranged the scarf across her shoulders. Hard to take, honey, she thought she could almost hear Aunt Rena say, this sanctimonious man. "Yes, I understand that. I'm prepared to find out about that."

"And Mr. Pugh?"

She looked straight at him. "Searcy is a stable person. Yes, he's had a stroke and yes, he's getting on in years. But he's a strong, sensible person. If his uncle Johnny went to prison he would want to know it. I believe both of us can handle whatever you find out."

The sun burned through the window, made it hard for her to look directly at this big man in front of her who she soon hoped to leave.

"You understand," he said, his voice softening, "I just don't want you to be shocked —or to suffer. I've seen too many clients do that. God knows, all of us have a black sheep or two in our families. Aunt Lily could probably tell you about some from our own." He paused. Elizabeth blinked, saw through the window the sun still burning, then, wordless, turned from the big man in front of her toward the door.

"She probably won't," John Shearer continued. "Though you might ask her sometime. She would never tell me, you understand. But I grew up on my grandmother, Rose's stories, and God knows, she —Rose — has lived an exemplary life."

Eleven: Miss Lily's Study

What a hideaway!" After returning from Houston to East Texas Elizabeth found herself in another room she would have liked to have had for her own. The very day she got back she called on Lily in the two story frame house under the shade trees at the end of the street. Lily had escorted her through the front hall, beyond the staircase —an old fashioned parlor on one side and large dining room on the other —to the back of the house into a small paneled antechamber. And then, after Lily pushed a button to one side of a false fireplace, into the hidden room behind it which seemed like a room out of one of her childhood stories, (at Lily's touch the panel simply slid open), three of its walls lined from top to bottom with books; novels mostly, but also poetry, story collections, old encyclopedias, many shelves of law books, a shelf with atlases and National Geographic and a history or two. An illuminated world globe stood in the far end of the room near the built-in-desk with Lily's I Mac on it.

Elizabeth said, "You've everything. You've the whole world here."

"This was my father's room," Lily said. "He literally hid himself away. As children we all wondered how he just appeared and disappeared, and Mama kept his secret, kept the curtains drawn over the back window so no one could see in from the yard. I was nearly ten before I even knew this room was here. He practiced criminal law, and he had some tough cases let me tell you, but he also liked to read and I think he may have used this space as much to escape from his job as to prepare for it. Anyway, after he died, I took it over." Lily cleared her throat, shifted from one foot to another, then sat down in the chair by the desk. " You're welcome to borrow anything you see. And I don't often make that offer."

Elizabeth said, "I don't lend my books either. And I won't borrow, though I appreciate your trust." On the wall with the tall glass window which looked out on the shaded back yard she eyed a long green couch, a good art deco reading lamp on either side of it. "But I would love to come over some afternoon when you're not using the room and just read."

"Any time you want," Lily said. " Tomorrow if you like. If I'm not in the house, I'll give you the key. Some of these books belonged to my daddy —" She pointed to the leather bound Poe and Dickens —" though I don't know how much he read in them —and some of the volumes of poetry belonged to my older sister, Vi, who died when I was little. Besides Daddy and me, she was the only one in the family who seemed to be a real reader. God knows, except for the Bible which she was forced to read on Sundays, Rose never read anything, or Mama either. This was one of Violet's favorites —" Lily pulled an old anthology of nineteenth and twentieth century poetry down from the shelf. "She wrote some poetry of her own, and they say she had committed some of these to heart."

"She wrote poetry?" Elizabeth asked.

"Yes," Lily said, " Wild Violet —Rose and Mama always called her Wild Violet —wrote poetry. I have some of it here." She pulled a cloth covered notebook from an end shelf. "I was always proud my big sister was a practitioner. As a book lover I'm just a recipient, but from the beginning I wanted to share my feelings about what I read. Teaching high school English was a way to do that. I just took to it from the start."

Violet's Notebooks

Although John Shearer had been more cordial, more interested than the first time she visited, he was still a little threatening. Yes, and arrogant. Elizabeth was exhausted after the trip to Houston which was broiling hot and welcomed the reading day in Lily's cool study. She had taken it immediately, the day after Lily offered. The first book she pulled from the shelf was a notebook full of poems and questions and poems which were questions.

"About Rooms," one of the headings read. "Which ones can ghosts get into?/ Those in old houses/Where dreams are prophetic?/Where it's too easy in sleep/To slip out of the body?" Well, surely this one, Elizabeth thought as she read what seemed to be the writer's own lines. Others on the page she recognized as lines from well known poets. Blake, Hopkins, Wordsworth, Yeats.

From Wordsworth, lines from THE PRELUDE (the entry was labeled) in which the poet had heard "low and wren-like warblings/ —ballad tunes/ Food for the hungry ears of little ones/And of old men who have survived their joy."

When she turned the page Elizabeth saw these broken lines were followed by a prose entry entitled, "Surviving Joy."

"I'm not sure I will," the first line read. "I'm not sure I'll be able to. What I feel from all this wonder is danger. Thrill in it. But I'm scared, too. Should joy scare you? Maybe so —maybe most of us are not strong enough to stand it. I wake sometimes terrified. I have dreams of being imprisoned in darkness (I don't know where.)"

What she was reading from, what she was holding in her hand, Elizabeth suddenly realized was Lily's sister Violet's journal, or one of them. Although it seemed as if she was snooping —she was she guessed —she fell onto the soft green sofa with it and turned page after page until well into the afternoon.

The girl was in love with a mysterious young man, a newcomer to the county, an oil rigger on one of the Shearer's Kilgore wells and a person of whom Violet's parents did not approve, at least not as a suitor for their daughter. Who was he, they wanted to know. Where was he from? Who were his people? From what Violet told them he didn't seem to have much in the way of schooling, though he read books, books by Walt Whitman, even one by Karl Marx, books that fostered radical ideas in young people, or so they had heard. In addition, the way he spoke, they said, was funny, his grammar wasn't always good and he didn't have East Texas manners. He had been seen in the company of ornery Mexicans and of rough white men. They weren't sure about his age, but he seemed older than most of the oil riggers, out of his teens, maybe even in his mid to late twenties. They wanted Violet to have nothing more to do with this interloper. If she weren't so wayward, didn't do so much running around, she would never have met him in the first place.

But, unlike her sister, Rose, who behaved as a young woman should —seeing friends she had grown up with, doing work for the church and learning from her mother and the colored help they employed how to run a kitchen, do cooking and canning, and how to oversee a household, she, Violet, was reading odd books or daydreaming and scribbling (God knows what!) or off on her horse her father was sorry he had bought for her and wouldn't have except that as a little girl she so loved to ride that he had thought caring for a horse of her own might teach her discipline and that someday she might want to enter a few shows and distinguish herself that way. But, what did she do but ride off this way and that and often to unseemly places, places far from home, places, like the oil field, where young girls did not go, and in which her presence threatened disgrace to the family and where she —and all of them —were in danger? Violet knew this.

"Why do I dream?" she asked. "Why do I dream so much?" She kept repeating the question. "In those dreams," she wrote, "I'm engulfed in crying. I don't know whose. His? A child's? I don't know. I can't see anything for the blackness. I'm lost. Who knows where. And the sound of sobbing is all I hear…But no matter, no matter. All of them be damned. And never mind the crying. Or the darkness. I will not have the joy of him taken away."

Elizabeth slammed the journal shut. This was not what she had come into Lily's wonderful room to read —it was none of her business and she was ashamed of getting into this girl's long ago private life. She wondered why Lily kept Vi's notebooks on the shelf anyway. It seemed the same as keeping love letters out for anyone to read. She would ask Lily. And she would ask how Violet died —and if it seemed Lily wanted to tell her —she would ask about Violet's life. It seemed all right to find out about that from Lily, but not all right to find out by reading a dead girl's journal.

"They were only a year apart in age," Lily said, "but they couldn't have been less alike or had destinies that were —well, for lack of a better word, more divergent. Rose —like Mama and Daddy —seemed determined to do what everybody in the county and town admired, while Violet lusted after everything that was foreign to it, including this strange man.

"No one knew where he came from, but he didn't talk like East Texas. He was an oil rigger on the Shearer's wells. A lot of local boys did that work when they got out of high school to make some good money in a short time. But some came from other counties, and some, I guess, even from out of Texas. So where this fellow was from was hard to say.

"I'm not sure even Violet knew. She was just hell bent on running off with him. She said they planned on going out west, that the young man had saved up some money. But first they wanted to get married. Mama and Dad, of course, wouldn't hear of it, and as things turned out, the man was arrested (I'm not sure what the charges were) and Mama and Daddy sent Violet away." Lily stopped to take a deep breath and then, with a forward motion, to rock in the storehouse chair. Elizabeth had shut the lid of the cedar chest where she had continued to search for — who knew what? —and sat upon it silently, attentive to Lily's words.

"She was pregnant, you see and they found out and Daddy took her, crying and screaming, into his new Studebaker and drove her to his cousins who lived in the hill country on the other side of Austin and they looked after her until she had her baby, a boy Daddy finally pressured her to give up for adoption. And then he brought Violet home and saw to it she stayed in the house. She was just seventeen, but she never got over losing the fellow she loved and then losing her baby. She took pills to sleep and one night she took too many."

Inexplicably Elizabeth felt she had always known this, though she had never wanted to. A chill ran through her as she asked, "Do you have any idea what happened to the baby?"

"Well," Lily said, "Daddy and Mama said they thought he went to some friend of Daddy's cousin, though of course it was supposed to be secret who he went to. Daddy and Mama made several trips back to see the cousin hoping to find out, but I'm not sure they ever did. Daddy hushed up whatever he learned I expect."

"What happened to the boy's father? Did he know Violet had been sent away?"

"I believe he did, but there was nothing he could have done because as I said, by the time she went to the relatives he had been arrested. I don't remember what for. Only know he was taken to jail. Later he was tried and sent to Huntsville. Daddy wanted nothing to do with the case."

Elizabeth couldn't speak, but did manage to stand up. She wanted an end to this revelation which she was sorry she had asked for.

Lily looked through or past her. "I think," she said, "we all just wanted to forget about the whole thing. I know I did. Even though I was just a tiny girl, even before she died, I knew something awful that had to do with my big sister Vi had struck the family. And that it just about broke our mother's heart. Years went by before Rose gave me any of the details. Rose, of course, married Mr. Shearer's son, had a couple of healthy babies and she and all of them became richer and richer. Daddy lost himself in his practice, though he gave up criminal law and only took civil cases. But, for a long time, Mama took pleasure in nothing, not even Rose's boys. And I was a burden. I had been born crippled which didn't help much. Had to wear high topped shoes until I went to school. I can hardly ever remember seeing Mama smile."

Twelve: Questions of Justice

*E*lizabeth wrote that over and over on her yellow pad. The title of her radio play had once simply read, "A Question of Justice," not multiple ones. What could the boy Violet was in love with have done? Was running drugs all of it? Did he get a fair trial? How long did he stay in prison? Then where did he go? And what happened to his son?

It seemed to her that not only should Mr. Shearer help her look for Johnny, but that he should attend to looking for a relative —albeit a distance cousin, from his own house.

This must be a nation —a world — full of missing persons. Why did she have this crazy desire to call them all home? What was in it for HER? What was her hang up? Was it because her own father had disappeared in the Depression nearly three quarters of a century ago? But, perhaps, everyone, or nearly everyone, had someone important to them disappear. Perhaps disappearance was a nationwide, or even world wide, phenomena. She didn't know.

Perhaps an obsession with the missing, and she admitted that she was beginning to be gripped by such an obsession, had to do with a deep rooted malaise connected to the fundamental, seemingly impenetrable mystery of why everyone was here in the first place. (This presupposed "purpose" of course, and maybe there was none. Just life, life itself, seemed enough.) Wasn't that why she always had been drawn to drama? Wasn't that why she wrote, then read her radio plays? To find out what it was all about, what was at the source or nearest to it, why some people had it easy and others hard and others, like Violet and her lover, after hard punishment for their passions, just slipped away. Slipped, as Violet's line read, "out of the body." Or, at any rate, disappeared.

The characters in her radio play began to have histories resembling Violet and her —what was he? "Sweetheart," she said aloud, pleased with the sound of it. What a lovely old fashioned word. No one used it anymore. That seemed important, the people coming to life more important than social issues. The title of her play changed again. She began writing *The Sweetheart's Story*. She didn't even change the names much. Violet became Viola and she gave the lover Aunt Rena's brother's name, Johnny, not knowing as she did so that Johnny was what it really was.

Well, why not, she asked herself, then later asked Lily what the boy's name was. "John something or another," Lily said matter of factly. She couldn't remember the last name. This had all happened when she was just a small child. Elizabeth laughed aloud at the rightness of it all. John, was, she told herself a common name. Even Searcy's investigator, Lily's great nephew had it, handed down from his granddaddy. She said to Lily, "A common name." And Lily said, "Yes, Rose married a man named John, too. An oil king's son and certainly an opposite to the other one."

Lily seemed flattered that Elizabeth wanted to use her sister's story in a radio play. "It always seemed so wrong to me," she said, "what happened to her. I feel better to know you want to tell her story. Or even something like her story. It's a way to try to make something out all the damage that was done over what everyone in those days called 'an illegitimate child.' As if there could be such a thing as an illegitimate child!"

"The wrong can't be righted," Elizabeth said. "Only explored, and brought to the attention of whoever tunes into it. That is, if I actually manage to write it. But that seems worth attempting. People do become agitated when they lose track of their history. The day I met you, you said that to me. So many have lost some of those who are close to them, sometimes even lose all traces of blood kin —here's a member of your family, Violet's boy, who is now lost to you, an aunt —albeit, a young one —he never knew."

"Yes," Lily said, "and I'm sorry we never made a connection. She smiled.

"In a world full of them, his name was Johnny, too. So I think you ought to use it for your radio play."

Elizabeth asked Lily then about the cousin who lived in the hill country on what she spoke of as the "wild" side of Austin (an appropriate place for "Wild Violet" she thought.) Asked if she remembered exactly where.

"In sparsely populated country," Lily said. "But I guess that includes a lot that's west of Austin. Ragged country. And Daddy told me the nearest town was just a wide place in the road with a post office and a general store."

Thirteen: Making Plans to Visit

The road directly ahead —both literal and metaphoric —was plain to Elizabeth. There was nothing to do but make plans for the next spring or summer to go to Austin, visit with C. C. and then explore some of the surrounding countryside. C. C. had told Elizabeth they could visit Louellen's property at Liberty Hill, northwest of Austin, which was, perhaps similar to the place where Lily's cousins had lived three quarters of a century ago. Elizabeth would call C. C. and make plans for a visit in the near future, if possible sometime within the next six months, just as soon as she could once again get away from L. A. She was already homesick, and here she was, in many ways still at home!

She was going to miss Searcy and his sweet little house where she felt so much herself and had such wonderful dreams. And she would also miss Lily and her hideaway where she had finally managed to read stories and poems from the shelves for almost a full day. At Lily's urging before she left she even borrowed a large volume of George Eliot she had just begun to explore. So big that it included three Eliot novels and so old it had pages that had to be cut. The book had not been read completely through by anyone. "You can give it back to me when you return," Lily told her, "it'll be a reason to come back here. I don't want you to send it back by mail. I've never trusted mail." Elizabeth had told Lily she had to go back to California, work a while for the station, try to finish her radio play. Lily had urged her to take the book with her, and she had complied.

It seemed her destiny to travel back and forth across landscapes, a displaced person, but to never really claim one for her own. "We'll visit Louellen on her property when you come," C.C. said when she called. As things had turned out Louellen and Nick hadn't waited for a years-in-the-future retirement to build a house on their property. They just went ahead and cleared the diseased trees, hired a contractor and were in the process of leaving Austin for a rustic home. For years they had run their computer business by phone and the internet anyway and they didn't have to stay in town to do that.

C. C. told Elizabeth the boys and their dogs loved the country, roaming the land, swimming and fishing in the river that bordered it, and Louellen had bought a horse. The house was roomy and attractive with many large windows and breathtaking views of vistas and oaks trees.

Elizabeth had never felt closer to C. C. She was like a sister and Elizabeth longed for the time when they could be together again. Re-live the world of their girlhood again. How different it was from the present.

Before she left for Houston where she caught a plane to L. A. she and Miss Lily helped Searcy get into Miss Lily's car and drove eight miles to the south to see Searcy's property, six pretty acres on a creek, just out of the "piney woods."

"If I ever build on this," Searcy said, "it'll have to be up on the hill. The creek would flood the bottom lands if we ever got hard rain. If anyone built near it, the house would have to be on stilts —which would be a possibility for someone who wanted a rough camp house near water. I've been meaning to get someone to come and clear the creek out. If I did, it would improve the value of the property."

"It's mighty pretty property," Miss Lily said. By the time she spoke she and Elizabeth had Searcy in his wheel chair and out of the car. With Lily trailing, Elizabeth pushed him through the gate and onto the path that led to the creek. Leaves crackled all around them; the summer had been so dry that many had already fallen. She liked to hear the crunch of them beneath the wheels of Searcy's chair and beneath her feet. And as they moved closer to it, the sound of the water bubbling over the rocks; it seemed almost to be speaking to her. Maybe it wanted to tell her that she should consider living near it. Too far from C. C. and her family she told herself, but said, "The creek sure is pretty. Searcy, if you ever wanted to sell, how much would you ask for this piece of land?"

Fourteen: Alone

*S*eptember. Santa Ana weather. Back in L. A. Elizabeth realized, as if for the first time, that except for C. C. and Searcy, (neither of whom were blood kin) she had no family. Colleagues, yes. A good friend or two among them, yes. But no one who shared her family history or her memories of those close to her in childhood. Aunt Rena gone like Uncle Leeland before her, like her mother's youngest brother, Bo, who had also brought her up, and yes, even like her tough mother, for the past five years also gone. She had no idea what had happened to her father and had never even considered undertaking an investigation. Oh, she had run his name through Google a few times, but grew discouraged when nothing on the search engine turned anything up and gave up going further as a waste of energy. For a short time she regretted never marrying and having children. Or at least never having children. Then before regret could make her maudlin or take a firm hold, or the hot winds off the desert could make her feel she was losing her mind, she threw herself into the writing of her radio play.

She found herself retelling Violet and her young lover's story, realizing that it was entirely possible that she was writing Aunt Rena's brother, Johnny's story, too. The time was right, the teens when Johnny ran away into the late twenties and early thirties (Violet's lover could have been described as "young" and still have been fifteen or sixteen years older than she), the setting in East Texas was right. Why hadn't Lily or her great nephew, John Shearer, ever suspected that the person missing from his family might be one of the persons missing from her own? Maybe Lily did suspect. Maybe that suspicion was partially why she was so interested in Searcy's quest. But then, in Big John Shine, Lily had a detective in her own family; if it had been crucially important to her, she could have used him to track down his great aunt's lover a long time ago.

Probably, Elizabeth told herself, Aunt Rena's brother just had a similar story. Probably there were hundreds of similar stories in other parts of the country and maybe even a few more in East Texas itself.

Then, in the old volume of George Eliot with the uncut pages she had borrowed from Lily, she found the letters —Violet's and one from Johnny himself. There they were before her, stuck in a page of *Daniel Deronda* that someone had only cut half way across. The moment she saw them it was clear to her that their stories were both meant to come to her and that she had selected them. She, after all, had pulled the volume that contained them off the shelf herself.

From Violet's Journal

He's been running drugs. I just found out. And he thinks the law is onto him —he says he thinks soon he's got to get out of here —he wants me to go with him —we'll go west he says, far. We'll get married. That scares me a little. People think I don't care what anyone else wants, but I wouldn't like to do it or to go without Mama and Daddy's blessing. I'll ask. If they got to know him I'm sure they would love him —how could they not? —he's all sweetness, really —well, sweetness plus manliness, something at his core that's really steely, really strong. He just did the marijuana run for money he wanted to send home to his family, his mama and little sister, all he has left and for money to save for his life ahead and to further his education. He came to Texas so he could make enough, but he couldn't always make enough as just a Roughneck. If Daddy got to know him, and what an inquiring mind he has, he'd see how earnest he is about a desire for betterment and that he's smart! Oh he loves to read (like me and also like Daddy!) He's given me so many exciting books and by writers that, before I met him I never heard of. He didn't have the money to go to college, but he'd still like to —and could someday, part time, even if we were married. Daddy, maybe, could help. If he knew him he'd see how sharp he is —and Mama, she'll appreciate how considerate, and that he never meant or means to harm anyone. Oh, he's impulsive and that gets him into trouble sometimes. He knows he made a mistake in the runs to Mexico and that the law may be on to him and he prays about it. He says he depends on the power of prayer to help him (he always carries The New Testament in his hip pocket and he's studied the whole Bible.) And he thinks now prayer can get us both through. We need to go west. He says when he asks the answers seem to come to him. "Enlarge my territory," his prayer says. We need to go forward into that whole open country — that's the answer that's come to him, he seems sure of it.

Out there. That's where our life is! And, oh, I'm ready. But I want not just God, but Mama and Daddy, too, to bless our leaving —no matter what they may believe about me, I know I'll need their caring. Oh, I do love John, and want to be with him always —but I also want Mama and Daddy to say they'll stand by us —come visit us and that we can always come to them, too. That it's OK for our family to branch out, take chances. That when John and I go West we will for Mama and Daddy and Rose and her husband-to-be and for whatever children they have be, as John says, ENLARGING their territory. ENLARGING THEIR LIVES (for good) is what John means, what he says the Bible means. Enlarging the future —and for all of us —too.

Did she know she was pregnant when she made this entry? Elizabeth asked herself the question.

J's Letter

When Elizabeth turned the page she found his letter.

Oh, darlin', baby, I can't ever stop thinking of you. Don't give up on me. I've got a lawyer on my side. He seems good, though the state just assigned him to me. (Your daddy might not like him. I don't know.) I'll get out of here. We can go somewhere where I'll find real work. I can take care of us, I know I can and maybe even send some back to my mama and little sister. That's what I meant to do when I left Louisiana in the first place. I've been too ashamed to write them. I meant to make a way for myself and to help them. I never thought I also might find someone else to share with. Nobody who understood like you.

It broke off there. Elizabeth remembered Rena saying, "Johnny was the kind of boy who wanted to make things big. 'Our life here is so little,' he always said. 'I want to make it bigger. I want to make it large. And for us all.'"

Part Two

Fifteen: Discovering a Spring

$\mathcal{U}$p the stream a way the men he had hired to clear it found the spring. The creek had been so clogged with leaves and fallen tree trunks and, shamefully, with the debris that campers had thrown into it, that they hadn't thought about even the possibility of a spring. It had been a long time since Searcy could recall being so excited —he would write Elizabeth about it right away. He remembered taking her to a spring in Arkansas when she lived with Rena and was just a little girl —so small he had carried her on his shoulders. They would hike to the spring, he had told her back then, and bring some good spring water to Aunt Rena. Odd that Rena was, through different connections, aunt to them both —aunt by blood to him and by marriage to Elizabeth who was almost a generation younger. Maybe the discovery was a good omen, maybe it would bring them luck.

Elizabeth had grown up —and grown old —to be an odd woman, displaced and alone. He never understood why she never married —she'd had men in her life he was sure —or why she traveled around the country as she did, a regular gypsy, a vagabond. Bad enough for a man to live a life like that, but for a woman it was he knew in the minds of some, a tramp's life, a scandal. He saw it differently. Some passion was in it. Some dream had directed her. He had never understood what it was or why it was important to her. He admired her for managing to make her own living. He just thought it sad that Elizabeth was a woman without a household, no progeny. No man, no child. She would never have grandchildren; (he wouldn't have them either, of course, but that was not because he hadn't tried.) No settling place.

Maybe, he considered, he could at least give her —or help her get —that. A settling place. Maybe she would even consider settling on a piece of his property. He remembered her asking about price. He was willing to sell some of it to her cheap, or even make a gift of it if she would let him. But he wouldn't tell her that now. He would wait until she returned. By that time they might both have a lead on Johnny. He was considering writing her a letter or even calling (it was hard for him to call, he had always been telephone shy) when he heard Lily's shuffle on the path. He wheeled himself through the kitchen and down the short hall to the living room's front door. His stroke, hard as it was, had after all, brought some blessings —reconnection with Elizabeth who he certainly considered kin —and Lily, long a neighbor, but now a real friend.

"Mr. Pugh," she said when she saw him —not right, he thought, that she still called him Mr. Pugh —"I have some news." She was holding a piece of paper. "My great nephew, Mr. Shearer's e-mail came just a few minutes ago and I printed it out."

Lily had been his communicator with John Shearer. He had considered installing a computer in the kitchen he now used also as the room in which he visited, ate, slept, sometimes read (not much, the local paper, some magazines with articles about gardening or fishing) where a lot of the time he just sat and looked out upon his backyard, the pecan trees, the little shed he used for storage and Bea's morning glory vine which grew over the fence and onto it, where he thought about things. But he didn't know if he was up to learning about using a computer just yet, he had never been much on buying the latest in electronic aides. Until he had a stroke he even used a manual can opener. The microwave, though he now thanked God for it, and even the new coffee maker had been real adjustments. Anyway, except for Elizabeth, he couldn't think of anyone much he wanted to contact by e-mail and was half afraid that if he started to reach out to people this way he would never actually see them or even hear their voices on a telephone (and shy as he had always been of talking on the phone he did like to hear the voices of others on it.) After Lily had volunteered to e-mail for him he had given her e-mail address to his county workers and the church ladies, and Elizabeth had sent it to John Shearer.

"Well, what does he say, Lily?"

When they reached the kitchen she handed him the sheet of paper along with his glasses which she picked up off the counter and at the same time told him, "He says he has some information on the prison interment of Johnny Brock."

His Uncle Johnny, his mother's and his Aunt Rena's much loved long lost brother; then it was true, he really had gone to prison. Huntsville, he supposed. The message said the information called for a meeting, that his findings should be shared personally. Maybe, Searcy considered, he had something that might be risky to divulge on the internet or even over the phone. "Well, I don't know what to do," he said, "I can't right now call Elizabeth back from California."

"I'll contact him, Searcy," she said. "Do you mind if I call you Searcy?"

He shook his head. "I've been meaning to tell you to do it."

"Maybe," she plunged ahead," I could even drive down to Houston to see him, that is, with your permission. I do still drive my car." As she spoke, she rocked in the wicker chair next to the daybed where now, night and day, Searcy took his rest.

"Do you hear what I do about the traffic? And all those one way streets. I wouldn't want you to have to cope with that." So his Uncle Johnny really had gone to prison, and this detective he had been hell bent on hiring had something that might serve as proof. He almost regretted what was probably a foolish longing, the childish yearning of an old man who still missed his mother and —yes, glad as he was to have his new friend before him —his beloved wife.

Lily smiled and set the rocker going with her good foot. "I like a challenge," she said.

"He really went to prison, Lily. I guess I wish I hadn't found that out."

"It happens in the best of families," she said. "If you make me a cup of coffee or let me make one for us both I'll tell you a story about my own."

After she was gone and the twilight came on, he lay on the daybed under the sheet she had thrown over him, the nearby fan oscillating. (Though it was hot, he wanted to keep the windows open, didn't want the air conditioner on.) They had shared a simple meal of scrambled eggs, toast and fig preserves —homemade from the tree in Lily's yard — more like breakfast than supper and she had helped him take off his shirt and, after he used the bathroom, get into a pajama top. He still had on the bottoms from the night before, (his shower worker wouldn't come until the next day.) When he was younger he had not liked this time of day, had not liked to see night come on, had found a sadness in it. But he didn't mind it anymore. The stroke had brought so many dark hours, maybe he had gotten used to them or at least learned not to be frightened when they took him to a different place. After the stroke hit him he had, in fact, gone down the tunnel, and pitch black it was. And when he came to the end had seen his mother, Aunt Rena's little sister ("Lucy, the healer," she had called her) smiling at him. He knew it was his mother though he could only remember seeing her in pictures. Why, dying's not bad he had thought, dying's not bad at all.

It was coming back to the living that was hell. At first he thought he would never be able to move anything —a leg, a hand, a finger, even, much less be able to speak or walk a step or two. Speech had finally come back to him, had come first, though for a long time the words tumbled out displaced and funny sounding. Walking more than a few steps with a three pronged cane had never come back, but if he had to choose between taking steps and making words, he'd take making words every time. If he couldn't make them, how could he ever have a friend like Lily? And if he were still walking she wouldn't be on hand to help him now. If he had been able to walk she might never have come to help him in the first place. He had seldom felt so at home with another person. His passion for his wife had also brought with it some tension, granted that it was of a kind that gave him joy, that let him know now and then life might be shot through with joy, that the chance for it was there, that joy wasn't just a myth. Exhilarating as that had been, he was now thankful that there was no tension of any kind in what he felt for Lily. She was simply his friend.

"Let's face it," he told her when they saw the sun setting over the morning glory vine and she announced she had to go home, "you and I are both getting ready to go home, to walk into the twilight." Then he laughed and corrected himself. "Or should I say you're going to walk into the twilight, Lily. I'm going to wheel into it. Or maybe just fall."

"That's classy. I'm going to be limping," she said.

"Then there we'll go," he told her, "wheeling—falling — limping —"

That afternoon she told him for the first time —and, except to Elizabeth, for the first time she had told anyone in a very long while —her sister Violet's and her lover, John's, story and told him it was a story Elizabeth also knew because she, Lily, had opened her Daddy's hidden room to Elizabeth (when had she ever let anyone else in?) and related it there. As she spoke, she saw Searcy's face cloud over and also saw it brighten when he said, "Why that John, your sister's John, might also have been my Uncle Johnny. That's possible you know." He thought it was funny he was paying her already wealthy great nephew to find out what possibly —just possibly —she already knew.

"Well, we don't know what finally happened to my big sister's Johnny. Or even what he was sent to prison for. When asked —and yes, Violet's John summoned the courage to ask him —Daddy, who told us nothing about it, wouldn't even take the case. We don't even know what finally happened to John and Violet's little boy. Whether or not there's a remote possibility he was also related to you is probably the last question we should ask. All in all, the fate of the missing fellow in your life and in mine is still a mystery. We don't know much."

He felt something inside him shift. "Maybe," he said, surprising himself with what followed. "Maybe it doesn't matter. Maybe what's important now is that we have each other to share the stories of our missing Johnnys with, —and that's a lot."

Sixteen: Bubbling

*B*ubbling. The water ever was. Both the sound and the thought of it brought comfort, brought back all his life to him, brought happiness. That afternoon the workmen at the spring directed Searcy toward it.

Hap-pi-ness. The sound of it unmistakable in the message the water was bringing to him. It had also been Aunt Rena's message, the one she didn't have to speak (though she did sometimes) because it was her way of being in the world. Probably, he thought, it was still her way, wherever she was.

Like his Aunt Rena, Searcy had never burned, or even flickered a little, with any kind of ambition. Not to make money —as his brother had —or to make anything really. Now and then, yes, a garden. (That was like Rena, too.) Though, of course, since the stroke he hadn't been able to follow up on it. Most of the time he was content just to be. That was all right. Rena had gotten that message across to him early. He didn't have to produce anything if he didn't want to, become anything more than what he already was, her nephew, his mother's son. Himself.

Content in his own being and in his relationship to other beings —Animal, Mineral or Vegetable. The name of a game he had played with his Aunt Rena when he was a child. He smiled when he thought about it. Yes, without asking or even particularly wanting to, he did grow through those relationships —animal, mineral and vegetable — but there was no strain in it. No special effort on his part had ever been required.

He changed, yes. He saw that, comprehended, but it had, except when he lost those he loved, been remarkably easy. Just this afternoon he had in a moment or two changed his thinking about finding his long lost Uncle Johnny.

Like his Aunt Rena, he lived for simple pleasures. Drinking his coffee. (It had begun to taste good again.) Eating supper. Sitting out under the pecan trees feeling the wind, if there was one, on his arms, his neck. Listening to Lily's shuffle on his front path, smelling the homegrown tomatoes she brought him, looking into the faded blue of her eyes and then the true blue of the flowers on Bea's vine. About it all, "Enough" was the word that came to him.

Yet, he did question. Just as Rena had. And in the last year the question that had come to him was this: Do lives have patterns? He thought about his Aunt Rena's, about Elizabeth's, Lily's, his own. His life, like Rena's

—like many, he supposed, maybe most —had been filled with loss. He lost his mother as a little boy, so young he could barely remember her. Scarlet fever. So many had it when he was a child. Back then the country was literally plagued. So many awful diseases. Typhoid. Diphtheria. Smallpox, even. His Aunt Rena brought his mother back to him in the pictures she showed him and the stories she told about the people in them. Later on he lost his little son and before his son, his first wife who died in childbirth (and he mourned her even though that marriage had never been just right.) Then he had been blessed with Beatrice before he lost her, too. Men were supposed to outlive women, that was the statistic. But all the women in his family were gone. He had kept Aunt Rena the longest. She had lived to be nearly a hundred —he couldn't complain about that. She had lost everyone she had loved, too —her only child, Uncle Leeland; even Elizabeth had drifted away. That is the fate of survivors, of course. If you live long enough losing loved ones, if you are lucky enough to have them, is what you do. Love and pain bound together, one the other's flip side.

But both he and Rena at least knew how the vanishing had taken place. Except for Johnny. Maybe just having that knowledge was what they were after. For completion. He remembered how his Aunt Rena used to work jigsaw puzzles. She was so patient. She waited to hold just the right shapes. She seemed to know if she fingered enough, just the right ones would finally come to her and the whole picture would fill in. Maybe that was why she lived to be nearly a hundred. Maybe her life required that length so that she could patiently connect all the pieces of it. But even at the end one piece was missing. Johnny. Her brother Johnny. His Uncle Johnny. Of story, of legend, even. Maybe he had wanted to find out what happened to his Uncle Johnny, had been waiting to find out, like Rena waited to fit together the pieces of her jigsaw puzzles, to make his knowledge of his mother's family (his heart's home) and his own life complete.

The sound of the water brought this knowledge to him. In his wheelchair, the workman by this time downstream, he sat very still listening. He heard a bobwhite's call, the leaves of the ash trees rustling and the fluttering sound of a few as they fell, summer being almost done. Heard the sound of the bubbling water which said Hap-pi-ness. Which said Fru-i-tion.

Completeness. That's what he had been after. What Elizabeth, in a different way from him was after, too. She had come to him, he thought, because she didn't want to lose what she had left of her family, and where she might find a place in which she could experience a sense of wholeness. She should have some of this property, share it with him, an acre —or more if she wanted it. They couldn't bring back those who were gone and they might never find out what had happened to those who got lost, who were just missing. But they could have this, this place to re-collect all that they were. All their pieces. He would have some papers drawn up. He was going to make Elizabeth a gift.

Seventeen: An Encounter With John Shine

*H*e hadn't counted on needing such a lot of money, couldn't believe the figure he now needed to raise —would he have to sell his land? — he hadn't counted on once again breaking down.

The visit to John Shearer's had begun it. That man who hadn't even wanted to take the case had for some reason suddenly been eager to go on with it and had wanted him and Lily to come down to Houston right away. And, without understanding why, he had agreed and found himself with Lily in her little car, his wheel chair in the back of it —crippled as she was Lily had put it in the back herself —speeding down Highway 59, through and past Lufkin and then Livingston until they were out of the pines and on one of many scary lanes that led into the heart of the sprawling city.

Lily was a good driver and they had made good time, taken just the right exit, parked without having to look for a space (Handicapped was in some ways a blessing) and found themselves in John Shearer's South Main office twenty minutes before they were due. Mr. Shearer had taken them in before others who were waiting. Lily was his great aunt after all. And after shaking his hand and embracing Lily, who he hadn't seen in a long time, not since his grandmother Rose's New Year's party he had said, he announced while nodding toward Searcy and tapping his Truth is Liberty sign, "I've found the truth, the rundown on this man, this man who disappeared from your family and who from the evidence I now have caused havoc in mine." Then he had picked up a document from his desk and from it, read, "John Brock. Arrested for drug dealing and assault. Interred in the Texas State Prison Huntsville, February 23, 1930."

The way he had run on startled Searcy. He first felt his head swimming again then and there. Dizziness was a danger signal and he knew it. John Shearer's voice had droned on and on about his mother's and Aunt Rena's brother, a man he had never known, a man who was only a story. Only a story. How had he gotten so caught up in whatever it was that had been the destiny of this man from a story, this ghost of an uncle from another time, from what was now almost another century? Why had he ever wanted to do this? But since he had, why did Mr. Shearer's words come to him as blows?

John Brock had gone to prison and for sometime.

Searcy had, after all, told himself that might have happened. So what if it had? All it meant was that because of some wrong he'd done, the man had suffered. One way or another everyone does. "John Brock," he heard himself repeating dumbly after John Shearer read that name from the paper he held in his hand, light glittering across it, reflected from the man's huge diamond ring. "John Brock, yes. Brock was my mother's maiden name."

John Brock had suffered at the hands of the state. Had his girl and his child taken from him. "Mr. Pugh," John Shearer had said, or Searcy thought he had said, "Here are the papers. I have the documents. Here is the proof." What does it matter, he had wanted to yell at him. But hadn't. Had only repeated "John Brock" over and over. Had only repeated the name.

"I'm sorry, Mr. Pugh. I didn't want this news either." John Shearer's voice he remembered had softened, was as he handed over the papers, consoling. "But you must see all the information is here, birth records, even a confessed account of his relationship with my grandmother's and Aunt Lily's sister. A tragic history." John Shearer had said that. "A tragic history for your relative. And," he had added, "mine." Searcy had not wanted to think there was any connection between his mother's brother and the lover of Lily's long lost little sister. "It was a long time ago," Mr. Shearer had said, "and not a reflection on any of us who were not in the world at that time." Then he had looked at Lily and added, "Or not long in the world at that time."

Searcy had not been able to answer. Stared at the papers John Shearer had put in his hands. The words blurred before him. He had thought of Elizabeth then and of Jabez's prayer that she had found, the one John Brock in 1915 had written down and he supposed said out loud many times, the one asking for a bigger life to come to him from God and for Good (God/ Good —that was one and the same, wasn't it?) He wished he had attended church more often or at least prayed more often. The ladies who visited and brought him things offered to take him to services but he didn't go. Funny that although his head was reeling, instead of the words he was supposed to read, he all but saw them before him. "Mr. Pugh," John Shearer's voice echoed, "you need to go over these papers thoroughly."

"Yes, yes," he had responded, though he knew he might not. At least not thoroughly. Knew he never wanted to read them, only wanted as soon as he could to get out of this man's presence, away from the laser slashes of light that seemed almost to strike as they bounced off his hand, away from this office with its expensive furniture, cherry wood desk, leather sofas, incongruous next to gilded chairs. "Yes, I'll go over them," he had heard himself say, had to say if he was to get out of there. He couldn't, after all, just blurt out, Lily, Lily, something's wrong with me. Please just take me home.

"Truth is liberty," he had heard John Shearer say as he pointed to his sign. "Now that we know it we can be free." Searcy felt himself sinking, as if he were under water. Free? These connections strung their lives together. How could any of them be free? He heard Lily thank John, say they should all see each other more often. Incomprehensible to him. "Your grandmother, she should come to see me," he heard Lily say. "You and your mother, too. Maybe at Christmastime."

The words brought back his memory. For a moment he had forgotten Lily's sister was this man's grandmother. Hearing Lily declare that came to him as a shock. Then when the big man took his hand he was again blinded by the glitter. No wonder Elizabeth recalled his name as Shine.

He would call Elizabeth as soon as Lily could get him out of this terrible place. The office. The congested city. Through all the snarls of traffic —away from this man who he hoped never to see again, away and back through the piney woods home.

Eighteen: What She Thought She Knew

When she tried to get to the bottom of her uneasiness about John Shearer she realized that what made her most uncomfortable was not his arrogance, or even his machismo or his moralizing about crime and liberty and truth. The thing that made her the most uncomfortable was that he made his assessments of others on the basis of what they had materially. He assumed Searcy's Uncle Johnny was shiftless, inferior, possibly even a criminal because he had nothing in the way of material goods. She knew John Shearer equated material assets with character. He didn't even take Searcy seriously because he judged him to be a man of not much means —a few acres of land, a small house in a small town, a meager pension and savings. He wasn't poor enough to be a criminal, of course, but he hadn't enough for his opinions or even his desires to carry influence of a serious kind.

The last time they had spoken and he had lamented the behavior of John Brock, Mr. Shearer had told Elizabeth he admired the man —he thought it was one of the country's recent presidents —who said that a man's first duty in life was to make a fortune. Elizabeth had been shocked by that. In her mind it followed that some women, those who had little sense of themselves, might think a woman's first duty in life was to find a man who had made a fortune and, if she couldn't do that, a man who at least wanted to. His grandmother Rose had done that, and as a result all in his family lived lives that were not only good materially, but, in his thinking, also morally. Elizabeth was sure that those who made a great deal of money were in John Shearer's view morally superior, and this belief not only put her off, it sickened her.

For reasons she had not been able to fathom, it scared her some, too. When she was face to face with John Shearer, alone with him, she always sensed some threat. She was not sure why, what her malaise was about, but John Shearer looked at her and often put her down in a way that made her feel violated. She was probably twenty five years his senior, she told herself, and yet, a sexual component seemed in it, one that hardly flattered her. There was no attraction, no tenderness, or even lust, in it, only what came across as the prospect of brute force, a wish for dominion. One he might not be consciously aware of —he was clearly not an introspective man —and one, she felt sure, he would give only mental and verbal, rather than physical expression to. (He was, after all, Rose's properly brought up, easily shocked, sanctimonious grandson.) Still, the idea of mental domination was scary enough. She was uneasy about seeing him again.

But she would tell no one. If she spoke about what she felt she was well aware of what the reaction of most would be. The fears of a woman who had lived alone too long, who would soon be called "elderly" and after that "old." An "old woman," and, therefore, discounted. Hysterical old woman, some would think, if not say. Probably always frightened of men.

Sometimes, you bet, she told herself and with good reason. But some men she had always trusted implicitly. Searcy was now one of these and she knew if she told him about what she suspected of John Shine, he would believe her. Still, she thought it best, for a while, anyway, to keep her feelings private. No matter what she said or how often she spoke, she would not be heard; as far as most were concerned she was not one of them —she was diminished, already a ghost.

She only admitted what she felt to herself after Aunt Rena once again appeared to her in a dream, this time holding the pink scarf Elizabeth stored in her top bureau drawer. "Put this on, honey," Aunt Rena said. "Everything will be all right."

A hysterical old woman, she could hear Lily's neighbors or Searcy's church ladies or Lily's sister Rose say. She'd never met Rose, of course, but she had her opinion of her. Aunt Rena was gone. Except for C.C. no one else was living who remembered she'd been in love. Several times. And with fine men. That she'd been too young for the first of them and too late for the other. That she had for years made a conscious effort not to think of either of them. No one would know she hadn't been skittish. Had been frightened only of the power, and what she feared might be the consequences of her own feeling. No one would know that she wasn't in the presence of Mr. Shearer, young enough to be her child, just a crazy old dame.

If there was no one to consider her for who she was, there was also no use in trying to persuade anyone. She only intended to see John Shine one more time to go over the documents Searcy had told her about and to make arrangements for payment. That office visit would be uncomfortable like the others, but she would get through it. Then she would never have to see John Shearer again.

Since this is so, she told herself, maybe I am being a little bit crazy, a little hysterical, that old Freudian word for a woman upset (no equivalent word for a man.) Deep down she thought she knew there was some basis for her fears, some possibility she didn't want to consider.

Nineteen: Going To C.C.'s

$\mathcal{S}$he wouldn't see him for a while. First she would visit with C.C. and together they would drive to Liberty Hill to look at Louellen's property. She would also make inquiries at local realtors about land that she might consider buying, if for nothing else, an investment, though she couldn't deny her fantasies of the simple one or two room cabin that one day she might put upon it. The cabin she would visit in spring and fall, those two good Texas seasons. In the spring she would gather wildflowers.

Yes, she knew some would call her childish. No matter. She could not give up this dream which represented her idea of "home." No matter if it was an illusion. She wrote stories, after all, and this place that she carried in her head, at the moment just another fiction, was essential to her.

She packed her suitcase carefully. She would need jeans or khaki pants for Liberty Hill, long sleeved shirts, sneakers, a cardigan or two, the kind of clothes she almost never wore in L. A. She didn't know why it took her so long to select these items from her closet, fold and place them between the books and papers that were always with her when she traveled, but only in the wee morning hours did she get to bed and even then, fell into a restless sleep.

The dream came, as had some of the other important dreams in her life, with a title.

At the Spring

"Come out from under the bed, Pumpkin," Aunt Rena said to her. "Searcy will take you there. Searcy will take you to the spring."

Rena's nephews, Searcy and Johnny, visited once or twice a year. She was shy around new people, especially those who took up Aunt Rena's time and attention.

Why did these men who Aunt Rena called "her little boys" have to come here? Searcy, Aunt Rena said was almost twenty, his brother, Johnny, even older. This morning Johnny had gone to town to see about buying a car from a man and Aunt Rena was busy canning fruit. Searcy wanted to go to A Thousand Drippings Spring —he had never been Aunt Rena said —and he would take her. She had always loved the spring where last summer on a hot day like this one she had gone into the icy water with Aunt Rena and Uncle

Leeland. "Searcy wants to see you. Come out now, Pumpkin."

Well, she had, she had —and he had smiled at her and taken her hand and said not a word about her crying and kicking the floor. And they had walked together to the Old Bus (Aunt Rena and Uncle Leeland's ten year old Studebaker) and driven down the hill and turned onto the dusty road and driven for what seemed to her miles, to the thicket that led to the water. And when they entered the thicket Searcy had picked her up and carried her on his shoulders down the dark path, pine needles brushing her cheek. When she looked up she saw the blue of the sky. And they went on and on. The path had no end.

And then all at once there it was, the water! And Searcy swung her down into it. And she screamed with fear, and then with delight. It was so cold.

She woke with a start. When she was an older child how many times had Aunt Rena asked — asked when she was resisting his visits, "Don't you remember Searcy?" (She didn't.) "Why, he carried you to the spring."

But she didn't. She didn't remember. It must have happened when she was too young. Or maybe she was just blocked from remembering because she was so jealous of Searcy and his brother — the way they took Aunt Rena from her, or the way she feared they would —and she didn't even know them. They lived in Louisiana where Aunt Rena had come from before she married Uncle Leeland, and she didn't even know really —although she had been shown on a map —where that was. And now, when she was in her sixties and thought of Searcy as nearest and dearest kin, she had remembered in a dream. Or had she? Had it been memory or just a dream? (Who was it that said, "Memory is a dream."?) And on the night before she was leaving for C.C.

Twenty: Hiding

*D*id a post office and one block of stores —a small grocery, a card and gift shop, a garage that also sold antiques —qualify it as a town? The chill and mist intensified the pain in her ankle, the one she had twisted before boarding the plane, and in addition, she realized she was getting a cold. It had been Searcy's health she had been concerned about, not her own. She could remember Aunt Rena in her dream saying, "You can be thankful your health is still good." Hers were minor ailments, of course. Before she boarded the plane she had waited for almost an hour before being allowed to move through Security and after she reached the Check Point and handed over her bag and shoes she was detained even longer. Was it from another life, her memory of traveling being care free? Being fun? Somehow the security personnel misplaced her shoes and when they were finally retrieved and given to her she turned her ankle right after putting them on. And she fell just before she crossed the threshold of the gate nearest the plane waiting for her on the Burbank field. She got up right away but her ankle hurt. She wondered if the fall had come to her a warning, one that meant to say: Turn back. Don't go

Well, whatever, it was too late now. On this damp November afternoon she had arrived, a strong smell of cedar in the air, wet cedar (the smell of fresh water, too, in the chilly mist), the storefronts, by this time, a half mile behind C. C.'s Land Rover off the dirt road through the open gate of Louellen's and Nick's property. After the dirt road turned into a scrubby field Elizabeth startled to the sight of leaping fires burning piles of debris. Was it also burning some of the cleared trees —those with oak wilt? When C.C. cried out she heard herself say that it was all right, that in drizzle it wasn't likely the flames would get out of hand. But what she thought of was hell. Hellfire. Were they entering Hades?

At the end of the road the rise of the straight up and down house surprised by its austerity, its plainness, its severe tall brick front —no curves, no porches. To each side of the road she took note of the oaks and cedars, all so small she thought of them as stubby. The trees, she told herself, don't achieve height here —only the houses can do that. What were the other trees? Mesquites? Ugliness in the landscape, but also an odd dwarfed beauty.

Not far from the house the longhorns' heads dipped into clumps of grass —four of them, tan and white, brown and white, a lone black —all of them grazing on the stubby clump of green. Very near the residence four dogs, a Pyrenees mix, a border collie, a shepherd and an oversized chow ran after each other, circling the house. Just frolicking, she wondered or protecting it?

With such guards, what was there to fear here? The mist that seemed to swirl around them, that seemed to rise out of the very ground? (Did that mist rising explain the soreness in her bones? The way she felt her heart beat?)

After C. C. parked and they were out of the car, the door opened upon the beauty of Louellen's face and the dark, lovely face of her husband, Nick. Nothing, she told herself. Nothing. Nothing, she nearly murmured aloud when she looked on at their boys, one blond as his mother, the other freckled and sandy headed. She spied the cats then. Half farm —half house cats? She asked herself about them as she remembered C. C.'s story. A gray, an orange tabby with a long body and small head, a thin black with stylized lines whose likeness might grace parchment paper on an art nouveau card. Then another feline down the hall —near what? A family room? —whose murky color she couldn't make out.

Upstairs then. Louellen soon had her and C. C. up them, touring rooms with large windows through which the sweep of land, miles and miles of it dotted with those dark, twisted oaks and yes, the blackish cedars, spread before them and in the distance, the other side of a river —the Gabriel River she was told, cotton mouths on its banks —a flat-topped plateau, a little mesa called Mt. Gabriel. Mount? Was there meant to be humor in that?

Yes, Aunt Rena's brother could have come looking for his son here and from this place the two of them might also have departed, "blazed a trail," the term her family members had so often used, farther west. Or, she considered, into which they may have just rooted —hidden. Could a disease that affects humans —not unlike the way "oak wilt" affects trees —come from that? A disease from the root? Rooted. She loved the sound of the word. Also its connection to "hidden." Roots were, after all, underground.

She stopped. Leave it alone, she told herself. Let it rest. Come back to the living, to these beautiful young people who are making a new home here. Running a business, schooling their children (one of the upstairs rooms was a schoolroom) in this hidden world, this fortress. "Louellen," she heard herself saying, "I thought you and Nick were saving all this for your retirement."

Louellen startled, looked at her with surprise (in Elizabeth's memory Louellen's face was ever serene.) "After what has happened in our world in the last years? Late in 2001 I asked myself, 'Louellen, what are you waiting for?'"

Elizabeth again felt her heart leap.

Danger! Danger! The word all but rang out. Fear drove so many, even those who exuded calm, had been the most vital. And in a world with so much killing, so much blood lust, why not? She knew fear now gripped her.

Aunt Rena, she wanted to say, this is what I have to tell you. I don't know why, I don't know why, but now I don't just perceive fear in those around me. I am afraid. I am afraid now, too.

"Are you all right?" Louellen asked. "Mom told me you haven't felt well. Let's go downstairs. I'll get you a Coke or a cup of coffee."

"I'm OK," she said. "It's just the weather. I have a cold and a little arthritis in that ankle I turned before I got on the plane." She knew better. The pain she felt in her bones warned her that something sharper, some sharper pain might lie ahead. Searcy after his Houston encounter with John Shearer might be seriously declining. When she last talked to Lily, Lily all but said so. Why hadn't she gone to him immediately instead of indulging herself in this side trip that she had thought of as pure pleasure? Why had she held back? What was she doing here? She should get to Searcy soon.

Twenty-one: Liberty is Truth

This visit to Louellen's new home, this reunion with Texas family, her gift from C. C. who wanted her to feel included, was one that she should have postponed. She should have gone to Searcy first. On her way to C. C.'s house she used her cell to call him and was surprised to hear Lily answer the phone. Searcy's blood pressure was way up and his doctor had him admitted to the hospital where he could be completely monitored and checked out. They couldn't take a chance on him having another stroke.

"I'll be there by tomorrow night, Lily," she heard herself saying. "I'll fly to Houston and take a car up from there." She went on to say she might stop to talk to John Shearer if she could get an appointment, that there were a few things she wanted to clear up. "But I'll be on my way up to Nacogdoches right after," she said. "I'll call Searcy in the hospital in the morning, but you tell him that I'm on my way, too."

That evening in C. C.'s upstairs guest room she took a pen to her journal. "Aunt Rena," she wrote, "I have so much to tell you. But first I have to see that man we should never have gone to, Lily's nephew, her oil rich sister's grandson John Shine." She was sure she had the name right this time, that is, if it wasn't John Slick. In her heart of hearts she believed there was a light on the "slick." Yes, she told herself, a shine.

Once again he struck her as less than cordial. "If you remember," he said, "I asked you how you thought Mr. Pugh would react. You said you believed him sensible and stable, in possession of his life and most of his faculties." This time he wasn't behind his desk. As if enthroned, he sat on the edge of one of his gilded chairs, she across from him on the hard black couch.

"Well, he was," she said, shifting from side to side. (She was chilly in her lightweight slack suit and on the cold leather.) "I guess what I didn't take into account, or enough into account, is that he is a victim of stroke. Fortunately, he has —at least not yet — had another —" She stopped to cough; her cold had taken a good hold, had become what Aunt Rena always called "the grip." "I take responsibility for this, Mr. Shearer. You were right, we should never have begun this search. I'm just here to tell you that I'm the one to hold accountable for the bill."

"I'm not concerned about it," he told her.

"I don't have a lot of savings," she went on, "but I can give you a thousand dollar payment and I hope we can work out terms for the rest. I realize you've given us a good deal of your time, and I don't want Searcy to have to worry about money."

She hadn't said what Lily had told her the night before toward the end of their conversation. That Searcy was worried about paying her nephew's bill, afraid that in order to do so he might have to sell his land.

He nodded. "Fine," he said, to her great relief. "I'm sure that will be just fine." Then he asked if she was staying in Houston overnight.

"No. No," she murmured quickly. "I'm going straight up to Nacogdoches."

"I'm sorry," he said. "I was hoping I could introduce you to my grandmother. I'm driving by to see her right after I leave the office."

She shook her head as she rose; he stood then, walked over to her and touched her hand. "I'd like to make amends," he said. "I can see my Aunt Lily and your Searcy are close."

She hadn't counted on the warmth. Perhaps she had just stereotyped him. The diamond, the boots, the expensive suit, the ostentatious furniture. He couldn't help his family coming into riches. And from oil. And generations before he was born. He couldn't help making more with what he began with. In some ways money may have even handicapped him. All those sanctimonious remarks, maybe he had felt expected of him, obliged to make. He couldn't buy taste. She shivered visibly, then felt her ankle give way.

"Look," he said, catching her under her arm as she started to fall, "you aren't feeling well. My brother has a major interest in the Holiday Inn at Calhoun, near Main. And my grandmother keeps a suite of rooms at the Warwick. I can arrange for a place for you to spend the night in either at no charge."

"No," she was quick to answer after she caught her breath.

As he pointed toward the window, the light from his ring struck her face. "I insist," he said in a forceful voice. "Look, the sun is setting. You shouldn't drive all the way to Nacogdoches in the dark. Mr. Pugh will be asleep by the time you get there. You can see him in the morning. Anyway, I have something more to tell you. And —" He paused. "There's something I want you to have."

By the time he said that she had risen and was walking quickly past him. Heard herself say as she turned, limping a little, but trying to quicken her step, "I'm sorry, I can't." "I can't," she repeated as she felt the metal knob on the door.

Then she was aware of him there beside her. "Look," he said again, touching her hand, then her shoulder, "I may not be what you think I am and you don't have to meet my grandmother. I'll call her to postpone our visit. But I insist on buying you dinner."

And there she was —as in a dream —in a dark dining nook near the bar on the second floor of the old Warwick Hotel, just off the main dining room, a place where she and her family had once eaten a Christmas night dinner, with this man whose presence she had from the start found both threatening and offensive. The Warwick —out of date by local standards —which still had the grace and charm that she always felt much of Houston lacked, was the last place in the city she would have imagined he would have taken her. But then his grandmother had an interest in it, kept a suite there in which he insisted she spend the night.

Was she actually sipping a bourbon sour, a drink she hadn't had in years? She had liked bourbon when she was young, liked it a little too much, but as she grew older found it aggravated indigestion and so gave it up. Fortunate probably. Had not really chosen to have this one, although the strong drink felt good to her throat. John Shearer had chosen for her as he had chosen the whole evening of which she was captive. She had simply succumbed. (Was that because that morning she had left C. C.'s in such a hurry she had forgotten to put on Aunt Rena's scarf?) When she commented on having good memories of the hotel, he replied that his grandmother's wedding reception had been there. "Rose," she had responded. "Your grandmother was Rose, Lily's older sister." He nodded. "My father, also a John, is her son."

"So you're a third?"

"Yes. But unlike the first or the second I didn't go in the business."

"An oil king's grandson who didn't go in the business? Why not?"

He shrugged. "I didn't have the aptitude —or, to tell the truth, a liking for it. I was more interested in sleuthing, in putting together facts that on the surface don't jive." He laughed. "My mother read mysteries. Always one on her bedside table and a paperback in her purse. Maybe my fascination came from wondering what she wanted from them. Or from all those old shows she put on the VCR. Who knows? Anyway, my older brother was in the business and my Dad. It was all right with me for them to run it." He stopped to take a large swallow from his Jack Daniel's —straight up, not even on the rocks —and then smiled. "That is, as long as I get my dividends."

"Did you know about your grandmother's sister?" she asked.

He shook his head. "Until this case came up I never knew my grandmother had any sisters other than Great Aunt Lily. Iris who was just a story moved away before I was born." He had only met her once or twice during the Holidays when he was a kid. His family didn't see Aunt Lily much either. He shifted his bulk when the waiter came with boiled shrimp and oysters on the half shell —that, yes, he had insisted on ordering —accompanied by silver containers of horseradish, cocktail sauce, a champagne sauce for the oysters and lemon slices. All served on a large platter packed with ice. Before he lifted an oyster onto her plate and then one onto his, he again touched her hand, this time the side of his ring scraping against it.

"Mr. Shearer," she couldn't help saying, making sure to get his name right, to pronounce it clearly, correctly. But also smiling —hoping to make a joke of what she knew she was going to say. She glanced down at his hand on hers, the diamond glittering. Somehow the sight of it directed her. "To use one of your favorite words, you are taking liberties."

He returned her grin with one of his own. "You may be right," he whispered, removing his hand from hers and plunging it into his breast pocket, pulling out a large yellowed envelope. "You may be right. But then I'm not married." He smiled. "I've always liked older women," he said, then paused to finish his drink. "And you are a challenge."

Was he making fun of her? No matter. She wanted to stand when he said that. Couldn't because of the way she was squeezed into the booth.

And then he thrust the envelope toward her. "Here," he said, "this is what I wanted you to have."

It was the last thing she had expected. Her father's death certificate, dated November 12, 1939, that and a small news item clipped from a San Antonio paper. Encyclopedia Salesman Found Dead In Boarding Hotel Room.

Prescription drug overdose the subhead cited as the cause. He had suffered from migraine headaches his landlady said and also from a heart condition. An overdose of medication for both had apparently caused his demise.

"Aunt Lily told me," he explained, "about your father's disappearance." He saw that she was trembling and reached over to touch her hand. "I expect I've taken another liberty."

"No. I'm glad to have this —grateful." She wiped her eyes with her napkin, then said, "I just have a cold."

"It seems to have been an accident," he told her. "I did a little research and when I found this story I thought you would want to know."

"Yes." She couldn't deny that. (It was even all right for John Shearer to hold her hand.) In assisting Searcy to find out the truth about part of his family's history she now had explicit information on her own. Growing up without a father had grieved her more than she had ever allowed herself to admit. Left a soft place inside her where tears easily welled up for almost any misfortune, hers or another's. But had toughened her, too.

John Shearer saw to it that she ate most of her dinner. She had left her oysters and only ate a few of the shrimp. Ordinarily she would have eaten all of them. She had ordered flounder. She loved Texas flounder, couldn't get it in California. After dinner John Shearer had seen her to her suite, cautioned her to drive carefully in the morning. And before she left he had called and sent a full breakfast to her room.

What did he want from her? She couldn't help wondering. She had told him she would pay his bill, assured him she would go over the papers Searcy was holding on the long lost Johnny and for Searcy's sake and Lily's —he had seemed genuinely concerned about both of them —try to put the best face on whatever information she found.

Had she misjudged him? She had been so sure of the way he felt about those without money —attitudes from people newly rich she had encountered when she was growing up. Perhaps she had projected her own prejudices, her own disdain for those whose lives seemed to be about acquiring riches. Especially, she told herself, those from oil. This man preferred to find the missing pieces of lives that made a puzzle as maybe the majority of lives do. Last night and this morning, too, he had been so good to her.

She was ashamed of herself. Ashamed of being sure that he wanted to dominate her, that he was all machismo. Had he changed? He had been a different person during her first visits to him —even toward the beginning of the one yesterday. What had changed him? The realization that his great aunt Lily and Searcy had become close? He had known about that for a while. Or was it that he saw her as frail? She had a cold, an injured ankle. A frail old woman.

And she had flirted with him. Which undoubtedly made her seem to him even more pathetic. She was going to stop it. Going to stop, period. Take a harder look at herself.

She hurt all over when she woke that morning. Her chest, her throat, all her bones, even her eyes hurt and she thought maybe she was running a fever. She had felt Searcy endangered and what had seemed strong in her also seemed at risk. Although she tried, she couldn't eat much of the breakfast John Shearer had sent. The Texas grapefruit, half of a Ruby Red, was the best thing. After she had sucked the last piece of it down her inflamed throat she took three buffered aspirin and told herself she would have to be very careful. She would begin by taking a really long hot bath.

In her Roman bathroom —she thought of it as Roman —she used several of the provided comforters, the bath oil, the oversized sponges, then the velvety towels, the hand cream and body lotion. Afterward she dressed carefully, as she had not on the day before. Her warmest beige slacks and long sleeved cream colored top. And, yes, this time she remembered to pull from her suitcase Aunt Rena's bright pink scarf. So large she could make a shawl of it if she chose. How could she have forgotten to wear it on the day before? She had left Austin in much too big a hurry. "Aunt Rena," she said aloud, "Your scarf will remind me to keep a check on myself." When Aunt Rena was alive and she a teenager, she had often told Aunt Rena to watch out, let her know that she was too open with people, reminded her how being so open got her into trouble. Both before and after Uncle Leeland Aunt Rena had made dangerous marriages with men she hardly knew. And in her nineties she took what turned out to be a nearly fatal trip back to Corpus Christi where she and Uncle Leeland once lived. (Said Uncle Leeland had come to her in a dream and told her to go.) She had made friends with a boy selling scarves she had met in the Kress's across the street from the bus station. (Said the Gulf Coast wind had blown her right to him.) And his baby brother had been mixed up with drug dealers, shot and killed by one of them and later she had been accidentally shot by another. Searcy had told her the whole story. Yes, Aunt Rena had recovered, but — Sometimes it was maybe not so good to be too open. Well, she, Elizabeth, had been, she decided as she threw the loud dime store scarf over her shoulders, too closed. She should learn to be more like her aunt who had managed to survive her bad choices and lived on to make some good ones. "Pumpkin," she could hear Aunt Rena saying, "you need to get out more —have a little fun. Take some chances. Give the people you meet a chance."

Like many who live alone, she often spoke her thoughts aloud. "Aunt Rena," she attempted to say —her throat so sore she hadn't much of a voice, "I'll try."

Twenty-two: I Can Hear You, Aunt Rena

*T*his is the way it was," Rena said in his dream. It seemed he had one dream after another of her —and for days and days. He'd been asleep for such a long time.

"Well," Rena told him, "this is the way it was, darlin'. I had to go back to Corpus Christi where Leeland and I had once lived because in my sleep he told me there was something there I had to find. When I got off the bus the wind whipped me. I'd forgotten it was so strong. I went in the Kress's store across from the bus station to buy a scarf and in the store I made friends with the young man who sold them whose baby brother was in trouble. And the trouble got the baby brother killed, darlin' and almost got me killed, too. But I came through it and after I did, I had a whole new family of friends. You can tell Elizabeth that." She was silent then and just looked at him in that soft way she had of looking.

Then she said, "You can tell her that when I was there through the new friends I made and through going through their sorrow with them and facing danger with them, too, I brought together all the pieces of my life. Worth risking the trip for I can tell you. Now you and Elizabeth, you're going to be all right and you don't have to worry about losing what you have."

Before he had this dream he had felt himself sinking into an awful darkness. Where was this black place and why did it have him who had so loved light?

When he first came home he had meant to call Elizabeth, but once there, he didn't call her. He had been too dizzy. Lily had helped him to his daybed where he'd told her he just wanted to rest. If he could, take a short nap. But everything was spinning. So he couldn't drift off. And, anyway, he heard Lily talking on the phone and the next thing he knew, saw her over him. Paramedics were on the way, she said to take him to the hospital. His doctor had given the order.

After Lily spoke to him he felt himself fall away. Down, down into the shadows and then into terrible darkness where he kept on falling and falling. Finally, there she was. Aunt Rena. Holding up a gold frame with his mother's likeness inside. Tapping one side of the frame with her finger —a sound as soothing as the sound of rain. Aunt Rena had taken him to buy a frame for his mother's picture when he was just a little boy. He remembered. He remembered. And here she was again all these years later at what must be the bottom of the black pit —or had there been an opening in it? Had he gone through?

He had chosen the frame for his mother's picture almost eighty years ago. Now here he was, an old man, dizzy and so tired —he had tried to rise from his bed and perhaps had stumbled, then fallen —through what? —into where ever he was now. Aunt Rena before him showing off a photograph of his mother in a shiny frame. Once long ago they had gone together to Kress's to find it. As they entered the big store, Rena had held his hand, guided him to the counter with all the frames. Asked him to choose one.

She seemed to be asking something again —he saw her lips moving —but this new place he was in was so silent. He didn't know what she said. Was he in a 20s film? Once, they had found the frame she now held, together. That had really happened when he was a little boy. He had chosen the frame for his mother's picture —his mother who had died and who he missed so terribly —when he was not even old enough for school. Almost a century ago. He was an old man now and tired. The trip to Houston to John Shearer, had done him in, and when he got home he had to lie down. And then he had heard Lily say the paramedics were coming. He had fallen into something. Fallen through something and Aunt Rena was before him in a silent place. Telling him —what? He couldn't read her lips; his eyesight hadn't been good in a long time and he didn't have his glasses. "Aunt Rena," he heard himself say, "you'll have to speak louder."

Up until the Houston trip his hearing had been just fine. He wasn't sure what had transpired in Houston, what it was that confused him and set his head spinning. Meeting Lily's nephew, Shearer, Shine. He hadn't liked the man. Hated his news. His mother's big brother imprisoned for drug dealing. That and the assault on an officer. His imprisonment contributing to the suicide of the sister of his neighbor and friend. Of the loss of a child and a grandchild for her mother and father. Most of all he hadn't liked the knowledge that he asked for all of this information.

More than asked. Paid for it. And would pay more. Writing that check might take most of what he had, the little buffer against disaster he had in the bank. He might have to sell his land. He remembered telling Lily that. He would try to keep it from Elizabeth, but here in this queer place he could tell Aunt Rena. Even after she told him about her nearly fatal trip to Corpus Christi, her lips were still moving. Would she hear him if he spoke? He framed the question to sound, a soft buzzing noise and the tap, tap, tap of Rena's fingers again on the frame.

"Honey," he heard her say, "you won't have to sell your land."

"I can hear you, Aunt Rena." He woke himself saying that. But he couldn't remember what it was in response to or anything that had gone before. "She must have been trying to tell me something," he said to Lily who was sitting next to his bed. "Probably," Lily told him, "that you are going to be all right."

Searcy liked, had always liked, looking into her face. Why had he never told her? Shouldn't tell her now when he hardly knew who or where he was. The room he was in didn't look at all familiar. Then he remembered. The hospital. The doctor had told Lily to take him to the hospital. "Lily," he said, "did anyone ever tell you you are a damn good looking woman?"

"I think," she answered, "all women are good looking to you."

Well, he admitted, Beatrice certainly was. And his mother in her picture, dark skin, honey colored hair. And black haired, blue eyed Aunt Rena, though plump, was pretty —as his first wife had been. Elizabeth, too, in an off beat way, her eyes the color of Rena's and her unruly salt and pepper hair.

His mother, Aunt Rena had said was a healer. Lucy, the Healer, a title almost. God given, Aunt Rena had gone on, her talent inborn. From the time she was a toddler she unknowingly healed others with her touch. Their mother, hers and Aunt Rena's, first realized this when as an eighteen month old toddler she wrapped herself around the legs of an old crippled man she came by daily selling whatever his garden had produced. When Lucy let go, those who witnessed said the old man who had limped for years walked away limping less. "That old man with the rhubarb, with the garlic and green onions, his arthritis improved all at once." Aunt Rena had told Searcy that, had said her little sister Lucy, his Mama, Lucy, had just the touch. All the people who were ailing, whether with colds and flu or with worse things, claimed to feel better after Lucy gave them a hug or a kiss or even brushed against a pant leg or stroked a hand. Searcy wondered if any of these old stories were true —if so, he could certainly use his mother now. People were so superstitious back in the olden times when there was so much in the way of poverty and sickness. When there were no cures and no money there had to be miracles. People had to have some hope, had to hear some good news, had to listen for it and to look for signs.

First his Aunt Rena in a dream —he guessed that's what it must have been —and then Lily had given him good news. He was sure Aunt Rena's news was good even though he couldn't remember exactly what it was.

Twenty-three: Women in His Life

*I*f he had been unlucky not to have known a mother, he was blessed with her substitute. Aunt Rena's love didn't cloy. And there was a dramatic flair, even a recklessness about her. A bright flamboyance like the pink in the scarf she had bought in Corpus Christi and that he had given Elizabeth. Hadn't that sunset color flashed through his dream?

But what good were dreams when you couldn't figure them out? Maybe it was enough just to imagine she was bringing him cheer. And cheering him on. Telling him she had survived that trip that nearly got her killed by a drug lord and not only survived it, but made new friends and through them pieced her memories together. Had he told Elizabeth that story? He couldn't remember, but even if he had, he resolved to tell her one more time.

The others, too, had brought cheer. His first wife. Then Beatrice. Then Elizabeth. And certainly Lily who was visiting this morning with a letter in her hand. "It's from Rose," she told him, "inviting me to a party at her house in Houston for Christmas. Says she'll have a surprise." Having a surprise, she went on to say, was not like Rose who as she remembered never liked surprises. Rose, Lily said, always wanted to think the world should be a certain way, that she could order it. But having a party was like her. She might go for months on end without ever contacting her relatives, but Duty, Lily said, was Rose's middle name. She had some kind of Holiday do every year. "I've half a mind," Lily said, "a little later on to have a party of my own. Maybe host a potluck —though Rose would think that tacky. Get the family to come here for a change." She told him she might even make a fruitcake by her mother's recipe, the one she brought back from a trip to New Orleans. "I only did that once," she said, "the Christmas that Daddy died. Might even use your kitchen if you'll let me. You're getting so much better you can help."

Searcy pointed to the papers John Shearer had given him. "I'll help you make that cake," he told her, "If you'll help me go through this pile of manure. Help me sort this mess out." When I can piece together what happened to Johnny Brock he thought —but didn't say (he didn't want Lily to know he worried about money) —I'll summon up the strength to also open your nephew's final bill.

They went through the papers together. The report from the prison and all the rest. The facts were these: John Brock was incarcerated for drug dealing. He was an unhappy, but cooperative prisoner. But after a year he broke out. After he received news from his girl telling him she was pregnant with his child and had been sent far away from home to have it. The post mark as from a place called Leander.

They said he had been apprehended in Bertrum County —which Searcy knew was west of Austin —that he was confronted by a Texas Ranger there, that he assaulted this officer and afterward was restrained and taken back to the state penitentiary. His sentence was for ten years. He was discharged after seven. He had been after a problematic year or two, a cooperative prisoner, a good worker, skillful at carpentry and with tools. At first he made benches for the prison kitchen, and after a time, benches and tables for other places in the prison —all secured to the floor so that they could not be used as weapons —and some for general sale, proceeds going to a fund for the wives and children of prisoners, which seemed appropriate Searcy thought. He wondered what his mother and Aunt Rena would have thought about this if they knew. Were grieving spirits possible? He had heard of vengeful ones. Ones who couldn't release themselves from earth, who couldn't fly free. But those who peacefully passed on were always spoken of as joyful and associated with light. Perhaps, though, not a spirit like his mother's. In a fever she had run from her bed to the river and gone down in a whirlpool. And perhaps not Violet who in a depression brought on by despair had taken too many pills and with them, her life.

So much chaos in the world. So much misery. He had been lucky. He knew that. He had even been getting better from his stroke. Then something had happened. He had gone down again. Could he now hang on? "Pray for me," he said aloud. And not just to Lily, but to all of them, all the women in his life.

Twenty-four: Getting Better

 *S*troke patients do get better, Lily had told him, and sometimes remarkably better, especially in the first six months, the first year —particularly if they work hard at it every day. Searcy walking across the kitchen on his three pronged cane wanted to demonstrate that. Wanted to show Lily he was a good patient. He knew she was trying to assist in the way she knew best. By giving instruction and then setting tasks for him to accomplish when he used it. He wouldn't disappoint her.

This morning they would begin to make the fruitcake, which after reading the recipe Lily had given him, he realized was a three day process. When he sat down at the table he would take hold of a nut with his weak right hand and with his good left, crack and pick from one after another until he had shelled all the pecans Lily had gathered for him from the trees in his backyard. And yes, in his own light filled kitchen —which also served as a sleeping and sitting room and where over the past months he and Lily had brought all of the ingredients. Tomorrow after the pecans were ready, he would help sift the flour. Lily would pour it in the sifter for him and he would turn the handle. And sift, not once, but twice. Elizabeth had said she would help, too, and Elizabeth had never made a cake in her life. She had admitted as much. "You're going to have a kitchen with two novices, Lily," he said.

"Three," Lily told him. "I haven't attempted this recipe in thirty years. But one thing is sure. I can read and so can you, and making this cake is mostly about mixing together what we read off the list, then letting it all sit. And we've got three days to do that. And precise directions to follow. Mama was above all else pree-cise." She handed him the nutcracker and a pick. "I don't think we can go too far wrong."

The fruitcake called for several dozen ingredients and on the day of its completion, it would be soaked in a good quality bourbon, wrapped in a soft cloth and stored for several weeks. Stored until New Year's Day when Lily's sister and her children and grandchildren would, hopefully, arrive and partake.

While Searcy and Lily began work on the cake Elizabeth, out in the storehouse, rummaged through Searcy's old chest for what she thought would be a last time. She was looking for something that would give her more information on the Jabez prayer. Something she could use in "The

Sweethearts' Story." She didn't find it, but she tucked the texts she had come across into a corner of her pocketbook and headed back into the house.

"First day," she heard Lily, who was reading from the recipe say as she came through the door. "Cut citron, orange and lemon peel in thin strings, cherries in half, pineapple in wedges. Well, we can do that," she said and handed Elizabeth a paring knife. As Elizabeth, standing at the butcher table, began to slice the fruit, she went over what she planned to tell them about what had happened in John Shearer's office. She might even confess to Lily the feelings she had once about him and the ways in which they had changed. And without making a big deal about it, she was going to set Searcy's mind at rest about payment. She was going to stay in East Texas longer than she had planned. Not just because she felt obliged, but because she realized that when she was with Searcy and with Lily she mended. Her cold was already so much better. The sleep she had in the sweet little bedroom she now thought of as at least partially hers seemed to have healed her. And maybe even the rewards of sleuthing had helped. (She had just claimed a reward from Searcy's storehouse. She had to keep it secret for a while, but she would tell Searcy about it soon.) She told herself this as she sliced orange and lemon peels and looked out at the blue trumpets of Searcy's morning glory vine. Yes, she was mending. She was at peace.

And also having fun.

Twenty-five: Aunt Rena, This Is What I Have To Tell You

*E*lizabeth wrote that on a page as she began a new journal that night in what had been Searcy and Beatrice's room.

Your brother, Johnny, Searcy's Uncle Johnny —he went to prison, yes (but not because he ever killed or even wounded anybody.) Unfairly many thought. And he had to stay there for years. He broke out once and assaulted the Texas ranger who found him and was sent back for a longer time. But he lived to get out and after he did, he went west. At first just west of Austin, because he hoped to find his boy there. And, afterwards, west as far as he could go. And he stayed there. And prospered. (He and I have that in common.) Finally, he even hooked up with his son —a miracle. And he lived to be an old man.

Why didn't he ever try to find you and the rest of the family? That's harder to say. Maybe he was ashamed of going to prison and was afraid if he wrote to you about anything, you'd find out. Or maybe, he thought if any word got out about it, some who had it in for him, might find him and send him back to Huntsville, or try to. It's hard to know. But he was one of the lucky ones. Finally things came together for him. I can tell you that now.

How did I find out? Partially by reading the prison report. And partially by something I found in one of Searcy's neighbor's books (believe that or not.) And then, just today, in a precious envelope with two letters inside that I found out in Searcy's storehouse. In a jewelry box that had belonged to Searcy's wife, Beatrice, at the very bottom of Searcy's keepsake chest underneath a stack of Beatrice's clothes. The box was locked, but its key still in place in a groove on one side. I believe when these letters came to Searcy's address —and someone in the Louisiana town where they were sent from knew what that was —I believe that when they came, Beatrice hid them. Who knows why? Maybe she thought the contents would be too unsettling for Searcy. Make him sad. Or maybe she meant to give them to him at just the right time. But never had the chance because she caught a cold and then just up and died.

The first letter, Aunt Rena, is to you. But that letter was never mailed. I found it enclosed in another letter written later by a different party. Before I clip them into this book (just to keep them safe for a while) I want to read them both out loud to you. For maybe you are somewhere near —I often feel you near —and listening.

Dear Renee,

(I guess he called you that.)

I'm writing finally to tell you what happened. To say something about it, anyway. There's too much to tell. I thought of you and Mama ever day, but I couldn't write. When the work on the oil rig played out I got into trouble. Caught by the Law for some trips across the border —which was paying me plenty —to pick up a plant some liked to smoke though it wasn't legal. And I got mad and had trouble with a Law Man after me. And that got me a lot of time in a big state jail. And I also had my money taken away so I could never send any of it to you.

But, Renee, that weren't the worst of it —there was a girl —so freedom loving —like you that way —like all of us in our family —and just plain loving, too. And smart. A reader. I brought her books. Pretty as her name. Violet. Dark hair. Like yours. Blue eyes —like yours, too —but darker. We loved each other, but her people didn't want us to marry —I wanted to take us West —and they sent her away. But I didn't know because by that time, I was locked up.

When I broke out I went looking for her. I'd found out where they sent her. Out to a place in the Hill Country way west of where we had been. I'd found out there was a child —that she'd had our child, a boy —but when I broke out of prison and went to the place where I was told she gave birth, I didn't know where she was or who had him. And I didn't know she wasn't there anymore, that she'd been sent home directly after he was born, that she'd taken a bunch of pills —oh, it's still hard for me to write it —that she had died.

Of course the Law found me and I didn't go back with them peacefully. A mistake. It only got me more time."

The letter breaks off here, Aunt Rena. Half of a page is torn off, missing. On the next one he talks about the darkness of the place when he returned to it. I guess he means when he finally got out of prison. Even in moonlight he says it was a dark place.

"The moons were pretty," he says, "like yellow eggs, those oblong moons. Over all the dark oak trees and the black cedars —and the mist, always a mist rising. I'll swear, Renee, it wanted to claim me. Take me. Sometimes I thought it had me by the legs, by the ankles, that it would rise up from the weeds and yellow grass and throw me down. Then one night —I know this sounds crazy —it nearly gripped me, nearly took me under. I was sick all

the time after I got there, one cough after another, and I ran a fever —but that's not what I thought would get me. What would get me I was sure came from the ground! Something bad must have happened there and the ground itself wanted to let me know. Or maybe thought I had done it.

"Well, one night I saw the horses, a brown colt and a white one. A palomino standing in the cedars. And I put my arms around the neck of one —first the palomino —and then the other — And before I knew it I was on the other's bare back and we began to ride. He took me out of that place that griped me. Out of —away from —Liberty Hill which, for me, Renee, wasn't liberating —and we just went on and on to a freight, where I dismounted and said goodbye, and then went on out of the state of Texas —and west —a long, long ride."

The sense of the letter stops there, Aunt Rena. Some pages must be gone. But the bottom of the last one says, *"Just as soon as I get an address I'll send it. Don't give up on me. I'll send money, too."*

And that's all. I found the letter that I just read enclosed in another and both of them in an envelope with Return to Sender stamped on it. The second letter I can't answer because there was no envelope with it, no return address. But it reads like this:

"Dear Great Aunt Rena,

You are really my great, great aunt. But my father always called you Aunt Rena as his father, my grandfather, did. So I hope you don't mind if I call you that, too.

My father passed away a few weeks ago. I found my grandfather's letter on a shelf in my father's closet when I was going through his things. I'm sending it to the address on the envelope, but I don't know if it will get to you. From the looks of the paper my grandfather's letter was written a long time ago. I don't know why he never mailed it or why my father never spoke to me about it. When I was little my grandfather did speak to me about you. He thought a lot of you and your sister, Lucy and wanted to help take care of you. But he had been gone so long he was ashamed I guess and then, maybe he thought you wouldn't be at this old address which I'm going to give a try. I've never been to Louisiana, but I did get back to Texas where my father's early memories were and which he and my grandfather had many stories about. My father's parents —that is, the people he thought were his natural parents (who he later learned adopted him) were killed in a wildfire which followed a windstorm at Liberty Hill where my father lived the summer they sent him to Bandera to camp. Afterwards he was placed in the county's home for children and they eventually located his father in Southern California. My father was almost grown up by this time, but he still grieved for the mother and father he lost. He told me that at first he and my grandfather were shy with one another, but they were so much alike that it didn't take long for them to become close.

My grandfather talked a lot about East and South Texas and about the Gulf of Mexico. I like boating and fishing and after he died —peacefully in his 95th year in his sleep —I considered buying Port Aransas property which I knew would be a lot more reasonable than here. But I gave up my plans when a big hurricane blew in —early in the season. This was in the early 90s. I can't remember the year. July. Maybe, like my father and grandfather, it has been my fate to skirt killer storms. In Liberty Hill, Texas my father missed the windstorm that brought fire and in Corpus Christi I missed the hurricane. And I may have missed worse. I saw a shooting on the steps of the Catholic cathedral the morning my taxi was taking me to the plane. (Drug lords the driver said had taken over some of the town.) I guess it left a bad impression. Anyway, after that trip I never went back to Texas to pursue my plans. Even if they had all worked out, it would have been hard to uproot my family. I'm married, Aunt Rena, and have two boys. So I just stayed on here near my father and grandfather's home.

I hope this finds you and that you are well. And that one day I will meet you. Both my father and grandfather would want us to be in touch.

  Respectfully yours,

John Brock, III

(I am John Brock, the third, but my grandfather always called me Johnny Boy Two.)

I'll stop, Aunt Rena. John Brock III's P. S. says that after his father and grandfather were reunited his father took his grandfather's last name, but didn't have to take a first; he'd been a John from the start.

Twenty-six: At the Spring

$\mathcal{E}$lizabeth was glad she decided to stay through New Year's Eve and Lily's party. She thought she would see John Shearer again, something she told herself she needed to do. And this time she would see him in a family context. She certainly wanted to meet the legendary Rose. And she had always celebrated her birthday on New Year's Eve, although she was actually born at 12:01 on January one.

Now here she stood with Searcy who she had spent her early life avoiding, the middle part of her life forgetting and in the last few years —much as she had come to like him —neglecting. Or at least she felt she had. She vowed not to anymore. Fortunately, Lily had been attentive. She was glad she had been able to give him John Brock's letter which pleased him so, and the one from John Brock's grandson. She saw him satisfied, but also saw she was right about him not wanting to search anymore. The youngest Johnny's letter had on it an unreadable return address. The words smudged out.

The three of them had come together —she slowly pushing Searcy's chair a quarter of a mile down the path that ran along side of the creek bed, almost dry from lack of rain, Lily with a cane only a short distance behind —until they came to the place where Searcy's workers, who had been clearing out debris back in September, found the spring. Thick layers of leaves underfoot —oak and ash, the tree branches bare —but pine trees, too, some bright green ones and cedars and near the place where they stopped to see water (a trickle, not a gush) coming out of an indentured place in the far creek bank's side.

"It's so clear," Elizabeth said as she pulled Searcy near a yellowing willow. "And look at the shine it puts on the pebbles." They were tan and brown and black and some were speckled. Some were even rose colored. Some, gray.

Lily lifted the lunch basket off Searcy's lap and Elizabeth threw the table cloth that had been on top on the ground. "I'm glad I put in those gourds," Lily said. "Before we leave we can use one as a scooper. I want to take some of those pebbles back. Just for luck" She had taken a seat on a tree stump. "But I'm not sure I can make it down into the stream."

"I'll get them for you," Elizabeth said.

As they ate sandwiches from the lunch basket, Lily sitting on her stump facing Searcy and Elizabeth on the ground, Lily talked about Rose's party in her huge Houston house. All the windows she said were hung with velvet draperies and on either side of the fireplace long velvet covered chaise lounges faced the marble coffee table and the front of the room. Odd, she said, the effect. And even odder, the person who was stretched out on one of the chaises, the party's surprise. Iris! The sister Lily barely remembered.

"Stylish and stylized," Lily said, "stretched out on that long chaise. And wearing a long, green Empire waisted dress with a matching headband. She was the Fleur de Lise, all right. Got up like a French queen. Maybe not accidental." She had, Lily said, married a Canadian, a man of French descent. And the surprise of her, Lily said, turned into two. "In a large needlepoint bag which she had parked on one side of the chaise she took out some pictures. Of Violet! (Or at least that's what she said.) A beautiful blue eyed dark haired girl child of maybe three or four and then of seven or eight. Who didn't look wild —or sad —at all, but wistful. Expectant. She gave one photo to Rose and one to me and I've taken mine to be framed."

As Lily spoke, Elizabeth took off her canvas shoes, rolled up her khaki pants and with one of the gourds in hand, walked down to and into the creek, bending to scoop out of the cold, shallow water dozens of the shiny stones.

Twenty-seven: Pieces of Land

*S*he brought C.C. a mason jar full of them —she loved their smooth feel; she had taken a bunch from Lily's New Year's table. Lily had used the stones as a base for her centerpiece of pine and holly and cedar they had gathered together that day down by the spring. Her old friend listened to her as she always had, ever since they were both fourteen, as she spoke about Lily's potluck and about Searcy's offer.

"I want to give this to you, Elizabeth," Searcy had told her the day they had lunched by the spring. "This piece of my land, the half acre here by the creek. We can have a little camp house constructed on it. A little house on stilts, like the one you once described to me. So it won't get flooded if the banks overflow from too much rain."

She had shaken her head and said, "This is yours, Searcy. You keep it."

"But you like it, don't you?" he had asked her.

"I like it. And the plans for the camp house too. But you'll have to include a ramp with a good, strong railing so we can all get into it. If you build a house like that I'll come, and as much as I like sleeping in yours and Beatrice's old bedroom, I'll stay in it. I promise you. And you can visit me. Lily, too."

To C.C. she said, "I couldn't take his land, not even a piece of it, though I had once wanted to. It's his only security. But I didn't lie to him. Whether or not he ever builds the camp house, I will always visit Searcy. Just as I'll always visit you. Seems to be my role," she said, "that of visitor passing through."

"So," C.C. said, "I'm fascinated. Tell me about Rose."

"Ordinary," Elizabeth said. "Very proper. On the dull side." She stopped to check herself, remembering her new rule about not judging others. "At least as far as I could ascertain. Wears super expensive clothes. Neiman Marcus clothes. She may be a lot more than those. I've no way to tell. She didn't stay more than half an hour."

"But she did come," C.C. said.

"Yes. And she even brought her share of the pot luck, a honey glazed ham."

"And her grandson, the detective?"

"Mr. Shearer. I was disappointed. He didn't show up. I so wanted to see him with his family. See how he related to his brother —his brother and wife were there. Reserved. Formal. Maybe John Shearer will remain the real mystery in my adventure." Maybe, she thought, I'll find out more about him at another gathering or maybe I'll never know what I should think of him —or just who or what he is. But just how many people do we ever really know about? "What I've decided," she said to C. C., "is this. Unless we have strong suspicion of threat —or unless they are running for office —we just have to give most the benefit of the doubt."

Twenty-eight: On the Coast of California

She shortened the title of her radio play, "The Sweetheart's Story." The title had become simply, "Sweethearts." She had revised in the room she'd taken in the inn across from the new luxury hotel near Aliso Beach, one of her favorite spots. Just yesterday she had found a piece of quartz there, an odd offering on a beach that, some of the time, didn't even provide shells. She couldn't help but wonder how the stone got there. Probably from one of the rocks on the shoreline. No matter. Gladness. That's what it brought, this white stone which she used now as a paperweight, its imbedded colors —amber, gray-green, frosted yellow and silver —all catching the light. Violet and Johnny now sweethearts forever in her play.

Natural forces had brought them together. Society torn them apart. And at Liberty Hill nature had taken its revenge, and then spoken to Aunt Rena's brother Johnny and sent him on his way —even provided a choice in horses, a light and a dark. He had ridden the dark horse. When she visited Liberty Hill nature had also spoken to her, sickened her and in the sickness given her a tip.

Who couldn't see the connections?

After her morning's work she crossed the street, walked down more than a hundred steps to the ocean and sat before it for most of the afternoon, getting up now and again to wade a little, but never going fully in. Watching a sail boat in the distance, thinking, I could do this right here every day of my life and be perfectly happy.

Still, if and when she had the means —in spite of war, disease, terror —there were places she wanted to travel. She yearned to step into more of this world of what she hoped were still often blue —if fouled and rising —oceans and seemingly endless sky. All of the Hawaiian islands, (she had only been to two.) Australia, New Zealand. Some spots on the wide skirt around Asia. The Mediterranean for sure. The Amalfi Coast. All of Italy —how was it she had never been? —and, after Italy, or maybe before, Turkey and Greece. There was good reason she supposed why it didn't seem her destiny to be a land owner, to have —what those she knew in Texas used to call — "a Place." She was not meant to be stationary, only to hold on to those who were. She would keep in close touch with Searcy and Lily, and as she always had, with C.C. For the time being her base remained here on the western edge of the continent and a coastline that from the first told her it had been waiting. And that she had come to love. She would be able to return to it often, at least for a while, because NPR had decided not to do away with dramas after all. She had just the day before signed a new contract with the station in L. A.

When evening came she returned to her motel, showered, dressed and took herself a few miles down the coast to a restaurant where she had a window table from which she could see all the boats in the harbor. The sight of one confirmed her choices, put to rest her remaining doubts and fears. Secured as serenely as it seemed to be, also caused her to smile, prompted her (almost) to wave. How long had it been waiting there for her, this skiff with its name painted on the side? Should she include it in her play? And —dare she ask the question? —whoever could it belong to? This saucy little ship.

The Johnny Boy II.

About the Author

Eve La Salle Caram is the author of five novels, those in *TRIO*, *A Corpus Christi Trilogy* and the interconnected duo of *The Blue Geography* and *Wintershine*. She is also the editor of *Palm Readings, Stories From Southern California*, a multicultural anthology of Southern California women. For the past twenty seven years she has taught Literature and Writing at California State University, Northridge and Fiction Writing in UCLA Extension's renowned Writers' Program where she won the Outstanding Instructor in Creative Writing Award in 2006. She also teaches at Los Angeles City College whose students helped inspire her novel *Rena, A Late Journey* and who asked her to write *Looking For Johnny*, the short novel that completes *Trio*. All of her books have been used in Literature and Writing classes in California and in Texas. With her UCLA Writers' Program colleague, award winning fiction writer and poet, Carolyn Howard Johnson, Eve will conduct writing classes in a villa near the Trevi Fountain in the heart of Rome. She is presently working on fiction inspired by a recent trip to Italy. A collection of stories, *Eight*, as well as a novel written in her youth, *Rushes From Girlhood*, are also forthcoming.

Website: www.palhbooks.com/evecaram.html

Email: ecaram@roadrunner.com

About Eve La Salle Caram's Books

Dear Corpus Christi

"Body and Soul resonate wonderfully in this accomplished and compelling novel. *Dear Corpus Christi* becomes an embodiment of all our loving contradictions, fusing the spirit of a place with the awful power of the blood."
Robert Love Taylor, Winner of the Oklahoma Book Award

"Eve La Salle Caram is interested in the past as it intersects with and illuminates the present and provides a sense of continuity. *Dear Corpus Christi* is a novel of honesty and grit."
Cecil Dawkins

Rena, A Late Journey

"Eve La Salle Caram has crafted a stunning journey across the century offered to us in the powerful voice of Rena, her ninety-year-old character who, in healing her past finds herself in a contemporary world of drugs and violence."
Maria Amparo Escandón, Author of *Esperanza's Box Of Saints*

Looking For Johnny

"How I love a novel that leaves me with something important, something intense, something more than I had when I started reading. Eve Caram's novels do that and now there is wonderful *Looking For Johnny*."
Carolyn Howard Johnson, award winning fiction and non fiction writer and poet